WALK

AMONG

US

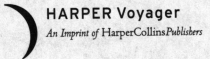

HARPER Voyager
An Imprint of HarperCollins*Publishers*

WALK AMONG US

THREE NOVELLAS OF THE WORLD OF DARKNESS

GENEVIEVE GORNICHEC

CASSANDRA KHAW

CAITLIN STARLING

WALK AMONG US. Copyright © 2020 by Paradox Interactive AB. All rights reserved. Printed in the United States of America. No part of this book may be used or reproduced in any manner whatsoever without written permission except in the case of brief quotations embodied in critical articles and reviews. For information, address HarperCollins Publishers, 195 Broadway, New York, NY 10007.

HarperCollins books may be purchased for educational, business, or sales promotional use. For information, please email the Special Markets Department at SPsales@harpercollins.com.

Harper Voyager and design are trademarks of HarperCollins Publishers LLC.

FIRST EDITION

Designed by Paula Russell Szafranski

Library of Congress Cataloging-in-Publication Data has been applied for.

ISBN 978-0-06-299405-9

21 22 23 24 25 LSC 10 9 8 7 6 5 4 3 2 1

CONTENTS

WALK

AMONG

US

A
SHEEP
AMONG
WOLVES

GENEVIEVE GORNICHEC

CHAPTER ONE

Clea caught sight of the flyer that changed her life on a bitter Sunday night in November. The words made her stop dead in her tracks and stare, and made her shuffle across the fresh dusting of snow on the sidewalk leading up to the empty building until her breath was so close to the window that it fogged the glass.

"Honestly—I'm really worried about you, hon," her mom was saying on the phone, which Clea pressed against her ear with bare, shivering hands. "Are you still not making any friends? It's almost Thanksgiving. . . ."

"I've made friends," Clea said mechanically, her eyes not leaving the flyer. Her other hand hung limply at her side, clutching the greasy paper bag that held the late-night burrito she'd bought for dinner as a break from campus food.

"Uh-*huh*," her mother said, unconvinced. "How about your roommate? Did you talk to your RA about getting transferred to another dorm?"

"No . . ."

"Ugh, *Cornelia*. Do you want me to call the school and—?"

"*No*, Mom," Clea said with disgust. She finally shook herself and turned away from the flyer, pressing herself against the window to take refuge from the snow under the building's small awning. "This isn't a *school*, it's a *university*. And even if I wanted you to call, like I'm some kind of *baby*, I—I wouldn't even know who you'd call in the first place."

"Residence Life. I have their number right here."

"*Mom*."

"All I have to do is call and—"

"*Mom*, I said *no*."

"Well, fine then. You know, I'm not going to be around forever, so if you don't advocate for yourself, one day no one will—"

"I've gotta go, Mom. I'm at the library studying for an exam."

"But I hear cars in the background—"

"Good*bye*," Clea snapped and ended the call. She stared at her phone for a moment or two before heaving a sigh and sending a follow-up text to her mother: *Sorry, I swear I'm fine. I love you.*

A moment later a check mark and the word *Seen* appeared under her message, but no response came.

She stuffed her phone back in the pocket of her coat and started to walk home—except she saw the flyer again out of the corner of her eye, the words stark red against a gray background.

Do you feel invisible? it asked. And then below: *Are*

you far from home? Do you need someone to talk to? Come to the Community Space, Monday night at 8:30 p.m. on November 3, for hot cocoa, doughnuts, board games, and more!

Clea examined the flyer more closely. It was printed in the proper colors but didn't have a club name or the university's logo anywhere, which was quite strange for Ohio State. But the event took place in this very building, which looked abandoned and was across the street from campus—maybe Res Life had rented out the space? Then again, it could be any number of clubs behind the flyer; everyone knew that the best way to get college students to show up was by offering free food.

She looked over both shoulders—something about being alone in a big city made her feel like she was always being watched—before ripping the flyer down and cramming it into the pocket of her parka. Then she took off down the street, still clutching the bag containing her now-cold burrito.

CLEA ARRIVED BACK AT HER DORM SOAKING WET, THE SNOW having turned to sleet halfway through her walk home. She waited for the elevator with three other people, and when it arrived on the ground floor, she stuffed herself as far into the corner as she could during the thirty-second trip. The others were glued to their phones and didn't seem to pay her any mind, but she was wet and felt like a drowned rat, so she tried to stay as far away from them as possible.

It wasn't just her bedraggled state that made her want

to fade away. She imagined her fellow students were judging her as the elevator *ding*ed on floor three; the rest of them were traveling to the upper levels of the six-floor dorm. Though she knew logically that they probably could not care less which floor she was going to, she imagined them judging her for not taking the stairs.

Her face flamed at the imagined insults—fresh from her own head—as she stepped out of the elevator, stealing a glance over her shoulder. The other students were still staring down at their phones, paying no attention to her whatsoever.

Clea wasn't sure which one was worse: being mocked behind her back or going so unnoticed that it was like she didn't even exist.

The elevator doors closed behind her, and she made her way down the hall toward her dorm room. *I'll have to microwave the burrito*, she thought sadly, the paper bag at her side completely soaked.

She could hear giggles and loud thumping music, which was not unusual for a freshman dorm, especially on a Friday night—but as she made it farther down the hall, she realized that it was coming from her own room. She'd known her roommate and friends were going out that night—just like every other—but Clea was sure they'd be gone by now, off to stumble down High Street to coerce upperclassmen into buying them drinks before being invited to any number of house parties.

Her heart sank and her hands began to shake as she hovered outside the door, listening to the laughter. She fumbled to get her phone out of her pocket and check the time. *Eleven thirty—maybe I could just go downstairs and*

eat in the lounge, and by the time I get back, they'll be gone.
Maybe—

But then the door swung open and her roommate Hannah's freckled face appeared, and she let out a shriek of surprise when she saw Clea on the other side of the door.

"Oh my *God*, you scared the *shit* out of me," Hannah said, clutching her chest so dramatically that Clea knew she had already been drinking. Hannah's face was plastered with makeup, her red hair in perfect waves, and she wore a short black dress with a lace overlay and stiletto boots. The rest of her entourage was dressed similarly and seemed to have been about to head out the door.

Clea pictured the lot of them tottering down the street in their heels, clutching their massive cell phones, shivering without their coats. It was the number one way to spot a freshman girl.

Two more minutes, Clea thought in dismay, as the scent of booze and hairspray wafted out of the room. *If I would've just waited two more minutes . . .*

Over her shoulder, Hannah's friend Delaney twisted her face into a sneer. "What were you doing just standing there, Cleopatra?"

"I—I—," Clea began, floundering. As if on cue, the soggy paper bag broke and her burrito fell to the floor with a very sad *plop*, causing salsa and sour cream to burst through the foil and splatter the geometric-patterned commercial carpeting at her feet. The girls erupted into raucous giggles.

"Ugh, c'mon, guys," Delaney said, ducking past Hannah and pushing past Clea, stepping over the burrito with disgust. The rest of the girls filed out after her, giving Clea smiles of fake sympathy before they got farther down the hall and whispered among themselves, snickering and stealing glances over their shoulders at her.

Yeah, Clea thought, *this is worse than not being noticed.*

Hannah was last, and she hesitated in the doorway. Clea cast her eyes down and moved aside, motioning for her to go; her roommate was a decent person when it was just the two of them, but she could never seem to bring herself to be kind to Clea in front of her friends. It was as if she were risking her social standing merely by association.

Clea's face flushed again. There was a time when she'd thought college would be different than high school, that a place as big as *the* Ohio State University wouldn't have cliques and drama and mean, mean girls.

It hadn't taken her very long to realize she'd been wrong.

"Sorry," Hannah mumbled without looking at her and then followed her friends.

Clea watched them pile into the elevator, and she could hear their giggles turn into flat-out laughter as soon as the doors closed. Unlike her imagined slights from the students in the elevator earlier, Clea was certain they were laughing at her. And Hannah never said anything in her defense, although Delaney was the only one who was ever mean to Clea's face.

Clea bent to pick up her burrito. It hadn't touched the floor despite losing some of its contents, so she dumped it on her desk, grabbed a napkin, scooped up the escaped condiments from the hallway floor, and threw them away.

Once the door had closed behind her, Clea breathed

a sigh of relief at the empty room and shrugged off her backpack and parka and plopped down at her desk. Then she cracked open a Mountain Dew from the mini-fridge— *How can your roommate drink that crap?* she heard Delaney say in her head—and reached for the remote control to Hannah's flat-screen television. It was too quiet in here; she needed background noise.

She ate her cold burrito—unable to risk encountering anyone in the lounge to heat it up—and watched the last thing Hannah had on, not really absorbing anything. When the burrito was gone, she felt worse than before, and her stomach protested. She tossed the greasy foil wrapper into the garbage and put her pop can in the recycling bin behind the door and avoided looking in the giant mirror mounted there. Her thin, mousy hair was still wet from the sleet, and the frumpy, oversized hoodie and jeans she'd been wearing for several days suddenly felt dirtier than before. She felt gross, and even grosser because she knew it was her own fault.

Passing her desk again, she stole a brief look at her art box, full to bursting with Prismacolor markers and pencils, ink pens, and kneaded erasers. It sat there atop a new empty sketchbook her mother had given her for graduation.

I wish, I wish, Clea thought, but every time she tried to create something, she couldn't bring herself to do it. Every time she tried, she failed, so she just stopped trying.

Clea turned away and flicked on her bedside lamp. She changed into the oversized T-shirt and sweatpants she wore as pajamas and brushed her stringy hair, willing it to dry before she went to sleep—she should shower, but it was too much effort at this point, and the thought of people *looking* at her freaked her out enough to avoid the communal bathroom until absolutely necessary—and settled down in her bed.

Since she slept a lot during the day and at odd hours, she kept a bag of earplugs in her nightstand drawer in case the noise from outside disrupted her, as it frequently did. Oddly, she found it was too quiet in the dorm tonight, as if everyone had gone out without her.

That was when she remembered the flyer.

Why had it caught her attention? It was the same as all the other flyers around campus, advertising all the programs and meetings and initiatives sponsored by the university. It was a whole *thing*, as if they knew that a majority of college students were struggling with their mental health. Clea figured that the university's flyers must work for some people, but she hadn't been able to bring herself to seek help from the school, even though the resources were certainly there.

She missed her therapist back home. It had been hard enough for her to open up to someone the first time, to get it off her chest how worthless and lonely and excluded she felt, and talking about it only increased the shame that came with being a perfectly logical person who struggled with mental illness. Yes, she knew she *should* get up and do things and make friends, but she couldn't and she didn't know why; yes, she knew it was pointless to worry about the things she worried about, like people talking about her behind her back and judging her wherever she went, but she couldn't make herself stop no matter how hard she tried. And it only got worse the longer she was here, in college, surrounded by thousands of students who seemed far more functional than she was.

So the thought of having to start from scratch and explain her shame to an entirely new therapist was terrifying. As long as the one back home kept prescribing her meds and seeing her on school breaks, that was just fine with Clea. It was enough to get her by in the meantime—or so she'd hoped when she'd first started college. Except it seemed like she needed help now more than ever.

But she'd ignored the beckoning of the university's numerous crisp, clean flyers begging her to look after her mental health. So why had this dingy off-campus flyer appealed so much to her instead?

Clea got up and crossed the room to her desk, where she'd put her damp parka on the back of the chair, and she reached into the pocket to extract the crumpled paper. Smoothed it out on her desk. Let the words draw her in, as they'd done earlier that night.

Do you feel invisible? it asked. She read the words over and over again until they seemed more accusatory than concerned. *Do you feel invisible? Do you feel—?*

Finally, Clea crumpled up the piece of paper again and stuffed it under her pillow.

She knew what she was doing tomorrow night.

CHAPTER TWO

———— ◆ ————

Monday dawned cold and dreary, and since Clea had been too distracted the night before to set an alarm, she slept through her morning classes and spent the rest of the day chewing over whether she was going to go through with it, whether she was *actually* going to get involved and go *do* something instead of hiding out at the library eating junk food and watching Netflix on her laptop until she was sure Hannah and her friends had already gone out, or wandering aimlessly about campus in the wee hours of the morning when she couldn't sleep.

Walking alone during those times didn't bring her the peace she expected it to. She was always on alert, never fully calm even when she was clutching her pepper spray. It was a small comfort in case something happened to her and she couldn't make it to an emergency post in time to slam the button and summon the campus police. The posts littered campus like friendly sentinels, positioned such that you could always see one if you were standing at another—helpful if you feared you were being followed, so you could punch the buttons as you walked to indicate your path.

But they were still just small pools of light in the darkness, and their presence didn't stop Clea from constantly looking over her shoulder as she meandered between classroom buildings and dorms, across the Oval and down to Mirror Lake, and back again.

The night was bitter cold, but she eventually found herself sitting on a bench on the campus side of High Street, across from the Community Space. She twisted the crumpled-up flyer in her hands and took deep breaths. The building looked as abandoned as it had the night she'd ripped the flyer from the darkened window. She hadn't even tried the door—maybe it was locked.

Maybe I ripped down the only flyer, Clea thought, keeping her head down to avoid eye contact with passersby while low-key monitoring other people who tried to enter the building. So far, there was no one.

I haven't seen any other flyers around campus. She put in her earbuds and took out her phone and tried to look busy so strangers might be deterred from bothering her, as she watched the door out of the corner of her eye. *Maybe I'll show up and there will be nobody else there and I'll look like an idiot. It's safer just to go home, then, isn't it?*

She put her phone aside; took another deep, shaking breath; and untwisted the flyer, smoothing it out in her lap.

Do you feel invisible? it asked her.

Clea sighed, thinking about her interaction with Hannah and her friends last night. *I've tried to be invisible to spare myself the pain that comes from being noticed, but is that really what I want for my life?*

Do I need someone to talk to?

It was dark outside, and Clea was cold. So she steeled herself, scrambled across the busy street as fast as she could, and walked over to the door, her fingers hovering just over the handle.

The building was still dark inside, so dark that she couldn't see in. Clearly, no one was there; this was all a mistake. Suddenly, she was glad she'd grabbed the flyer, as proof that she hadn't hallucinated this whole thing from a secret need for companionship.

She dropped her hand and sighed. *Stupid, stupid, stupid. I'm just going to go home.*

But when she whirled around to leave, she crashed into someone who had been coming up behind her, slamming her nose into his chest.

"Whoa," he said, stepping back.

"Oh my God, I'm so sorry," Clea muttered, stepping aside, her hand covering her nose. Her eyes flickered to the person's face, and then down, then back up to do a double take. She couldn't help but stare.

The man was at least six feet tall, pale, and blue-eyed, with a close-cropped beard a shade darker than his sandy-blond hair, which was tied in a short ponytail at the nape of his neck. He was dressed in a hoodie and jeans and had a giant tote bag slung over each shoulder.

"You don't have to apologize," he said. Clea couldn't place his accent. She could feel his eyes on her as he continued, "I ran into *you*, after all. Are you all right?"

Clea shrank back and lowered her hand from her

nose, averting her eyes to the sidewalk again. She nodded mutely.

"Scuse me," someone snapped from behind them, and they moved aside simultaneously as a dark-haired girl with a forearm crutch breezed past them, opened the door with her free hand, and disappeared inside the building without sparing them a passing glance.

So the door *was* unlocked.

The blond man regarded Clea with an uncertain half smile. "Are you here for . . . ?"

"Um, yeah," Clea said, holding up the crumpled flyer. "This is the right place, right?"

"Ah, it sure is." The man's face lit up into a friendly grin, and he opened the door and gestured for her to go in before him. "Come on in. You're a little early—we're still getting things set up, I'm afraid."

Clea only hesitated a moment before she walked inside, expecting to have to fumble for a light switch. She stopped short when she saw that the room was indeed fully lit, and she turned around to look at the front windows, confused; she now realized that they were heavily tinted, which is why the building had seemed so dark and abandoned before.

"Early?" she managed as he slipped in the door behind her.

He nodded at the flyer in her hand, which she looked at again more closely. "It says eight," she observed.

"It says eight thirty," he corrected gently in his strange accent, pointing to the corner of the page, which had been worried away by Clea's twisting and crumpling.

"Oh," she said. *I'm such an idiot.*

"It's fine, though," he said, brushing past her to enter the room. "We're glad you're here."

Clea stole a glance at him as he made his way across the room, which was full of long folding tables and rickety folding chairs. The only other person in the room was the girl who'd pushed past him, and she sat in one of the chairs with her crutch leaned up against the table and her backpack under the seat. She hadn't taken off her coat, but Clea could see she was wearing a black hoodie with some emo band's logo on it, her hair partially covered by a slouching black beanie. She was playing a game on her Nintendo Switch; she must've pulled it out of her bag the moment she sat down, having entered only seconds before Clea and Mysterious Tote Bag Man.

"You can have a seat, too, if you'd like," the man said as he plopped said tote bags down on the front table and started extracting some cups, plates, and napkins, and then all manner of snacks after that: tins of gourmet cocoa powder and boxes of fresh Buckeye Donuts from one bag and several very old board games from the other.

"I was in charge of supplies," he said with a smile, his startling blue eyes darting up from his work just for a moment to observe Clea. Then he frowned a bit and turned to the dark-haired girl. "Hmm, if the door was unlocked—was there anyone inside when you got here?"

"I thought I saw a lady in the back, but I didn't get a good look," she replied without looking up from her game.

As if on cue, the back door opened and a red-haired woman entered the space, wielding a large hot-water dispenser. It was one of the big silver ones Clea recalled from her churchgoing days as a child, and although she remembered them being heavy—especially when full—the woman carried it effortlessly.

"Welcome," said the woman, who had an accent similar to the man's. She plopped the water dispenser down next to the tins of cocoa, turned to Clea and the other girl, and said, "You can help yourselves. First come, first served."

Clea made the slightest movement to get up, but the other girl said, "I'd rather wait for everyone else to get here," and Clea leaned back in her chair and nodded, although the doughnuts called to her, the siren's song of fresh pastry. Not necessarily because she was hungry but because she was uneasy and wanted something to do with her hands, something to put in her mouth so she wouldn't feel like she had to talk.

"Suit yourself. We're expecting a few more people," the man said, "but it's early yet." When neither Clea nor the dark-haired girl responded, he said something to the woman in a language Clea didn't recognize.

Clea didn't look up from her hands, but she could feel the woman's eyes on her. The redhead was almost as tall as the man, dressed in tight black jeans and tall black riding boots, and a tunic-length cable-knit sweater in heathered grays. She was as pale as her companion but wore precisely winged black eyeliner, subtle smoky eye shadow, and deep red lipstick, all so expertly applied that it seemed like she'd just walked out of a fashion magazine.

Clea was immediately suspicious of her, because she wasn't sure someone so objectively beautiful would be able to identify with the feeling of being invisible. Suddenly she felt that the flyer had been a false advertisement; it was clear to her that at least one of the people running this meeting had never been in her shoes.

The dark-haired girl had finally looked up from her game and was observing the woman and man talking through narrowed eyes, and she turned sideways slightly to lock eyes with Clea for just one moment—long enough for Clea to know that she was thinking the same thing.

Then the moment was gone, and the girl looked back down at her game, but not without offering a reluctant "Jade Mendez."

Clea managed a smile. "Clea Albright."

"Cleo?"

"No, Clea. Short for Cornelia."

"That's a weird way to shorten Cornelia. Do people ever call you Corny?"

"Only when they're making fun of me."

"What about Cleopatra?"

Thinking immediately of her roommate's horrid friend Delaney, Clea forced a smile. "Only when they're *really* making fun of me."

"Well, that's a shitty thing to do. Cleopatra is an awesome name."

"Yeah, I guess, but my name's Cornelia."

"Yeah, I got that. I'm just saying."

And that was the end of the conversation.

Thankfully, other people began to wander in: a few lonely students like them, a few well-groomed people in suits, but also a few homeless people who made a beeline for the cocoa and doughnuts, which the man and woman offered up graciously. At one point, the city bus stopped just outside the building and a few more people trickled in, immigrants from the suburbs on the other side of town, each one all alone, addressing the man and woman at the front of the room in halting English.

One of them sat down to breastfeed her fussy baby: a new mother dressed in raggedy clothes, her features gaunt, eyeing the doughnuts and cocoa from across the room. At that point, the redheaded woman picked up the box and brought it over to her, offering it out and saying, "Please help yourself. You must be hungry."

The woman smiled but looked uncertain and said something in another language Clea didn't know. But surprisingly, the redhead responded in kind, and the woman's face lit up and her eyes filled with tears as she accepted a doughnut from the box.

Before long, the room was nearly full—although still awkwardly silent besides the man and woman greeting any newcomers—and Clea finally decided to get in line for cocoa and doughnuts. She turned to ask Jade if she wanted anything so she wouldn't have to get up, but the girl gave her a vicious look as if she knew exactly what Clea was about to say. Jade then got to her feet and grabbed her crutch, moved swiftly across the room, and somehow made it to the line before Clea was even out of her seat.

Clea got in line behind her and grabbed a pumpkin spice doughnut and a cup of cocoa. When she noticed Jade fumbling to pick up her own doughnut and cup at the same time, Clea opened her mouth to offer help at the exact moment Jade stuffed the doughnut into her mouth to carry it, grabbed her cocoa with her free hand, and stormed back to her seat.

"I don't want your help," Jade muttered when they

were both back in their seats. "I can't fucking stand people feeling sorry for me."

"Good thing I don't, then," Clea replied without looking at her. The words had come out before she could stop them, and she braced herself for a scathing retort, but when she turned to give Jade a sideways look, she could swear the girl was smirking.

"Welcome, everyone," the man said when eight thirty rolled around and the time finally came to start . . . well, whatever this was. "My name is Finn, and this is—"

"Ingrid," the redhead said. Clea could tell even from the back of the room that the woman's tight-lipped smile was forced.

"We're so glad you all could come today," Finn continued. "Ingrid and I formed this community support group because, since we're new in town ourselves, we recognized a need for this sort of thing. As we all know, Columbus is not only home to a diverse group of people in every sense of the word but the city is also expanding pretty quickly. It's easy to get lost in the shuffle—you wouldn't be here otherwise."

The people in the room remained mostly silent; most of them, Clea thought, were probably new in town as well and took him at his word. She herself wasn't overly familiar with the city yet, having grown up several hours away. She also hadn't strayed far from campus in the past couple months since the semester began.

"Some of you may feel isolated," said Ingrid. "Maybe you moved here alone for a job, or you moved here for a spouse and don't know anyone. Maybe you're struggling with mental illness and are having trouble finding help.

Maybe you came here from far away in hopes of a better life. Maybe some of you are here, in this city, for reasons beyond your control—hell, maybe there's a *lot* in your life that you feel is out of your control. You may feel invisible; you may even feel powerless."

She paused, and the room was quiet, expectant. Clea leaned forward in her seat involuntarily, waiting for the *but*.

"But," said Ingrid, "we're here to tell you that's not so. And even though, unfortunately, there's only so much we can do for you in one night, we hope you stick around. Our flyers for this meeting spoke to you all for different reasons, but in the end, the reason you're all here is the same."

The silence in the room was absolute, but Clea had goose bumps. Ingrid's hammer had hit her metaphorical nail right on the head.

Finn held his hands palms up and smiled reassuringly. "Now, we won't go around the room and introduce ourselves—we know that can be painful for some of you." He seemed to look at Clea directly when he said this, and she looked away.

"For today," said Ingrid, "we'd just like you to enjoy your snacks and maybe meet someone new. This group is called the Common Cause, and Finn and I are your community coordinators. We really hope you come again next week. We don't want to bore you with a lecture today. Just trust us when we say that we can help you. You don't have to participate in anything you don't want to—for now, just hear us out. That's all we ask."

Clea felt an overwhelming sense of relief. When they

had started talking, she had been afraid she'd be forced into doing things like icebreakers and team-building exercises. Things where she'd have to *talk* in front of *other people*. At least it seemed like Finn and Ingrid were smart enough to know how to avoid scaring off an entire group of misfits.

People had started to leave one by one, so Finn added, "We've rented out the space for the night, so feel free to stay as long as you'd like. It's cold outside." He directed this last bit to the homeless people who had been lingering anyway.

With that, it seemed their speech was over. Some more people started to leave, especially when a bus pulled up. Others went up for second helpings of doughnuts and cocoa. Very few seemed to talk to the others.

Ingrid had a look on her face like she thought the people leaving were all ungrateful, which went against everything she and Finn had said earlier. But as soon as she noticed Clea eyeing her surreptitiously, her expression smoothed into something unreadable.

Jade hadn't made a move to get up, but she'd taken her Switch out again, leaning her elbows on the empty table in front of her as she gamed. She'd apparently already tossed her doughnut plate and cocoa cup into the trash. Clea hadn't even noticed her eat the food, but then again, she hadn't really been paying attention. Plenty of other people in the room had wolfed down their first round of doughnuts and gone back for seconds already, and Clea rather wanted to be one of them. She hadn't eaten dinner yet. She could almost taste another pumpkin spice doughnut on her tongue.

But fear of judgment was very strong for her when she was forced to eat in front of other people, and it was that very fear that kept her in her seat and made her turn to the girl next to her instead.

"Do you . . . want to play a game?" Clea hedged.

"I'm already playing a game," Jade said without looking up.

Clea shifted and the folding chair creaked beneath her. She was suddenly overwhelmed with the sudden urge to go home, but it was too early yet; Hannah might still be there, and Clea never texted her to ask whether or not she and her friends were around. She didn't want to annoy Hannah with these texts every night, so she always just assumed the worst, even if it turned out they were getting ready in another person's dorm room that night. It unsettled Clea to have to live like this, for the only time she was ever comfortable was when the dorm room, her *space*, was her own. It made her anxious that she never knew what to expect every time she came "home."

Maybe I will *get another doughnut,* Clea thought, *and then go to the library and watch Netflix.* She never went anywhere without her laptop for exactly this reason.

But as soon as she moved to stand, someone plopped a tattered box containing Candy Land on the table. Clea's startled gaze moved from the box up to the face of the person standing across from her and found herself looking at Finn.

"Were you going somewhere?" he asked, the picture of innocence.

"J-just to get another doughnut," Clea managed.

"It's okay if you were; you're free to leave," he said with a smile.

Clea shook her head. "I wasn't going anywhere. Just—just to see if there were any pumpkin doughnuts left."

Finn's smile widened and his eyes crinkled at the corners. "Those are my favorite. I have to admit, I was tempted to eat a few of them on the way here."

"You and what's-her-face didn't touch the food," Jade observed with a sidelong glance at the pair of them.

"Well, that's because the food is for you all," Finn said cheerfully. "Ingrid and I will only give away what's left, so please eat up. There's a lot left, and we don't want to take it all."

As if on cue, Ingrid—who was deep in conversation with the breastfeeding mother she'd addressed earlier in another language, her infant now asleep in its sling across her chest—got up and grabbed one of the half-empty boxes of doughnuts and pressed it into the woman's hands. The woman shook her head and tried to force the box back on her but eventually relented, causing Ingrid to produce the first genuine smile Clea had seen from her.

"Are you guys a cult or something?" Jade asked all of a sudden, lowering her Switch and narrowing her eyes at Finn.

His smile was still plastered in place and didn't lose any of its good humor, although his own eyes narrowed slightly.

"Of course not," he said. "Common Causes are springing up all over the Midwest. Cities are growing, but technology has isolated us from one another. That's why websites like Meetup exist, you know."

"Right, I know." Jade rolled her eyes. "That's how I found you guys. That's why I'm even here."

Clea started. So that's why people from all over the

city had shown up tonight. She *hadn't* torn down the only flyer.

"But that's just proof that technology brings us together, too," Jade continued. "I game with people all over the country, and they've become my friends. I talk to them all the time online. So it's bullshit to say that technology isolates us. It *connects* us."

"Then why are you here?" Finn asked without a hint of spite in his voice—just genuine confusion, the need to understand where her argument was coming from. "Why did you come tonight . . . I'm sorry, what was your name?"

"Jade."

"Why did you come tonight, Jade?" he repeated, more softly this time.

At this, she finally lowered her game and sighed. "Because it's great to have friends online and all, but every once in a while, I just want to, like . . . eat dinner with someone, you know? To not do everything alone all the time."

Finn seemed satisfied by this answer, so much so that Jade rolled her eyes when she caught his expression and went back to her video game.

"I'd wager that you're not the only one in this room who feels this way," he said, and he looked to Clea with raised eyebrows. "Which is why we made this group in the first place. We saw a need, and we're trying to fill it."

Clea only nodded.

Finn looked down at Candy Land. "It's a shame. I picked up all these games at the thrift store on the way here, and it seems no one is sticking around to play. Ah, well."

"That's because Candy Land is lame," Jade said without missing a beat. "And so's guilting us into trying to stick around."

"Oh, *is* it lame?" Finn asked, seeming genuinely concerned. "We didn't have it where I grew up. It looked . . . I don't know. Cute?"

"It's for babies," Jade deadpanned at the exact same time that Clea said, "I mean, it's cute, but . . ."

They exchanged glances, and then Clea deflated and added, "But I mean, yeah, it's kind of for babies."

"Oh," said Finn. He looked almost comically disappointed. Across the room, Ingrid looked up at them as she started gathering the party supplies and moving them to the back room. For some reason, the scowl that flashed across her face made Clea change her mind.

"But we could totally play," she said hastily, shooting Jade a look. "Right? One round isn't going to kill us."

Jade pulled a face but stowed her Switch back in her bag and said, "Fine. Just remind me how to play. I haven't even *seen* this game since I was like six years old." She stood up and walked around the table to sit next to Finn and across from Clea.

Finn smiled at them, and the sparkle in his blue eyes made Clea smile back. It felt unfamiliar on her face, and Finn seemed to sense this, because he smiled even bigger, the corners of his eyes crinkling again.

"All right, then," he said, shimmying the lid off the ancient box and examining its contents. He pulled out four warped game pieces, barely recognizable as plastic gingerbread men. "I'll be blue."

"I call green," Jade said immediately, extending her palm, and Finn put the green piece on her hand.

Before Clea could say anything, she heard the *screech* of a chair being pulled up beside her.

"Red," said Ingrid as she snatched up the corresponding game piece and sat down.

Clea looked at the three of them and sighed as she held out her hand to Finn. "Well, then. Guess I'll be yellow."

"AREN'T YOU GUYS CARRYING ANYTHING OUT?" CLEA ASKED several hours—and several different board games—later, as the four of them exited the building and Finn locked the door behind them.

"Ah no," he said cheerfully as he turned the key. "We left it in the back room for next week." He gave her and Jade a hopeful look. "You *will* be back next week, right?"

"Same time?" Jade asked before Clea could respond.

Finn nodded.

"I'll be here, I guess," said Jade. "This actually wasn't terrible."

"Why do I feel like that's a pretty high compliment coming from you?" Finn said jokingly.

"Because it probably is," said Ingrid. Her face also attempted to rearrange itself into a genuine smile but failed so spectacularly that Jade just gave her a dark look.

"Clea, you too?" Finn turned to her, eyebrows raised.

Clea hesitated for just a moment before nodding. "Yeah. Yeah, I think I will."

"It was wonderful to meet you both, and thanks for staying. We promise next week won't be so boring," said Finn.

Clea and Jade smiled uncertainly, and an awkward silence ensued.

"North Campus or South?" Jade asked all of them, shifting on her crutch.

Finn nodded to his right. "East. We're off campus in the University District."

"North Campus," said Clea.

"And South for me," said Jade. "Well, Clea, wanna walk with me as far as the Oval?"

It was a longer route than her usual shortcut, but Clea nodded, and they waved goodbye to Ingrid and Finn as they crossed the street.

Once they were across and back on campus, they walked for a couple yards in silence before Jade said under her breath, casting a brief look over her shoulder, "Does any of this seem weird to you?"

"Weird?" Clea asked. Jade walked surprisingly quickly, and she was already struggling to keep up. "You mean Finn and Ingrid?"

"I mean the whole thing, but yeah, them most of all."

"They seem nice to me. Well, Finn does, at least." Clea looked back and saw that Ingrid and Finn were still standing in front of the building, deep in conversation, but Finn noticed her staring and smiled and waved. Clea flushed and waved back before turning around.

"You *like* him," Jade said.

"I do not," Clea huffed. "He's just . . . nice and paid attention to me. Those aren't the only two qualifications for liking someone. At least not the way you're talking."

Jade's eyebrows shot up as if she hadn't expected Clea to say something so perceptive.

"My clinical depression comes with a side of extreme cynicism," Clea added dryly at the look on Jade's face.

"Probably the only good thing about it. Otherwise, I'd just go around getting my hopes up all the time."

It was then that she realized that she'd just told a total stranger she was mentally ill, but Jade didn't seem particularly surprised about her big reveal.

"I mean, you're not wrong," Jade said. "But the guy is *too* nice. He probably just wants to get in your pants."

The thought made Clea uncomfortable. "I don't know. Even if he did, I'd say no. I just . . . don't feel that way about guys."

"You're into girls?"

"No, I don't . . . I don't think so?"

"Oh. 'Cause I am."

"Oh. Uh, cool."

Clea wished she could just roll with people telling her things like this, just as seconds earlier when she'd let it drop that she was depressed, but she couldn't think of anything more to say. And as the silence stretched on, Clea wondered if Jade was taking her response the wrong way.

"So," said Jade, shifting awkwardly on her crutch, "who *are* you into?"

"No, I'm just—I'm not *into* anyone," Clea blurted. "Not like that. I mean, I imagine myself falling in love, but anything like—anything physical doesn't do much for me, if I'm being honest." She shut her mouth abruptly. *Did I just make things worse?*

But Jade was giving her a crooked grin. "You're ace."

"If you mean asexual, I mean, I'm not comfortable calling myself that because to be honest, it's hard for me to feel *anything* these days."

"Because of depression?"

"Yeah."

"It happens. Well, see you next week."

"See you," Clea said awkwardly as Jade veered left toward South Campus.

Why am I so awkward? she thought at Jade's retreating back. *"Oh. Uh, cool." Seriously, Clea? Could you have sounded any less enthused? She probably thinks you hate her now.*

Clea had her bag packed for her nightly wanderings around campus and would've been happy to walk with Jade a little bit farther—if only to make up for that comment—but she was already too far to call after her, so Clea trudged off into the night on her evening trek around campus.

But after an entire evening of interacting with other human beings and feeling halfway comfortable among them, the cold, empty streets seemed even colder and emptier than other nights. Clea stuffed her hands deeper into the pockets of her parka and put her hood up, keeping her head down as she walked, ever grateful for the somewhat comforting blue lights on the emergency posts she passed.

She didn't know how long she walked, in circle after circle, from North to South and back again. She crossed paths with fewer and fewer people, and it was only when she stopped seeing clusters of students stumbling home from the bars that she decided it was probably safe to head back to her dorm.

She was about halfway there when she realized she was being followed.

Footsteps behind her—she could hear them. She came to a faltering stop in the middle of the sidewalk. The hair on the back of her neck prickled and goose bumps rose on her arms as she suppressed a shiver and whirled around to see a flash of deep red, almost like the color of—

The street was silent and empty behind her. The red she'd seen was just a sign for one of the buildings.

But I could've sworn . . . it looked almost like—like Ingrid's hair.

Why would she be following me?

She stood frozen on the sidewalk and regarded her surroundings for a long moment—glancing at trees, light posts, benches, anything someone could hide behind. But they were all lit up by the bright lanterns that lined all the campus streets. There wasn't even the shadow of a figure lurking behind any of these objects.

But I thought . . . never mind. It was probably nothing.

Steeling herself, Clea let out a long, shuddering breath and started walking home again as fast as she could.

CHAPTER THREE

———— ◆ ————

It took every bit of Clea's willpower to leave her room the next day, as if going out the night before had spent all the energy—or *spoons*, as her therapist said—that she had. If it hadn't been for the constant threat of Hannah's friends dropping by in the evenings to get ready for the bars, she wouldn't have mustered the will to set foot outside.

She fumbled on her nightstand for her meds and shoved the pills in her mouth with a grimace, swallowed them dry, and waited to start feeling things again, right on schedule.

She skipped class Tuesday morning and stayed in bed, staring at the ceiling. She heard Hannah's alarm go off, heard her roommate rummaging around, getting dressed, collecting her things, and shutting the door behind her when she left.

Clea lay there for hours afterward.

Then, when it got dark, she got up, pulled on some

clothes, and packed her own backpack for her nightly wandering. The flyer from the meeting the night before was still crumpled up in the pocket of her parka; she felt it as she reached into her pockets for her mittens and stilled as her fingers brushed the paper.

"You may feel invisible; you may even feel power- less . . . ," Ingrid whispered in the back of her mind.

Clea took the flyer out of her pocket and tossed it in the trash.

Just before she zipped her backpack, she grabbed her sketchbook and stuffed it inside, not really knowing why she did it. There was a sort of fluttering feeling in her chest, something she couldn't quite pinpoint, and it was that feeling that made her act.

She headed for the library, bought a pastry and a coffee shake at the café on the ground floor, and headed for the tenth floor overlooking the Oval. Lanterns dotted the crisscrossing paths across the grass, where students walked along like ants from where Clea had plopped herself down in one of the comfy chairs.

Settling in, Clea reached down to pull out her laptop and lose herself in Netflix shows for the next couple of hours, but her fingers found the sketchbook instead. She stiffened, having already forgot she'd packed it. *Depression sure does a number on my short-term memory*, she thought humorlessly. Nevertheless, she extracted the sketchbook and opened to the first blank page and pulled out a graphite pencil from where she'd stuck it in the book's coils several months ago.

Several months ago, when she'd smiled and thanked her mom, and her mom had replied, "This isn't to say I support you being an *art* major. I'm saying, I know it's something you like to do, and you should stick with it. But on the side. Not as a career."

So Clea had chosen psychology for her major instead, but her lack of interest in the subject was stifling. The irony of that wasn't lost on her, either.

"*. . . You may even feel powerless. We're here to tell you that's not so.*"

She thought of Ingrid. The way she very clearly didn't *belong*, the way she tried to pretend to empathize with people she couldn't possibly understand, the way she tried to be *normal*. Her red hair and pale white skin. Her lilting accent, her forced smile, her cold eyes.

You're being awfully judgmental of a person you just met, said a more sensible voice in the back of her head.

Clea ignored it and started to draw.

AND SO THE WEEK FADED INTO THE WEEKEND AND MONDAY dawned yet again, as Mondays do, and Clea found herself struggling to decide whether or not to attend her second Common Cause meeting.

Maybe Jade won't be there, and I'll have to sit all alone. I wish I'd asked for her number, she thought as she sat at her desk and half watched Netflix, freezing rain battering the window in front of her. Her eyes strayed to where her sketchbook sat atop the unread textbooks on the corner of her desk, and she sighed. As much as she'd wished that her inspiration, her will to *create*, would come back after that one night when she managed to draw for the first time in a year, it appeared to be a fluke.

Worthless, she thought as she took her meds.

She closed her laptop and managed to read through some of the chapters she'd been assigned by her English professor. Thus far in her college career, Clea had managed to eke out the bare minimum effort required not to completely flunk out, but by no means was she doing well in her classes.

Honestly, calculating how many points I need not to fail is almost as much effort as just doing the work, thought the part of her brain that was riddled with anxiety at the prospect of actually flunking out of school. But the thing about depression and anxiety—as with most mental illnesses, or so she heard—was that they tended to cover their ears and yell *La-la-la!* when logic reared its ugly head.

You should get a note from your therapist, and maybe your professors will give you extensions, her mom suggested after her first month of school, but Clea refused. It wasn't how long she had to do the work; it was that she couldn't *make* herself do it. Extending the deadlines for her assignments would only prolong the inevitable.

Lazy, her brain whispered to her. *It's just because you're lazy.*

After dinner, Clea packed up and went to the library to stall, and as eight thirty crept closer and closer, she hemmed and hawed and pulled out her sketchbook again. Looked at her drawing of Ingrid. Closing the sketchbook with a sigh, she made the executive decision to attend the meeting.

"I'm doing it," she said under her breath as she took the stairs down from the tenth floor. "I'm doing it, I'm doing it, I'm doing it." As if saying it aloud would make it true, would make sure she couldn't turn back.

She crossed the Oval and made her way down High Street and crossed to the off-campus side of the street as she drew closer to the Community Space. The building's darkened windows still made it look abandoned, and there was no sign of Jade. Once again, Clea hesitated before reaching out and opening the door, which was unlocked.

She took a deep breath and went inside.

"Clea!" Finn exclaimed as he bounded toward her like an excited puppy. "You made it. We're so happy to see you."

"We're delighted, actually," Ingrid drawled from behind him as she opened up several boxes of Buckeye Donuts.

Clea recognized a few familiar faces from last week, but she couldn't recall any names; Jade's was the only one she'd learned, she realized. Jade, and Ingrid, and Finn. The only people who'd stayed. But Jade was nowhere to be seen, and Clea's stomach lurched at the thought of having to go through this meeting alone.

Clea sat down in the same place as she had last week and shrugged off her backpack and parka, placing the former beside her and draping the latter over the back of her metal folding chair as she covertly surveyed the room.

It was clear that a lot of people were just here for the free food—the reason Clea herself had stayed in the first place, of course, so she couldn't judge, especially if those people were homeless—but the meeting was certainly less crowded than the week before. Had interest just dropped off, or had Finn and Ingrid not advertised at all this week?

Maybe they've already gotten what they needed, whispered a suspicious voice in the back of her head. A paranoid voice that told her Jade had been right at first, that this *was* a cult, a trap, and that she should flee as fast as she could.

But no, there were some new faces, Clea realized. More guys her age, looking more awkward than she felt. Wearing black band tees or geek shirts, baggy jeans, some gangly and loose-limbed, some chubby, but all with bad hair and scraggly, patchy beards.

One of the guys—of a similar build as she, wearing a stained anime T-shirt, with thick glasses and dark curly hair—caught her eye and gave her a small smile. Clea tried to arrange her face into a smile in return before turning away instead.

So judgmental, the sensible voice chided her. This guy wasn't bad-looking. Maybe he was a decent person. But Clea could barely handle her own shit, so she didn't want to give him even an inch.

Beggars can't be choosers, her depression said scathingly, and Clea pressed her lips into a firm line. It occurred to her that if Jade didn't come, Clea would be the only woman of her age group. And what then?

As if on cue, Jade breezed through the door. Her eyes landed on Clea, who gave a little wave, like Jade wasn't going to remember her—and then Jade made her way over and sat down next to her.

Next to her. Like they were friends or something. Clea felt a flash of validation. She wanted to call her mom all of a sudden and be like, *See? I did make a friend!* Then she remembered that last week, *she* had been the one to sit at the opposite end of the table from Jade. But then, they'd been complete strangers at the time.

"How was your week?" Clea asked. She hoped if she just acted normal, Jade would forget the awkwardness of their parting the last time.

"Fine. I should've got your number, though," Jade said as she shrugged out of her coat.

"My number?" Clea twisted her hands in her lap.

"Yeah, your number," said Jade. She sat down and ran a hand through her short black hair. "Remember how we established last week that we could both use a friend to do stuff with? Or are you not tired of being alone all the time?"

"Right. I mean, yeah, I am."

Jade studied her for a moment, and then her expression turned hard and she reached to pull her Switch out of her backpack. "I get it. I came out to you, and now we can't be friends because you think I'm hitting on you."

"That's not it at all," Clea said defensively.

"Man, Clea, and here I thought you weren't just like everyone else." She sank back in her chair and turned on her game.

I'm not, Clea wanted to scream. *I'm not, I'm not—I'm so much worse, but not in the way you're thinking.*

Before she could open her mouth to say anything, Finn announced from the front of the room, "All right, everyone, come grab your cocoa and doughnuts—we're about to get started with this week's meeting."

Clea made to get out of her chair and noticed Jade wasn't moving.

"Do you want me to grab you—?" Clea offered.

"Not hungry," Jade said without looking up from her game.

Wordlessly, Clea shuffled up to the front of the room and got in line with the others, plopped her doughnut on a paper plate, and caught Ingrid's eye at the end of the line from where the woman stood handing out cocoa—out of earshot of Finn, who was making small talk with the cluster of awkward boys, many of whom stared up at him in unconcealed awe.

Ingrid's cold eyes shot from Jade to Clea, and she leaned forward, proffering a cup of cocoa, and said off-handedly, "Having a lover's quarrel?"

Clea blinked a few times and swallowed heavily. Ingrid arched an eyebrow at her, her perfect red mouth curving into what she probably hoped was an understanding smile but, to Clea, seemed more smug than anything, because *what could she possibly understand about me? Nothing. Just look at her.*

"I don't know what you're talking about," Clea said stiffly. She took the cup of cocoa out of the woman's hand and nearly ran back to her seat, thinking of the drawing she'd made in her sketchbook. A chill ran through her, and she sipped the cocoa in an attempt to staunch it, to no avail.

When she glanced back at the front of the room, she saw Ingrid studying her with that same smug look, and she averted her eyes back down to her Styrofoam cup and took a long swig of cocoa.

By then, the last of the group had grabbed their drinks and doughnuts, and Finn and Ingrid moved the table to the side and stood at the front of the room. A hush fell over the small crowd; maybe twenty people had stuck around to eat.

"Last week we told you that we weren't going to make you sit around listening to lectures," Finn began with an easy smile. "This week is a bit different—"

"It's not a lecture. It's more like . . . life advice," Ingrid said. "Consider Finn and I your life coaches, if you will. Just for a night."

A murmur went through the group, but no one spoke up directly. When the buzz subsided, a look passed between Finn and Ingrid, a beat of silence.

"Show of hands," said Ingrid to the assembly. "How many of you have ever felt invisible?"

The new guys all raised their hands. After a moment, Clea tentatively did the same. In the end, the only person who hadn't raised their hand was Jade. But then again, she was still playing her Switch.

Ingrid fixed her with a stare. "Hmm. Is that so, Jade?"

"Yeah, I've always felt *too* visible, if you know what I mean," Jade said bluntly, without looking up.

"And why is that?" Finn asked kindly.

Jade put down her game, reached over, and lifted up her crutch. "Because I'm gay and disabled. No matter how much I *want* to blend in, I can't." She cast a sidelong look at Clea. "And I have a feeling I'm not the only one who feels that way, honestly."

Clea's face began to heat up, and she shakily lowered her hand, and the rest of the room followed suit. Every face had turned to look at her. She had never wanted so badly to disappear.

"I m-mean," Clea stammered, "it feels like all the times

I want to be invisible, I can't be. I feel like I take up too much space. And all the times I want to be seen, I just get ignored."

"Aha, and there it is." Finn clapped his hands together loudly, and everyone faced the front of the room again. Clea exhaled shakily and pressed her cold hands to her hot cheeks, taking deep breaths and giving him a look of silent gratitude.

"There *what* is?" Jade demanded.

"There's where we can help," said Finn, smiling, as if this were the simplest answer in the world. "You see, you may think that being invisible is a curse, but I choose to think of it as more of a superpower."

"A . . . superpower?" Clea said, lowering her hands from her face.

"Yep. I mean, there are superheroes who can turn invisible. Think of what you can do with invisibility. You could go anywhere, do anything, and go completely unnoticed."

"Okay, sure," said Jade, "but that's if you're talking about *literally* being invisible. Not other people making you *feel* invisible."

"Yeah, seriously," said one of the guys, a greasy-haired kid in a death metal T-shirt with an illegible logo. "Why would we *want* that? I thought the whole point of this group was to help us feel *less* invisible."

"The point of the group is to foster camaraderie among people who may be feeling that way," Finn said amiably.

"That sounds pretty unhelpful to me," Jade drawled. She picked up her crutch again and waved it at him. "So, like, as a highly visible person, am I free to go? I must've misread the flyer last week—clearly there's no place for me here."

A murmur of agreement ran through the room, and another one of the guys—a gangly young man with blue hair, several piercings, and a large birthmark spanning half his face—said, "Yeah, same."

Finn rubbed the back of his neck, abashed. "That's not it. It's just the theme of today's talk, that's all."

Ingrid put her hands up. "I'm not sure why Finn decided to phrase it the way he's phrasing it, but that's not what we're saying. We're trying to create a safe space for everyone who joins Common Cause. We're saying that it's *okay* to be who you are, even if who you are is an introvert who has trouble making friends. Does that make sense?"

The group was quiet, contemplative. A few of the guys were looking at Ingrid with renewed interest and in some cases lust, which made Clea's stomach twist uncomfortably.

But she wasn't really focused on this conversation—something in her had shifted at the word *superpower*, and it kept invading her mind. She struggled to pay attention.

"So you're not necessarily going to help us learn how to make friends," Illegible Metal Band Boy was saying.

"That's something you've got to learn on your own, I think," said Finn, once again confident after Ingrid's clarification, "but you could start by making friends right here in this room. What do you say?"

A couple of the Awkward Boys—as Clea had started calling them in her head—glanced at her and Jade and looked doubtful. Jade took notice of this and set her face in a sneer to stare down any of the group who dared to make eye contact with her.

"So back up," said one of the guys, and when Clea turned slightly to look at him, she saw it was the same guy in the anime shirt she'd made eye contact with earlier in the evening. The chair creaked as he leaned back in it, attempting to look haughty. "From my experience, being invisible just means that the girls you like never like you back and stuff like that. I don't see how that's a super-power, like, at *all*."

"If the girl doesn't like you back," Jade said loudly, "that means she *has* noticed you. She just doesn't *like* you, Nice Guy Syndrome."

"The name's Brendan, actually."

Clea's eyebrows shot up and she glanced toward Finn and Ingrid, wondering if they were going to step in, but they both looked on with thinly veiled interest. The Awkward Boys all gave Jade identical contemptuous looks, but Brendan actually looked contemplative.

"That's a fair point, though," he said thoughtfully. "I guess what I meant to say is the girl you like doesn't notice you, either. So she can't like you back, right? Because she doesn't even know you. You're not putting yourself out there. You're not even giving yourself a chance. So you can't even complain, y'know?"

"That makes sense to me," Clea said quietly, looking to Finn. "So you're saying we should give ourselves a chance and try to be noticed? Especially by the people we like?"

Finn opened his mouth to speak, then closed it again. Once more, his smile faltered just slightly. "I mean, not exactly—"

"What Finn is saying," Ingrid interrupted, "is that you don't have to change who you are in order to be accepted.

That's what we're getting at. So what if you're an introvert? So what if you have social anxiety?" She gestured around them. "Within these four walls is a place for everyone. And this city is so big that it can be hard to find people to identify with. So let's start here. Let's start with getting to know the people in this room, and maybe those of you who are shy or feel invisible will have less trouble reaching out to others out there in order to find the people you fit in with, and those of you who feel *too* visible or *too* different will know that there are people out there who won't judge you. This is only the beginning. These are your first steps. Does that make sense?"

Clea grudgingly had to admit that it did. This sentiment seemed to be shared by the rest of the group, even Jade, who folded her arms and cast her eyes to the ground, mollified.

"Right, right," said Finn. "The world needs invisible people just like it needs fast-food workers. We can't all be rich, or who would flip the burgers?"

"That's gross and classist," said Jade, and Ingrid pursed her lips like she agreed.

Finn raised his hands, palms up. "What I'm saying is that there is a way to take advantage of being invisible. It's more like . . . not everyone can be a stage actor. You need stagehands working behind the scenes, or the production will fail. Does that make sense?"

Jade made a face. "I mean, it's *less* gross . . ."

"So," said Ingrid, clapping her hands together, "in the spirit of my friend Finn here digging himself into an ever-deeper hole—"

Finn gave a good-natured guffaw and shrugged, which

endeared him to Clea somewhat; she wished she could take being called out with the same grace, especially when she could barely handle the imaginary callouts she was always scolding herself with in her own head.

"—tonight, let's play a game," Ingrid finished. "Let's go around the room, and Finn and I would like to hear about what you would do if you were invisible."

"Literally invisible or, like, the same things we're doing now?" Brendan asked.

"Literally invisible," Ingrid confirmed. "Who wants to go first?"

As they went around the room, some people gave the standard answers—mainly robbing banks and stores and spying on people. One of the Awkward Boys shamelessly announced that he'd use his powers of invisibility to spy on women in the locker room.

"*Wow*, you're disgusting," Jade said loudly, and even Ingrid wrinkled her nose in distaste. Clea, who was still trying to think of a response that wouldn't embarrass herself, didn't even react.

"Okay, smart-ass—what would *you* do?" the guy sneered.

"Oh, that's easy," said Jade, leaning back in her chair and folding her arms. Unlike Brendan earlier, she was genuinely haughty. "I'd be a vigilante."

"That's what I was going to say," said Brendan, who hadn't gone yet.

"What kind of vigilante?" Finn asked. He'd perked up a bit from where he stood beside Ingrid, a spark of sharp interest in his pale eyes.

"The kind that serves justice," Jade said. She stared him down, expression set in stone. "The kind that fucks up rapists who think they've gotten away with it and beats up wife beaters and child molesters and anyone else who preys on the innocent. The kind that stands up for people who can't stand up for themselves. The kind that punches up."

A slow smile spread across Finn's face and not the kind smile that Clea had been so used to seeing. For a moment, his expression had a hint of sadistic delight in it, like he was imagining all the things Jade was saying, picturing them in his mind.

Savoring them.

"That's a very good answer, Jade," Ingrid said, and even she was smiling. But unlike Finn's, the usual sharp edge to Ingrid's smile had softened, like how she'd looked when she'd spoken to the breastfeeding mother at the last meeting. Clea noticed that woman was suspiciously absent and hoped she was all right.

"I think I'd be more like Robin Hood," said Brendan, unprompted. "Stealing from the rich to give to the poor. Same idea, less violence. Or like Batman."

Finn's eyes darted to the boy, and in a beat, he was back to his normal, cheerful self. Clea wondered if she was the only one who noticed the look that had just passed across his face.

"That's a good answer, too," Finn said cheerily. Then finally, his eyes moved to Clea, the last person in the room who hadn't responded. "And what about you, Clea?"

Clea twisted her hands in her lap and looked down at the table, at her empty plate and Styrofoam cup. "I . . . I honestly don't know."

"Really? You had all this time to think of something,"

sneered the pimply boy who'd called Jade a smart-ass. "You're the last one to go."

Jade opened her mouth to retort, but for once in her life, Clea didn't shrivel up at a taunt; she kept her eyes on Finn and continued:

"I think I would try to use my literal powers of invisibility for good." She took a deep breath. "But I don't know. I really don't. Because I think you don't really know what you'll do with a power until you have it, you know? So what's the point in even thinking about it now?"

"I mean, she's not wrong," said Brendan. "Like people who talk about what they will do when they're rich, and then they get rich and blow all their money on stupid shit."

"That's a fair comparison," said Ingrid, with a wave of her hand. "I suppose."

But Finn was still looking at Clea, grinning. "That's a pretty wise answer, too, Clea. Good job."

"She just couldn't think of anything else," Pimply Boy said, rolling his eyes.

Clea clammed up, again desperately wishing she could take being called out with a little more dignity. Instead, her shoulders slumped and she looked away. *Is this what the point of this group is going to be, then? Forcing me to be visible by making me feel like an idiot? Is this what my "first steps" are going to be to get over this feeling? Like peeling off a Band-Aid?*

Clea didn't know if she could handle it.

When she didn't say anything, Jade jumped to her defense. "At least she didn't say the first perverted thing that came to mind, unlike *some* people."

"But Clea does raise a good point," Finn said. "So I'd

like you all to think on this for next time. Really *think* about what you'd do—not the first thing that comes to your mind. Give yourself some time to digest it.

"And please feel free to come up here for more cocoa and doughnuts for the road! Otherwise, same time next week."

As people got up and started to file out of the Community Space, Brendan came over to Clea and Jade's table and said, "Hi, I'm Brendan."

"You said that, *actually*," Jade said.

"Ah, I'm so glad you're all together," Finn said, bounding over to them. He leaned over the table and watched as the rest of the group left in a herd and said in a low voice, "You three had the best answers of the group. I was wondering if you'd all like to join me for coffee on Friday evening and talk more about this? That is, unless you're hitting up some parties or something this weekend." He laughed. "I wouldn't blame you in the least, honestly. I'd actually be a bit jealous—I can't say I've met many of my fellow grad students who like to party. We're all far too busy."

Brendan, Jade, and Clea gave one another the exact same look: *Us? Get invited to a party? Yeah, right.*

"I thought you were giving us a week to digest?" Jade said, her dark eyebrows rising up under her bangs.

"Your answers were thoughtful enough without any further need to consider them. So if you don't mind waxing philosophical with me for a little bit longer without the . . . ah . . . *peanut gallery* interfering, I'd appreciate it. Philosophy and psychology are hobbies of mine, and it's rare to get a chance to speak with people with such interesting viewpoints."

"More interesting than 'spy on women in the locker room,' at any rate," Ingrid said under her breath.

"Sure, why not?" said Brendan, turning to Clea and Jade. "What about you guys?"

Jade looked over Finn's shoulder at Ingrid. "If she's there, I'm out."

"How charming you are." Ingrid's smile took on its usual forcedness.

"It'll just be me, then," Finn said without missing a beat. When Jade muttered her assent, he looked to Clea. "What do you say?"

Clea inhaled deeply through her nose. All eyes were on her.

"Yeah, sure," she said. Not because she actually *wanted* to talk about her answer—which, as Pimply Boy had accused, she had rather come up with on the fly—but simply because she was caving in to peer pressure.

And what else was she going to do on a Friday night? Her usual?

"Great," Finn said, pulling out his phone, unlocking it, and passing it to Jade. "If I could please get your phone numbers, I'll start a group chat. Don't worry, I won't blow up your phones—the most you'll get from me is the time and place of our meeting. I was thinking, there's this coffee shop in the Short North that's open pretty late. I assume you all have classes during the day."

The three of them nodded, and Jade passed Finn's phone to Clea, who put in her number swiftly and passed it to Brendan. Their fingers brushed for just a moment, and he gave her a small smile and made brief eye contact as he took the phone from her. Her heart turned over in her chest, and she swallowed and smiled back.

"I should get your number, too," said Jade to Clea. "Could you write it down for me, so I don't have to dig up my phone?"

"For sure," Clea murmured.

Brendan had given Finn his phone back, and Clea thought for a moment that he was going to ask for her number as well. She breathed a sigh of relief when all he said was "Okay, guys, I guess I'll see you Friday."

"See you," Finn said, waving, as he and Ingrid moved to the table in the front of the room to clean up for the night. Jade and Clea stood and put their coats on, waved goodbye to both of them, and exited the Community Space.

"Well, that was weird as fuck," Jade said when they crossed the street back on to campus and were roughly in the same place they'd been last time when they parted.

"Was it?" Clea asked. "It didn't seem too weird to me."

Jade gave her a look as if she expected Clea to say she was joking. When Clea continued to give her the same blank stare, Jade sighed.

"Well," she said and headed left toward South Campus, "I guess I'll see you Friday."

"See you," Clea said, starting off in the opposite direction and into the wind. The cold bit her face so harshly that she pulled her scarf up over her nose and walked faster, desperate to get back to the warm safety of her dorm.

At the same moment, she realized it was too early and her roommate and friends might be there still. She realized that Brendan was walking in front of her and slowed her pace so she wouldn't catch up with him. When the wind became too much, she stopped short and veered left, heading toward the library instead.

Another night alone was better than crossing paths

with Hannah's friends, that was for sure. They'd only gotten more vicious since the Burrito Incident.

But in the back of her mind, the thought prickled her: *What would you do if you were literally invisible?*

And for a moment, as she thought of her roommate's vicious bestie, of Delaney's jeers and taunts, of Hannah and their friends snickering in the background—and she let herself think of the things she could do to them if they couldn't see her, she wondered if she really would use her powers for good after all.

CHAPTER FOUR

H ey, Cleopatra, do you ever get out of bed?" a voice
jeered. "Or do you just lie around all day like a
slug?"

Clea thought she had dreamed it at first. She was curled
up on her side, facing the wall. She took deep breaths and
didn't react to the comment except to open her eyes and
then narrow them, clenching her fist around the corner of
her pillow.

"Oh my God, shut *up*, Laney," Hannah hissed. "She's
still asleep."

"It's almost dinnertime. On a *Friday*. What a freak. Is
she, like, narcoleptic or something? Or just seriously that
lazy?"

Clea had, in fact, been up for so long the night before
that she'd been awake to hear Hannah's alarm go off for her
eight a.m. class. She'd been at the twenty-four-hour science
and engineering library, filling her sketchbook with . . . what
had she been drawing? She could barely even remember.

She could hear the scowl in Hannah's voice. "She's out just as late as we are most of the time. Give her a break. I didn't hear her come in this morning, and I got home at, like, five." Hannah yawned as if on cue. "Good thing I got to take a nap this afternoon. . . ."

"Out all night? Doing *what*? Does she even have friends? Or is she just hiding somewhere like a sad sack? She must've had a wild night out to have gotten back later than you. Maybe she has a secret fuck buddy," Delaney added sarcastically, with a horrible laugh.

"Jesus, Delaney, lay off," Hannah said. Clea could hear her zipping up her backpack; she must've just gathered the last of her things. "What the hell did she ever do to you?"

The door opened and closed, but Clea could still hear their muffled voices as they made their way down the hall. Only when she heard the elevator *ding* did she drag herself into a sitting position and reach for her phone.

Jade had texted her several hours ago, the very first text she had ever sent Clea since getting her number on Monday after the meeting: *Dinner today? I just wanna talk before the coffee thing tonight. Don't worry it's nothing bad lol*

And then, about an hour ago, Jade had followed up with: *Didn't mean to freak you out, just wanted to touch base about Prettyboy before tonight cuz I have a feeling about him*

Clea didn't have to ask who she meant by *Prettyboy*.

Sure, dinner sounds good, Clea texted her back. *Sorry. Was in class.*

That's a long-ass class. Where to eat? Jade responded almost immediately.

Somewhere on High Street so we can take the bus down to the coffee shop? Clea typed and followed up with her first off-campus choice: *Cane's?*

Sure, can't say no to chicken fingers lol. Time?

Seven? Since we're meeting at 8:30 for coffee and I need to shower

Sounds good, Jade replied, *meet there?*

Yep

OK, see you at 7

Kk, see you there. Clea typed out her answer and hauled herself out of bed, swallowed her meds dry, and undressed.

She pulled on a robe; grabbed her shower caddy, towel, and dorm room key; and poked her head out the door. The hallway was mercifully empty, so she made sure the door locked behind her and scurried as fast as she could to the bathroom's communal showers. They were the bane of her existence since college began. She tended to use the showers only in the very early mornings when she'd gotten back from her wanderings, or not at all—not until she got disgusted enough with herself that her revulsion outweighed the thought of anyone potentially making fun of her in her robe.

But tonight she was braving it because she *was* actually going out, to meet *people*, in the Short North of all places. She didn't think she'd ever be the sort of person who got invited to hang out there, but here she was. The thought warmed her along with the hot water as she washed her hair.

She finished showering, wrapped her hair in a towel and pulled on her robe, and made her way back to her room—only to find the door open and voices coming from within, causing her to stop dead in her tracks, clutching her shower caddy in both hands.

Hannah must've forgotten something—and sure enough, when she and Delaney exited the room, Hannah was stuffing a bottle of perfume into her bag.

"Y-you don't have to lock it," Clea said as they exited the room and Hannah reached for her key.

Hannah looked surprised to see her but slipped the key back into her pocket and said, "Okay, cool."

"Look at that—it lives," Delaney sneered at Clea as they brushed past her.

Hannah said nothing, only gave her roommate a fleeting, pitying look over her shoulder.

Something in Clea began to crumble. No—to *burn*.

What would you do if you were literally invisible?

"You know what, Delaney?" Clea said quietly, facing the door.

Both of them stopped and turned around. It took them a second to realize that Clea had just spoken to them.

"What, Cleopatra?" Delaney jeered, taking a few steps toward her. The crust of thick mascara and layers of eye shadow made her blue eyes look small and beady, her blond hair with its long, dark roots seeming to glow in the fluorescent hallway lights. She looked like some sort of luminous sea creature as she stood there grinning her horrible grin.

Clea turned her head sideways and stared her down. "I hope one day karma bites you in the throat, and you don't even see it coming."

Delaney made a choked sound of surprise, then let out

a loud guffaw. Then she took a few more steps forward and got right up in Clea's face—so close that Clea could smell the alcohol on her breath—and said, "We'll see about that, Cleopatra."

Then she whirled around and stalked off with Hannah, and Clea went back inside and closed the door behind her, leaning against it, her heart hammering in her chest.

She'd done it. She'd really done it.

And Hannah hadn't said a damn thing.

When she was able to pull herself together, Clea got dressed and used Hannah's expensive blow-dryer to dry her hair. Then she grabbed her backpack, bundled up in her parka, and headed out into the chilly evening to meet Jade.

"THANKS FOR MEETING ME," JADE SAID, AS THEY BOTH SLIPPED into a booth with their trays of food: lemonades, a basket of chicken fingers and fries, the best dipping sauce Clea had ever tasted, and a big slice of Texas toast.

"Of course," said Clea. She was still feeling a bit off after her confrontation with Delaney earlier, so she was a little shaky being around another dominant personality like Jade. This was also the first time she was actually sitting down and having a meal with another human being since she started college. Clea was always hypersensitive to how much she was eating compared to people around her, but Jade had explained that there had been a giant cookie tray in her dorm's lobby that afternoon and she'd stuffed herself on them. So she'd ordered her food in a to-go box and was currently picking apart her chicken tenders into dipping-sized bits "to get the most sauce per square inch onto the chicken."

Clea was too hungry to waste her time doing that, but she agreed with the general idea. She'd asked for an extra dipping sauce herself, after all.

"So do you have, like . . . a weird feeling about any of this?" Jade asked eventually. Her eyes were such a dark brown, they were almost black and focused on Clea so intensely that she shivered.

"Not really," Clea admitted. She finished off her first chicken strip and took a long sip of lemonade. Jade's eyes didn't leave her the whole time. After a moment, Clea put her drink down and continued, "I mean, not about Finn, at least."

"But the other one. That Ingrid girl. She gives me the creeps."

"Yeah." Clea shifted in the greasy booth. "Me too."

"Really?" Jade asked, raising her eyebrows. "Are you just saying that to agree with me, or do you really think so?"

Clea almost crumbled at the accusation but stood her ground. If she could stand toe-to-toe with an antagonist like Delaney, she could surely stand up to her own sort-of friend. "You think I'm just a sheep, huh?"

Jade shrugged and picked apart another chicken tender.

Clea had never shown anyone her artwork before, but then again, she'd never had much to prove. Swallowing her anxiety, Clea wiped her hands on a napkin, unzipped her backpack, pulled out her sketchbook, opened it to the page where she'd drawn Ingrid the other night at the library, and slid it across the dirty table to Jade.

"Holy shit," Jade said, wiping her own hands before pulling the sketchbook closer. "Did—did *you* draw this?"

Clea nodded. She watched Jade take it in, let out a deep breath, and then slid the sketchbook back across the table.

"Why does she look like . . . that?" Jade asked, gesturing at the drawing.

"It just came to me." Clea closed the sketchbook and put it back in her bag, then resumed eating her dinner. "I thought it was fitting."

"Well, it's like . . . I mean it's *really* good."

"Thanks."

A couple moments of silence passed. Jade picked up her lemonade and put the straw to her lips, looking thoughtful.

"I just think we need to stay on our toes," Jade said at last. "I wasn't kidding when I said these people could be a cult. Think about it. . . . I mean, there's a chance that this is not just a support group for the disenfranchised. It could be more like a recruitment tool for something a lot more sinister, you know?"

"Like what?" Clea asked. She didn't know many other people her age who talked about *disenfranchisement* and *recruitment*. Then again, she admitted, she didn't know many other people her age. Still, Jade was truly fascinating.

"I don't know, but I'm going to find out," said Jade with certainty. "Like, I haven't seen any flyers up around campus since the first meeting, right? And then all these scumbag boys show up. Maybe Finn and Ingrid are starting to advertise online. On, like, seedy message boards. What do you wanna bet half those guys are Internet trolls?"

Clea thought of Brendan and said, echoing her own sensible inner voice, "That's awfully judgmental."

Jade rolled her eyes; she was clearly thinking of Pimply Boy. And now Clea was thinking of him, too—a bully like

Delaney, emboldened because they thought Clea was an easy target.

"Just . . . Clea, listen." Jade leaned in. "Ingrid seems like a piece of work, but Finn? The dude's got charisma. However tonight goes, please promise me you won't just take him at his word."

She really does think I'm a sheep, Clea thought, offended. And then, her brain whispered, *But you are, aren't you?*

And then another thought:

She seems to genuinely care about me.

And when was the last time Clea was able to say that?

"I will," Clea said. "I promise."

THE COFFEE SHOP IN THE SHORT NORTH WAS BUSTLING AND cozy, and Finn and Brendan were already there when Jade and Clea got off the bus. Finn waved them over to where he sat in the corner once they'd gotten their beverages—a small cup of tea for Jade and an iced white chocolate mocha for Clea—and they settled down in the comfy chairs in a separated area of the café.

"Thanks so much for coming tonight," Finn said. He was wearing dark jeans and a button-up, his blond hair smoothed back into a ponytail, his beard freshly trimmed. "It's great to see you three outside of that crappy old building. How has your night been so far?"

"Pretty good," Clea said, and Jade and Brendan made similar noises. What Clea really wanted to ask Finn was where he was from, but she wasn't sure if that would be rude, so instead she said, "So uh, Finn, are you a student too?"

"A graduate student, actually," he replied. He was still smiling, his blue eyes crinkling at the corners. "I finished my undergraduate degree in Europe and I wanted a change of scenery."

Europe seemed pretty vague, but Clea nodded anyway instead of asking him to elaborate.

"I was lucky enough to meet Ingrid during orientation," Finn went on, "although her graduate program is in social work while mine is in computer science."

"Are you guys a couple?" Jade pressed, with a significant look at Clea, who pretended not to notice.

Finn looked back and forth at all three of them and made a gesture that was half-shrug, half-nod. "Well, she was one of the first people I met when I moved here. You see, Ingrid was very passionate about starting up a Common Cause when she heard about it, and that passion inspired me, too, so we hit it off. You know how sometimes you meet people you just click with?"

Brendan and Clea made vague gestures of understanding—clearly lies, since neither seemed to have clicked with anyone before—but Jade didn't look convinced.

"Anyway," Finn said, clapping his hands together the way he did to get people back on track during Common Cause meetings. "I asked you all here because I really liked what you had to say the other night at the meeting, and I was wondering if you'd be interested in helping me out with a project I'm working on."

"A project?" Clea asked.

"What kind of project?" Jade's tone was a bit more suspicious.

"Well . . . it's sort of a secret," Finn said quietly, leaning forward—both so they could hear him and so he could reach into the messenger bag at his feet and pull out a laptop.

Jade gave Clea a meaningful look, and Clea thought she could read her friend's mind: *Told you it was a cult.*

"I have an email list," Finn said, his voice almost lost in the noise of the café, "of two hundred of the richest people in the state. I'm writing emails to ask them for donations to the local domestic violence shelter, but I need every email to be unique down to the subject line so these people won't just delete them as spam, you know?"

"Huh," said Jade. Clearly this wasn't what she was expecting.

"So I was hoping that, between the four of us—we each write, what, fifty emails?" Finn said, opening the laptop. "I can email you guys profiles of these folks and the link to the donation site right now, if you want. But I know you're all busy, so feel free to say no. It's just, if we send out the same email to a bunch of people, it's more likely to be marked as spam. If you tailor it to them, they'd be more likely to read it."

"I mean, finals aren't for a few more weeks, so I'm sure I could help," Brendan said, and Clea nodded.

Jade even shrugged and said, "Sure, why not?"

"Great," Finn said with a grin. "What are your emails, please?"

They told him, and he typed them up.

"All right, excellent," he said. "Now, I'll email you all a link to the email account we're to be sending them from and a list of donor profiles so you can make every email unique.

I'll also pass along a link to the donation website. But please just copy and paste that link, don't click on it yourself—it'll disrupt the final data for how many clicks we get."

They all nodded. Again, Jade looked a little wary, but all she said was, "This is . . . surprisingly kind of you to be doing, Finn. You got some kind of connection to the shelter, or are you just a do-gooder?"

Finn flashed her a grin. "A little of both, actually. It's important to Common Cause to give back to the community in any way we can, and I thought this would be a great place for our chapter to start. Plus, judging by your answers the other night, I thought you three, of all people, might be interested in helping the less fortunate."

"Even me?" Clea asked in a small voice, for her answer had been uncertain.

"I just had a feeling about you," said Finn with a twinkle in his eye. "I figured that, even with your answer, you're the kind of person who would punch up."

Clea felt a rush of heat to her face and took a long sip of her iced beverage.

"What about Ingrid?" Jade asked. "Why isn't she helping? I thought *she* was the one into social work. Doesn't like helping the less fortunate, does she?"

Finn blinked a couple of times and said, not unkindly, "You know, Jade, I'm a little confused as to what you have against her."

"She just rubs me the wrong way," Jade said, casting a look to Clea. "And I'm not the only one. Show him your sketchbook, Clea."

Clea froze, her straw still in her mouth, and shook her head mutely.

Jade lurched forward and grabbed Clea's backpack before she could react, and before Clea knew it, Jade had flipped open her sketchbook to the drawing of Ingrid.

Finn was completely still, his eyes not leaving the page. After a moment, he reached out a rigid hand and took the book from Jade, his expression inscrutable.

Please don't turn the page, please don't turn the page, Clea thought desperately, for she'd added some far more embarrassing sketches to her collection as of late. But luckily for her, Finn's stiff expression forced itself into something a little warmer. "You drew this?"

Clea nodded silently.

"Incredible," Finn breathed, his eyes not leaving the page. "Why—can I ask why you drew her like this?"

"It's just—how she came to me," Clea said in a small voice. "I don't want to say more than that. I know she's your friend. Or your more-than-friend. Or whatever."

Finn's hand tightened on the edge of the sketchbook, and his gaze finally moved up to Clea. She felt like he was staring into her soul.

"It's okay to be honest," he said gently. "I'd like to know, in case she's deterring people from our cause, because that's the most important thing."

"More important than your sort-of-girlfriend?" Jade asked skeptically.

"Can I see?" Brendan asked, and Finn looked to Clea for affirmation. At a loss, Clea nodded, and Finn passed the book to him.

"Whoa," Brendan said, holding the sketch up, facing Clea, and gesturing at it. "Did you draw her as, like, a vampire?"

"What was your first clue?" Jade asked sarcastically, cupping her shivering hands around her steaming cup of tea. "The fangs or all the blood?"

Clea flushed and shrugged as she reached out to take the sketchbook back from Brendan. He let her, and she stuffed it back in her bag. "She just kind of has that . . . *feel* about her, you know? I don't know. It just came from my mind. Don't read too much into it." She gave Finn a desperate look. "*Please* don't tell her about this. I'm really embarrassed."

"Why?" Brendan asked. "It's a really cool drawing. Can you draw me as the amphibian guy from *The Shape of Water*?"

"And me as a werewolf?" Jade asked.

"And me as a zombie?" Finn asked with a grin, but in her mind, Clea still had the look on his face the moment he saw the drawing of Ingrid—had that been *fear* that flashed across his face?—and she could only force a smile in return.

They talked a little bit more after that—about this, that, and the other; where they'd come from and what they were studying—until Finn finally came back around to the point.

"You three, I'm so happy to have met such bright kids," Finn said cheerfully.

"Kids?" Jade scoffed. "You're a grad student. What are you, twenty-three?"

"Actually, I'm twenty-six, but I feel like there aren't that many years between us. You're all so mature."

Jade rolled her eyes. "Thanks, *Grandpa*."

Brendan burped as if on cue. The rest of them snickered, and even Finn smiled.

"If you're twenty-six, did you take a couple gap years before grad school?" Clea asked.

"Many of us go to school a little later in Europe," Finn explained. "After high school, a lot of students choose to take a few years off to work before we decide whether or not to go to university and what we want to study."

"Wish it was like that over here," Brendan grumbled into his coffee, "instead of making us choose what we want to do for the rest of our lives when we're eighteen. I'm still not even sure I'm on the right track."

"Tell me about it," Clea said with a sigh.

"There's always time to change," Finn said, giving her a significant look. "It's never too late to turn things around, Clea. And you're all so very young. You have plenty of time." He held up his laptop. "I very much appreciate your help on all this. If you'd have time, I'd love to have all the emails sent out within the next week or so."

"I'm just not sure what our answers the other night have to do with this," Jade said all of a sudden. The suspicion was back in her voice. "With the emails thing, I mean."

"Your answers told me that you wouldn't mind doing something for other people," Finn said, stowing the laptop back in his bag, "without any credit. In this case, asking for donations for the less fortunate, on behalf of a charity. They'll never know it was you, but you will have done some good in the world." Again, he seemed to be looking at Clea more than the other two. "I do believe you might enjoy it. In fact, I'm not sure there's anyone who's better suited to this sort of work."

Clea felt her face heat up, and she looked away.

"I guess that makes sense," Jade said reluctantly, and Clea and Brendan nodded.

When the four of them left the coffee shop, Finn waved goodbye and disappeared down the side street where he said he'd parked his car. As Clea and Jade headed for the bus stop, Brendan said from behind them, "Hey guys, I drove, too—do you guys want me to drive you back to campus?"

Jade and Clea looked at each other. Clea was about to say yes, but then she remembered that Jade would be getting dropped off first since she lived on South Campus, which would leave Clea alone in the car with Brendan for longer than she was comfortable with.

"But freshmen aren't allowed to have cars," Jade said.

Brendan shrugged. "I'm a commuter student. That's kind of how I ended up at the first Common Cause meeting. . . . It's kind of hard making friends with other freshmen when you don't live in the dorms, y'know?"

"It's hard making friends, period," Jade agreed.

"I mean, I'm cool taking the bus," Clea said. "Thanks, though."

Jade looked like she wanted to argue, but she hesitated a moment before shaking her head. "Yeah, I'll just take the bus with Clea. Thanks for asking, though."

"Okay, suit yourselves," Brendan said and started walking away.

As Jade and Clea made their way to the bus stop, Jade said abruptly, "I could've used the ride, you know. I'm having a high pain day and the bus stop is a few blocks from my dorm. But I didn't want you to ride the bus alone."

Clea stiffened. Jade was leaning more heavily on her crutch than usual. "I'm so sorry, I didn't know—"

"You were really quick to turn him down, and I've been through worse, so I didn't want to make it into a big thing," Jade muttered as the bus pulled up. "I know it's hard, but maybe stop and think for a minute how your anxiety-induced decisions affect your chronically ill friends, huh?"

"Chronically . . . ill?" Clea asked feebly as they boarded the bus, swiped their IDs, and sat down. "What do you mean? Is that why—?"

"Yeah."

"I never wanted to ask." Clea nodded at the crutch. "I figured you'd just tell me it was none of my business."

"I mean, you're not wrong. But I feel like this should've been enough of an indicator for you that maybe walking is a little difficult for me." She held up her crutch pointedly.

Clea was abashed but also a little bit angry. "How was I supposed to know you're having a . . . having a 'high-pain' day if you don't tell me? Invisibility is my superpower, not mind reading. You've gotta *tell* me these things. I feel like I've been pretty open about my anxiety and depression. You think I'm gonna judge you?"

Jade let out a dark laugh, then sighed. "I guess you're right. It's just hard to talk about. People either think I'm faking or exaggerating or just being lazy. . . ."

"You're preaching to the literal choir," Clea said.

They sat in comfortable silence the rest of the way, and Clea got off at Jade's stop, even though it would mean a longer walk for her back to North Campus. The night was especially cold, but Clea found she didn't mind it.

"I've got more health problems than I can count," Jade said out of nowhere when they were almost at her dorm.

"I literally had to pester the doctors into diagnosing me with fibromyalgia. They wouldn't listen to me. Said I was too young."

"That sucks," Clea said and meant it. "My parents thought my depression was just teen angst. I begged for years to go to a therapist and get on meds, and even then, they wouldn't take me until my school counselor recommended it."

"Looks like we have more in common than I thought," Jade said with a crooked smile as they approached the door of her dorm. "Well—see you Monday at the next meeting?"

"See you," Clea said, and as Jade disappeared inside and Clea turned to begin her long trek north to her own dorm, she remembered her assignment from Finn. Felt her face heating up as she remembered his words.

"They'll never know it was you, but you will have done some good in the world. I do believe you might enjoy it. In fact, I'm not sure there's anyone who's better suited to this sort of work."

Clea quickened her pace, eager to find out if he was right, and wanting more than anything to believe him.

CHAPTER FIVE

⸺ ◆ ⸺

When Clea got back from class on Monday afternoon—after barely leaving her room all weekend, composing emails for Finn's campaign deep into the night, forgetting to shower or eat—she stood in the doorway of her dorm and stared, her backpack falling limply at her side where she'd began to sling it off her shoulder.

Someone had dumped an entire burrito on her pillow, unwrapped and facedown, the sour cream and taco sauce and oil from the ground beef soaking into the fabric of her pillowcase.

And all she could do was stand there, shoulders shaking, willing herself not to break down.

Don't cry, she thought, stiffening her upper lip as tears welled in her eyes. *Don't cry, don't cry, don't cry.*

She had been up all night to finish emailing her list of donors, and the zeal of *doing* something had not worn off by morning, so she'd decided to go to her freshman

English composition class and Psychology 101. However, she'd almost fallen asleep in the latter and had been looking forward to going back to her dorm for a nice long nap before her Common Cause meeting.

Still trying fervently to hold back her tears, Clea shuffled into the room, kicked her backpack inside, closed the door behind her, and took the pillowcase off her pillow, maneuvering such that she turned it inside out around the burrito and used it as a sort-of bag for its contents. Beneath it, her heart sank at the sight of the grease and condiments soaking into her actual pillow.

She picked up the pillow in one hand, the dripping pillowcase in the other, and went down the hall to throw them in the trash room. Willed herself to keep it together in case she ran into Hannah—or worse, Delaney, the likeliest culprit of this cruelty, although Hannah must've been a willing bystander to have let her into the room to do it.

The smell of burrito still lingered in her room when she returned, making her stomach churn unpleasantly. When was the last time she'd eaten? She couldn't say. The smell of food made her sick, but she knew she should probably eat something before the meeting tonight.

As if on cue, her phone buzzed in the pocket of her parka, and she pulled it out and read the umpteenth text from Jade she'd received since Friday morning:

Clea. Please respond. Please tell me you didn't send those emails.

Her heart lurched in her chest, but she didn't reply to the text.

The first had arrived Saturday morning, and the text was so long that it almost took up Clea's entire screen:

Hey, so I looked up some of these people on the donor list before I started this project. Some of them really are super-rich, but others, they're just regular-ass people, and the info he has on them in these profiles for us to go off is like . . . really invasive. So I would maybe hold off on doing his "assignment" and we can talk to him about it on Monday, k?

Then, after Clea hadn't responded, she'd added: *Look them up if you don't believe me.*

She hadn't. She'd just kept writing and hitting *send*.

And then, Sunday morning: *Clea. Just talked to Brendan. He clicked the link that Finn told us not to click, and it crashed his computer.*

And Sunday afternoon: *Listen, this is really messed up. Brendan did some more digging on his parents' computer at home. Some of the "donors" on this list are like sex offenders. Some have criminal records and a history of domestic violence. Some have been arrested for other stuff, too, like robbery and assault. What the hell is Finn playing at, asking people like them to donate to a shelter? This is so fishy.*

Clea? Hello?

Clea still had not looked up any of the donors herself, regardless of Jade's warning. Nor had she clicked the link, out of respect for Finn telling her not to—and in case Jade was right.

She just kept writing and sending emails. She didn't know what made her do it. At first it had been because Finn wanted her to do it, and it was the first time someone trusted her with such a task, thought *she* was the only one who could pull it off, and she didn't want to disappoint him.

But then, as the texts kept rolling in from Jade, another

feeling took over: a kind of sick thrill. It was clear to her at this point that Finn had lied to them, and the thought made her a little uneasy. It even crossed her mind that what she was doing was illegal.

Yet she didn't stop. Because maybe the other "regular" people on the list were like Delaney—not necessarily criminals but evil in their own special way.

And if any of her recipients were dumb enough to click the link, maybe they deserved what was coming to them.

Karma.

And that was enough to make Clea keep going.

So, HAVING NOT SLEPT AND NOT HAVING ANYTHING BETTER TO do, Clea went to one of the dining halls and forced some food down, wandered around campus as night fell, and finally made her way to the Community Space.

She was the first one at the meeting, and instead of lingering outside and seeing who else showed up, she went right in. She was the first one there—the only one, it seemed, besides Finn, who was setting up an array of cocoa and doughnuts that, compared to the past two weeks, seemed significantly reduced.

"Clea!" Finn said. "I'm glad you're here first. I'd like to have a word with you."

"Um, sure," Clea said, putting down her backpack and jacket in her usual spot at the table she shared with Jade.

Finn bounded over to her, grinning. He was wearing a dark flannel button-up and black skinny jeans, his long hair pulled back in its short ponytail.

"Clea, your emails are brilliant," he said. He pressed

his hands flat on the table and leaned in toward her. "Yours have had more clicks than even mine. I *knew* you could do this."

"Th-thanks," she stammered, but felt pleasantly warm at the compliment.

"You wouldn't mind taking over Brendan's portion of the emails, would you?" he asked. "I'm afraid he had a bit of trouble."

Clea nodded mutely. "I—I mean, of course I will."

He grinned at her. "I very much appreciate it."

"I—of course." She looked around. "Where's Ingrid?"

"Ah." Finn stood up straighter and took his hands off the table, steepling his fingers. "I . . . I'm afraid Ingrid and I have gone our separate ways."

The warmth Clea had been flooded with a moment before turned to a sudden chill. "Oh. That's . . . I'm sorry. Can I ask why?"

Finn shrugged. "It just wasn't working out. It happens sometimes, you know?"

Clea nodded, even though she didn't know. She was saved from responding any further by Jade entering. She stopped just inside the door, her eyes moving from Finn to Clea and lingering on the latter with annoyance.

"Jade, welcome," Finn said with a smile. "Your emails were wonderful. I've just asked Clea to take over the rest of Brendan's. He won't be joining us any longer."

Clea's eyebrows show up. *Jade sent emails, too? After telling me not to?*

But now Jade wouldn't look at her. Instead, she glowered at Finn.

"Yeah, because his computer is busted from clicking

on that link," Jade said, giving him an accusatory look. "Just what were you having us do, Finn?"

Finn studied her for a long moment before a slow smile spread across his face. "It's actually quite simple, Jade. I was giving you the tools you needed to punch up, via a low-risk operation from the safety and comfort of your own home."

"Under false pretenses," Jade shot back.

"Yes and no. It's easy to *say* you want to make a difference. But I've found that many people aren't willing to do what needs to be done. They just need a little push in the right direction." Finn mimed giving them a nudge.

"By lying to us," Jade said bluntly.

Finn still hadn't lost his cheerful demeanor. "Well, I take it you looked up some of the people you were emailing. It seems to me that the reason you're most upset is that I did lie to you, and I apologize. I'm just not sure you would've done it otherwise. . . ." His smile took on a slightly sharp edge. "I see now that I was wrong. Tell me, did you send your emails before or after you realized it?"

Jade shifted on her crutch and gave him a scathing look but said nothing.

"Ah. And there it is." Finn pulled up a chair and sat down across from Clea, and Jade sat down next to her, still glaring at him.

"I'm sorry. I got all your texts," Clea said to Jade without looking at her. "I just . . . didn't want to stop."

Jade pursed her lips. "Neither did I. The more I found out about the people on the list, the more I *wanted* to do it. But the link . . ." She looked at Finn. "What does it do?"

"Let's just say that clicking the link still results in donations to the domestic violence shelter," Finn said, and then added after a moment, "involuntarily."

Clea felt a bit sick. Sending emails was one thing—but *stealing*?

Jade seemed to feel the same way. "But—can people track the emails back to us? To our computers?"

"Could we get in trouble?" Clea asked apprehensively, since this hadn't previously occurred to her and the thought of the police showing up at her dorm and leading her away in handcuffs, with Hannah looking on in pity and Delaney cackling in the background, was enough to make her break out in a cold sweat.

Finn shook his head. "The email logins I gave you are encrypted. There's no way to trace it, I assure you." He raised his eyebrows at her and grinned. "Does that mean you'd be willing to take on more assignments like this?"

Clea and Jade looked at each other, neither quite knowing what to say, but they were saved from answering when some of the Awkward Boys showed up and headed straight for the doughnuts, talking among themselves. Finn leaped up to greet them.

"You sent your emails?" Clea whispered to Jade, giving her a sidelong look. "After blowing up my phone all weekend telling me why I shouldn't?"

Jade sighed. "I guess maybe I was trying to convince myself more than you. Don't judge." She turned to look Clea dead in the eyes. "I had my reasons. We'll talk later."

After they'd all gotten their fill of cocoa and doughnuts and Finn had answered the question of "Where's the hot redhead?" several times from the Awkward Boys, Finn proceeded to go on a little bit about superpowers again, but this lecture was slightly more lackluster than the one the week before. It was more of the same stuff from the first week, about feeling invisible and how you could still have your voice heard and that you'll always have someone to talk to at these meetings every week. Everyone seemed rather unimpressed, but Finn delivered his talk with his usual zeal, as if he didn't notice how bored the group was.

Clea had a nagging feeling that he wasn't trying anymore. Maybe he'd already gotten what he wanted, but she couldn't put her finger on what that was.

When the meeting was over, Jade, Clea, and Finn were the last to leave.

"So I'll be sending more assignments your way," he said to them as he locked the Community Space behind him, "if that's all right?"

Clea and Jade nodded, and Finn waved at them as he went off in the other direction. Once they were across the street, Clea saw him give the rest of the doughnuts to a homeless person before disappearing down an alley.

"I'm not doing this because it makes me feel *empowered* or anything," Jade said after a while. They'd already passed the point where they would need to walk their separate ways, but Clea had decided to follow Jade back to her dorm and then walk home from there.

"Oh," Clea said, waiting for her to go on.

"I just . . . I knew I'd stumbled on to something weird from the very first meeting," Jade continued. "And now I just want to see how deep the rabbit hole goes, you know? I want to get to the bottom of this. I want to know who he is and why he's doing it."

"But he already told us who he is, and he's doing it because of the less fortunate—"

"That can't be all, Clea. That's too simple. There has to be something more."

Clea looked down at her sneakers, soggy from their snowy walk home. For a moment, she wondered if Jade was right, but she quickly pushed aside the thought. It was scary to think that Finn had ulterior motives considering the less than legal ways he was going about championing his cause . . . if "helping the less fortunate" was *really* his cause. If Jade ever got to the bottom of it, Clea might not even want to know the truth.

Because what scared her more was the possibility that she wouldn't care either way.

"Do you have any ideas?" Clea hedged, fearing the answer. "Or like . . . proof?"

Jade sighed. "I don't know. I just have a feeling."

"Well, maybe he's like Robin Hood."

"Or maybe he gets off on conning innocent college kids into doing crime. Either way, I'm gonna find out."

Clea was silent, but what she wanted to say was, *I'm happy not knowing.*

Because the truth was that writing those emails had made her feel . . . something. Purposeful. She couldn't remember the last time she'd been so engrossed in a project—even a drawing project—for so long that she'd forgotten to *eat.* It was a miracle she'd remembered to take her meds, although having an alert on her phone definitely helped.

Maybe I should do that for meals, too.

"You know there's nothing about Common Cause out there, right?" Jade asked after a long silence. "No website, no social media, no nothing. They told us at the first meeting that these groups were popping up all over the country. But if they are, there's no proof. I wonder what they're playing at." She took a deep breath. "And I wonder what *really* happened to Ingrid."

"Do you think it had something to do with my drawing?" Clea asked meekly.

Jade arched an eyebrow and gave Clea a long look that said, *Seriously?*

Clea, who was used to such looks, shrank a bit. "Right. Of course not—it's just a drawing, right?"

"A really *good* drawing, but yeah. I don't think it had anything to do with Finn deciding to cut ties, y'know?"

"Right," Clea said, thankful for the validation. But she still remembered that look on Finn's face when he saw it . . . and then Ingrid was gone the very next meeting? It seemed like too much of a coincidence.

"By the way, do you have an extra pillow I could borrow?" Clea asked as they approached Jade's dorm.

"I don't—I'm sorry. I've only got the one," Jade replied. "Why?"

Clea gave her the short version of the newest Burrito Incident and finished with "It was my roommate's friend. It's because she's been picking on me since the first week of class, and I finally stood up to her and told her karma would get her one day. And the next thing I know . . ."

"Well, your roommate is just as much of a piece of shit, then," Jade said. "Look, if you want to come stay with me sometime, my roommate has hardly been there since she started dating this guy who lives off campus. And she's decently cool—I'm sure she wouldn't mind it if you threw a sleeping bag on top of her bed some nights and crashed here."

"Thanks," said Clea. "If it gets any worse, I might take you up on it."

"Cool," said Jade, hovering near the door to her building. "And, Clea—just be careful, okay? With Finn? It really seems like he likes you, and like . . ." She made a face. "He really is kind of a lot older than us, you know?"

"I don't like him that way," Clea said stiffly. "I told you that the first day we met, remember?"

"Yeah, but that doesn't mean *he* doesn't like *you* that way. Although maybe it's just that you're so, uh, *good* at this whole 'crime' thing."

"Yeah, right." Clea pressed her lips together, shaking her head. "See you later."

Jade sighed. "See ya."

After Jade disappeared inside, Clea headed back to her own dorm. It was nice of Jade to offer her a place to stay, but Clea doubted she would ever take her up on it. She'd gotten so used to being alone—it was nice to have her space while Hannah wasn't there, to the point where it was worth it to put up with Hannah when she was.

At least, that's how she'd felt until the burrito.

As Clea walked home, she had that familiar nagging feeling that someone was following her. A few times she looked over her shoulder and thought she saw a flash of red just disappearing behind the corner of a building or tree. *But last time I thought I saw something like that, it was nothing, just a sign; this whole campus is scarlet and gray. . . .*

Clea shook herself and quickened her pace. *I wish I really could be invisible so I could stop feeling so . . . exposed.*

Like I'm being watched and judged and—and hunted *all the time. Even though it's nothing. It's always nothing.*

But what if it's not? The thought shook her concentration and caused her to almost trip, but she regained her balance and walked even faster, and the feeling of being stalked still remained and the hairs on the back of her neck stood up as she hustled to her dorm. Once safely inside, her heart still beat erratically.

Her dorm room was blessedly empty when she entered—save for that still-lingering smell of taco meat—but the weight of her weekend as an insomniac suddenly hit her with its fullest force. She barely made it into her pajamas before she fell into bed, balling up an extra blanket to use as a pillow, and fell into a fitful sleep.

CHAPTER SIX

———— ◆ ————

The weeks passed.

Clea wrote more and more emails and received private praise from Finn every week at the Common Cause meetings, which were increasingly lackluster—so much so that Clea and Jade both stopped going. But that didn't mean they'd broken things off with their fearless leader.

Your last batch of emails was fantastic, Clea, Finn texted her often. *So many clicks. You're really very good at this!*

That alone was enough to make Clea keep going. She started ignoring every other text from Jade—the ones about the digging she was doing on Finn and her suspicions about Common Cause. The part of Clea's mind that agreed with her friend, the part that was curious about what Finn was *really* up to, was blocked out by the pride she felt at his compliments on her work, and she didn't care if what she was doing was wrong.

The fact was that her sudden fervor for doing *something* had fed into her need to do other things besides sit around and watch Netflix, so she ended up going to class and completing nearly all her assignments. She even stayed in her dorm room and flat out ignored Hannah and her friends when they were around.

"Did you like your burrito, slug?" Delaney taunted Clea the next time they saw each other after the incident, but Clea only raised her eyebrows and gave Delaney a surprised, blank look, like she had no idea what the bleach blonde was talking about. Delaney's sneer faltered just slightly at that, before she muttered "freak" and left the room.

Is this what it feels like to be a normal person? Clea thought as she turned in her last English comp paper online. *Is this what it feels like to have the motivation to do things that regular people do every day without any effort?*

And then worse: *Am I really depressed? Was I really just lazy?*

Jade, of all people, was the one to force that thought from her mind one night as they were eating dinner at Cane's. "You take meds, yeah?"

"Yeah."

"Have you ever tried to go off them?"

"Of course I have."

"And what happened?"

Clea shook her head. "It wasn't good."

"That's because you need them. You have a chemical imbalance, Clea, just like I have a chronic illness. It's not our fault. We can't help it, and it's nothing to be ashamed of. We just have to, you know . . ." Jade shrugged. "Live."

"But then why am I so functional now?" Clea said,

taking a long sip of lemonade. Her voice was dangerously close to a whine. "Why couldn't I have been this functional the whole time I was on meds?"

Jade shrugged again. "I don't know. Maybe you'll always have your ups and downs, girl. I know I sure as hell do."

"But I *like* this feeling," Clea said, pushing the rest of her dinner away. She hadn't had much of an appetite lately and, as a result, could only eat smaller meals, which Cane's was not. "I don't want it to go away."

"Even if what started it was illegal phishing activities for a suspicious dude?" Jade said loudly and laughed when Clea shushed her. "Oh, c'mon. Don't act like you're not enjoying it." She folded her arms on the table. "It doesn't take a genius to see the change in you. How much more energy you have. How much more . . . I don't know . . . *comfortable* you seem. You realize that?"

Clea put down her lemonade and tried not to beam as she lied, "Not really, no."

"Oh sure," Jade said. *"Sure."*

By the week before finals, Clea was almost caught up on most of her assignments for class. One night when she sat at her desk, switching between writing donor emails and completing a psych paper, Hannah bustled in—alone for once—to gather some of her things, and she stopped and gave Clea a sideways look.

"Have you lost weight?" Hannah asked suddenly.

"Maybe," Clea said without looking away from the screen.

Hannah slung her boxy Swedish backpack over her shoulder and gave Clea a friendly smile. "What's your secret, girl?"

Like they were best friends. Like after an entire semester of standing by while her friends gave Clea hell, just because she lost a few pounds from her brain being so busy she'd been forgetting to eat every now and then, she was suddenly worthy of her roommate's regard?

Hell no.

Clea gave her a blank look. "I don't know. I guess I've been, like, manic?"

Hannah opened her mouth, but no words came out.

"Yeah, I think it might be an eating disorder at this point, actually," Clea said, with mock sincerity. "But when fat people have eating disorders, we get congratulated for losing weight, so why fix what ain't broken?"

Her eyes bored into Hannah, searching for a response, until the latter had to look away.

"Um, that's not true at all," Hannah said, making a face. "That's actually a really fucked-up thing to say."

"Oh? You think so?" Clea feigned genuine surprise.

Hannah shifted, tried to deflect. "Maybe you should see campus counseling."

"But I mean, it's working, isn't it?" Clea blinked at her, trying her very best at this point to keep a straight face.

Hannah opened and closed her mouth again and then opened the door. "Well, have a good night . . ."

"Bye," said Clea, who allowed herself a tiny smile as the door shut behind Hannah.

THE FRIDAY NIGHT BEFORE FINALS WEEK, AS THE SNOW FELL heavily outside, Clea finished up the last of the emails Finn had sent her way and texted him for more. After nearly all of Saturday passed without a response from him, Clea started to feel a bit antsy.

His reply came Saturday night: *Sorry, that's all I have! But you've done so well. I'm really impressed.*

Her heart sank. But the three little dancing dots on her screen indicated he wasn't done typing yet.

Although there's something else I'd love your help with. Meet at the Community Space tonight if you're free? Say 9? Just for a minute? It's an assignment better talked about in person.

Yeah! Clea replied. But then she hesitated and followed that up with another text: *Can I bring Jade?*

I'd rather it's just you, but if you'd feel more comfortable with her along, the more the merrier, Finn replied. *It's just, I'm not sure she'd be too keen on this one.*

Clea shifted in her desk chair. The thought of meeting Finn alone made her nervous for reasons she couldn't quite put her finger on: Is it that she didn't trust him specifically or the thought of being alone with any man that made her so anxious?

Could we maybe meet at the coffee shop again instead?

Of course, whatever you're comfortable with! Tomorrow at 9, say?

Sounds good. See you then.

Clea let out a deep breath and put her phone down. She spent the rest of Saturday and most of Sunday studying for finals in an attempt to keep herself distracted from wondering what Finn's next "assignment" was, so when she got off the bus near the coffee shop that night, she was nearly shaking with excitement.

She almost didn't catch that flash of red out of the

corner of her eye—stark against the snowy streaks—but catch it she did, as it disappeared down an alley. Clea took a shaking breath and told herself she'd imagined it and pulled open the door to the coffee shop. The heat of the interior and strong smell of espresso greeted her like a warm hug.

"Clea! Come sit." Finn flagged her down as soon as she walked in, and when she sat down across from him, he slid her an iced white chocolate mocha across the table. "You look great by the way."

"Oh, wow, thanks—and thanks for the coffee," she said. She hadn't eaten much that day—she'd been too excited— so she hoped the drink wouldn't upset her stomach. Plus, it had been hard to pick out something to wear that night because all her jeans were a little loose and her hoodies felt more like giant potato sacks than usual, but she flushed at his compliment nonetheless.

"It's been a few weeks, hasn't it?" he said. "I've been dealing with a couple of things, so Ingrid has taken the Common Cause meetings back over."

Clea started. "But—I thought you two had gone your separate ways?"

"That's true," Finn said. "But you see, I've gotten pretty busy with schoolwork, which is why my lectures became a little, ah, lackluster. You may have noticed."

"I mean . . ." Clea shrugged a shoulder.

He looked abashed for a moment before perking up again. "But you know, I thought to myself, this *is* Ingrid's field of study . . . and I find that she draws more of the crowd. So she's taken the reins, so to speak. So maybe it's a good thing you and Jade haven't been attending, since I know how you both feel about her." He said it with no bitterness, as if he were merely stating a fact.

"I don't—I never—Jade was the one who *really* didn't like her." Clea took a hasty sip of coffee, and her stomach churned. "Is this about the drawing?"

"Oh, heavens no. But in any case, since you mentioned drawing . . ." Finn folded his arms on the table and leaned in, his own cup of black coffee sitting untouched beside him. He took a piece of paper out of his sleeve and slid it across the table to her, facedown.

Clea detached herself from her straw and made to flip the paper over, but Finn's hand covered hers before she could. His touch was cold, and it made her shiver.

"By now I think you've realized that the things I've asked you to do have been . . . less than legal. I hate to say that, but it's the truth. More important, it's for the greater good," he said quietly. "Are you willing to take that one step further?"

Clea's blood pounded in her ears. If she said no, would he stop giving her assignments? And if he did, would she stop being so . . . alive? Would she just revert to the person she'd been only weeks ago? To the "slug," as Delaney so eloquently put it? She shuddered at the thought.

But if she said yes . . . how bad could it be? His hand was so cold on hers.

"Can you tell me what it is I have to do before I agree to do it?" she asked, fearing the answer.

"Of course. That's a very fair request."

Clea let out an internal sigh of relief.

"You see, my artistic skills are sadly lacking," Finn said, looking a bit ashamed. "But I have a bag of spray paint in my rucksack, and I need you to draw this symbol on a building."

He released his hand from hers and allowed her to flip the paper over. There was a strange symbol there, and beneath it was an address.

"What does it mean?" Clea asked.

"There have been people coming to town lately that have been threatening everything we're trying to build here," Finn said, running a hand through his shoulder-length blond hair, unbound for once. "People who didn't care about this city before I got here. I'd like to remind them whose domain this is."

"Domain?" *What a strange word,* she thought. *Like a predator marking out his territory.* She looked down at the symbol again. *And I guess I'm the marker.*

"There's a caveat," Finn added. "This *must* be done during daylight, and for this location, the best time to go unnoticed is dawn. But you must *not* do it under cover of darkness. That's what makes this whole operation risky."

The address was for a location on High Street, but it looked unfamiliar to Clea. She didn't dare take out her phone and look it up, not in public. Comparing it to the address of the coffee shop, though—which was on the same street—it was farther south, closer to downtown. Was it still in the Short North? Clea was uneasy at the thought of being so far from campus in the wee hours of the morning. Did the buses even run that early?

"At this time of year, dawn is later than you'd think," said Finn, seemingly reading her mind. "You should be all right. And the location isn't particularly visible."

"Then why even do it?"

Finn smiled grimly. "Because the people I want to see it will see it there. Trust me."

"*Trust me . . .*"

But why should she?

Because . . . because I was invisible.

And he sees me.

And sees what I can do.

And it matters to him.

And, she realized, *because it matters to me.*

Clea took a heavy breath. "You can count on me." She stuffed the paper into her pocket. "I'll do it tonight."

CLEA TOOK THE BUS BACK TO CAMPUS AFTER THEIR MEETING, her backpack heavy with the black spray paint cans. Unable to sleep when she got back to her dorm, she did her nightly wanderings around campus for the first time in about a month, braving the bitter December winds to try to keep herself busy until dawn. Even bundled up in a hat and scarf to cover her face, the chill bit into her like icy fangs all over her body.

It turned out the buses *weren't* running anymore—and she didn't want to take them anyway because it would be too noticeable—so she began her trek south to the Short North again, that long stretch of High Street dotted with art galleries, boutiques, and bars just north of downtown. Eventually she passed the coffee shop, cold and long closed up for the night; she ran into few people and kept her head down from the wind—and eye contact—when she passed them.

At this hour, they were certainly doing the same—

everyone is invisible this late . . . until they choose not to be.

Finally, she reached her destination, and she pulled the scarf tighter over her nose and mouth, both to hide her face but also to keep her warm. It was an art gallery, and a high-end one at that, down a side street. *Thank God for that,* Clea thought. But she was still wary. She checked and double-checked the address, making sure it was the right place. The addresses matched perfectly.

She took out the first can of spray paint with shaking hands. Took off her glove, put her forefinger on the nozzle. Took a deep breath. Drew the symbol. Then drew it again. Over and over until tiny symbols coated the art gallery's window.

The sky in the east was turning a brilliant orange by the time she was done.

Adrenaline coursed through her veins as she began the long trek home, the empty cans rattling noisily in her bag, her breath heavy and hitched as she walked faster and faster, not running for fear of slipping on the icy sidewalk.

"Hey, you!"

Clea stumbled at the sound of the voice from behind her—her breath caught in a small gasp as she slipped on an ice patch—and her heart stopped for a moment as she righted herself and began to sprint, not looking back.

She felt more than heard her pursuer gaining on her. Her chest heaved as she willed herself to go, go, *go*, and the only thing she could think of was to plant her feet on the spots of bare, salted sidewalk and snow to keep herself from slipping on the ice—

"Let her go—it's almost up!" another voice said, this

one different than the first, and Clea suddenly realized she had *two* pursuers. Oh God, that was it; she was going to jail—

There was a long break between buildings as she crossed a large, empty street that was closed for construction, but barricades enclosed the narrow stretch of sidewalk on both sides to protect Columbus's heavy pedestrian traffic. On her right, the orange sunlight was so bright now that she had to put a hand up to shield her eyes against it.

When she reached the other side of the street, a horrible screech sounded from behind her and she found herself sliding to a stop. After several heavy breaths, she turned around and saw that her pursuer had stopped halfway across the street and was backing up, hissing and covering the side of his face with one hand—the side facing the sunrise. From where she stood, she could see that the skin of his hand was blistered and burned. And when he lowered his hand and staggered backward to rejoin his friend, who was hiding in the shadow of a building on the other side of the street, she could see that the skin of his face was in equally bad shape.

Confused, Clea's eyes met her second pursuer's. It was a kid not older than she was, in an anorak and jeans, and he was giving her a look of utmost loathing.

Then he bared his *fangs* at Clea—actual honest-to-God *fangs*. The empty, sunlit sidewalk sprawled like an impassible river between them, and he regarded her with the utmost hatred as he dragged his friend to his feet and they both fled the way they'd come, keeping to the shadows as they ran.

Clea's mouth was open, but all she could do was take

short, ragged gasps, like she was choking on air. Her stomach churned, and she doubled over and dry heaved onto the sidewalk. She wobbled forward and sank onto a bench, willing herself to take deep breaths.

That couldn't have just happened. I must've imagined it. But I didn't.

When she managed to get her heart rate down, she hauled herself to her feet and started back down the sidewalk, trembling beneath her parka. The rattle of the cans in her backpack was deafening. A few times she thought she heard sirens behind her, but when she dared to glance over her shoulder, she saw only the lightening sky, no blue-and-red blinking lights.

Jade was right, was all she could think. Not like Clea could tell her friend what just happened. Who'd believe her? And if she were Jade, the next thing she would do would be to stop playing along and just meet with Finn. Demand answers. Be forceful about it.

But Clea was not Jade. And this thing with Finn—whatever it was—was all she had.

When she was about halfway home, her frozen fingers fumbled to get her phone out of her pocket so she could send him a text:

Done. What's next?

CHAPTER SEVEN

———— ◆ ————

And that was how Clea ended up sitting across from Finn in the coffee shop at the end of finals week with another backpack in her lap and a small sheet of paper with a different address in her hand. His whispered details of her next assignment echoed over and over in her brain on an endless loop.

"Clea?" he prompted as she peered into the new backpack. Her heart jumped up into the general vicinity of her throat when she saw that its contents matched what he'd just asked her to do, and she realized he wasn't kidding.

Finally, she zipped the backpack shut and swallowed down her disbelief.

"Are you—is this—?" The hand that held the address shook so badly that Clea ended up tucking both hands in the pockets of her hoodie. Her iced white chocolate mocha sat untouched on the table in front of her.

"I thought you'd be able to pull this one off while you're on winter holiday—you're from Cleveland, right?

This is right in your neck of the woods," Finn said, his eyes searching hers for some mirror of his excitement. When he didn't see it, his smile drooped.

It's too much, Clea thought, clenching her fingers around the paper in her pocket. She willed the words to come out of her mouth. *It's too far. This is going too far. Graffiti is one thing, but this . . . This is . . .*

"This is arson," she whispered.

Finn didn't have anything to say to that, but Clea could see the gears turning in his head. He laced his fingers on the table and opened his mouth to speak.

Clea cut him off before he could.

"I almost got caught the other night," she said. It seemed like a million years ago she'd vandalized the art gallery. In the five days that had passed since then, she had taken all her finals and packed up her dorm room for her monthlong winter break. Hannah was already gone, but Clea's mom wasn't coming to pick her up until tomorrow morning.

"You almost got caught?" Finn looked concerned. "Did you run away?"

Clea shifted in her chair. Thought about her pursuer's skin *burning in the sunlight* in the middle of the street, about her other pursuer leering at her from the shadows with his—with his *fangs.* She swallowed the lump in her throat.

It was a trick of the light. And the sun was coming up, so maybe he—maybe it would've been suspicious to be chasing a girl down the street in broad daylight. Yes. That must be it.

Finn was looking at her expectantly. Clea couldn't bring

herself to meet his curious—and increasingly concerned—gaze.

He'd think I'm crazy.

And if I'm crazy, he might not trust me anymore.

And this is all I have.

She took a deep breath. "I did."

Finn broke into a smile. "Good for you. How did it feel?"

"Good," Clea said, and she meant it. Finally, she raised her eyes to meet his. "It felt good."

"I'm sure it did." Finn leaned back in his chair, looking pleased. "And this will feel good, too. If you have any other questions about it, please don't hesitate to ask. I'm all ears."

It almost sounded like a dare. Like a test—a test she would fail if she wanted more information or justification for the deeds she was being asked to do for Finn's cause.

Whatever that was.

Luckily, Clea didn't particularly care about that. What she did care about was never, ever going back to the way she was before, and Finn's assignments were the only thing that had ever worked. The only thing that had given her purpose.

"I only have one question," Clea said before she could stop herself. She took her hands out of the pocket of her hoodie and wrapped them around the new backpack. "It's just—the people we're doing this stuff to—are we the good guys?"

Finn paused for just long enough to make Clea think she had royally screwed up—but then he gave her the approving smile that had coerced her into committing fraud and vandalism, and he said, "That is the best question you could've asked. You see, everyone thinks they're the good guys, but we both know life isn't always that simple. Everyone thinks their way is the true way. Everyone thinks they're the hero of their own story. But not everyone can be right."

Clea held the backpack tighter against her chest.

"Let's just say they've done worse to us than arson, Clea," Finn said darkly. "Far worse."

"But it's like the old saying, *'An eye for an eye makes the whole world blind.'*" Clea looked down at the backpack. "If you keep fighting violence with violence, when do you win?"

"When we punch up hard enough, I suppose," Finn said, mimicking an upper cut with his fist. Clea didn't know what to think of that, except that there were clearly bigger things at stake than her committing arson . . . and she *really* wished she'd asked Jade to come with her tonight.

But she thought about the way she felt after sending those emails. After making that graffiti. The thrill. The rush.

She knew there was a lot Finn wasn't telling her. But that was okay.

Whatever this "cause" of his was, it wouldn't matter, *didn't* matter to her. All that mattered was the sense of *purpose* he gave her and how it made everything else in her life make sense, too.

"All right," she whispered. "I'm in."

LATER ON THAT NIGHT, HER MIND STILL BUZZING WITH EVERY-thing Finn had told her at the coffee shop, Clea sent Jade a text: *Hey, sorry I haven't replied. Finals week sucked. I basically had to do an entire semester's work in like two weeks because I was so far behind.* It wasn't a total lie.

She followed it up with: *My mom is coming to get me tomorrow morning. Do you want to get breakfast or something before that?*

Because the fact was that Clea felt like a dam about to burst, and she knew at the first sight of Jade, she'd spill everything. Finn hadn't told her *not* to, after all.

Clea had set the new backpack Finn had given her next to Hannah's bed, and it stared her down from across the room. She swallowed heavily. Deep in her heart, Clea needed validation that she was doing the right thing, and she honestly didn't know if Jade would give it to her. More likely, she'd say, "I told you so," and tell Clea she was crazy for listening to Finn.

So Clea sat there on her bed in her mostly packed dorm room, staring at the phone in her hand. Willing it to vibrate. Minutes passed. Should she follow it up, send a third text? Should she add, *I really need to talk to you* or something? If someone texted Clea those words, she'd want to talk right at that moment, or she'd worry about it. But Jade didn't have the same anxieties.

Clea frowned. When was the last time she'd seen Jade? It had been a couple of weeks. And the last text Jade had sent her had read: *I just tried texting Brendan, and he doesn't know who I am. Wtf, I thought we were cool. Maybe he changed his number but still, idk. Think he's just trolling me?*

Clea honestly had no idea.

Maybe she doesn't want to be my friend anymore. The

old insecurity gnawed at Clea's gut. *And it's my own fault. Right when I need her the most . . .*

No, she couldn't despair, couldn't fall into that hole of paranoia and self-loathing again. She'd come too far for that.

And tomorrow night, Clea would prove how far she'd go.

WHEN CLEA'S ALARM WENT OFF IN THE MORNING, JADE STILL hadn't responded. Clea got up and dressed, and went to the dining hall before it closed for winter break. She didn't have much of an appetite, but she ate what she could—half a waffle and a small glass of milk—then went back to her dorm and brought her bags down, and stood there, shivering, to wait for her mother by the curb.

They made small talk for the entire two-hour drive back up to their Cleveland suburb. Clea was distracted, and she knew her mom could tell.

She unpacked her bags when they got home—all but the black backpack, which Clea stowed under her bed. She spent the rest of the day trying to distract herself with Netflix, to no avail, until finally her mom called down that dinner was ready.

"Hey, Mom," Clea said as she picked at her food, "you have cold-weather running gear, right? From when you used to run?"

Clea's mom's fork paused just above her tuna casserole, and her eyebrows shot up. Clea's dad paused with a forkful of food halfway to his mouth.

"Oh, honey," her mom said approvingly. In her prime, she'd been a distance runner and had done something like three marathons, or so Clea recalled, even though her mom understandably wasn't in the best of shape anymore since she'd had some health issues. "Is that how you've been losing weight?"

Clea forced a smile and nodded. "I usually just go to the gym at school, but I'd like to keep it up over break."

"Well, you can use anything you want. I'll dig them up for you after dinner," her mom replied, beaming. "And we'll go shopping this weekend to get you some of your own stuff. Have you been running in those old Vans sneakers? You can always borrow my shoes, too. They're much better for you. Won't give you shin splints. I think the rest of what I have might fit you, too. Oh, honey, I'm so proud of you for getting active."

"Thanks, Mom," Clea said, with as much feeling as she could muster, although she felt a stab of betrayal in her heart. Her mom was just like Hannah. *Not valuable unless I make myself smaller, huh? Would you have ever told me you were proud of me otherwise?*

She choked down the rest of her tuna casserole, but it left a bitter taste in her mouth. When she excused herself, she cleaned her plate and went back upstairs to her room, and her mom arrived a short while later—still beaming— with a pile of her old running gear, which Clea accepted with as much enthusiasm as she could.

And that's how she ended up with a bunch of thermal underwear, a lightweight Nike-brand balaclava, and a solid pair of running shoes for her assignment that night.

After that, she took out her sketchbook and started to draw; it was the only surefire way to clear her mind. She drew Jade as a werewolf and Finn as a zombie.

At around four in the morning, she put her sketch-book aside. She got dressed as silently as she could, put on the black backpack, snatched her mom's car keys off the kitchen counter, and slipped out of the house.

It was either do the deed now or spend all of winter break thinking about it.

She entered the address Finn had given her into her phone and drove for about an hour, crossing through downtown Cleveland to the suburbs on the other side of the city to an area she recalled was pretty affluent. There were several century homes—mansions, more like—each sprawled on acres of land. When she got to the one marked on the address, she pulled her car into a wooded parking lot a little ways down the road and crept in silence toward her destination.

"There's a nature preserve on the other side of the property," Finn had told her, bringing up a map on his phone. "Just there. If you park here and find the path, you'll have more cover to get back into the woods. If you approach from the front yard, there's way too much open space."

Clea found the path easily enough and followed it, fumbling with the night vision goggles Finn had given her. It wasn't quite sunrise yet, but her mom got up at seven and left for work at eight, and if she waited until dawn to head out, she'd never get back in time. She'd just have to take the chance.

Besides, the Cleveland weather had for once truly blessed her. Her mom said that it had snowed the week before, but it had all melted, and in true Ohio fashion, it was now above freezing, but still cold enough for Clea to wear a scarf. If she waited any longer, who knew what the weather would be like? The last thing she wanted to do was leave tracks in the snow.

She veered off the path and crept through the woods until she spotted the back of the house: a large brownstone mansion, with ancient diamond-shaped glass panes. There were no lights on outside, but there was clearly activity inside; the outlines of people moved about, shadows against the curtains in almost every room. The back of the house had an enormous window, looking over the backyard, laden with heavy, closed curtains.

Good.

What was *not* good were the black-clad figures she saw circling the house. They looked normal enough in the low light—almost *too* normal—but Clea could see the guns in holsters at their belts and she swallowed heavily, making sure to keep to the shadows of the treeline where they couldn't see her. They were circling the house at a leisurely pace, but there weren't very many of them; it would be easy to get closer, but to get close enough to do what she had to do would be a little bit trickier.

One step at a time, Clea, she told herself. *One step at a time.*

She watched the guards, trying to pick up on some kind of pattern, some kind of opening. She counted one, two, three guards as they made their rounds, but that was it; whoever was inside clearly wasn't too concerned about a threat tonight.

Clea steeled herself and crouched down, unzipped her backpack, and took out its contents.

Then she tightened the scarf around her face, stepped

out of the safety of the woods, and crept forward. The yard was large, but it was interspersed with old pines and a hedge or two, so she used them for cover as she made her way closer to the house, timing her movements between small gaps in the guards' rotation.

A canister of gasoline in one hand. A box of matches in the other.

The closer she got, the more she could hear. It sounded like the people inside were having a party of some sort. She could hear low music, voices talking and laughing, a few people moaning—though with pain or pleasure, Clea couldn't tell.

She took a shaking breath. *It's almost dawn. How are these people still partying?* She hadn't expected anyone to be awake at this hour, and she hadn't expected there to be guards, either. This complicated things.

Then the back doors opened, and Clea's heart jumped into her throat. She ducked behind a hedge and froze as two figures emerged, each dragging a long black bag behind them.

"These ones weren't much fun," one of the figures lamented, dropping his bag. He sounded drunk.

"They never are when they're willing," the other said, sounding less than sober herself, and laughed. "Can't believe they almost lasted until sunup, though."

"Hey," one of the guards shouted. "Is it our turn to go inside yet?"

"You guys have another hour," came the reply.

"It's *been* an hour," said another guard, poking her head around the corner of the house. "There's nothing happening out here."

"Orders are orders."

Clea didn't move a muscle for several long moments. She couldn't look away from the body bags that had been dumped so unceremoniously outside.

They've done worse to us than arson, Clea, Finn's voice whispered in the back of her mind. *Much worse.*

These words and the sight of the body bags strengthened her resolve—and plus, she noticed with a start, all three guards were now arguing with the other two who'd dragged the bags outside, and the coast was suddenly clear.

This was her only chance.

Clea dashed out from behind the hedge and around the corner of the house, her heart pounding in her chest. As she ran, she unscrewed the cap from the gas canister and began to circle the house with gasoline, her heart thumping so loudly and quickly that it felt she was about to burst with adrenaline.

Fuck exercise and caffeine. *This* was the biggest rush she'd ever felt.

When she was nearing the back of the house again—and the door where the five people had been arguing—she saw one of the guards start to round the corner and sprinted the other way, and ducked behind a hedge just before the guard passed her, muttering under his breath.

Clea watched the rotation again from where she crouched, looking for an opening as she had last time. Her mouth was dry and her heart pounded in her ears as she observed.

The wooden doors were closed again. They were down to two guards now, and Clea judged that at the pace they were walking, they were both on the sides of the house, leaving the front and back open.

Now, to finish the job.

She dumped out the rest of the canister by splattering it on the old wooden doors—the most likely place for the fire to catch—and set the canister itself right outside the door in the puddle of gasoline. Then, with shaking hands, she struck a match and tossed the entire box in the puddle before dropping the lit match beside it.

The fire roared to life, and moments later, a cry of alarm went up inside the house.

By that point, Clea had already dashed halfway across the yard, but something made her stop: sunrise. The beautiful sky in the east, the reds and oranges of daybreak over the treetops reflecting the fire at her back. It made Clea slow her pace, her breath fogging in front of her as she took it in. She had never seen anything more beautiful.

Then she turned back toward the house.

And the sunrise had nothing on what she saw now.

Her plan had originally been to drop the match and then run as fast as she possibly could, but instead she ducked behind the nearest hedge and stared. Took in her work.

The house was engulfed in flames by now. The gas canister had long melted, and the fire had even spread to the body bags outside the door. Inside, the screaming reached a fever pitch as people flung themselves out of windows and doors, clothes aflame, trying desperately to escape.

Every part of her wanted to turn from the horror, but she found that she couldn't look away. The people came out with their fancy, elegant, *heavy* clothing aflame, and they were burning up more quickly than she would've thought. And the instant they were caught in the first rays of sunlight, even the few who had escaped the actual flames started to burn where their skin was exposed, like the person who'd chased Clea down the sidewalk, their mouths open as they screamed, revealing—*fangs*.

Clea's breath caught. It was the same thing she'd seen on the street that day.

I didn't imagine it after all.

Or did I? Some of the people—some of the guards, even the two who'd been outside when Clea had struck the match, who were desperately trying to put the others out—seemed like regular people, but they were burning, too.

They didn't notice her as she stepped out from behind the hedge and looked on, her hands balled into fists at her sides as the people—the *creatures*—burned around her, the fire roaring at their backs.

I did this. I can't believe I did this.

She let out a hysterical giggle. Gasped in surprise and clapped her gloved hands over her mouth. But she couldn't suppress another, and then she was laughing and she couldn't stop, and before long she was doubled over and howling as the house and the creatures burned before her. She laughed until she started to hear sirens in the distance.

And then finally she ran.

She sprinted down the trail as fast as her legs could carry her. The cold-weather running gear was a great excuse in case she happened to be intercepted by rangers for using the park before sunup—she was just on her morning run, just back from college, wanted to go before her mom had to go to work because she didn't have a car, nothing suspicious about that—but that wouldn't help her if someone had followed.

She didn't stop running until she got to her mom's car.

She unlocked it, ducked inside, and drove out of the park, and she didn't breathe until she was speeding away in the opposite direction, chest heaving, head spinning.

Then she caught sight of the smoke and flames billowing into the sky in her rearview mirror, and Clea began to laugh again—slowly at first, and then more hysterically, until she found that once again she couldn't stop.

She wished she could've stayed to watch the house burn all the way down.

By the time she started to see fire trucks and police cars speeding in the direction from which she'd come, sirens wailing, she'd already integrated into the usual morning traffic and was able to get home undetected.

Which wasn't to say that her heart didn't stop every time she heard a siren. But when it passed and her heart started again, all she could do was laugh and laugh.

By some miracle, she was home by the time her mom was up for work, and she slipped back inside unnoticed, replaced her mom's keys right where she'd left them, and slunk back up to bed. Before collapsing into a deep sleep, she sent Finn a text:

Done.

CHAPTER EIGHT

———— ◆ ————

Clea slept for most of the day, physically and emotionally spent. She awoke close to dinnertime, and her entire body ached from her early morning sprint; she told her mom as much when she was called down for dinner as an excuse for having been in bed all day

When she checked her phone, she saw that Finn hadn't texted her back. She tried not to let it worry her too much or make her feel bitter. She'd only just committed a felony for him, after all.

She stared at her phone for longer than she was willing to admit, replaying the night before, trying not to dwell too much on the implications. So Finn had sent her after some—*creatures*. The same creatures that had chased her down after she'd tagged the art gallery. Finn was clearly fighting against them, that much was certain. But what did that have to do with the emails?

She thought back to the monsters going up in flames. Then she thought of her drawing of Ingrid, and her brow furrowed. She hadn't wanted to even think the word *vampire*, but there it was, suddenly stuck in her mind. Had she ever seen Ingrid during the day? Had she ever seen *Finn* during the day, for that matter?

Fangs. Body bags. Burning up in the sun.

Impossible.

But at least she could rest easy knowing that she'd set a match to a den of *monsters*, although part of her wondered if she would've been capable of doing the same if she'd been certain that the people inside were human.

Deep down, she really didn't want to know.

Because it had felt *good* and she'd do it again in a heartbeat.

After a while, Clea decided to leave her phone upstairs so she wouldn't be constantly checking it for a response. After dinner, she watched an old Western with her dad, and around ten at night, they both shuffled upstairs to go to bed. Her mom was already asleep.

Clea certainly was still tired, despite having slept all day. But when she plopped down on her bed and picked up the phone from her nightstand, she saw she had a few texts from Jade, several missed calls, and a voice mail that had been left just five minutes earlier.

Hey, sorry I didn't reply. I'm still on campus if you're still around; my flight home doesn't leave until tomorrow.

But I've been doing some digging after the thing with Brendan and I am like 1,000 percent convinced Finn and Ingrid aren't who they say they are.

Finn isn't answering his phone, but I got ahold of Ingrid because she was in that group chat Finn made, so I'm gonna try to get some answers out of her.

Hello?? I'm sorry I didn't text you back.

Oh my God, you're not going to believe this.

Clea? CLEA

Clea hit *play* on the voice mail and raised the phone to her ear with shaking hands to listen. At first, there was only silence; then there was a sound like something sliding; and then she could hear Jade's labored, ragged breathing.

"Clea, oh my God," Jade whispered, "oh my God, it's working; my phone is working, oh my God. Please—please pick up—I shouldn't have come here—I think she's gonna kill me. I'm in the basement of the—of the place where we had the—" Her voice broke into a sob. "I don't want to die, I don't want to— Oh God, no! Get away from me—"

The voice mail ended abruptly with the sound of glass crunching, as if the screen of Jade's phone had been smashed beneath someone's heel.

By that time, Clea was already on her feet.

She called Finn as she pulled on her coat. He didn't pick up. She called him again and again as she put on her hat and boots and grabbed her mom's keys for the second night in a row and started the car, not caring how much noise she made on the way out.

She called him at least twenty more times as she made the long drive back down to Columbus, hands shaking on the wheel.

Jade is in trouble and it's all my fault.

If I would've listened to her in the first place . . . if I would've told her what was going on after I did the graffiti . . . if I would've tried harder to get in touch with her before I left . . . if I'd warned her . . .

She had just passed the first couple of exits for Columbus by the time Finn called her back. It was past midnight.

"*Where is she?*" Clea demanded as soon as she picked up his call.

"Clea, slow down," Finn said calmly. "Where's who?"

"Jade!" Clea shrieked. Tears streamed down her face, but with one hand on the wheel and the other on her phone, she couldn't wipe them away. "Why—why weren't you picking up?"

"I was busy. Why would I know where Jade is?"

"Because Ingrid has her," Clea sobbed.

"And what makes you think Ingrid is so dangerous?" Finn's tone was polite, but it had a slight edge.

Clea thought frantically of the drawing and of the flashes of red that had followed her and the *fangs* and the *fire* and all of this tumbled together in her mind, but she couldn't say the word out loud—just like the last night at the coffee shop, she couldn't risk Finn thinking she was crazy. Not after what she'd just done.

"I got this—I got this voice mail, and—she had tried to reach Ingrid," Clea went on. "Jade thought she knew something about you guys, something important—I'm driving down now; I'm almost back—she's in danger; I *know* she's in danger—"

"When did you get this voice mail?" Finn asked sharply, with a hint of worry.

"Earlier tonight. Does the Community Space have a basement? Jade said she was in a basement."

"Well, yes, but— Clea, if you get there before me, don't go in there. Wait for me outside; do you hear me?"

A long pause ensued, in which Clea lowered her phone

and wiped the tears from her eyes. When she put the phone back to her ear, she found Finn still waiting patiently for her answer.

"Clea," he said gently. "Please. It's for your own safety. Promise me."

Clea took a deep, shuddering breath.

"I promise," she lied and hung up.

COLUMBUS HAD BEEN HIT WITH A MINOR SNOWSTORM IN THE day or so since Clea had left. The side streets adjacent to High Street were blessedly empty—unlike when class was in session—so Clea found parking easily enough just a block away from the Community Space and made her way there. Her body was stiff, sore, and cold, but she pushed herself forward with determination.

The front door to the Community Space was locked. So she ducked into an alley and went around to the back door, which was also locked. But the building was old and the back door had a glass panel on the top half, so Clea went back to the alley, grabbed a piece of cracked cement off the ground, and slammed it as hard as she could against the glass. It shattered easily, and she reached her gloved hand inside and unlocked the door.

A month ago, she might've hovered outside the door, hemmed and hawed, and maybe actually waited for Finn to get there. But it occurred to her as she slipped inside that she'd smashed the window and hadn't thought twice about any of it. Breaking and entering was nothing compared to last night—especially when her friend's life was on the line.

The vestibule of the building was dark when she entered, the only light coming from the dim streetlights shining in through the outside door, which she shut behind her. To her right, there were three steps leading up and a door that must've led into the Community Space. But directly in front of her was another door, which was unlocked; when she opened it, she saw stairs leading down, a flickering bulb at the landing. Then the stairs turned, and she didn't see where they went.

Great, so this is the part where I die, she thought, hesitating for a moment before starting toward the basement stairs. She couldn't hear any sounds coming from below.

She hoped that didn't mean Jade was dead already.

Every step creaked beneath her feet as Clea descended. The walls of the narrow stairwell made her claustrophobic; there was no railing, but she wouldn't touch the sides, which were concrete and damp and looked slimy to the touch, making her feel like she was walking straight into the belly of some slavering beast that had burrowed deep into the cold ground beneath the street. Her heart hammered in her chest.

It got even colder as she descended. When she reached the landing beneath the flickering light, she could see her breath fog in front of her. The stairwell ran straight into a brick wall at the bottom, but there was an opening to the left so one could enter the basement. There was no light coming from below.

Clea broke out into a cold sweat beneath her coat and stepped off the landing. The stair beneath her foot creaked so loudly that she froze, expecting something to creep out of that darkness at the bottom of the stairs.

Instead, she heard a low, pained whimper and the sound of something shifting.

Clea's breath caught. She pulled her phone out of her pocket with quivering hands and swiped the lock screen, her finger hovering over the flashlight button.

"Jade?" she whispered, still frozen with one foot off the landing.

There was the whimpering sound again, and then a woman's croaked, muffled "C-Clea?"

At the sound of her voice, Clea dashed down the stairs, not caring for the sound she made, and flicked her phone's flashlight on as she bounded headfirst into the darkness.

She stopped short at what she saw inside.

Her flashlight shone upon Ingrid, curled up on the floor, her hands bound in front of her, her face and the side of her head smeared with blood, a thin strip of cotton tied around her mouth. Her cable-knit sweater and leggings were filthy and caked with blood, her eyes wild and terrified.

Clea staggered forward mechanically, like a zombie. This didn't make sense. *None* of this made sense.

Holding her phone aloft to light the way, she reached down and pulled off Ingrid's gag. The woman immediately hissed, "Clea—you have to go. She's a fucking murderer. I found—I found her last victim in this basement a few hours ago when I came down for a mop. She's gotten rid of the evidence, but you *have* to believe me—"

Clea shook her head back and forth slowly. "No. Wait—"

"There's no time," Ingrid said, her voice cracking. "Just leave me here and get out before she comes back, or you'll be next—"

"Before *who* comes back?"

Then a single light bulb flickered to life overhead and a voice from behind Clea said, "On the contrary—Clea has nothing to fear from me."

Ingrid froze in terror, and Clea stiffened and flicked off the flashlight on her phone, stuffing it in her pocket. Then she turned, slowly, to see Jade standing in the corner, leaning casually against the wall. Her short, dark hair was perfectly in place, her jeans and flannel shirt pristine down to her spotless Chuck Taylor sneakers.

She was very much alive . . . in a manner of speaking. Her complexion, normally a rich olive, was ashen, her cheeks colorless.

And when she opened her mouth to grin, the tips of a sharp pair of fangs rested cheekily on her bottom lip.

Clea could only gape at her.

"You were magnificent, girl," Jade said, a fervor in her eyes as she stepped forward and reached both hands out to grasp Clea's. Jade's skin was cold, so very cold, and Clea nearly flinched away at her touch. "God, I wish I could've been there to see the looks on those old Camarilla fucks' faces when their fancy mansion lit up like the fucking sun."

"I don't—I don't understand," Clea stammered, pulling her hands away from Jade's icy grip. "You're— Are you—?"

"You'd say vampire, but we call ourselves Kindred," said Jade. She looked down at Ingrid with loathing as she bent down to resecure the woman's gag. "That's what you wanted to know, isn't it? Well, there's your truth. Too bad you won't live long enough to tell it. Just like Brendan."

Clea started. "Brendan is—?"

"What are you doing?" came Finn's startled voice from the doorway, his wide eyes on Ingrid. He, too, had his fangs bared.

The bottom dropped out of Clea's stomach.

Both of them— They're—

Jade sneered, "Doing what has to be done. Your little girlfriend here has been sniffing around for answers since day one. She would've blown our cover wide open. Did I not tell you to get rid of her weeks ago?"

"She could be an asset to our cause," said Finn through gritted teeth.

"Or a birthday gift for Clea," Jade shot back. "Or did you think you'd be an only childe forever?"

The sight of Finn being admonished by a woman an entire foot shorter than he was startled Clea, but it wasn't more shocking than the realization that Jade—her friend, a perfectly normal gamer girl who shared meals with her and offered her a place to sleep and always spoke her mind and who *cared* about her—was really the one in charge.

Shared meals. She'd seen Jade with food, but had she ever seen her *eat* it? Come to think of it, had she ever even seen Jade *or* Finn in the daylight?

Clea felt like the world had just been turned upside down.

"What's going on?" Clea asked in a small voice, looking to Finn. "I don't understand. I don't understand any of this. If you're—if you're a— Was it all a lie?"

"No," Finn said vehemently. "I'd never lie to you, Clea. It just—it wasn't the whole truth."

"All that stuff about being *special* and being *so good* at doing everything you asked me to do—was that the whole truth, too?" Clea demanded, tears springing to her eyes, because oh, that was the answer she feared most, the answer that would completely pull the rug out from under her feet.

She didn't know what any of this was, but she needed to know that the things she'd done had been every bit as important as Finn had led her to believe. She needed that truth like she needed air.

"Of course *that's* all true," Jade said, gesturing around them. "You're the most promising person we've met in this whole damn city. That's the whole reason we're throwing you this birthday party."

"And you—" Clea turned to Jade. "Are we really friends? What about your—your—?" She gestured to Jade's crutch, abandoned in the opposite corner of the room.

Jade cast a glance at it and sighed. "It wasn't all a lie. I was chronically ill when I was mortal. I met my sire online like fifteen years ago. He wanted to *fix* me." She looked down at her hands, clenched and unclenched her fists. "But I didn't need to be fixed. My illness didn't make me any less worthwhile, any less *valuable* as a human being. But that asshole offered me what no doctor ever could: a permanent end to the pain. So I let him turn me into his ghoul even though it sounded horrible to be a vampire's servant, but . . . I was good at my job, and I liked it. I liked the power. I wanted more. So I let him Embrace me."

She balled her fists and looked back to Clea, grinning, fangs flashing in the dim light. "And then I killed him."

Clea stepped back, shaking her head, and looked again to Finn for answers.

"I never lied to you, Clea," Finn said from the doorway, shifting. "We're the good guys. We're the Anarchs. They're the Camarilla, the old order who'd throw us to the wolves without a second thought. There would be no *us* without *them*."

"Oh, come off your high horse. Our friend Clea here doesn't need convincing," said Jade, who was looking at Clea very closely. "She doesn't care. Does she? She did it all anyway, only knowing a fraction of the truth."

Clea was at a loss for words. She hugged her parka tighter around herself and took a deep breath. Then another. In. Out. Inhale. Exhale. She couldn't stop shaking. She squeezed her eyes shut.

"Oh, yes. She did it all anyway." Jade came up close to her and added very quietly, "And she'd do it again, wouldn't she?"

When Clea finally opened her eyes, she saw Jade looking up at her from a few inches away, giving her a crooked smile, her dark eyes alight with mischief.

"Yeah," Clea whispered. Then her voice gained strength. "I would."

Jade stepped back from her and raised her voice back to its normal volume. "I know you would. That's why you get to join our team—if you want. I won't say the Embrace is painless or that you'll even make it through. But you're the perfect candidate."

"To be—turned into—one of you?" Clea asked, blinking furiously.

"You got it." Jade smiled. "And honestly, there's not a better friend I'd want by my side for the rest of time, y'know. You thought I was in trouble and got in the car and drove two hours down here to make sure I was okay." She shifted. "I mean, that was a lie. Obviously. But after Ingrid stumbled down here and saw something she shouldn't have—and after what you did last night—I knew now was the time. I couldn't wait a month for you to get back from break. But so you know, once you've turned, I'll need to keep you down here until the bloodlust has worn off. That's why I've provided your first meal, right here."

Ingrid's eyes went wide as saucers and Finn made a sound of protest, which Jade cut off with "End of discussion."

"But I—but I get to choose?" Clea asked meekly. But then she swallowed, stood up straighter, staring at the dirty floor. "Right? I get to choose."

"I mean, I guess," Jade said with a shrug.

"Would I—would you kill me if I said no?" Clea jerked her chin nervously down at Ingrid. "Would I end up like her? And like—like Brendan?"

"Not necessarily," Jade said. "Brendan was an accident. Ingrid was snooping. She made it quite clear she doesn't approve of what we've been up to. But you—Clea, you're our friend. You've proven yourself. And it's always helpful to have humans on our side, to do . . . Well, the things you've been doing."

"Ingrid would do those things, too," Finn said desperately, "if you only let her—"

"The fuck I would," Ingrid said through her gag, giving him a savage look. Finn wilted and looked away.

"Which is why you're going to die," Jade said and looked back to Clea. "But why wouldn't you want this? It's like what you're doing now, only *better* because you'll be immortal. Besides, this has been everything for you, right? Your whole thing. Your whole purpose. You'd still be sitting in your dorm room feeling sorry for yourself if not for Finn and me. We changed your life. We *gave* you that purpose. We *made* you."

Clea thought on that for a long moment, then lifted her head and looked Jade dead in the eye. The other girl scowled and raised her eyebrows.

"No. You just gave me the tools," Clea said at last, raising her chin. "I made myself."

For a second, she thought Jade was going to lunge forward and rip her throat out, but before either could move, Finn piped up from the doorway, "She's right, Jade."

"So she is. But she does still have a choice to make," Jade mused, her lips curling up slowly into a smile as she spread her arms wide. "So what'll it be, Clea?"

CHAPTER NINE

———— ◆ ————

One Month Later

Tonight was the night.

She almost hadn't gone through with it, had almost told Jade to call it off. But then, when she went back to her dorm to start tailing that night's victims, she ducked into the supply closet and overheard their entire conversation as they walked down the hallway to the elevator on their way to the bars.

"So you haven't seen your roommate since winter break?" Delaney said.

"No, but I know she's been coming back," said Hannah. "She's been taking and leaving stuff, but I haven't seen her."

"Maybe she really did find a boyfriend."

"Or girlfriend."

"Ha. Fat chance she landed either. *You* wouldn't date her, would you?"

Clea could hear the reproach in Hannah's voice. "Being bi doesn't mean I try to date everyone I meet."

Delaney laughed that horrible laugh of hers. "I mean, keep telling yourself that. . . ."

"How am I even friends with you again?" This time Hannah's disdain was palpable.

"Your own good fortune, Han," Delaney drawled. "If you're *really* lucky, you won't see her for the rest of the semester. Just a couple more months and you and I will be roommates. It's gonna rock."

There was a *ding* to signal that the elevator was on their floor, and Clea put her hand on the doorknob of the supply closet and leaned in, ready to spring toward the stairs and follow them once the elevator took them down.

"Yeah, as long as you don't leave nasty, dripping burritos on my pillow when I piss you off." There was a hint of warning in Hannah's voice and maybe even a little bit of regret.

"She deserved it," was the last thing Clea heard Delaney say, loudly, as the elevator doors closed. "Maybe she's dead. RIP, Cleopatra. And good riddance."

The last of Clea's doubts dissipated as she headed down the stairs. She caught sight of the two of them leaving through the dorm's front doors and waited about thirty seconds before following. She figured she'd be unrecognizable to them even if they did turn around; her hair was stuffed under her hat, her scarf covering the bottom half of her face, and more importantly, she'd traded her baggy jeans and sneakers for a pair of black skinny jeans and ankle-high Doc Martens and her parka for a black anorak.

She was just another college kid.

She was invisible.

The frigid January wind whipped against her cheeks,

and Clea put her chin down deeper into her scarf to brace herself against the cold, and pulled her hat down lower over her face, but not so low that she couldn't still see her quarry. A block ahead of her, Hannah and Delaney finally picked a bar and disappeared inside.

Clea stopped, smiled, pulled out her phone, and sent a text with the name of the bar and a description of the two: a pretty redhead with short hair, wearing a tunic-length sweater, leggings, and riding boots, and her shorter, spray-tanned friend whose bosom strained against a tight dress, strutting confidently in stiletto boots, her hair long and straight, dark roots stark against platinum blond.

Then she made her way silently to the end of the dark alley where she'd been told to wait. She stuffed her hands deeper into the pockets of her coat and shivered—not with fear, not with anxiety, but with anticipation.

Less than an hour later, Jade appeared, arm in arm with Hannah, who was giggling drunkenly and stumbling.

"My car is back here, parked on a side street," Jade said, half supporting the redhead. "We can cut through here."

"Okay," Hannah said, but as soon as they stepped into the shadows of the alleyway and were far enough from the street not to be seen, Jade made short work of her. The girl didn't even cry out as Jade's fangs pierced her neck, and within moments she had passed out.

Clea looked on silently from the darkness. Jade hadn't acknowledged her yet, but she drank her fill and left Hannah's body slumped against the cold brick wall of the alley.

"Is she dead?" Clea asked quietly as Jade approached her.

"Nah. I like her," said Jade, giving her a sidelong

look. "Which I hope you'll be cool with. The other one is technically my gift to you, since you wouldn't take me up on my original offer. I think I want this one for myself."

Clea had hung around long enough to know what Jade meant by that, and she shrugged. "As long as she doesn't end up like Ingrid. She's not a bad person. She's just . . . well, a sheep."

"A couple months ago I would've said that was the pot calling the kettle black." Jade snorted, then crouched down and cupped Hannah's chin. "Trust me. I have my ways of keeping her quiet."

Clea could see why. Jade had a strange gravity that had drawn Clea to her even when she was posing as a college kid; now, with her mask of humanity completely off, she was even more charismatic than before. Clea was fairly convinced that Jade had the ability to make anyone do anything she wanted. It didn't hurt that she was dressed to the nines in dark-wash boyfriend jeans, Chuck Taylors, and a crisp flannel button-up. Her short, dark hair was styled artfully beneath an olive-green beanie.

"That sure is a look," Clea observed.

"I could say the same about you," Jade said with a grin, nodding at her outfit.

Then they heard Finn's voice coming toward them from the sidewalk, and Jade and Clea looked at each other and grinned before ducking deeper into the shadows.

"You didn't bring a jacket?" Finn was saying to someone.

"Didn't want to carry it around," Delaney replied. "I'm used to it. We do this almost every night. Usually I can find a guy to loan me one."

"Ah. Well, if I'd worn a coat, I'd lend it to you. I don't get cold too easily."

"Yeah, I bet you're used to this. It must be much colder in Switzerland."

"Sweden."

"Whatever." Delaney shivered. "How much farther?"

"Not very far now—like I said, it's right off campus. We can cut through here since you're so cold, though." He stopped at the mouth of the alley and gestured her forward. "Ladies first."

Delaney brushed past him without hesitation, but her steps faltered as the darkness spread around her. "Hey. You got a light on your phone or something, Andy?"

"It's Anders," Finn said with a sigh, having given her a fake name, "and no, I'm afraid I left my phone at home."

"Ugh." Delaney reached into her clutch and fumbled for her phone; at the same moment, she almost tripped over Hannah's legs. "What the hell—?" Her voice took on a note of terror. "Han—Hannah?"

"Oh dear," said Finn in his most sympathetic voice. "She doesn't look well."

Delaney's voice rose an octave. "I'm calling the cops."

But when she tried to walk past Finn, he blocked her way. She moved to the other side and he blocked her again effortlessly, causing her to step back and glare at him.

"I have pepper spray, freak," she warned him, her hand still in her clutch as she stood over Hannah's unconscious body as if to protect her friend from him. "You'd better not try anything, or I swear to God—"

"Didn't your mother ever warn you not to follow strange men to parties?" he asked, his friendly smile contrasting his words. "Ah, she did, didn't she? That's why you have the pepper spray. That's very smart. But maybe it would've been smarter to stay in and reconsider your life choices."

Delaney's jaw dropped, her hand frozen in her clutch. She stared at him like he had two heads but didn't move a muscle.

He took a step toward her and put a hand to her cold cheek, still with that reassuring smile on his face. "You really are a stunning woman, Delaney." His hand dropped from her face, and the smile dropped off his own.

"With beauty like yours," he added frostily, "it's a shame you're such a bully."

Delaney still hadn't moved, except to curl her upper lip as she asked, "Who the fuck do you think you are?"

"Great question," said Jade's disembodied voice from the opposite end of the alleyway. "Clea, would you like to tell her?"

Delaney's head whipped around, and her eyes scanned the shadows for the source of the voice. "Who the fuck is that?"

"Maybe you should show her instead," Clea said loudly, stepping out of the shadows.

"Cleopatra? What the hell—?" Delaney gaped at her and stepped back, whirling back around to face Finn. "What is this? What are you—?"

Finn's hand clamped down hard on her shoulder and he leaned in close to whisper in her ear, "Sorry, I can't promise this will be quick *or* painless."

Then Clea felt Jade brush past her like a gust of wind, and Delaney didn't even have time to scream before Jade grabbed her arms and forced them behind her back and whipped her around to face Clea, whose face was lit up in the dim light of the alley like something out of a nightmare.

Clea stepped closer so that she was inches away from Delaney's face. "You asked who we think we are?"

At that moment, Jade's fangs pierced her throat, and Delaney's mouth opened in a soundless gasp and she tried to twist away. But Jade's grip tightened as she drank, digging her fangs in more savagely than she'd done with Hannah, and she forced Delaney to her knees within seconds.

When Delaney went limp with shock and blood loss—her eyes wild and terrified, her breathing shallow—Clea leaned down and gave her a bone-chilling smile.

"We're karma," she said.

"Bet you didn't see us coming."

FINE
PRINT

CASSANDRA KHAW

MAN

◆

The last light left a wet slick of gold upon Duke's desk, a hulking antique liberated from the estate sale of a disgraced English lord. *Vampire*, the auctioneer had confided, pleased to have such gossip to market, clearly a skeptic but too much of a showman to let it do more than faintly stain his act. *The lord was burned alive for suspicion of being a vampire.*

That was all he needed to say.

Duke stroked a thumb along the mahogany, down to the charred edge antipodal to the corner on which one of his two guests sat perched, smiling, serene, and deeply cat-like in her languor. He stared. The woman was art. Exquisite if slightly unearthly, the buttery sleekness of her black leather skirt as faultless as her complexion, both absent of any evidence of cellular degradation. To Duke's eyes, she looked like something prototyped for the consumption of the far-future elite, and when she smiled, he thought of wolves.

"Duke Guillo. God, I hope that isn't a real name."

Opposite him sat an old woman in a charcoal suit, white-blond hair teased to stratospheric heights. Moonlight lapped through the slats of the blinds behind her, tiger-striping her round, unsmiling countenance. She tented her fingers, tipped her head one direction and then another before flashing an ophidian smile.

"What's real in the era of deep fakes?" Duke countered, uncowed, and though something in the basal strata of his psyche flinched, he kept his expression level. He armored his expression with a shit-eating, country-boy-done-cosmically-well smile, leaned back in his chair, legs kicked out straight. "But that doesn't matter, does it? I'm going to have to change names a hundred times over the next millennia."

Both women laughed.

This wasn't how it was supposed to go.

"No," said the older of the two. "What do you think being a vampire means exactly, Mr.—what was it? Guillo? What powers, what obligations, what *pleasures*"—and the woman closed her jaw around the word with so much ecstasy, Duke shivered despite himself—"do you think the status comes with? Before you worry, this isn't a test. You'll still be Embraced by the Clan of Kings, but I am curious about what you expect."

"Besides all the goddamned power in the universe?" Duke's attention rose to the ceiling, the crepe plaster resplendent with a replica of the Sistine Chapel's ceiling. Or an approximation, at any rate. Duke had decreed a few changes: Bill Gates to be sainted, Steve Jobs to be deified, and every last one of those anachronistic seraphim—the round-cheeked cherubim and their attendant angels—to be dethroned by a roster of hip-hop celebrities, nymphets in latex and rappers gorgeted by thick gold chains. "It means never having to worry about time. It means *having* time, time enough to pursue every idea to its logical end. Technology has always been about one generation passing on the tools to another, and you know what? It sucks. *I* want to be the one who shepherds my work into its final form. And if I don't have to worry about death, I can do that. I can make it happen."

Silence followed his panting denouement, resinous, cold from the fluorescent lighting that had activated on cue—like clockwork, a mechanical voice reeled out the hour and the extrinsic temperature and stock market predictions with the gravitas of prophecy—exactly at the stroke of seven. Duke realized then, with shuddering clarity, that his was the only breathing he could discern. But that wasn't right, was it? He'd done his research. As best he could, at least. The old woman, Mara, everyone else he'd been trotted out in front of, they'd all been so opaque, so reluctant to seed him with even the most basic data. The ghouls—and that was what Mara was, like it or not, even if such labeling of her fine-boned face felt anathema—were always alive. Altered, ageless, but irrefutably alive.

And yet . . .

"Oh, Mara, my dear, I think we might have made a mistake about Duke."

"I believe so as well." Heterochromatic eyes met Duke's, one green, one a duck-egg blue, spoked with gleaming clusters of nickel like it was full of shotgun shrapnel. Mara smiled glossily, blandly, without even the courtesy of polite interest.

"He would be so much happier with the Tremere, wouldn't he? Or another of the more scholastic clans. The Toreador might find art in his obsessions too. There is something so wonderfully tortured about this side of—"

"No!"

"No?" said the old woman.

"Fuck. That." Duke slapped his palm onto the desk with each word, ricocheting to his feet, chair slamming into the wall behind him. "Fuck being around another bunch of dreamers. I want *power*. Fuck the rest of them. I don't want to be around more idiots for an eternity. Jesus Christ, have you been in Palo Alto lately? Have you seen the kind of smug assholes who've come to town? Fucking precocious geniuses who can't even figure out how to get their dicks wet let alone land VC. I don't need to be around people with their own ideas and no clue how to actually make them happen. I want people to just fucking *listen* when I tell them that this is optimal. That my way is *the* way. Not even the right way. But the definitive technique for getting shit done. I want . . .

"I want them to *bow*."

"Like I said, Mr. Guillo, this isn't a test. We're sold on you."

"Yeah? Then why does it feel like you're fucking with me? You really think I don't know what you're trying to do? These bullshit power games are transparent as fuck."

"I swear, Mr. Guillo. No games. A bit of friendly professional teasing, perhaps. Besides, your talent with—what was the phrase again, Mara?"

"'Big data,' ma'am."

"Big data. Yes. Your facility at deciphering big data is astounding. Whatever your other faults, your predilections, your lack of reason—"

He bristled at that. Duke's constitution for insults was dependent on whether he believed they were true. Call him abrasive and Duke would have clarified he was an asshole. But reason—crystalline and innocent of cheap emotion—was his oeuvre.

"Hey, *listen*—"

The old woman did not.

"We are deeply interested in your ability to quickly break this world down into its discrete parts. With your talents, my people can be assured of uninterrupted and well-demarcated access to the kind of victuals it needs." She fluttered a bony hand, the skin brindled with liver spots and glutinous, puddling in the creases, ugly in a way Duke would never be, not if he could help it, not with this deal he cut. "Never again will my little family need to ask, 'Does anyone know where exactly can we find provincial Belgian teenagers on short notice?'"

"Exactly. And that means you assholes aren't getting any of this genius unless you meet my terms."

"I could not forget if I tried. You've been so insistent. Insolent, even. To which I'd point out you're not the only tech genius in the world. We could find a replacement. Maybe a subpar one, but one with a better personality. Yes, it might take more time, but time is something we have an abundance of." The old woman sank her chin into the cup of an open palm and flapped her spare hand as Duke, ready for the counterattack, cleared his throat to speak. "Don't worry. It won't come to that. We remember what you asked for and we're happy to oblige. The house in Iceland, done to your specifications. The Tesla. The harem . . . God help me. Are you sure you don't want us to include a few willing boys and nonbinary people? You're not hideous. There'd be people interested. Even if your performance might not be up to standard."

Outside, a procession of fire trucks and ambulances slow-danced through traffic, ululating at top volume: *Business is to be had so make way, San Francisco; give passage in case the clientele die in transit.*

"Fuck. You."

"Even when I cared for such things, you wouldn't have been my type."

Mara laughed, a sound poorly syncopated, eerie and erratic and unmusical.

Duke's expression hinged shut. He knew when he was being intimidated. Different environment, different actors from what he was accustomed to, sure, but Duke knew a professional shakedown when it came for him. And with the boardroom swagger he'd spent a career meticulously cultivating, Duke enthroned himself again at his chair, head cocked at a warning angle.

"Listen," he demanded again, trying as best he could to ignore the infinitesimal way the women's smiles expanded, their disdain no longer covert but worn as mockingly as a stolen medal. "This deal isn't done. I can still walk. I will walk if you don't fucking treat me like an equal."

The old woman laughed then, the sound high and mellifluous, hardly the croak of someone flash frozen at the cusp of senescence. "Here's the thing, Marmalade."

Duke stiffened. *Marmalade*. It had been months, years, decades of clench-jawed personal reinvention and no small amount of time spent high on illegal psychoactives, since he'd last heard the nickname. *Marmalade*. Spoken in that specific, singsong diction. Marmalade, like Duke had never found his way out from the back roads of Alabama, dirt-poor, not a whiff of good to him, no hope, not even the promise of military service because, God help him, he couldn't run three blocks back then without falling apart. Marmalade, because his mother—bless her black heart—thought it was *sweet*, how he used to cry.

"You could pull out," she said, her smile, perhaps, a fraction longer than previous. "You absolutely could. But I don't think you'd be happy if you made that decision."

"Are you *threatening* me?"

"No," said the old woman. "In the same way you're not threatening us. Rather, what I meant by this statement is, if you walk away now, you turn your back on everything you've worked so hard to piece together, this arrangement with all of its collateral pleasures. You will grow old, Marmalade, which seems like a terrible thing to suffer given your family's genetic predisposition toward pancreatic cancer, glaucoma, poor liver health. *Alzheimer's*." The last she said with particular relish. "Old and blind with a mind like a sieve, everything frightening because you can't remember how to take an unassisted shit. Just like your granddad. You remember him, don't you?"

Her grin opened into teeth.

"You're too hungry, Marmalade, to be happy with an end like that. Up until the day you drop dead, your heart would still be jackhammering in its cage, wanting more,

more, more out of life, and knowing you're never going to get it.

"But such isn't for me to say. This is your choice, of course. So, what will it be? You still intend to walk if I don't treat you like one of the big boys?"

Duke did not hesitate, said the words before the old woman could cross to the end of her sentence.

"Abso-*fucking*-lutely."

That laugh again. "Marmalade, you delight me."

"Duke."

"What?"

"That's my name," Duke said through gritted teeth. "That's my goddamned name and you can start there."

"Earlier in our conversation, you implied you weren't *attached*"—and here, her voice lowered and became conspiratorial in cadence, the gap between each syllable intentionally elongated—"to that name and were, in fact, looking forward to experiencing iterations over the many, many centuries to come."

Some quality in Mara's mismatched eyes changed, the pupils engorging. She ran her tongue in an orbit around burgundy lips, a vulgar gesture that, if performed by just about any other woman, would have read to Duke as an invitation. But all it did was frighten him. It felt profane, somehow. Monstrous. Nonetheless, the epiphanic terror did nothing to dilute Duke's bravado.

"*I'll* be the one to choose what I'm called. So remember this: my name, my terms.

"Also, fuck you."

The old woman guffawed and Mara joined her in a scintillant unholy chorus.

"Fine, Mr. Guillo. All the things you want, every last condition and sub-clause. It will be everything you asked for." The laughter deliquesced into a warm smile. "And, Duke, let me just say: I am so looking forward to seeing what you will do with it all."

SEVERAL DAYS AFTER THE FINAL MEETING, DUKE'S LAWYER called to inform him that the paperwork, as far as he could tell between the ceaseless redactions, was sound. Every clause was met, every sub-clause acknowledged and initialed. He saw no loopholes or any malignant terminology snuck in. Whoever the other party was, he'd said in his quiet, clipped tones, they were very careful to remain within the letter of Duke's stipulations.

"Nothing weird at all, then?" he asked his lawyer at the close of the call.

"Not unless you count the fact that they're firm about *their* restrictions lasting into perpetuity. Ordinarily, there's a statute of limitations. But—"

"It's fine," said Duke.

"It is anything but fine. The clauses extend to anyone who might inherit or have any link to your assets, Mr. Guillo," said his lawyer, baritone still operatic despite the poor reception. Duke could picture him very clearly: little round glasses atop a beak of a nose, mouth slightly pursed. His lawyer was not a big man, was, in fact, exceptionally small for someone who claimed thoroughbred Dutch parents. What he lacked in stature, however, he made up for in presence and a predilection for expensive suits and imposing furniture. "Children, spouses, business partners.

I'm not sure what else. And I imagine you do have plans to have progeny, correct?"

"Something like that."

"Then, Duke . . . ," he began, stopped, started again with a flutter of exasperation. "Duke, I've been your lawyer for a long time. We're friends. And as someone who sees you as more than a paycheck, I have to tell you that it is hard to do my job without sufficient information. Are you in trouble of some kind? Because if you are—"

"I swear, it's fine. Don't worry about it."

"Corporate law is not my specialty, but I have friends I can refer you to. They're excellent at the field. . . ."

"Really." Duke couldn't help but chuckle, warmed by his lawyer's effusive concern. The little man prided himself on being a shark, a veritable monster, yet here he was clucking like a worried aunt. "It's okay."

"Duke."

"I promise everything's fine."

A long pained sigh unwrapped through the phone line. "If it somehow ends with you murdering your boss, I'm not taking your case. Not even if you double my retainer."

"What if I triple it?" said Duke.

He counted to five before his lawyer answered. "No."

"You thought about it."

"I'm still running a business." Another sigh, this one more aggrieved, less manufactured. His voice whittled to a troubled murmur. "You'll tell me if you get in trouble, right?"

"I'll think about it. Send me the paperwork to sign." Duke ended the call before his lawyer could object, and sat back in his massive chair, the silence a velveted weight.

Into perpetuity, the lawyer had said. It made sense. Intimidating as the words were, Duke understood the caution, the incontrovertible necessity of them. Functional immortality meant new rules, new needs. You had to account for centuries-long machinations, plans cartographed on the movement of empires, the crescendo and collapse of economies.

And having pondered this, Duke relaxed into the work of tying up all the loose ends of his mortal existence, a task bracketed by calls to and from members of his old fraternity. It was the latter he cared about more than anything else. These were his boys, his brothers, his best friends to the bilious end, and moving on without at least one last hurrah was not a thing he could conjecture. By the end of the hour, plans were made and locked in stone. There would be a celebration, a final blowout, one last bender to send Duke on his way. It would be at a penthouse belonging to a white Californian man named Louis, who'd shared several of Duke's classes when the latter was flirting with a detour into Eastern philosophy. No one in their circle knew precisely what Louis did for money; he seemed effortlessly rich. No one asked, either. Friendship meant ignoring the uncomfortable details.

A flurry of logistical banalities later, it was time for the bacchanal. The Wolf of Wall Street had nothing on what followed.

There was an excruciating amount of drugs present at the event, more even than what was traditional among his circle of friends, and Duke, to the delight of his frat brothers—a large majority of whom found jobs in complementary if not competing firms—indulged with gusto.

The old woman had been explicit about how the Embrace would annihilate existing predilections, and while Duke could not tell if she was grossly dramatizing the situation, he understood it couldn't be all fiction. Changes would happen, both physiological and metaphorical.

So he imbibed aggressively, chasing psychedelics with hundred-dollar pours of rare whiskey until the world began to gyre, firmament and floor losing delineation, thickened to an ombré of moving colors. At some point in the evening, someone called out the arrival of strippers, but by then, Duke couldn't care less.

"I'm going to miss you guys," he slurred, toppling gracelessly sideward onto a cream-hued couch. "I really am."

Someone propped him upright, draped an arm over his shoulders.

"Then stay," said a male voice, shrugging with so much conviction that the motion jogged his voice.

"I can't, Louis." The name surfaced, tasseled with the largely eroded memories of their collegiate years: the bars, the strip clubs, the fake IDs, the shenanigans, the debauchery, the women. Louis, preternaturally self-possessed, had never been as awkward as the rest of them, and Duke recalled envying his confidence. "I already signed that contract."

"Ah." Duke felt the slow metronoming of Louis's head beside him. "They're going to make you pay a percentage of their relocation package, aren't they? Fuck that. You got money. Just cut them a check and tell them to fuck off. The hell Iceland has that San Francisco doesn't?"

"Hot blond women."

"Fuck you—we've got that in spades."

"Bottle blondes, though."

"Come on, man."

"It's not that. It's—" His voice emptied.

"What?"

A male voice shouted for the strippers to peel out of their lingerie. The music went from Billie Eilish to Marilyn Manson, levels adjusted so the latter's trademark scrawling wail glittered like new ice. "Did I ever tell you where I came from?"

"Like, your family? I think you said you were from Lafayette."

"Someplace like that," said Duke, a bit of his pubescent accent creeping in. Louisiana had made more sense than Alabama, what with the romanticizing of New Orleans, the noted presence of French immigrants. There were two types of country: Hollywood and hick. Duke knew where he belonged and what he'd prefer to be associated with, so when teenage Duke decided on reinvention, he threw down with all things Cajun. "Hated it like hell."

"Can't blame you. The only places worth anything in America are the coastal cities. And the Gulf doesn't count. Everything else? Pure swill. Sorry. No offense." A long pause, broken up by drags from a blunt. "Hey, is it true that people in the boondocks never, ever leave? They just stick there forever? Growing old. Being scared of the outside world."

"That's a thing that happens, yeah." Duke exhaled through his teeth, the world still smeared in his vision, leaking oil-slick colors at the rim.

"Everyone popping out kids at eighteen. Trailer-park living. Lots of meth."

Duke thought of every dead cousin and every uncle, his or otherwise, pickling trauma in cheap bourbon and cheaper 'shine. And his brother, missing in action, gone for years now, leaving Duke to a family worth less than the lip of grime on an old deep fryer. "Unless you get a scholarship somewhere or end up in the military."

"How often'd that happen?"

"Not enough."

"Man." Louis passed the joint over. "That sucks."

"You have no idea."

"Hey, it's a privilege and an honor to have grown up white-collar with try-hard parents who think that money can compensate for neglect. I will take my purebred ignorance over growing up in a swamp, thanks."

Duke guffawed even though he rankled at the way Louis had said *purebred*, at the fact he'd said the word so glibly. It reeked to him of patrimonial fetishism, a just-about crush on the spirit of eugenics. But Duke knew his manners, and Louis, Jesus help him, wouldn't ever go as far as to commend the practice. They were both raised better than that. He was sure of this, Duke told himself. Thus reassured, he let his laugh thin to a chuckle, then a sigh, like an opening act.

"I would take that too. In a heartbeat. Call me Moby, call me white Jesus. Call me anything you like. I'd kill for that kind of life. And this new gig, it might give it to me. I want what you have, man. And I don't mean the money. That I've got already. I want"—Duke dropped his voice to a confessional whisper—"I want the way you know none of it is ever going to be taken away from you. I'm so sick of being scared."

The last word slid loose before Duke could think it through. He froze, joint touched to the flap of his lower lip as he tried to will the clock hands back. His only hope was that Louis was just as febrile with recreational analgesics and wouldn't think twice about what Duke had divulged.

"Huh," Louis said with a lilt that told Duke he was percolating the recent admission.

"If you even think about calling me a wuss—"

"I am sincerely offended. Do I look like the kind of guy who'd judge a frat brother for his vulnerability?"

And Duke thought *yes*.

"You tell me," he said instead, voice stiff.

"I wouldn't," said Louis, earnest as the freshly baptized. "Not in a million years. I know where my loyalties lie, you know? 'Brothers for life.'"

"'Brothers for life,'" Duke whispered right back. Love, bright and grateful, engulfed him in that instant. "Thanks."

"So, what are you scared of?"

It came out in a deluge. The volume of Duke's voice, already low, became crushed by the terror that had sat locked for so long in the vault of his neocortex. To his lack of surprise, even laid bare under the light of another human being's attention, that fear remained awful. "Being priced out of San Francisco. Being—"

"You don't even live there, man."

"Heh. Doesn't matter. Same deal, same fucking deal. Being overwhelmed by all these new technologies because I'm not twenty anymore and I can't just mainline Adderall to keep up with everything. Being stuck in my discipline. I am *good* at what I do, Louis. But keeping up with everything that Silicon Valley churns out? I can't. My job takes all my bandwidth. If people decide they don't need my expertise, I'm going to end up in an entry-level WordPress position."

"Hey, don't knock WordPress." A finger wagged in the periphery of Duke's vision, a hand stole the joint from him. "I know people who have made a very good living selling templates."

"Dude, I don't know if you're fucking with me."

"Does it matter?"

"No," said Duke. "But that's exactly the point. I'm scared senseless of being old. There is so much I want to do, but not enough time for all of it. This opportunity in Iceland, it's going to fix some of that."

"They going to make you immortal? If that's the case, I hope there's a referral program."

Duke paused, inhaling through clenched teeth, the noise a sharp whistle. His vision had begun to steady, portending the necessity of more whiskey, more weed, more distractions. Not yet, though. Clarity was suddenly very important.

"What if . . . ," Duke began, hesitated, the magnitude of what he intended so heavy, so ponderous, his tongue numbed at the concept. He tried again, wetting his mouth as he did. "What if."

No luck.

"What are you trying to say?" Louis's countenance remained abstracted, vague curvature and architectural cheekbones, no detail asides from those. Duke couldn't recall what color eyes the man had, whether he was filamented with scars, if he'd had stubble or even the right face for a beard. There was nothing but an impression, one that amounted to the name Louis and fuck all else.

And one day that was all he would ever be: spare change in the pocket of Duke's eternity, a few dilute memories. The revelation was a liver shot, knocking the breath from Duke as he stared at his friend. However, that did not have to be the case. Duke could, if he was willing, swear Louis to secrecy, reveal the truth behind his departure from Palo Alto, and plead with his sire to take in his brother-by-oath as well. The two of them were peers, matchless, at the top of their current game. One head was always better than two, and would his employers not be pleased to have twice the manpower committed to the Sisyphean ordeal of enumerating the world's population?

At the same time, Duke was still metaphorically in gestation, still only a candidate for immortal life. A mere neophyte. Without clout or any value except what was prescribed to him by his sire—an idea that chafed terribly, but Duke wasn't naive enough to expect immediate status, demands or no. Nor was he foolish enough to think such a misstep would go down well with the administration in charge of his new life.

Maybe in a few years, or even a few decades.

Would that be so bad?

And it would give Louis time to steep in his specialty, develop new skills, gain a freckling of age spots, be humbled and improved by the passage of time. He would be more grateful that way, more comprehending of why Duke had made the decisions he did. A respect for your mortality, Duke felt, was mandatory in the process, and Louis, with his endless swagger, could use an existential crisis or two before being proffered forever.

Besides, they were never that close to begin with, Louis always at a judicious remove from the rest of them, not as in need for the structure the fraternity offered, the support, the security. But one way or another, he was still his brother, and Duke would love him like the sibling who'd left home too early. On days when he was feeling honest, Duke envied his aloofness. On other days, he resented that distance.

"Nothing," said Duke, sweeping his guilt at the thought under a rueful chuckle. "I'm just high. Speaking of which, I think I'm going to go home and sleep it off. The fucking plane ride is going to be awful otherwise."

He pried himself from the sofa, patting Louis on a bony shoulder as he went. Before he could disengage, a hand bangled his wrist and tugged.

"Hey, Marmalade," said Louis, breath cool against the rim of Duke's ear. "You did good."

"What?" And then: "What did you call me?"

"Marmalade." He could almost feel Louis's mouth rictus. "Ain't that what your mama used to call you?"

"How did you—" It was stupid. Saying those words. Duke knew, had known from the first swaying, singsonged syllable why and how Louis knew that nickname, yet he couldn't stop himself. "How did you know?"

"I've never been more glad for someone's self-centeredness. It would have sucked, having to kill an old friend for being a nice guy. But in the end, you didn't disappoint. You stayed true to your inability to think about anyone but yourself. Ugly behavior, but goddamned appropriate."

Louis dropped his grip.

"You're one of them," Duke said, hating himself for needing to verbalize the obvious. "Or, like Mara—"

"No. Not like Mara. Never like Mara. Don't fucking try to put me on her level," said Louis, his tone jovial despite the vitriolic objection.

"Okay," said Duke, backing away, all the while fighting the primordial instinct to offer his belly, give in to the hope that if he had to die, it'd at least be quick. He wet his mouth, swallowed. "Okay, man."

"Good. Now go home, Marmalade. Tomorrow's going to be a big fucking day."

DUKE SANK DOWN ON ONE KNEE AND THEN THE OTHER, BENT back over the lap of a small Indian woman, her hair a drowning torrent spread over his eyes, his face, the black strands fragrant with something Duke could almost put a name to, would put a name to if it weren't for how the light was wicking from his vision.

He had expected more ceremony. A subterranean chapel gaudy with the regalia of the Ventrue, artifacts ensconced in the walls, tastefully backlit for effect. A speakeasy, cleared of its regular clientele, and a jazz band in the background like voodoo loa in attendance. A baroque museum, closed off for the evening, rife with old people in Venetian masks, smiling like they'd come to star in *Eyes Wide Shut*. Something cinematic. Not this. Not a second-floor apartment in downtown San Francisco, two blocks from Divisadero Street, the old woman and Mara engaged in small talk while a stranger bled him dry . . .

Rain, Duke thought suddenly. She smelled of a storm taking its first breath, the air turned crystalline. Of the week he'd spent in Mumbai, alternately riveted and fearful of the monsoon as it swept over the city, more alive than anything America had readied him for. Weakly, Duke reached a hand to palm the Indian woman's skull, a lover's intimacy, but his arm went slack partway.

He tried again. It felt important, somehow, to do more than recline limply as the woman exsiccated him, to be an active participant in this brutal, glorious, rapturous event. Except that, too, was more effort than Duke could muster. He was dying far too quickly. The revelation troubled him less than he'd expected it to, and for a moment a paring of Duke's consciousness felt the urge to panic over the fact.

Cool fingers rapped his cheek.

He blinked, looked up through an ink-dark lattice of hair into the face of the old woman, her expression clinical.

"Help me settle a debate that we've been having, Marmalade," she said, her touch arrowing downward along to the point of his jaw. "I told Mara there is no way that you even recall my name. I look too old, after all, for you to care about the idea of recalling my identity. As far as people like you are concerned, I'm scenery, at best."

She laughed in that profoundly unsettling fashion of hers and chucked him under the chin, as though he were a precocious nephew and she, a proud grand-aunt.

The light was growing skeletal. Duke's vision narrowed to spokes. The old woman was right. He couldn't remember her name. His heartbeat became thunderous, the organ of its origin thrashing within his ribs, and Duke would have wailed for release if not for the overwhelming sublimity of this death. Though some animal region of his brain continued to rage, the rest of him was beginning to succumb, melt into a darkness that tasted so peculiarly sweet.

"No answer? That's all right. We have eternity, Marmalade, for you to learn how to bend and scrape and lick my boots. You'll wish you had asked."

A wretched relief flooded him as his cognizance of the situation leached away, and finally darkness came. Duke, barren now of any thought, of any emotion but an infantile gratitude, tumbled toward the encroaching oblivion, eager to be done. No more fear, no more self-doubt.

Then a slender wrist pried his mouth apart.

"Drink," commanded a voice.

And he, half sure he was already dead, complied anyway.

MONSTER

———— ◆ ————

D uke woke up.

This surprised him, as he had no recollection of entering sleep or of anything more concrete than the tectonic certainty he'd enjoyed himself slightly too much. Duke roused slowly, in increments, with none of the vigor he was once accustomed to: an old man, his bones leaden with sleep. His disorientation grew as he took in the alien crispness of the air, a mineral smell that scrimshawed itself into the back of his throat and left his mouth dry and stinging with frost. The light was wrong too, lustrous yet diffused as if poured through a ripple of clear water. Duke knuckled at his eyes with a hand, gaze combing the high walls that framed him, the black-out blinds along one narrow window, an adjacent stairwell curling upward to a loft of a second floor.

The stucco walls were white, foliated at intervals with sheets of slate-gold glass and no other ornamentation, which was, Duke decided as he levered himself into an upright state, the reason for the strangeness of the lighting. Still, nothing could account for the decor: ascetic, rendered in cream and taupe, and almost entirely nonexistent. From where he sat, Duke could see a marble banquet table, its gleaming surface jet-black; a chair; and a hive of computer terminals and servers waiting for his attention. Some distance away, standing alone, a silver fridge that could have held two full-grown adult male bodies with space left to rent.

But nothing else.

His eyes went down and for the first time, Duke came to realize precisely what he was sitting in.

It was a coffin.

"Of fucking course."

Like the rest of the house's sparse furnishing, it was black, gorgeously burnished, angles razored, the sides as thin as cardboard. An inadequate layer of velvet cushioning lay beneath Duke, the house's only nod to the vanity of human comfort. This was the home he had asked for. He recognized it now. The design, on the most molecular level, was his, but it had metastasized since, had been reinterpreted through the lens of a funeral director or, more specifically, an asshole with an intent to vex.

"Fuck," said Duke, dragging shaking fingers through his limp hair. "Jesus fuck a cat."

His blasphemy echoed disturbingly, the acoustics of his accommodations folding the sounds onto themselves so the reverberations came slightly out of sync. Duke shuddered, inexplicably embarrassed. His gaze dropped again, landing finally on the yellow Post-it note taped to the foot of his coffin.

It said *We're watching.*

"Welcome, Mr. Guillo. We've been waiting."

Duke jolted at the satin purr of a woman's voice, its accent nominally Scottish, just enough of that burr to make her appealing but not enough to obstruct understanding. She was tall, as sleek as new tech. All of her was. From the shining topknot to her makeup to the catsuit she wore, the material reflective as oil, pebbled like skin. Even the smile, measured and patinaed with a daub of gold, gleamed like cutting-edge innovation.

"Who are you?"

A split-second pause. "We are your staff, Mr. Guillo."

We. She had definitely said *we*, Duke thought. His focus clarified. He realized then there was not one woman but six in straight-backed attendance, each of them slim and sleeved in identical catsuits, every one of them dark-haired and calcium-complexioned. They did not smile. Duke, after a moment, realized their eyes were all the exact same shade of verdigris.

"Staff?" said Duke, unsure.

Five of the women looked to the first of them to speak.

"Yes," said their spokesperson, the corners of her mouth raised by a fraction. Duke could decode no warmth from her countenance, no interest, nothing but clinical professionalism, the smile entirely ornamental. "We're here to do whatever you need us to do."

"Well, I've never had an orgy—"

Her expression frosted over. "We are your staff, Mr. Guillo. Not your harem."

"In that case, you can get the hell out," said Duke, trying and failing to find equilibrium. God only knew if he looked as much of a wreck as he felt. "I don't need random strangers in my fucking house."

"I'm sorry," said the woman, in a tone that told Duke otherwise. "But that isn't going to be possible."

"You said you're here to do whatever I want you to do. As far as I can tell, that's complete bullshit. You've said no twice already."

"That's because you were not operating within the framework given, Mr. Guillo. We can do things for you if they fit the mandate we've been assigned."

It then dawned with gruesome vividity what role precisely his so-called staff possessed: they were his wardens.

He raised a one-fingered salute.

"Fuck. You," said Duke, shimmying out of the coffin and onto his feet, his usual sneakers gone, replaced by two-toned brogues that were at least a decade out of fashion.

"Come on, you gotta be kidding." Duke fisted a hand uselessly at his side. "My— Oh, you went through *everything*."

His clothes were different too. Gone was his normal wardrobe, exchanged for a three-piece suit in shades of concrete, the fabrics peculiarly uncreased. Historically, Duke was a restless sleeper, and the outfit should have been rumpled beyond salvation. But it was not. Even the tie, a plain banner of glossy black satin, lay smooth along his pearl-buttoned shirt. Duke shucked the jacket and rolled up his shirtsleeves, scowling. Being manipulated was one thing, but to be subject to such gross personal revision? It wasn't merely a violation of privacy; it was *rude*.

Especially given the nature of the personage who'd likely orchestrated it.

But at least the women who had likely denuded him were hot.

"That stupid—"

A monitor in the cluster atop the banquet table winked to life.

"Mr. Guillo. How *are* you doing?"

"You goddamned—" Duke paused, realizing halfway that he was, metaphorically speaking, reading lines off the wrong script. "Where's the old hag?"

Mara smiled with as much width and temperature as the edge of a new pocketknife, a perfunctory flash of humanity. She wore no makeup, her hair knotted into a loose bun atop her head, an oversize hoodie half zipped; the garment slouched over a pale shoulder as Mara steepled her fingers. There was a band T-shirt of some kind underneath, but the angle of the camera made proper identification impossible.

"It's morning here," she said.

Right. The old woman was a vampire. As was he now.

"Where the hell am I?"

"In the house you requested."

"Bullshit," snapped Duke, stalking closer to the monitor. Mara's voice rebounded through the house, projected by hidden speakers, her easy alto hollowed out by the architecture's eccentricities. "You might have started with the blueprint, but this is clearly not my fucking—"

"Your design included too many windows," said Mara. "We kept one out of respect for it. But even with the right technology, you're putting yourself at risk of UV exposure and we don't want that, Marmalade."

"Don't call me that. Where's the other shit? That kitchen

is just Hannibal Lecter's fridge. There's no TV, no other furniture, *definitely* no harem—"

"You have everything you need, and everything is in accordance to the specifics of your contract."

"Bullshit—"

"You shouldn't have *skipped*"—Mara spat the word, viperous—"the fine print, then. The 'luxuries,' as defined in Section C6, will be delivered at the end of the initial product cycle. So it was written. So it was notarized. You signed off on this, Marmalade."

"I said don't call me that!"

She smiled again. "You're not my master."

"Fuck you. Also, what is this bullshit with the fine print? Who the fuck sticks shit like this in a contract?"

"Undying predators who have lorded over the commerce of your people since time immemorial." Mara bared a tooth. "Or businesspeople with a shred of sense. You decide what fits your personal mythos better."

"Listen here, you—"

"Marmalade," said Mara. "We don't have to make this difficult. As it stands, we are both cogs—one beloved, one disproportionately useful. Both, nonetheless, expendable. It would be more expedient if we cooperated, especially given that this is a necessary orientation."

"Then don't fucking call me Marmalade."

"Fine."

"*Fine*," said Duke, feeling as though he'd lost somehow, a revelation that infuriated him even more than his continued inability to piece together the last few days, the few weeks.

He groped for a new topic. "How long was I out?"

"Depends on your definition of *out*," Mara said.

Throttling a juvenile impulse to withhold information, Duke said through clenched teeth, "I don't remember anything."

"You were very hungry."

"I— Can you not *fucking* talk in riddles?" He stopped in front of the screen, hands jutted forward, palms upturned. "You're already making this a *really bad day*, so just tell me: What the fuck happened? I don't— Just— Can you help me understand?"

"You were Embraced," said Mara, voice suffused with an abrupt, nearly carnal longing. "You were hungry. Then you were asleep. At some point, things were done to ensure that you would survive . . . and survive passage to this ridiculous house you requested."

Duke had her, then. "You're really just talking about all this on a public transmission? Man, that old bitch is going to take your face off."

Something like hunger bloomed in Mara's countenance, enveloping every feature, so naked in its intensity that Duke averted his eyes. "You'd like that, wouldn't you? To have me on my knees, begging my mistress to stop hurting me, to just let me *die*. Well, I'm afraid this is a closed network, Mr. Guillo. And very well encrypted."

"There are still risks, you fuckhead."

"So you say," said Mara, and she laughed that uneven, shrill hyena sound again.

Desperate for respite, Duke cleared his throat and blurted the first thing to arrive at his mind. "So, I'm in Iceland?"

"You are in Reykjavík, yes." Mara ceased laughing

with dizzying abruptness. "Although I'm still not sure why you asked to be relocated there, of all places."

"The Northern Lights," said Duke, happy to have the conversation turn recursive, to have an opportunity to blather needlessly, instead of listening to Mara and becoming disquieted by her lunatic exaltations. "I've always wanted to see them. But more than that, Iceland's modern. It has good internet. It has smart people. Everyone's literate. They publish more books here, per capita, than anywhere else in the world, you know? And when summer comes, the sun doesn't go down. I've always dreamed of that. Endless golden days, with nothing to do but—"

"In case you've forgotten, sunlight will kill you."

Duke hesitated. Fucked over again. The thought upset him less than he thought it would. He'd heard variations of such conversational warnings before, mostly from his doctor, who'd remind him each year that there were vanishingly few vices he could enjoy without future repercussions. Don't smoke. Avoid liquor. Stay out of the sun or die.

Same ideas, different bodies.

"I'll figure it out," Duke said. "Sunblock's a thing."

"If only it were that easy, the world would have different masters. But it's also a moot point."

"What?"

"The sun isn't merely anathema," explained Mara with rising glee, leaning into the camera. "It puts you to sleep. You're nothing but a corpse in the light of day, a well-preserved one so long as you don't leave the casket open."

"Wait. Does that mean I'm going to be unconscious for months?"

"Oh. Yes," Mara said. "But I wouldn't worry about that. Instead I'd focus on making the systems you promised my boss."

The blatant instruction gored through Duke's fugue, digging down to where an old welter of righteous fury boiled.

"Fuck. You."

She sighed. "Not this again."

"Fuck you and your piece-of-shit boss. Fuck this *Shawshank Redemption* bullshit with the wardens, and—"

On the monitor, Mara propped an elbow onto the table and laid her jaw into an open palm, a faultless impersonation of her master's mannerisms. Nothing in her expression indicated contrition, never mind intimidation. She was amused by Duke, which, in turn, pissed him off.

"And you wonder why no one loves you, Mr. Guillo."

"Hell is that supposed to mean? I've been rolling in pussy since college."

"*Have* you?" said Mara. "Our records suggest different. In fact, everything we have on you indicates you had trouble socializing with your peers. The only people you got along with were your fraternity brothers. And somehow that was still an improvement over your high school life."

"You get your rocks off on this, don't you? This is what turns you on. You fucking *leeches*. You think you have the monopoly on power? Well, I've got news for you." A lesson he learned early: contingency plans were important. Duke bared a mean, tight-lipped smile. "You don't have as much of an upper hand as you think. All this bullshit? You're going to regret it."

"What makes you say that, Mr. Guillo?"

Her cadence, he decided, that was what irritated him most. The tempo she'd elected to use, the choices she made in regard to where to plant emphasis. It chafed at him with its nursery rhyme swing, and he couldn't wait to throw it back in her face.

"I've got fail-safes planted across the internet. If I don't check in, videos are going to be released. Your boss is going to get doxed so hard, Area 51 will know the exact chemical composition of her daily shit." Duke folded his arms. "I'm going to tear down your precious Masquerade around your ears."

Take that, you bitch.

And yet his threat found no purchase in Mara's expression. Her smile incremented in width.

"Really?" She sighed again.

"Really," Duke growled in answer, a bit less sure of himself.

"You think you're the first person who thought they could threaten us? You sweet summer child," she spat. "You don't know what you're messing with. My master—"

"Can suck my cock."

"I thought she told you already: you're not her type."

"Yeah, I bet I know what kind of ass she likes," said Duke, leering. "Got to say, she doesn't have bad taste."

"If I were you, Mr. Guillo," said Mara, composure smoothing into affectlessness, "I'd think less about what my master's preferences might be and more about the work you need to do. You have very limited supplies within your house. I'd hate to have your next shipment interrupted."

"Are you threatening me?"

"You keep asking that. You're very insecure, aren't you?" said Mara, resecuring her hair as she spoke, pins sliding delicately into place along that shining dark. "Each time you think you're being threatened, you go on the attack."

"Answer my fucking question."

"I wonder where it came from," she said, decidedly *not* answering his question. "Were you hurt as a child, Mr. Guillo? Were you often bludgeoned? Punched? Told to lie over your mother's knee as she pulled out the belt? What is it? What makes you so frightened of conflict?"

"You want to come over here, bitch?"

"You say it like the word should hurt. I'd rather be a bitch—teeth, talons, and only two generations down from a wolf—than something like you." Her voice held flat as tarmac as she spoke, her face without inflection. "And besides, a threat, Mr. Guillo, is a statement of intention. It is a word that describes the possibility of danger. It isn't a guarantee; it is just a warning of what might come. By those definitions, I am not threatening you. I am providing you a public service announcement."

"You're not providing me a goddamned thing. I know what you are. You're just the *help*. You're not even that. You're furniture. You're the crack whore at the back of a highway gas station. I know what you are. How dare you even think about talking to me like that?"

Mara sighed once more. "I hope no one misses you, Mr. Guillo. It'd be a shame if anyone was stupid enough to do so."

The monitor went dead.

Duke stood in the cold silence, his hands fisted, proverbial cock in hand, with nowhere and no way to spend his rage. Taking out his fury on the electronics would have been too indulgently onanistic, a puerile act. Greed supplied its own reasons too. The merchandise was state-of-the-art government-grade technology. Whatever his employers' other faults, they didn't skimp on equipment. To someone like Duke, raised to worship at the court of cyberpunk made manifest, wrecking such gear would be like torching the Louvre.

And besides, those women were still here, still watching. So he didn't. Chose instead to shout *fuck* at oscillating volumes, until the answering percussions irritated him too much to keep going. Then Duke sat himself on the hard-backed chair he'd been given, stared quietly at the nucleus of wires and screens and gently beeping equipment, the exhaust from them cool on his fingers, and went to work.

It didn't surprise him to find an absence of safety measures. No firewalls, no keyloggers, no sheathing of surveillance programs—not even basic heuristic software to record his streaming habits. The computers were as clean as the last bone on a convict's plate. *Good,* he thought. At least they respected his skills enough to waive that formality. Still, because of the diptych of principle and paranoia, he disemboweled the systems, cleaned them out twice, and then loaded up his own suite of apps.

Closed network, his ass.

Without looking up, he said, "Hey. Can one of you girls get me a Coke?"

"No. You wouldn't like what would happen if we did," said the spokeswoman, a long curve of black leather and bone-pale skin at the rim of his peripheral vision. How'd she get so close without Duke noticing her approach? She wore—and Duke glanced down to be sure—boots like any good femme fatale. Four-inch heels, with a flash of steel at the base. He should have heard her coming.

You should have done lots of things, baby, crooned his dead mother's voice. Two years dead, and still she had opinions on his life.

"Could we all stop with the cryptic weirdness for just one second?" said Duke, raw-nerved, unhappy. "What the hell is wrong with a Coke?"

"Most Kindred cannot, without effort, consume anything but blood."

"I'm a tough guy. I'll manage," said Duke.

"You would not."

"Just buy me a fucking Coke. Or hell, get me some fucking coke. At this point, I don't care."

The woman, her name still a blank gap in his head, did not reply, but Duke heard, to his disproportionate delight, a thin little sigh as she strode noiselessly away. Victories were victories no matter how petty, and given the situation, Duke refused to begrudge himself small pleasures. His gaze drifted. Four of the six women were in view, standing—just *standing*—randomly arrayed through the house in clear observance of him, their posture as rigid as ever. Their hands were positioned oddly: one held over another, fingers curled and interlocked, like choir girls onstage.

"Weirdos," he mumbled.

With nothing else to do, his programs still installing, he stood up and went to the fridge, a reflexive action rather than anything motivated by genuine hunger. Later Duke would wonder if it was to distance himself from the boreal scrutiny of the women. For now he needed to move.

Both of the refrigerator doors were swinging open before Duke could get another thought in. For his trouble, he discovered a dearth of shelving, little poles instead latticing the white plastic interior of the fridge. From those hung a crowd of medical blood bags, each of them calligraphically labeled.

Green eyes.

Mongolian ancestry.

Sarcoma patient.

Burn victim.

Child savant.

Duke leafed through the containers, condensation ribboning around him. Their epithets grew weirder: *Geriatric Synesthete. Roswell Conspiratorialist. Allergic to the Color Red.* Duke paused at the last.

"Allergic to a color?" he said aloud, craning his arm into the back of the fridge, fingers groping around until they closed on the hook of the blood bag farthest inside. The onslaught of choice was paralytic, especially without the context of familiar experience. A small part of Duke, which he staunchly kept sequestered away, was screaming, had been screaming since he'd woken up in a coffin, and would, Duke suspected, keep screaming until the sun imploded.

But the rest of him had no intention of humoring a breakdown.

Duke freed the bag and studied the label with an anthropologist's detached curiosity.

Blond woman.

"Damn right that's my type." He glanced over his shoulder. "No offense."

The women were missing, vanished into the quiet.

He looked back at the container and experienced a sudden wrenching aversion to its content, a horror so visceral, he nearly dropped his acquisition. The blood was an aortic tomato red, unpleasantly and improbably fresh. He wondered briefly if it had been ethically sourced and if such practices were an option; Duke could see an entire cottage industry for that.

Like Netflix for blood, he thought, and barked a laugh into the cold, unmoving quiet.

Obsessing over the minutiae of his new unlife quickly accomplished what he had hoped it would: It distracted him. The dread melted into a more nebulous malaise, a sense of ambient wrongness, disconnected from any particular source. In that state, it became a much simpler enterprise to rationalize away his initial reaction to the blood: He was nervy, a dog in a new environment. Animals loathed change.

Emboldened, Duke returned the blood bag to the fridge and patted the pouch like it was the ass of an attractive coed, a bit of private delinquency. His mouth twitched as he shut the doors. Mutinous acts didn't require audiences, he decided. They just needed to be. And if he could enact one, he could steer others to completion. The Camarilla had no claim over him. They were his employers. Sponsors, at best, assisting in his immigration into a new existence. He was his own man. Whether they liked it or not.

And that previous spasm of terrified repulsion?

Cortisol malapropism. That's all.

Duke went back to the computers, already composing

a checklist of things he intended to replace. The chair, first of all. It wasn't unappealing as far as furniture went, the blackwood inlaid with pagan carvings, horned wolves and beatific dryads, and saints of the wild woods. But it was much too old-school for Duke's tastes. And, throne-like as it was, it lacked in one critical department: ergonomics.

He hooked a leg over an ornate armrest, went to Amazon, undid his tie, placed several expedited orders at frankly criminal expense, checked on the local takeout services, sighed loudly over how paupered he was when it came to dining options, commanded the sound system to play Nine Inch Nails, before finally ringing up a few old Bay Area contacts.

The first one answered immediately.

"You are so lucky it's the weekend, man."

Duke grinned. "Fred, how are you doing, dude?"

"I am so goddamn high. This chemist chick at the party is apparently trying to come up with a line of, get this, healthy poppers. I don't fucking know how it'd work, but I am so on board with the fact that she's giving out free samples."

Seventy-six men in their fraternity and eight had gone into law. Of the number, Fred was the only one to make judge, all despite—or because of, Duke wasn't sure, not with everything he'd heard of the pressure cooker that was the field—his infatuation with deviant living. It helped that Fred was built big, a mammoth of a man with a boisterous laugh and a better smile, the Irish in him evidenced in the golden-red hair, the green eyes, the put-on theatrical brogue he swore was unique to the small village of his grandparents' distal birth. Today it was out in full effect.

Fred beamed into the phone camera, neck garlanded with glow stick necklaces, pomaded hair dusted with what looked like granulated cotton candy.

"How can I help, man?"

"I need you to get in touch with Tony."

He watched as Fred staggered around the bend of a hallway, out into the graffitied alley behind the club, exchanging quick kisses with two Slavic women before at last according Duke his full attention.

"Yeah?" Fred mopped his face, still grinning. "I thought you were going off-grid?"

Duke swallowed, flicking a look over the top of his monitor. "Where the fuck did you hear that?"

"Your Facebook? Duh? Shit, what are they dosing you with over there in Iceland? We had a whole conversation about this in the comments. You were trying to take a step back, evaluate your life, experience Iceland without thinking about how Instagrammable it was? You don't remember?"

"It's coming back to me," Duke said. He saw no point in contesting the statement, especially given his suspicion on the matter. The San Francisco Camarilla wanted him cut off, an unwelcome and unfortunate development he'd nonetheless made provisions for. "But you know how it is. A few days off-grid—"

"A week," Fred chortled.

"—and you start thinking about how much you miss the world, you know."

The tiny screaming voice incarcerated in the back room of his head grew fractionally louder. Duke ignored it. He rode the propulsion of his own lies forward, convinced that if he kept going, he wouldn't need to stop and confront the ever-expanding pit of panic that had moved into his stomach.

"I can see that. Social media, it's the best drug. Hey, you on TikTok—"

Duke waited until Fred talked himself to another standstill before asking again, "Tony. We got to talk about him."

"Tony! Yeah! Wait. Which Tony? Tax Guy Tony or Coroner Tony?"

"Neither. Streaming Services Tony. I need you to get in contact with him for me. Can you do that?"

"Does a judge shit in the woods?"

Duke considered the question. "Yes?"

Fred guffawed, a raw bray of a laugh, ecstatic, and slapped a palm against his own thigh. "I miss you, man. When are you coming back to San Francisco?"

Never, Duke thought.

"You know how it is with a new job. Can't start thinking about vacations until you've put in at least a year."

"Look, dude. I know I have no jurisdiction over anything out of the state of California, but fuck me, if they're going to chain you to a desk for a year, I am going to move Heaven and Earth to make sure you can ride out here to San Francisco for Christmas."

"That'd be nice." A kind of pained tenderness bloomed in Duke as he spoke, and he was struck again by the finality of the mortal condition. In a few decades Fred would be another obituary. His accomplishments might survive him, his years in the judicial spotlight, but no one except for Duke would remember his laugh, his willingness to crusade for the rights of a frat brother he only saw annually at their reunions. "But right now I just need you to get in touch with Tony."

"Are you in trouble, man?" Those green eyes, bright even through the shitty transmission, clarified. His voice lowered with concern. "Because if you are—"

"I'm fine," said Duke. "I just need to make sure that I continue to have the right leverage over my piece-of-shit employers."

"Are they underpaying you or something?"

Duke laughed. "Nah. But I promise I'll let you know if I need you to come to my rescue, okay?"

"Promise?"

"Promise." And feeling like he owed Fred more than a passing call, like he owed the fraternity as a whole, for their indulgence and for their affection, their stalwart presence, Duke added: "Hey. How about we do the next meetup in Iceland, huh? My place. We can take a truck out to see the Northern Lights or something. Drink beer with the puffins."

He regretted the proposition the moment he said it, but now that he had, there was no way to recall the invitation, not without sounding like a dick. Fred pursed his mouth at the camera, and Duke, very momentarily, suffered a jolt of hope. But it died as Fred reeled out his booming brassy laughter, an earthquake sound jouncing through the long strange halls of Duke's new habitat.

"Everyone but Louis, anyway. I don't know if I want to see him again," said Duke when Fred's laughter had seeped away. "What do you have against Louis?"

"Nothing. It's just—" *He's a monster,* Duke wanted to say. A monster like he was except worse—or better, depending on the framing—because he allowed himself no pretenses on the subject, and something in Duke railed against the concept of allowing such competition in his house.

Competition?

The word had surfaced without prompting, a thought as vicious as the crack of a bullwhip, and on reflection, Duke discovered he did not like its implications. He did not like thinking about what kind of competition Louis represented, as there was only one logical answer to such meditations. As with anything that discomfited him, however, he only lingered on the disquietude for a quick count of heartbeats before sullenly, firmly, dispatching it from active contemplation.

His smile broadened.

"—Jill, you know?"

Fred rumpled his tanned brow, the skin right under the thatching of red hair the complexion of buttermilk. "Jill?"

"Yeah."

Jill did not exist, of course. No doubt there was a Jill whom Duke and Fred must have bickered over, some fine-boned artist or long-legged accountant-in-gestation, lost now to memory. But Jill, as an impediment to hospitality, was a fabrication and a gambit besides.

"Ah," said Fred, when it became apparent Duke wasn't about to elaborate further. "Jill. Yeah. I remember now."

Duke relaxed, loosed the breath he hadn't needed but was holding out of habit. "You know what I'm talking about, then."

"Totally. Louis has stolen a few chicks from me, too, so trust me, I can empathize."

The rest of the call faded into a slurry of small talk.

Eventually a woman—tall, with imperious cheekbones, hair a glimmering maritime curtain—came to extradite Fred from his conversation, and the off-duty judge said his good-byes, swearing they'd talk again and with less deplorable frequency.

Then he was gone. The silence rushed eagerly back, a roaring presence, its resonance compounded by the knowledge of how it could be filled. Fred, unfiltered and uncouth and unrestrained, had made the room alive for the half hour they'd sat chatting. Duke missed it already.

He drummed a finger on the glass-encased mouse, the device as impractical as his chair: a drop of cream suspended in ice.

At least that was done.

Tony was notified and some of Duke's unease was, if not fully mollified, partially emolliated. It was a beginning. An awkward start. But Duke would take what he was given. He sat up straight, then laced his fingers and cracked the knuckles as he raised his arms into an overhead stretch. Duke let his hands fall again, landing nimbly on the keyboard.

"It's a start," he said aloud, mouth fissuring involuntarily into a smile.

The quiet did not correct him.

BEING A VAMPIRE WAS LESS LUXURY THAN DUKE HAD BEEN LED to believe.

The second floor, which he'd hoped would be stocked with wonders, was barren of anything approximating furniture: a blank horizon of white tiling, unremarkable save for the gray pellucid lights indented into the ceiling.

And another yellow Post-it note.

This one said, *Watch out for marmalade, Marmalade.*

He had frowned quizzically at the message. The house, Duke discovered, was lousy with notes, each of them more enigmatic than the last. They were taped to the underside of tables, in slants of deep shadow. Nowhere they would be immediately visible, which puzzled Duke. If they were meant as instruction, however cryptic, the notes should have been more accessible. It stood to reason as well that the old *cow* could be simply fucking with him, like a cat with a broken-boned bird. Whatever the case, Duke had no plans on playing the industrious hermit. This task they'd given him was asinine, and though he recognized that compliance was a necessity, he wouldn't start on *that* chore until he'd dug his roots into the city, made this place his.

What *really* nagged at him, no matter how hard he tried to suppress his trepidation, was the fact that he saw no accommodations for the women and, worse, no indication of how they could move so discreetly through the structure. Duke couldn't stop picturing them in the walls, arms folded over their breasts, eyes still wide and green, luminous as stars in that claustrophobic dark.

Duke shoved the thought down, shivering.

He spotted a slim obsidian cabinet adjacent to the door leading out of the house, the wood bracketed by stainless steel and anchored to the floor by cast-iron claws. Inside, a navy-blue parka with an oversize hood, furred boots, woolen socks, several scarves, and a scatter of thermal undergarments, some of which were designed for women, not men. It made Duke wonder who'd lived here before him, if this house he'd pictured for himself wasn't as singular as he had thought, if he himself was nowhere as exceptional as he had envisioned.

The notion depressed him. The house, with its myriad eccentricities and pointed deviancies, its lack of basic appliances, already scratched at Duke; and the introduction of the idea that it, with the insult of its many problems, wasn't even built for him specifically made the space frightening.

We're watching.

Duke, after pacing tense spirals through his accommodations, up and down the two floors, occasionally pausing to forage for more notes, concluded he needed to move. He needed to get out. See the city. Learn the environment. His problem, Duke told himself, was a lack of traction. He was free-falling without a harness through a new mode of existence. If he could just anchor himself, equilibrium would return, sure as the oblivion at the tail of every life.

Assuaged, Duke went to dress himself for the outside, feeling all the while as though he were ransacking a mausoleum. The thought did nothing to alleviate his mood. Squeezing a toque over his head, scarf raised to cover his mouth, Duke turned to find that woman again, six inches from his face. He hadn't realized before, but she was taller than he was, tall enough to need to stare down the ridge of her nose for eye contact.

"What?" said Duke.

"Are you planning to explore Reykjavík?"

It felt, to Duke, like a threat, a sensation he immediately took umbrage with.

"Nah. I'm just trying to catch some waves in the sea," he snipped.

The woman smiled tepidly. "I wouldn't advise that."

"Look, if I'm going to be stuck here," said Duke, "I don't want to be stuck here like some Podunk Amish kid with no idea of the world outside."

"If you want, we could drive you."

Duke raised a hand in objection. "No offense, but that's a bit too 'Prisoner's Day Out' for me."

"Mr. Guillo," said the woman, and there was no description for what followed, save that her smile sharpened. "You are *not* our prisoner. You would know if you were."

Duke held her eyes. "Well, when that day comes, we'll see who emerges from out of the bloodbath, huh? Now move."

She complied, taking a side step to the left. Duke swaggered past her and into Reykjavík, excitement and a pang of fear jostling for purchase on his heart, a drip of hunger underneath it all.

The breeze wailed through the open door, stole through the small gaps he'd accidentally left in his winter armament, and burrowed deep into his marrow. Yet he did not goose-pimple from the cold. He did not shiver. His body did none of the things necessary to warm itself. Instead the frost settled in layers, sinking down, filling him, until he lost the words for warmth. Duke stood in the glacial air, flayed by the wind, part of him afraid, but the rest?

The rest of him didn't care, transfixed by the view he'd emerged into.

He knew cities and flatlands and deserts that bled into the dusk-wounded horizon, gold along the prairie and gold along the sky, a seam of red conjoining them like a throat gashed open. Duke understood and loved the temples of

San Francisco's commerce, her maze of alleys, the variegated houses climbing the steep curves of her hills. At the right hour, it reminded him of a pop-up picture book, the lights blinking amber and holy.

But this, though, this was different.

Reykjavík, vividly roofed, its houses so *relaxed*, untroubled by even the prospect of needing to optimize real estate, stood ringed by basalt ridges, their summit hachured with snow. The city spilled its colors onto a polished-glass sea and Duke, hand to his mouth, was humbled. Beauty rarely gave him pause. All his prior experiences had conditioned him to covet beauty. To desire it, to compulsively scheme up tactics for owning things others found mutually beautiful. Late-stage capitalism bred its own hobbies.

The city, nominally domesticated, alien, and jeweled with ice, was a sight he could barely hold in his mind yet, let alone conjecture possessing. Not that he had any mayoral ambitions, having seen what politics could do to a man. But in terms of property, of societal place, even that seemed far-fetched. He didn't belong here, not in this edifice of unapologetic tundra, barely altered by the centuries.

Yet all that did was make Duke love the city more.

He swallowed, a kid on his knee in front of a prom date stratospherically out of his league. Reykjavík was so beautiful. He took in the city line: Harpa at the coil of the ocean's mouth, blue green, its body mosaicked with lights; a crenellated spire rising in the distance, a church whose name eluded Duke for the moment, and that was okay.

For that nebulous width of seconds, Duke was content, unable and unwilling to ask for more, overwhelmed, drowned by the largesse of the universe. Happy in a fashion he wasn't sure he had ever been. Happy and whole. Then the wind picked up again, and the snow came, cauling the city, and Duke, up till that point stupefied with love for the natural world, hunched into his coat and began to walk.

Ten minutes into his exploration, a lonely one only interrupted thrice by the sight of another person, several things occurred to Duke, chiefly that he'd been remiss in deciding on an itinerary, and he had no clue where he was going, much less what he wanted to do. He had aspirations of finding sustenance, but he had only a sallow concept of what that entailed. Blood was on the menu, of course, although Duke hadn't yet formulated an exact opinion on his recent nutritional requirements. At a remove, it had sounded romantic. Confronted with the practicalities of his new diet, Duke felt daunted.

The house was stocked with a surplus of the substance. He could ostensibly backtrack and sample what he'd been given. Begin slow. Experiment at his own pace. But could blood go stale? And if it could, wasn't it worth canvassing Reykjavík for a farm-to-table option, so to speak? Especially for that first transcendent sip. He didn't put it past the old woman to provide him something dismal. Just for laughs.

And how did someone actually *hunt*?

The more Duke brooded over his circumstances, the more questions he unearthed. Both Mara and the old woman were very forthcoming on certain things, incredibly obtuse when it came to others. The Masquerade was paramount: Maintain secrecy at all costs. Dignity, too, was essential. Comport himself with appropriate grace. There was no sin worse than vulgarity. Except for indiscretion.

No mention on whether he could eat food, drink wine, enjoy his original vices, or if blood would become his overwhelming motivation, his one pleasure.

Only way to learn.

Duke turned a street corner, only to balk as four people erupted from a bar, laughing as they went, fluting at one another in a mix of what Duke presumed to be English and Icelandic. Their accents, combined with the violence of the omnipresent wind, made them indecipherable. Their body language, nonetheless, was amiable, and one—a bottle blond, who couldn't have been older than twenty-one, still growing into his rangy frame—even proffered Duke a gold-banded black cigarette. He demurred, unprepared to gauge the effects of nicotine on his undead body.

"You guys know where the supermarket is?"

The quartet exchanged looks.

The blond—they were all blonds of varying gradients, really, but that one, who Duke had singled out as *the* blond—studied him with an impassive expression.

"I know where *a* supermarket is."

The group splintered into friendly drunken laughter. Duke joined in.

"Okay, can you tell me where a supermarket is?" said Duke.

"You're not from around here," said one of the girls, bespectacled and green-eyed. She hooked an arm around the blond's elbow and half hid herself behind the man, peering from behind the bend of his shoulder. He patted her on the head. Siblings, Duke decided. "Where did you come from?"

"America," said Duke.

"Which part of America?" said the girl.

Duke considered the question, hoping as he did that no one would pay any mind to how little steam feathered from his mouth when he spoke and how, sometimes, he forgot to breathe entirely.

"New Orleans," he said with an exaggerated prime-time drawl. Better a familiar name than one that wasn't. Fewer questions that way, Duke had learned. "Came here on an exchange program."

"You look too old to be a student," said one of the women in the remaining pair, an exquisite-looking couple, both of them intimidatingly tall, gorgeously attired in lush fur coats, and somehow upright despite the snow and the four-inch heels of their boots.

"It's a work thing," said Duke, appraising the two women. He revised his original opinion of them. They were not lovers, he decided. There was certainly a sororal relationship ligamenting them and that, Duke suspected, was what he mistook as a romantic connection. But not lovers. Sisters of some nature, although he couldn't put a finger on its specific variety.

"Really?" A coquettish laugh that Duke loved immediately, although his affection felt somehow hollow to him, reflexive rather than reactive. "I guess this isn't the right time of year for tourism."

"Eva, don't chat up the American," said her friend.

"Why not? He seems nice," retorted Eva.

"Stranger danger," offered the blond's sister, only to be swatted by her brother, *his* expression kind.

Between drags of his cigarette, he told the group, "Give him a break, Anouk. The man is probably fresh from the plane, tired, hungry." A pause as he looked Duke over, one eyebrow raised high, and Duke smiled, abruptly and likely disproportionately thankful for the unexpected ally. "And cold."

"So damn cold," said Duke with a laugh.

"Doesn't change the fact that he creeps me out," said Anouk, glowering openly now. "No offense, but something about you screams *predator*."

You're not wrong, Duke thought, smile luminous, but any rebuttal he had died stillborn, strangled between his teeth, Eva speaking before he could.

"I'm sorry." A dismissive flap of her dark-gloved hand. "But she's like that with everyone she doesn't know."

"Just trying to keep you safe," Anouk retorted.

"You don't see Sven trying to swaddle Margret in silk," said Eva.

Sven—the perfect name for the blond, Duke thought—shrugged a bony shoulder, cigarette flicked into a snowdrift. "That's because I care."

"I question that," countered Anouk.

Duke interrupted, sensing old tensions, a progression toward some pointless argument first begun in the infancy of their friendships and kept alive till today. He hadn't the time, the want, the space to see such nonsense through.

So he said: "Look, you guys seem great, but you're right. My plane landed, like, two hours ago and, no offense, but I just want to get a sandwich and go home to sleep."

"Fine. Fine. Whatever. But he shouldn't go to *that* supermarket then, Sven," said Anouk, tone brisk, expression discontent.

In deference to her graphic dislike, Duke withdrew a step. "Why not?"

"Gunnar works there," she said in a tone heavy with incontrovertible finality, a sidelong glance directed at Duke, features cool and faintly contemptuous. Duke couldn't quite tell if her disdain was meant for him, Gunnar, or the world as a cohesive whole. "You don't want someone's first experience of Reykjavík to be *Gunnar*."

"Fine, fine," echoed Sven, winking at Duke, who winked back in return. "In that case, take a right, two lefts, and then a right again. You'll end up in a 10-11."

"It's expensive," warned Margret, still shy, still snuggled behind her brother.

"But it'd be open," said Anouk, her arms flung out to herd her companions away. "Which is what's important. Now, let's go. We want to make the actual party, don't we?"

Duke tacked on a bright smile. "Man, I'm lucky to have met you guys. What are the odds you'd know that someone in a random supermarket—"

"There are less than a hundred and fifty thousand people in this city. The odds are very high. Everyone knows everyone." Eva sighed. "Good night. Enjoy the city. Ignore my friends."

"Say hi if you see us at the bar this weekend!" called out Sven.

Duke waved and moved on, the conversation percolating through his subconscious. A hundred and fifty thousand people. That was less than a neighborhood in San Francisco, smaller than any borough he'd ever resided in; Reykjavík had a population bordering on provincial. He would need to practice concern over the coming years.

Sauntering down the route he'd been given, Duke congratulated himself on having intercepted the four, and on being congenial enough to glean so much so easily. Had he been more reticent, less amiable, or unattractively unkempt, he might have found himself in trouble one day, expecting his future actions to melt into a nonexistent metropolitan clamor.

The wind lost its urgency. Without the gale, the snowfall gained a pleasant dreaminess: relentlessly thick, but the individual flakes seemed to waltz through the air, rendered into gilt by the streetlamps, and Duke couldn't shake the image of having been shrunk down and fitted into a snow globe. Any minute now a face, distorted by glass, would bear down on the sky, peering myopically for Duke. It would be the old woman, laughing and triumphant.

So striking was the thought that Duke jolted his head up, half expecting to see the harridan's visage eclipsing the night. The orange-tinged dark met his wild stare. He sighed. She had him jumping at shadows. His jaw tautened. Duke would see her pay for it.

His gaze dropped to find softly luminescent lime signage in the shape of the phrase 10-11, with the zero swapped for a caricatured clock, its hands about ten minutes from eleven. Duke eyeballed the green-and-white image for another handful of seconds before, at last, the joke tolled in his understanding and he loosed a soft "Ah!" in recognition of the iconography's intent. Comforted by the universality of puns, he loosened his scarf and strode into the store.

MILLING THROUGH THE SUPERMARKET, ITS ANEMIC LIGHTING doing little to improve the appearance of the salad bar,

Duke rediscovered, to his astonishment, a childhood affection for such places. His parents were skinflints, preoccupied with themselves and the business of a household they hadn't wanted, Duke an obligation undertaken with great resentment, but once in a while, whim or whiskey would lead them into taking Duke's hand and walking him into a supermarket. There, in the cool dry air, he would be allowed free rein to select one purchase for himself. His prize, of course, could not exceed a few dollars in value. But that wasn't the point.

The point was, he could choose anything within reason, be it dozen-for-a-dollar confections or a small plastic dinosaur, and ask that it be taken home with him. Whatever he chose, it would be his and his alone. His parents, for all their other faults, respected that covenant, at least.

Duke smiled, unexpectedly nostalgic, as he ladled potato salad into an opaque plastic container. The girl hadn't lied. The prices in 10-11 were cutthroat. Duke, thankfully, was inoculated. Between the time spent and money made in the Bay Area, he could afford the experiment. He could let himself think of supermarkets as magic parceled in easy-access consumerism.

He browsed through the aisles, full of aimless wanting, aware of a need, but picking out basic condiments and pastel-colored bags of potato chips, fruit preserves, some bread, an armament of sodas, bags of salted nuts, instant noodles from brands he didn't recognize, and—as a grudging concession to the specter of health—fruit. Better to have variety than not. Duke wafted past the more traditionally Icelandic groceries, his eyes combing their labels with great suspicion. No small amount were vacuum-packed meat of indeterminate nature.

Them, maybe? Was *that* what he craved?

Duke couldn't tell, but he shoveled one of each into his basket nonetheless.

Haul acquired, Duke made his way to a counter manned by a saturnine kid in his mid-twenties, blue eyes bruised with black liner, hair brilliantined into a slightly malformed pompadour. It drooped like half-melted wax.

Duke tried on a smile. "Just this."

"Mmm."

The cashier began ringing up his purchases.

"So, I heard this place was pricey." Duke couldn't help himself. With the milquetoast ambient music, the excitement of being in Iceland and some quantity of alive, and the positive interactions preceding his visit to 10-11, he wanted to talk, his Southern congeniality leeching to the surface. "They weren't kidding."

"You could have gone to Nettó." The cashier's lilt kept its bored monotone.

"Yeah, well. I'm still learning my way around Reykjavík. I just moved, you know?"

"Mmhm."

"I heard that Iceland has this traditional rotting shark dish?"

The cashier rolled his eyes with grandiose enthusiasm, a teenager's raw drama. "Yes, we do. And puffin. And whale. Do you want me to show you how to get to the glaciers, too?"

"If that's your side work, sure." Duke searched him for a name tag. Gunnar, said a plastic oblong. *How many people were named Gunnar around here?* Deciding to have some fun, he said, "You're Gunnar, huh? I met some of your friends today."

There it was: a darting of interest in those deep-set eyes. "Was it Johanna? What did she say about me?"

"Not much," said Duke, a sly grin in play. "She was too busy singing my praises."

"You? Too old for her. But maybe she doesn't hate me as much as she says if she's willing to talk about me."

"Maybe."

"Maybe she might like me more than she says too."

"Could be." Duke looked him over and lied again. "Could well be."

"Yeah," said Gunnar, jouncing his head, lips thinned to a downturned line. "She does."

Duke nodded. "I think she knows that too. If that helps."

"Mmm." A pause followed. "Get a UV lamp."

Duke chuckled at the suggestion. "I don't really mind the night."

"Eh," said Gunnar. "You and every vampire here."

Fear prickled the hairs at the back of Duke's neck and he steadied his smile, although he was immediately beset by paranoia, a hundred contentious scenarios arranging themselves for perusal. Foremost in his concerns was the sudden certainty that Gunnar, despite his lackadaisical posture, his wilting coif, was a vampire hunter and this was the prelude to a fight.

Were there really vampire hunters?

Were there even other vampires in the city?

Duke didn't know and his lack of knowledge did nothing to winnow his mounting anxiety. It showed, he realized, in his body language, as Gunnar, previously so ambivalent, raised both eyebrows, forehead crumpled from the motion.

"No. I don't mean real vampires," he said with some ill-disguised contempt. "*30 Days of Night* is just a movie. None of that is real. We do have hours of perpetual midnight, but again, none of that other shit is real," Gunnar sighed, voice relapsing to a bored drone, jabbing a plastic bag at Duke.

Meekly, Duke took the bag and began putting away his groceries, the cheap white plastic distending under their weight.

"Obviously not," he said when he trusted himself to speak without a waver in his voice. He wondered if he looked dead under the fluorescent lights. Duke wondered if he looked dead, period.

Gunnar gestured at Duke's shopping, the irritation slopping from his expression, baring a look of judgment. "Are you having a party?"

"Yeah."

"I thought you just got here."

Duke shrugged. "You can have friends, you know?"

"I guess." Gunnar aped his shrug. "Doesn't matter to me."

"Is it true that everyone knows everyone in Reykjavík?" asked Duke, slinging the bag along the bent trench of his elbow, embarrassed by how much he wanted that fact to be more than apocrypha. In his heart of hearts, he missed small towns, the ease with which one could make connections.

"Why?"

"Just something I heard."

"I guess?" said Gunnar, irritation once again reinstalled in its customary seat. Between the ease with which the man's face crannied with wrinkles and his adolescent expressions, Duke reconsidered his estimate of Gunnar's age. Either he was precociously wizened or inappropriately juvenile. Neither of these options were flattering. "There are only so many bars you can visit around here. Eventually everyone meets everyone."

"Have you ever encountered anyone weird?" asked Duke, swiping his card when prompted.

"Weird how? Like you?"

Another shrug, another unexpected ventricular flutter. Duke was learning to startle at his own physiology and the odd times his organs reacted to stimuli. How much of those autonomous functions he had taken for granted! His lungs, his heart, the mechanisms that allowed for heat generation. Briefly he pondered his alimentary systems, the task of convincing his digestive tract to work, to move what he'd eaten. And the whole concept of disposal, that was even more esoteric a process. Duke pushed down on his musings, stared at Gunnar with cordial expectation.

"Yeah," he said. "Like me."

Gunnar twitched a shoulder. Even his derision was tiring of Duke. "Eh. I suppose. You tourists are always so surprised by everything."

"Okay, I meant more like . . . people whom I share a resemblance with."

"You mean short?"

Duke, who had never considered himself short and was, in fact, of the opinion he was taller than average, blinked once, twice, poleaxed by how he hadn't noticed the gap between their heights. Gunnar, slouched and running to bone, still almost had five inches on Duke.

"Sure. Why not?"

Gunnar raked a look over Duke. "*Eh.*"

If he'd seemed blasé before, Gunnar now looked entirely done with Duke's presence, and the brittle smile he wore suggested he'd tell Duke as much if it weren't for the obligations of his employment.

"Have a nice night?" said Duke, moving to exit.

"Eh."

And that was that. Duke traced his route back home, thinking the entire time how strange it was, how comically bizarre that he now lived in what amounted to a borrowed showroom. His good mood tapered to gloom the longer he walked. The house was a joke. The coffin, the fridge crammed with blood bags, the bizarre notes like the walls had become tumorous, those strange silent women. It was surreal. But until he fully understood the parameters of his own life, it seemed defensible, at least. Adequate if not ideal.

Maybe he could start with dead bolts, Duke thought to himself, when he finally reached the front door. Dead bolts and a careful scan of the walls, just to be sure there weren't crawl spaces there. He let himself in, having not locked prior to his exit, and the silence inside felt physical, almost, a clinging layer of dried fat.

"Plants," he said aloud. "Maybe plants too."

Duke then ferried his groceries to the fridge, enumerating his list of planned household purchases as he did. A portable stove, maybe. If he could indeed eat without consequence. A sink too. And whatever it was that he might need to identify hidden electronics. First chance he got, Duke planned to strip the place of its monitoring equipment. The old woman would need to get her kicks from someone else.

What *was* her name, though?

He pondered this while tossing out satchels of chilled blood, sifting through them at random. *Diabetic Irish woman. Man with gigantism. Soccer mom.* Duke folded cross-legged onto the floor, the bag nestled on his lap.

A trash can. He'd need that, too.

Still deep in his own ruminations, Duke lacerated a bag of potato chips with a nail, a puff of salted air emerging as he tore at the wound in the plastic. He extracted a thin yellow curl, bit down, and savored the familiar crunch. The taste, though, was absent. Where he'd expected maple Dijon and the unnatural umami of the snack, there was nothing. A cardboard-like flavor, which shocked him to no end, as he could *smell* the chip: the salt and the processed starch, the flavorings. He bit down on another chip and discovered, to his dismay, more of the same offensive blandness.

"Fuck."

Duke, flustered, yanked out one of the black bottles of soda he'd bought and knocked back half in a long earnest swallow. It burned the whole way down. Like the potato chips, it tasted of nothing. No, worse than nothing: an insipid chemical slurry with only one redeeming merit. It was, thanks to the weather, still cold. Duke set down the bottle and mopped his lips with the back of his hand, deeply unsettled by the panic fizzing in his belly.

Gracelessly, he clawed through his shopping, found

the potato salad, and ladled out a mouthful with his hand.
Duke swallowed the clump of starch, barely chewing.

Nothing.

Ash, just ash, with a crunch of skin, sure, but otherwise, a mealy nothing and the oily tackiness of cheap may-
onnaise. The bread was no better, not alone, not swollen
with the fruit preserves, the latter jellied clots in a swamp
of indigo-dark syrup. Duke changed tactics, decided, as
the jittering in his hands worsened, adrenaline somehow
still in production despite the loss of everything else, that
he'd compromise. Forget taste. Ignore flavor. Eating didn't
need to be a pleasure. It just had to work.

Because what Duke was discovering with each desperate bite was that his hunger had no bottom, no limit.
Roused by his attempt at its fulfillment, it grew, billowing, building, until he became wholly his appetite, a thin
veneer of skin over a void as gluttonous as any rich man's
greed.

Duke crammed fruit and chips and flatbread down his
throat, choked down ribbons of jerky, inhaled nuts and
uncooked noodles, calved butter with his nails and licked
the keratin clean. He ate without attention to taste, gorg-
ing himself, hoping to capitalize on quantity.

But it only made him hungrier.

Of all the things he'd experienced in the last few days,
of all the conversations he'd had, of all the wonder and
horror he'd recently witnessed, it was *this* realization that
broke him, *this* that set his teeth chattering on edge. The
hopeless inanity of it, the sheer ridiculous stupidity, un-
corked a well of baying hysteria. Duke rocked back and
began to laugh in convulsive gasps until his throat lost grip

of the tempo and he was left burbling with both hands clasped over his mouth.

His stomach writhed and leaped. Due to his agitation, it wasn't until vomit, cold and sour, had surged up into his mouth that Duke recognized the physical upset as more than just nerves. He shot then to his feet and staggered to the bathroom, flinging over the toilet bowl, just in time to empty a stinking cascade of waste into the water. He groaned, an elbow propped on the seat, forehead rested on a palm. Potato chip flecks constellated his puke. His head throbbed. Whatever was going on, it stung worse than any hangover he'd endured in his life.

Your limpid system is not working, he reminded himself, and wasn't certain if he'd inculpated the wrong bodily function and if the revelation, inaccurate as it could possibly be, comforted or terrified him.

Groaning, Duke raised his attention to the joint between the toilet seat and its lid. Behind the wide plastic oval there was a flash of yellow. Another note. He snatched it from where it'd been double-taped to the tank.

Warned you.

The debacle had an auxiliary effect.

He was very, very hungry.

As soon as he became aware of this, the hunger changed shape. He'd been conscious of its presence when he woke. It had been a twinge then, a mild discomfort readily ignored. It had grown slowly in urgency over the next few hours but never in a fashion Duke would have considered significant. Peckish, he would have described himself. Eager to eat.

But now the hunger was something else, red-raw, panting with avarice, a thing alive and furious to have been sidelined for so long. It flensed him, rode him like a god come to roost, fountained through every nerve ending until Duke rattled with his appetite. Duke had wanted things in his life, coveted successes, lusted for women, dreamed and despaired over insurmountable goals. All those desires felt paltry beside this hunger, idle schoolyard fancies beside the solar heat of this singular craving.

Duke stumbled upright again, wholly possessed by his monomaniacal appetite, and raced to the fridge, its doors still open. Inchoate, he descended on the first blood bag he grasped, not pausing to decipher IV tubing or whatever inane label was affixed to it. Instead Duke bit down through the plastic, torquing the container away, molars and motion finally accomplishing what he'd wanted. Blood seeped onto his tongue and—

He choked.

It was wrong, wrong, foul as offal scooped fresh from a corpse, cloying as old honey, an ingot of gore on Duke's tongue. Was this what he was doomed to? An eternity of subsisting on this utterly wretched diet? He swallowed and swallowed and swallowed, nonetheless, fighting the urge to vomit, no pause between each gulp, the plastic crushed in his fist. When he was done, he leaped for another bag, mutilated it in the same fashion, and drank it all down with a drunk's shamed abandon. As he lurched from the third bag, however, nausea overrode hunger.

Duke collapsed as his body fought to evict the unwanted substances, fluids gushing from his nose, his mouth, his tear ducts. Halfway through, he stemmed the flow, held on to what was left. Miraculously, the process did not incapacitate him. Duke, after the initial paroxysms, rolled onto his elbows and, using them as ballasts, kicked his way into a crouch. From there he began an agonizing crawl toward the door, a brushstroke of blood left in his wake, his only thought the refuge of a hospital. Common sense wailed for him to stop, that he'd be less than welcome at a medical facility when the personnel learned his heart did not beat and his lungs were vestigial, useful solely for speech.

But the alternative was untenable.

Duke did not know if his body's insistence on purging itself would go on until he had disgorged his organs, the layers of necrotizing muscles—or not, he had no clue—inside him, the veins, and when there was nothing remaining, the bones themselves. Duke had no plans of finding out. He succeeded, to his own surprise, at wriggling into his coat. Pulling his toque clumsily over his head, the wool closing an eye even as the rest of the material soaked up the blood, Duke took an uncertain stride forward and collapsed, straight into obsidian-clad arms.

"I told you you wouldn't like it," thrummed a voice recently familiar, the words pitched low and soothing. "Now close your eyes. We'll take care of you."

A SHORT, SWEET-FACED MAN OPENED THE DOOR. HE HELD A clipboard in the crook of his elbow, had a stethoscope draped around his neck, and were it not for how young he looked, his calm manner and adherence to stereotype would have been enormously comforting. But as it stood, there was something about being there, quietly scrutinized by someone who couldn't have been out of medical school for more than a year or so, that left Duke uneasy, and a little self-conscious of how filthy he looked.

"Hey," said Duke, mopping his lips with the back of a hand. The clinic unsettled him with its white walls and minimal furniture, the latter insectoid in design and entirely in matte burgundy. The spokeswoman—he'd ask her name later, he owed her that much—had led Duke through the necessary procedures, and then did what she could to make him presentable, all without complaint or interest, only the calm briskness of a trauma nurse.

Then she left, her heels still making no sound at all.

"Sorry about the mess," said Duke.

"Trust me," the doctor said, "I've seen a lot of blood coming out of a lot of orifices."

Duke laughed despite himself, a broken noise that embarrassed him immediately. "I bet. I didn't think Reykjavík saw a lot of violence, though."

The doctor sat himself on the battered stool beside Duke, nodding amiably, a polished tag declaring his name as Orri Helgason. "It doesn't. But violence isn't the only thing that causes hemorrhaging. You'd be amazed as to how inventive human beings can be when it comes to accidentally hurting ourselves."

"I can imagine." The laugh came easier this time. "I don't know how you guys do it."

"Immersion therapy," said Orri with a wink. "Get bled on enough and you just become used to it. Now, let's see."

Duke jackknifed away as the young physician reached for his jaw, earning a pause from the other man, a frown bent into place.

"Mr. Guillo . . ." he said, hand still outstretched.

"I . . . I don't know if I can let you do that." Duke tried for a weak chuckle, mouth fluttering at the corners, undecided between a grimace or a snarl, feeble regardless of its intended shape. "What if I'm . . . contagious?"

A mealy cover, but the best he had at the moment.

"You're just hungry, Mr. Guillo."

And it was the manner in which the young doctor had said the word *hungry*, so very softly and so very carefully, that ran ice down Duke's spine so he froze in position. Orri's smile held as he winked again at Duke, both hands brought down around the head of his clipboard.

"You're like me."

Orri wiggled his fingers on his clipboard. "Not quite. My blood's too thin, so to speak, for anyone to want to call me family. Your, ah, relatives, in particular, would laugh at the idea. But in more general terms? Yes. Yes, I am. You're safe here, Mr. Guillo. Ish."

Something in the pith of Duke's psyche cracked, splintered under the gentle pressure of that ill-deserved compassion, offered without expectation, kind without reserve. His expression must have divulged his internal rupturing, as Orri's smile, until then so nonchalant, brittled with concern.

"Really, you're safe here," he said again. "This place is meant for our kind. It's lacking in many ways, but we make do. The forensic facilities are excellent, however. And we have an attached crematorium."

"Crematorium?"

"Mistakes happen."

Duke sagged, the unexpected prosaism of his situation,

though significantly less distressing than the last few days, was nonetheless as disorienting as everything else he had recently endured. This was not the unlife he'd anticipated, always pendulating between banality and abject alien terror. Nothing as luxurious as mythology had intimated. In some ways, it was worse than the life he had shucked. At least in that one, he had resources. In that one, he had no clue that the monsters under the bed were real.

"I'm going to lose my mind," he whispered. "I went to this place called 10-11, and—"

"That's your first mistake. No one should go there. The prices are absurd."

Another nervous tremble of laughter. "Yeah, I figured. I tried to eat some of the things I bought there. I drank the soda, ate the chips. Threw up. And then I was so hungry. They'd filled the fridge with, uh, *wine*, if you know what I mean. I drank that. I started throwing up again. I didn't know our kind had food allergies."

Orri rapped a cheekbone with a knuckle. "Firstly, you shouldn't be eating *normal* food anymore, so to speak. How do I put this? What you and I are, we have rarefied tastes. We prefer our nutrition *liquid*. Unless you make an effort of will, your body will refuse anything else. You throw up."

"Figured that out the hard way, doc. No one fucking told me anything. If I knew—"

"But you didn't. Which means your sire wanted you to find out for yourself."

"Why?" A pause. "And what about the other stuff? If I'm supposed to be on a liquid diet, why am I throwing that up too?"

The doctor's good humor elided itself from his face then, and he sighed, fingers pinched around the bridge of his nose. "To answer your first question, I don't know. I don't ask, either. The Blue Bloods always have their games, and I make it my business to stay as far away from them as I can."

"So why are you helping me?"

"Because they told me too." Orri stood.

"*What?*"

Again, Duke felt that initial chill, exacerbated now by the pity grooved into his physician's expression. Orri did not look unsympathetic to Duke's situation, but he looked as though he'd seen enough real emergencies to not break form for one stranger's personal ruin.

"I was told to make sure to watch out for you in case you messed up, provide assistance, and then stay out of it." Orri scratched at the back of his neck with a pen, high forehead rucked with genuine distress. "Sorry."

"You're scared of them."

"Fucking terrified," said the doctor without inhibition. "As you should be too."

"Then help me."

"No."

"You're a smart man," said Duke, possessed by both a sudden wordless fear and the lurid certainty that if he missed this opportunity, if he failed somehow to communicate how exigent his predicament, he would be squandering his one chance at getting, what? Help? An alliance? Camaraderie? Duke was too exhausted to attach the correct words to his want. But he knew it was important. "You know what they say. Together we stand, divided we fall."

"There are less than four hundred thousand people in Iceland. Of that number, only a handful share our, *ah*"—Orri made that sound, the singular *ah*, an exquisitely gentle pluming of air that meant he was rummaging for euphemisms, the exact same way each time—"unique health conditions. Not enough to begin a revolution and definitely not enough to risk things for a stranger."

"But that's the fucking thing about revolutions. They all start with one person—"

"No," said Orri firmly. "They start with one shared idea, and yours is one I will not share. I like what I call a life these days. I'm really sorry, Mr. Guillo. You're on your own. My only advice is keep your head down. Try not to piss anyone off. And look, if it helps, here's a freebie to answer the second part of your earlier questions: your, ah, family is even more particular about their libations than anyone else. Each of you eventually develop a taste for only, ah, specific vintage, and no other. I don't know if anyone's told you anything, and I'm pretty sure they have not. But you'll learn precisely what you want. When you do, please refrain from consuming anything else. If you do, it'd be this—"

Orri fluttered a hand at the slaughterhouse floor of Duke's front.

"—all over again. When that happens, though, don't come back here. It will pass, and we can't risk you causing more questions."

"That it? That's all the help I'm getting from you? 'Figure out what you want to eat and never come back'?"

"Yes," said the doctor. "For what it's worth, I really am sorry."

Duke nodded. He knew a lost cause when he saw one. "Thanks, doc," he said. "I guess I'll go home."

EXCEPT HE DID NOT.

Instead Duke staggered down again to the main street, head stooped, parka clutched in a blue-veined hand. He had lost a glove in the last assault by the wind and given up, at that point, on parroting human sensibility. Let the locals think he was impaired by drink or drug, that he was inviting hypothermia and frostbite on behalf of an inadvisable vice. He was too tired to care.

The snow built until it gained a luminescence of its own, washed with lights from the shops of Laugavegur: a mottling of halogen gold on solid white, the frilled spar of the city's largest church a distant shadow. It was pleasant in its inhospitable fashion: starkly, bleakly magnificent, true to every Nordic detective series Duke had watched. But the storm continued to churn, and soon it became ice and the flicker of streetlights.

We're watching, the note had said.

Duke wondered how closely.

"Seven Nation Army" boomed through a door as it swung open an inch from Duke's nose, spilling two women in enormous coats, the material fringed with piebald fur. There was the smell of cheap liquor worked into the grain of even cheaper wood: the universal attar of any dive bar, and Duke, starving, badly in need of a win, eased past the women and into the establishment. Lucky for Duke, it was dark enough to camouflage the poor state of his clothing, and too crowded with drunks for anyone to pay attention anyway. The ceilings were low, and the single dance floor teemed with bodies: most young, every one of them effortlessly lithe. Duke wanted a drink so badly, he'd have wrung a dishrag dry for a drop. Not that he could any longer.

But, maybe, this was the place to harvest something better.

The hunger writhed in him, urging him forward, onward, *keep going, keep going,* a compass erratically realigning to the north of what he needed. He could taste it, almost. That precise—what had Orri said?—libation, yeah, the bestial appetite inside him coveted. Duke couldn't put a name to it yet, but he knew he was close, close enough.

His elbow grazed the swoop of a woman's bare spine and he jumped as though singed, pivoting awkwardly in the tight space, a tottering diagonal half step nearly leading him into a collision with a man. But the man caught Duke with a laugh and a hand applied to the divot of his shoulder blade.

"Hey, it's the American," said the man with glee, and it took Duke a second to tether the voice to a name.

"Sven," said Duke. "How ya doing?" He was genuinely glad to see him for a reason he couldn't yet parse.

"Can't complain. Alcohol on all the shelves. Pretty girls all around. A new friend found again. Life could be worse, you know?"

A warm smile bled onto Duke's face, slow in its conception, sudden in its growth. Sven clapped Duke's arm, his own grin making for a matching set. And despite everything that had happened, optimism kindled in Duke.

A few more contacts like Sven, and maybe Duke wouldn't starve of connection, might have the life he wanted, armed and armored with allies.

Sven leaned in.

"So, you made an impression on Eva," he murmured into Duke's ear.

"That's what I'm afraid of."

"Because of Anouk? Don't worry about it. She's all bark, no bite. If Eva really likes you, Anouk'll let her do what she wants."

"Even with an American?"

"You can find out yourself," said Sven, Duke realizing too late what it meant as the other man pushed him lightly. "Go get your girl, brother."

Momentum and, likely, the commotion that preceded it, made it impossible to withdraw. The woman—Eva, unidentifiable from the back and bereft of her winter gear—had taken notice. Duke gave her a once-over as she turned to study him. She stood several inches taller than Duke, balletic in her elegance, magnificently leonine, with an ice-blond mane and a clinging black dress, blue eyes like a clear summer morning. Every bit Duke's type. Every bit *any* man's type. In the presence of such preferred beauty, Duke, in a previous life at least, would have rolled out the right lines already, coke or compliment, whatever she might have wanted to wheedle. But this version of Duke only mumbled to himself and ducked his head, stupefied by circumstance, more awkward than he could recall ever being.

"Hey," he managed.

She looked him over, one corner of her mouth crooked up. "Hey yourself. I was just talking about you."

Her accent was local—although, he realized now, the lilt was dusted with an American twang; she must have done college overseas, somewhere coastal. New York, maybe. Its chimerical nature, regardless of origin, was charming, and Duke thawed slightly, enough to measure out a shy smile.

"So I heard. I hope the things you said were good."

"The best," said the woman. "But now that I've actually seen your face, I feel like I should go back and tell them I've revised my opinion."

Amusement lit in him. "Oh?"

"Absolutely. Like Sven said, it's a small city. We all run into each other again and again. Always good to be nice for that reason."

"What do you really think of me, then?" said Duke.

"You're interesting." Her grin bloomed.

"*Just* interesting?"

"At *least* interesting." Eva winked. "So, what's your name?"

"Duke," he said. "Nice to meet you."

The woman jounced a finger at Duke. "You're wearing far too much for a winter that's so mild."

"Am I?" He couldn't tell if she was teasing. The room was equal halves those in their winter gear and those in club finery. "I guess so. I came from California."

"I thought you said New Orleans."

"Good memory," said Duke, not missing a beat. "But that's my hometown. California was my last stop. And yeah, I guess I'm still getting used to the weather here."

"You really chose a good time to move." Eva swayed closer, her interest entirely undisguised, a hip bone touched to Duke's thigh. "But you know what? One way or another, you should take that off."

Her hands flew to the zipper of his coat before he could intervene; a downward tug made a window to the gory mess caked under his down-cushioned exterior. The smile fled from her face. To Eva's credit, charity, as opposed to terror, was her first instinct in the wake of an emergency.

"You're bleeding. We need to get to a hospital. Did someone hurt—"

"*Quiet.*"

Later, Duke would wonder if his next action was coincidence or evidence of self-actualization. I think, therefore I am. In his case: I think, therefore my Blood kindles with the obscene power that is the Kindred's heritage. A certainty of effulgent purpose roared up in him, magma through dead arteries, spreading through vascular tributaries until it clotted at his throat. *Shut up,* Duke begged, holding her terrified gaze. *Please,* he thought. *Please, please.*

The woman quieted immediately, though her eyes stayed wild with panic.

"Come on," said Duke. "Let's go outside."

A hand flew to her mouth and Eva shook her head.

"Eva," said Duke cautiously, zipping up his coat, a hand extended in entreaty.

At the sound of her name, she shrank away, inching backward, both hands steepled over her mouth, head wagging with increasing vehemence.

This was wrong, Duke knew. He should allow her to walk away, to leave, to escape what had to be an impossibly terrifying situation, take advantage of her muteness to flee himself. But he was so very hungry. A condition he'd temporarily forgotten in his recent consternation but now, oh, it was roiling in him, an appetite nearly bathyal in scope. Duke stared mutedly at Eva's naked throat, the marbling of cartilage and muscle along the graceful bones of her shoulders, and was subsumed by his want for her, her skin, her warmth, the blood beating hot.

Throughout his life, Duke had adhered to an economical approach when it came to matters of ethics, particularly on the subject of the opposite sex; agendas didn't always necessitate discussion, and commitment was invariably subjective. But consent, though, that he required to be mandatory, and preferably accompanied by boundless enthusiasm. Eva, he knew, was in no state to supply that. Her eagerness was a product of compulsion. Yet he couldn't help himself. One drink, he compromised. One tiny sip. That was all he'd take.

"*Follow*," he said, and he let her lead them outside, though not before detouring first to acquire her own jacket, a gallantry that nonetheless felt entirely hypocritical to Duke as he pressed her into a wall of an alley, mere seconds after their exit.

Eva gasped into his neck, body molded to his, while he fumbled at her hair. How he wanted her then, with the snow veiling them both, her skin nearly molten beneath his fingers, the smell of her a better intoxicant than anything he'd sampled in his sordid life. Duke kissed her, hard enough to bruise, savoring the benediction of her mouth, the normalcy of passion, however empty it was. The ritual of desire was reassuring, calming, panacea and placebo both, even with Eva trembling and terrified. He recognized what was coming, what he'd done in turn, and the clarity of that knowledge broke him like glass.

But not enough.

Not enough to stop.

He bit down.

Not on her neck, as he'd intended, but the jut of her lower lip.

Eva moaned.

Duke had planned to stop there: one sip, no more than that, a small reprieve from the emptiness at his core. But he couldn't, wouldn't. What was it that people always said? Just the tip? Except it never was. That one concession always precipitated the momentum for more, and if anyone disagreed, well, they shouldn't have been complicit in the first place.

What a monster he had become.

He couldn't stop, though, even with the flood of self-disgust, his threadbare principles too little, too superficial against the cavalcade of his gluttonous desires. Duke cupped his hands around Eva's face, took as much into his mouth as he could, all the while berated by the one small part of him still cognizant enough to understand that this was coercion, an unforgivable violation.

But he was so hungry.

And Eva was enjoying this, wasn't she?

Duke recalled his own circumstances, the masochistic ecstasy of desiccation, and unlike his own parent, he wouldn't drain Eva completely. He'd stop. Soon. Besides, it wasn't like this was *pleasurable* for him. Her blood, like the blood he'd sampled before, was repulsive. Eva's lashes fluttered against his cheek and he swallowed hard, bracing as the relief of that warm fluid gave way to immediate nausea.

His gorge rose again. Duke flung himself away, palm over his mouth. Briefly, in the cresting nausea, he found himself with the fantasy that this was his repulsion incarnated into a physical response, and was overwhelmingly grateful at the delusion. Maybe he wasn't that much of an animal yet. Duke clung to that delusion as his undead biology expunged itself of Eva's blood, Orri's warning recalled too late. What had the doctor said? That Duke's kind— his clan, the Ventrue—could drink from only one specific phenotype?

Something like that.

Blood geysered from him, thick coagulated rivulets, streaming between his fingers, warm still. He dry-heaved once, twice. Then more came, bubbling between gasps, no matter how hard Duke tried to hold it down, rivers and rills of red, clotted despite it only being moments since consumption. Then after another minute, a new problem introduced itself:

Eva was screaming.

Not loudly, thank fuck, a keening wail obscured by the wind and her knuckles jammed into her mouth, a child's expression of abject horror, performed with the hope no one would hear, counterproductive as that was. Because silence wasn't always an option, not in the face of a real life monster, not with your lip chewed raw by a recent stranger, your brain still fogged from his power.

Duke looked up into Eva's eyes as her voice slimmed to a whimper, the girl sliding down to a shaking boneless heap.

"Please don't hurt me," she whispered.

"I won't. I'm sorry. I didn't mean it. I did not mean it. I'm sorry. Please stop. It's okay. I'm sorry. Please.

"Please, *please*."

She inhaled, preparing again to scream. Every warning that Duke has been prescribed—by Mara, by Orri, by the commandments of common sense—surfaced to conscious attention. If he didn't stop her now, this would be it. Someone would come. Someone would *see*. And if not a mob of Icelanders, then it'd be some Scandinavian Camarilla hitman who would show up to stake Duke for the sun.

Duke wasn't ready to die.

But no one had prepared him for this causality of indiscriminate feeding or dealing with consequences, truth be said. All his life, he'd escaped recrimination on account of being white, good-looking, and, in recent years, statistically rich. Unfortunately, this phase of existence saw no merit in those traits. Things were going to end very poorly if he didn't act now.

So, like a kid aping his forebears, he did the only thing he could think to.

He tore his wrist open with his teeth and pressed the wound to Eva's mouth, his frame enveloping hers, sheltering her from the ice, them from view. At a glance, they might have resembled an amorous couple without sufficient respect for the climate, and hopefully, that would be enough to dissuade anyone from interrogating them.

"It's okay. It'll be all right. Just . . . drink," said Duke, as Eva's tongue explored his skin, its tentative examination quickly giving away to active suction.

His world constricted into sensation and the two stayed there, devoured by the ice, for what would soon feel like not long enough.

DUKE HAD LITTLE RECOLLECTION OF HOW THEY'D REACHED home. There was a cab, at some point, and a transaction

conducted entirely in Icelandic, and Eva coiled in the
back seat, and her legs around his, and her mouth at his
wrist, and both of them laughing, voices low and sweet
and warm. The taxi driver had dialed up the music at one
point, and Duke had chuckled in delight at his sense of
discretion, while Sinatra belted out how he did it his way
and with no compromise.

More memories came, stop-motion and disrespectful
of chronological order: Eva leading him inside, both of
them wobbling like fawns. One of them—Duke wasn't
sure whom, couldn't be sure—had tried going upstairs,
only to be whistled down by the other.

And there had been her skin, and wine on her breath,
and her hair in his fingers, against his mouth, and her
teeth shearing through the flesh of his arm. Yet somehow
that wasn't right either, not the pleasure of her attention,
not anything. Duke was incomplete, starved still of what
he needed. *She* wasn't sated, but she was getting what she
wanted.

Duke was getting nothing.

He blinked at the ceiling.

On the bright side, his head didn't hurt.

Duke rose for the second time from his coffin, and
found Eva draped over the side, lips still wrapped around
the knob of his left wrist. The eroticism startled him. As
a teenager, he'd fed on the Dracula mythos, enjoyed *True
Blood* without irony, read too many of the Anne Rice books,
enough to be embarrassed. Yet, confronted with the reality, he felt abashed. Her makeup was smudged. She'd gone
raccoon-eyed from whatever they'd done over the course
of the night. Her face had gained as well a childlike quality

in sleep, a fragility that transformed Duke's sheepishness to genuine shame. In a fit of emotion, he leaned down and skimmed his fingers along her resting cheek.

"Hey." Eva stirred, lashes white-gold over blue eyes. "Hi."

She stretched, detaching from Duke's wrist with a lurid smack of her mouth, tongue lightly stroked over her upper lip. Her gaze was unfocused, the look of an addict in the embrace of their vice. Eva lowered her arms and smiled at Duke as if he'd taught the world the word *love*.

"Hey," she said again.

Duke walked his gaze up and over Eva's head, to the trail of red-brown blood beginning at the fridge, the doors *still* somehow ajar. The mess was far from inconspicuous. It wasn't restricted to the floor, either. The walls bore his handprints, and the streaks where he'd stumbled and slipped on his own fluids.

Had Eva not noticed?

He tensed at the idea she might have not, bracing for the moment when she did and her languorous worship morphed into screaming terror once more. Another memory stirred: Eva, balling herself as she sank to her feet in the alley, whimpering, over and again, "Please don't hurt me."

Did she forget, or had his blood erased any concern outside of the next hit? Instinctively, Duke understood it was the second, the revelation so uniquely horrible that he immediately relegated it to his subconscious, unable and unwilling to cogitate on the implications. Duke wasn't a stranger to drugs, had no prejudice against their consumption, but he'd seen people spiral into obsession and how deep such lusts went.

And if petty narcotics could drive someone to larceny, what about the blood from an immortal being?

Not for the first time, Duke wished he'd been less antagonistic toward the old woman and her assistant, or even the peculiar staff he'd been given. Unfortunately, it was too late for reconciliation, and even without Duke's own pride as an impediment, he knew they wouldn't forgive him the first volley of insults. So better to keep on with what he was doing and pray his natural aptitude for adaptation would carry him through. Not that he had any room for extensive strategy, not with this hunger to manage, his appetite alive as any animal's, muzzled for the moment but present, waiting, restless.

"What's wrong?" Eva's brow rucked.

"I was wondering if you remembered last night," said Duke, cautious.

"I remember." And her smile returned, pretty and nonchalant. "It was something else, wasn't it?"

"Yes, it was." Nothing of what she had said encouraged him. Duke remained guarded, as flummoxed at his circumstances as he was before this line of questioning, Eva's features divulging nothing but an affectless fondness. "I'll be honest, though. I don't remember all that much."

"You're an *alfar*," said Eva with glee.

"What?"

"*Alfar*," said Eva again, enunciating the word with more care. "A foreign cousin, anyway."

"I don't know—"

"God, you don't have to lie to me. I know you're one of the huldufólk," said Eva, her delight finally turned physical. She clambered into the coffin with Duke, a harlequin smile on display, the grin revolting in its width. "You're one of the hidden people."

He flinched away, wincing at her fervor. "What?"

It was the only thing he could think to say.

"One of the hidden people," said Eva patiently. Their faces were inches apart, close enough that Duke could see the patterns of his blood on her cheeks: where it had dribbled, where it had soaked into the fretwork only beginning to spider across her skin. "An elf-thing. My grandmother talked about them all the time, and I know, we're not supposed to actually believe in that. But I was always a little sure. And now you're here."

Duke's first instinct was to laugh and not kindly, the concept so ludicrous, he wanted to berate her for suggesting it. By the next moment, he retired the impulse. Elves *weren't* more far-fetched than vampires. More important, here was a happy fiction Eva had created for herself. What did it matter that it was inaccurate? She was there and docile and that was what mattered.

"You got me."

"I knew it." Her smile was satiated, lazy. Eva sat back once more, both arms crossed along the rim of the coffin, her features joyful. Her attention wandered the house, pausing on the charnel in the kitchen before drifting along. When her gaze finished its circuit, it returned to Duke and her expression remained unaltered.

"How?"

A lithe one-shouldered shrug. "The blood, the teeth. There are a lot of stories about the hidden people, some of them dark. At least, that's what I remember."

"And those dark stories, you're not afraid of them?"

"As a girl, sure. I screamed. I had nightmares." Eva sighed, lower lip pinched in her teeth. "But as an adult? Not so much. There's something appealing about the dark, you know? The world is ending. Might as well be on the winning side."

What Duke wanted to say was that he understood, empathized with her attraction to the macabre. The void had its allure, particularly when gift-wrapped in latex, and even more so when nihilism stood as the only other option. The words did not come. Instead what emerged was:

"Careful. The things that go bump in the night might want to eat you."

"Let them." Eva laughed gauzily. "I might like it."

Duke studied her in silence, a radical idea cohering. "Is this universal among the Icelandic? I know your people have endless nights. So I'm wondering if you're all naturally goth."

"We're people, not a stereotype," chided Eva. "Not everyone shares the same kind of passions. We—"

"Yes, okay. *Fair*. How about your friends, though? Are they, you know, of goth-y persuasion?"

"What *are* your plans, Your Excellency?"

Duke swallowed a laugh. "Your Excellency?"

"You are a duke, after all," said Eva, without missing a beat.

"Heh. Well. I was wondering if your friends might be as open toward being indoctrinated into this life." He gestured feebly. The house wasn't a feast hall, hadn't any finery, couldn't be mistaken for a place of power, even with both eyes closed and an optimistic attitude. "I'm still redecorating, I'm afraid. And I don't want to force you to do anything, but yeah, if you have friends who might like what you're feeling—"

"They'll love it." A pause. "They'll *love* you."

He studied her carefully, an echo of last night's guilt throbbing in his chest. Duke recalled, with far too much clarity, how easy it had been to win her over, to quiet her, to sedate her into adulation. He remembered how it had felt to impose his will, the basaltic force of that exchange, how there had been no resistance at all, not even the hummingbird flitting of a captive spirit. She had simply stoved in.

Duke looked over at the fridge, still leaking gouts of cold.

"Bring them over."

A CONSCIENCE, DUKE LEARNED, WAS REMARKABLY EASY TO IG-nore under the shadow of desperation. Had he any lingering moral quandaries, they evaporated by the time Eva returned, hours later, freshly changed, with an entourage of her friends, the three he'd met on the initial freezing walk.

The trio were dubious until the first draught.

And then it was easy.

In an hour, the three were soporific, drunk on whatever compound it was that now percolated through his blood. Duke, between feeding his new retainers, unsure but unrepentant, charged each of them with a responsibility: one to comb the house for hidden electronics, one to clean, one to purchase a ticket out of Iceland for Duke.

His hunger worsened, a blade ticking under the steeple

of his ribs, tunneling further with each hour. It had become manageable once more, if barely, a gnawing discomfort that, for the time being, could be set aside in the face of more important concerns.

But not for long.

Duke would need to figure out his specific dietary requirements, what classification of blood would allow for untroubled consumption. The doctor had cleared it up. One flavor, one genus of individuals and no other. As his new minions busied themselves with their tasks, Duke wrestled with an unpleasant prospect: he needed to call either the old woman or Mara. The alternative was drinking a path through the refrigerator and that, to Duke's wry surprise, was an option worse than the dissolution of his pride.

So he choked down his pride, and rummaged through the house, found a phone number among the yellow notes.

He called from the computer.

Mara picked up almost instantaneously, more polished in appearance than she had been the previous time they'd spoken: sleek blazer, starched shirt, hair immaculately bunned, a monochrome Rembrandt.

"We're still waiting for your first commit, Mr. Guillo."

"Oh, go fuck yourself."

She laughed that shrill, uneven laugh of hers. "Why? Because you'd like to but you know you cannot? And now you're hoping I'll act as a proxy for your cock?"

Her venom, transparently lethal, stole the wind from him.

"Very catty," said Duke.

"Glad you noticed," said Mara. "Where's our first commit, Mr. Guillo? We have a *contract*. And more than that, I thought you had a passion, a want to survive the centuries, a marrow-deep urge to see your work to its completion."

"I do. And I will," he lied. "But I have a problem."

"Your lack of class?"

Duke swallowed his comeback, said in its place: "My inability to eat safely. You didn't tell me there were restrictions."

"You didn't ask," said Mara.

"Fine. I'm asking now. If you want me to do anything, I need to be able to eat. Nothing happens on an empty belly. So tell me what kind of blood I can drink."

With oratorical gravitas, Mara made her reply.

"Nope."

"What?"

"I have no idea."

"Fine. Ask your damn boss."

"There's no need."

"Jesus Christ, stop fucking with me, Mara. What the hell do you want me to do? Drink from every bag until I get it right?"

Her laughter ricocheted again, and the acoustics of his house limned it with metal this time, as sharp as nails on rust. "It would be the smartest idea you've had yet. But to answer your not-question, I'm not messing with you. I'm telling you the truth. Every Ventrue's predilection is specific to them. No one assigns you your preference. It's not like Hollywood, where you're taught to believe young is beautiful, blond is good, blue eyes are better than brown."

"You really needed to get those blows in, huh?" said Duke, teeth clenched.

"Hardly my fault that the truth hurts."

"I . . . As much as I like arguing with you, can you just tell me what you mean? If no one 'assigns a preference'"—Duke carved air quotes for emphasis—"to me, how the hell do I figure out what to drink? Nothing is going to happen if I drop dead."

"Well, you wouldn't drop dead. You'd just go catatonic."

"Thanks. That's a load off my shoulders. I'm so happy to know that I won't be dead, just an invalid." Duke balled his fists, counted to ten. "For everyone's sake, please help me."

The viciousness drained from her, and somehow the pity that replaced it was worse. "I wish you had better listening comprehension. I *can't*. I meant what I said. It's all specific to the individual Blue Blood. The best I can tell you is that it often seems to tie to something important to you. What matters to Duke Guillo? What do you care about most? Who do you care about most?"

"Computers? Sex? Weed?"

"Those are *things*. Material pleasures. You don't connect with them; you desire them. For once in your life, think in context of other people. Who are you closest to?"

"My weed dealer?"

"If you're not going to try, I have better things to—"

"My frat brothers?"

As soon as he spoke the words, he understood. Something clicked, turned in him like he was a lonely lock, and the horror it loosed asphyxiated him. Brotherhood. Yes. *That* was what he craved. It seemed so obvious in hindsight, his abject need for fraternity to matter in what he ate.

What.

Not who.

Not exactly.

Duke reeled at how easily his brain realigned around this new revelation, its casual devaluation of anything—there it went again, slicing the humanity from his choice in victuals—he could construe as food. He called up memories, happy ones, of his frat brothers over the decades, willing those luminous recollections to overcome this animal hunger, but all they did was make him hungry.

And he was so very, very hungry.

It was then Duke realized something else:

The blood he wanted was already here.

Not cocooned in plastic, not cold, not congealed to shadow, too thick to sip, but still running hot in living veins. The smell permeated everything now, a warm coppery musk, and Duke had no clue how he'd missed it before. As though leashed by a string to its source, his attention twitched across the room until his eyes rested on the blond who'd offered him a cigarette, who'd stood up for him, pushed him to chase joy, to speak to Eva.

In answer to his scrutiny, Sven looked up from his mop and his bucket, beamed, waving a still-mittened hand.

Duke stared slackly, mesmerized.

"Everyone else? Take the rest of the day. You.

"You, I need you to stay."

WHEN DUKE WAS DONE, THERE WAS LITTLE ANYONE WOULD have called a body. In a way, this proved a boon. Corpses were intrinsically difficult to hide. A hundred and seventy pounds of meat, memory, and muscle. Two hundred and six bones. Rubbery acres of gray-blue intestine. Such things were hard to grind down, especially in volume.

But for Duke, it would not be a problem.

He snapped a fluted tibia in his hands, worked a finger, and then his tongue, in the marrow, scraping the cavity for any last vestige of matter. Duke knew he should feel guilty, did so to some extent, a neglected lobe of consciousness aware that he'd not only recently murdered a man, he'd devoured him.

More or less, at any rate.

Duke hadn't actually *eaten* his victim, not in the normal sense, at least. Not that he didn't try initially, to his misfortune. He'd compromised, in the end, on emulating a spider, suckling on the meat and the muscle, wringing the arteries of their harvest, squeezing every ligament and stretch of tendon in his mouth for the last drops of blood.

Either way, for all the guilt that Duke knew he should experience, mostly, he felt full.

Duke lolled a drowsy look over the patchwork maze of bones spread over the floor, the skull in pottery shards. One death. He was owed that much, wasn't he? In a life in which he had to prey on the living, one death seemed inevitable, a casualty of self-education. Besides, the human species itself was unapologetically omnivorous, and it rarely questioned how the steak on the supermarket shelves was produced. Cows died to feed stockbrokers.

Stockbrokers could well die to feed something else.

The ecosystem was circuitous, ouroborosian in how it tied life and death, death and life, and now, life and undeath. Convoluted as his justification was, it was enough to calm him. And the blood, too, so much of it. That helped too.

Duke exhaled.

"Mr. Guillo," said a woman's voice. "Would you like us to take care of this?"

He thought about it for a moment.

"Yes," said Duke, beginning to succumb to lethargy. "Yes, please."

It was time to sleep and after that, to leave.

MEAT

D uke bulldozed into Keflavík Airport, swearing under his breath, *fucks* issued rapid-fire. Eva called out behind him, begging him to wait as she parked the car. Reflexively, Duke slowed, her panic too palpable to ignore, but lengthened his stride again before even his next redundant intake of air. He didn't warrant Eva's devotion, he reasoned, having secured it by illicit means, an accident of power. Moreover, he knew he was bad for her. Addiction, as a gestalt, provided no remuneration, and something of a hemophiliac bent was likely worse. In this respect, he was doing her a favor.

Better to vanish now.

Better to walk away, give her and her friends an opportunity to recuperate, forget, and deal with the sudden disappearance of the fourth member of their quartet.

Better to run before his wardens took notice, grateful as he was for their willingness to tidy up his mess. Better to go. Better to escape.

"Wait."

He turned at the sound, mimed helplessness with an exaggerated shrug, said "*Stay*" with as much force as he could, then jabbed a thumb at the inside of the airport before falling in step with an Asian family and striding indoors. Duke made an immediate beeline to his counter, passport slid across its polished top before he was even asked to do so.

"*Duke* Guillo?" said the attendant: a mousy thing with watery blue eyes, blond hair in thin ringlets, like an aging starlet displaced from the Roaring Twenties. Pretty in her heyday, but otherwise unmemorable. The bone structure prohibited it. "Is that a title or your first name?"

A memory of the old woman rose up, unwanted, unbidden. *God, I hope that isn't a real name.*

"First name," said Duke. "Got a brother named King and a sister called Queenie. It was all the rage in the South."

Lies, all of it.

"Really?" said the woman. Her tag broadcasted her name as Evelyn. It seemed fictitious, a moniker picked from a hat. "I wasn't aware of that. Which part of the South do you come from, sir?"

"Lafayette."

She glanced down at his passport. "It says that the passport was issued in Montgomery, Alabama."

"Well, I spent some time there."

Her smile declined in temperature. "Which part of the South do you come from, sir?"

"Lafayette," said Duke again, his expression static.

"I see."

"You know, the way *I* see it," he added, regretting, for multiple reasons, his initial evaluation of her. For one, it was a miserly view. Evelyn *was* attractive, just older than Duke liked them, which was to say she couldn't pass for seventeen in good light.

For another, Duke needed all the friends he could get right now.

He continued. "The South's basically the same thing all over. It's just a question of what kind of food you like better."

When he wanted to, Duke could honey his voice, let the accent thicken in the vowels, and smile like he was raised Pentecostal, together with a ranch of older sisters, each of them more picky about their brother's manners than the last. This talent had opened doors and legs for Duke, and though he wouldn't ever admit to it, Duke saw it as his devil's Hail Mary, his can't-lose last-ditch solution. He winked at her and waited, prayed under his breath.

If his charm had any effect, Evelyn showed no initial evidence of it. Her front-desk smile kept its glacial shine. Yet her eyes held Duke's just long enough to resurrect his optimism.

"If you say so, Mr. Guillo." Her eyes dropped to the monitor. "Hm. I'm afraid there's a problem."

"Yeah? Don't tell me the system has me confused with a real duke. That happens some—"

"You're on the No Fly List, Mr. Guillo."

"I'm sorry?" Hope rotted in his chest.

"You're on the No Fly List, Mr. Guillo," she said again, no change to her diction. "Sorry about that."

"Wait. Whose No Fly List? It's got to be a mistake. I haven't done anything wrong. I don't even have outstanding parking tickets—"

But he knew.

We're watching, a little yellow note had warned Duke.

It occurred to him then that the Camarilla, so stuffy, so fanatically obsessed with appearance, were exactly the sort to be able to recriminate him like this. Duke wasn't going to be intimidated, though. He'd said so. Plus, there were always ways to circumvent the system.

"Really," he said again. "It's got to be a mistake."

"Mr. Guillo, I'm going to have to ask that you step aside so I can serve the next customer."

He glanced behind him. There was no one there.

"Evelyn, come on."

"Mr. Guillo, I'm going to have to ask—"

Duke flung himself on the counter, halfway to panic. "Please check again for me. I need to get back to America. My sis, she's alone and she's sick. When she left home, our parents told her not to come back. I'm the only one she's got—"

"What is she sick with, Mr. Guillo?"

"Sorry?"

"Your sister," said Evelyn. "What is she sick with?"

He hesitated.

"Mr. Guillo, I really do need you to step aside so I can serve the next customer."

"No one else is fucking here!"

Duke hadn't intended to shout, hadn't wanted to draw attention, knew better than to piss off customer service— especially in an airport, with security all around—but the phantasmagoric awfulness of the last few nights had chipped away at his reserves of decorum. Worse yet was the memory of that stupid note, bolted now to the forefront of his consciousness, reminding him of his impotence.

We're watching.

A power move, Duke knew what it was. That didn't stop it from working.

"Look, are you just trying to shake down the tourist? Is that it? I'll pay. You want me to give you more money for a seat? I'll pay. Fuck, I'll pay double." He pawed through his wallet, credit cards raining out of their sleeves.

"Mr. Guillo, calm down."

"Triple. I need to get out of Iceland."

"If you do not calm down, Mr. Guillo, I'm going to have to call security," said Evelyn, unmoved by the hysteria. Statuary might have shown more passion as she closed Duke's passport, placed it atop the counter, and slid it an inch in his direction in emphasis. "Have a nice day."

"I want to talk to your manager."

"Sir." Not even Mr. Guillo anymore, he noticed. Just *sir.* Tense and clipped, impersonal, deeply uninterested in him as anything but a transaction to be firmly closed out. "I need you to leave."

Her dismissal rocked him. Duke took his passport and sleeved it in a coat pocket, stared at Evelyn for one last long wild-eyed minute. He felt hollow again, latheringly hungry. It pulsed in him, that appetite, a muscular tick-tocking, as though of an atrophied heart vainly struggling to keep time. Duke knew, understood without exception, that he should back down. That this was his one chance to withdraw gracefully, and any further interaction he might initiate was an act of spite and subject to censure.

But he reached inward anyway, down into his blood.

"Come on. You can make an exception for me."

It rose, cocksure, hipshot, every recollection he had of

being enough, being powerful, being the biggest dog on the field. The power shone with a cocaine luster, which was all right by Duke. He appreciated the familiarity. It made the sensation—that ephemeral infant instinct to weaponize his confidence, turn his charm on the literal offensive—easier to direct. Duke took a breath he didn't need and by the time he let it go, he felt messianic, high on the world singing him his hosannas.

"Evelyn, *please*. Come on. For me."

Duke wasn't sure what he was expecting, but he knew what it was *not*: Evelyn, smile still on parade, pointing a slim finger up at the camera above her counter, the matte-black device abscessed with red lights.

We're watching, said the note.

"Fuck."

He peeled from the desk, vertiginous with terror, the tiled floor seeming to carousel slowly beneath him. The light was cold and blue tinged. He hadn't noticed it before, but the light worked like a whetstone, giving everything an edge.

"Are you one of them?"

"Sir?"

"Tell that old corpse I'm not afraid of her. I'm getting out of here and she can't stop me."

Her smile became dazzling. "Next, please."

THE MOON, GIBBOUS AND ENORMOUS, WATCHED AS EVA AND Duke drove home to Reykjavík. Despite his misery, the uncertainties frissoning through him, Duke couldn't help but gawk at the lunar manifestation, the satellite an ominous shade of distant autumn. Like everything else, it had to do with the framing. In parallax with skyscrapers, he wouldn't have thought twice about the sight. But here, without civilization to lend perspective, the moon loomed like a warning, and Duke could see how his ancestors, clinging to one another, afraid, so very afraid of the dark, might have believed there was something numinous about the heavenly body.

Something terrible.

The tundra stretched on.

Eva broke the silence first, reaching for the radio. She wandered between the channels until, rather inexplicably, she found a station playing country music. A man wailed about the comeuppance liars and gamblers were to expect, that God would come to cut them down.

"You were going to leave me," said Eva as the singer's voice gave way to his guitar. "Here. Alone. Without you."

"Eva, I . . ." A glib answer leaped to his tongue and was dismissed. The moment seemed portentous. "I was going to come back."

She drove another mile in white-knuckled quiet. Another voice replaced the first on the radio, singing of the divine's country, and how the Devil came to Georgia but refused to linger.

"You weren't," said Eva.

"I don't know. How about that? I don't know what I was going to do."

"Why did you want to leave?"

"There are people here who want to hurt me, I guess?" said Duke, an elbow braced against the cold window. "I just didn't want to be stuck here."

"We'd protect you," said Eva, her own hurt palpable.

He laughed. He hadn't intended to do so, hadn't wanted to injure her, not with what he'd done, with her friend dead, with everything building to catastrophe. Though it was all *chemical*, Eva remained the closest thing he could name as an ally.

Nonetheless, her presumptuousness had caught him off guard and he'd laughed, a lunatic noise, shrill and tortured.

"Like fuck you could," snarled Duke, buoyed along by momentum. "Who do you think you are? You're just a couple of mortals who drank my blood. And seriously, who the fuck do you think you are? You're nobody. You'd die if she showed up at your door. You would be nothing, you fucking idiot. She'd just turn you into pulp. Just like I did to—"

Your friend.

He choked down the denouement of his rant.

Eva said nothing.

"If you leave . . ." said Eva after another few miles, voice careful, a cup on the brink of shattering. "Will you make sure we can still have your blood? There were the bags in the fridge. We could empty those out."

"I don't think that's a good idea."

"Please."

Duke squeezed his nose bridge in a hand. "No. Just no. Seriously, whatever you think it is, it's basically just the drugs talking—"

"Did you spike—"

"Did I spike my blood? I don't know, Eva. Is that something people can do? Because I don't know. I don't fucking know anything, okay? Just. I don't know."

"Okay," said Eva. And then again, in a softer voice: "Okay."

The lights of Reykjavík sloped into view, a string of pearls along the black throat of the sea. Exhaustion settled, heavy as regret, and Duke thought he could feel the dawn veer closer. His eyelids faltered.

"For what it's worth," said Duke, "I'm sorry."

Eva did not answer until they'd closed on the city limits.

"Do you even know what you're sorry about?"

Duke thought about her question.

"No."

"I thought so."

FOR MOST OF DUKE'S LIFE, THE SUBJECT OF WAKING HAD RARELY merited comment. He knew he slept hard, had had it commented upon several times by previous girlfriends, who'd marveled at his obliviousness to a midnight earthquake, and he knew he woke with verve, which was why his first night as the undead had startled him as much as it had. But never in his existence had awareness come with such sudden violence.

He screamed.

His larynx recognized his circumstances before his consciousness could catch up. Duke screamed a high, dry noise that went on even after he'd run out of breath, the sound razoring from his spent lungs. It hurt. He felt flayed, cut open, pinioned and ribboned into delicate strips of flesh, and it was not until another minute had passed that it dawned upon him that it was precisely what had happened.

"What are you doing?"

A face and a corona of wild blond hair crept into sight.

"What we need to do," said Eva, very seriously, her mouth pursed in focus.

Duke tugged at his restraints. He lay splayed in his coffin, legs and arms draped over the edges, tied to something he couldn't quite see. His neck, too, was bound, a thick wreath of rope pressing on the esophagus, and his skin felt cool, dead, waxen.

He was bleeding.

Someone had sliced him open from wrist to elbow, knee to ankle, and there was the sound of his blood impacting plastic. He twitched a foot and banged the side of it against the mouth of a bucket.

"The fuck is this?"

"You were going to leave," said Eva, her frown deepening. "You were just going to walk away."

"Get out."

His fear surged in him, tidal, rose and suppurated through the pores of his skin. Duke wanted his so-called lushes to leave, but more than that, he wanted them to share in the fear black-blooming in the pith of him. He wanted them to go, to leave, to free him from his imprisonment. Mostly, though, he wanted the pain to stop. He wanted the terror to end, to let go, so he could breathe and that animal part of him, screaming and incoherent, would shut up and let him *breathe*. There was not enough air in the room, not enough in the world.

But Eva only shuddered, a delicate frisson, and lowered herself out of view.

Duke heard a splash in the bucket, the ecstatic sound

of someone drinking deep, and a sigh by the end of that
endless swallow, hoarse yet pleased.

Another face entered his vision, its hair immaculate,
its expression calm.

"I told you that you would know if you were a prisoner," said that rich, low voice with its familiar mildness,
its lack of interest.

He knew then there was no leaving now.

Nor would there ever be.

IT WENT ON FOR DAYS.

It went on until Duke forgot how to number the
hours, the transition of the seconds, hunger evolving into
his solitary concern. At first it had felt like an unexpected
ally, come reluctantly to support him against a shared ad-
versary. But hunger, like greed, like any human vice, was
loyal to nothing but itself. His appetite became cavernous,
became the whole of him, and very quickly, Duke lost interest in anything but the now-omnipresent awareness of
the fact that he was starving.

Had circumstances been even slightly different, this
status might have precipitated an escape. But Duke, already hungry from the start, bound and bled so many
times, could only lie there, nearly catatonic from the
paired horror of his exsanguination and the advent of an
endless golden summer.

They freed him, eventually, although Duke couldn't
be sure as to when. To his inexplicable embarrassment, his
captors took care to make him *comfortable*. Blankets were
found. Rags. Cushions. Things to improve the ergonomics

of his enforced bed rest. At some point through his delirium, he thought he heard a conversation.

Eva: "He's going to die if this keeps up. And so are we."

"You won't," said his staff's spokeswoman, purring and warm. "It'd just be unpleasant to be weaned off his blood."

"But I don't want to be. None of us do. How can we fix this?" said Eva.

"I appreciate an honest woman." A brief silence. "And to answer your question: very easily. It looks like Mr. Guillo there asked for some old friends to visit. Intercontinental food delivery service. Who'd have guessed that was a thing?"

Duke longed to protest, to say something, anything, or just make, if he couldn't muster eloquence, a nonsense sound. Anything so long as it could be construed as an objection.

His frat brothers were coming.

The knowledge engorged in him and he could not tell if it was hunger or fear that he felt as consciousness waned again.

THE DOORS BANGED OPEN AND ARTIFICIAL LIGHT CUT A STEEPLE across the murk of the floor, tiles sticky, still crusted with Duke's blood. Bodies crowded the door, shoving for entrance out of the cold. On instinct, Duke shrank away, pressing into the wall, torn between wanting to lurch forward and to hide. His Renfields would always find him, he knew that. There was only finite space in the house.

Despite his knowledge that resistance was pointless,

even destructive, some vestigial corner of him still kicked at the thought of being pinned down, weaned on. For a while he had fought, but eventually that seemed too much trouble, *was* too much trouble for Duke. Besides, they came occasionally with blood he could consume and Duke, at that point, had no shame about whoring his veins out for a drink. So he let them bleed him and did what he could to master the way his mind screamed at the violation. In this fashion, he could retain some ghost of control. In this manner, he could say he had autonomy still.

But it wasn't his retainers who walked through the door.

The scent that wafted into the house was delicious, was nothing like he'd tasted on the root of his tongue. It was joy, it was light, an olfactory hallelujah, life condensed into an aroma so appealing, he surged from his hiding spot before he could think about what he'd done.

"Duke?" said a voice.

Recognition flicked a switch in his starved psyche, deadened the magnetism of that smell long enough for Duke to whimper, "Get out."

"Dude. What the hell? We flew out here for you, remember?"

"Please get out." He skirted the borders of the light, still keeping to the walls. The bodies at the door had moved inside, their frames in silhouette. Here and there, however, the light found the profile of a nose, a familiar tense smile. Fred stood at the forefront, bigger than Duke remembered, an out-of-season Santa hat jauntily astride his head.

"Get out," repeated Duke, desperation fissuring his voice. "Please."

"Duke! The hell is going on here? This place stinks. I always knew you were a piece of crap when it came to taking care of yourself—"

The door bolted shut behind the men.

Duke lunged.

THE MONITORS FLICKERED ON. IT WAS THE OLD WOMAN AGAIN, her face in close-up, every fold, every wrinkle in stunningly high resolution, replicated across every screen in the house. She wore red lipstick like a gashed throat, the only daub of color in a regal monochrome ensemble. Diamonds frothed beneath her chin.

"Marmalade," she purred.

Duke jerked his head up, a startled animal or a guilty child.

"Please," he said. It was the only word he could shape. *Please.* Someone else had said *please*, had screamed the word, had held on to the syllable as Duke dug down, through a haze of capillaries and red veins, until the noise shrank to a gurgle. *Please.* They'd all said *please*, had begged. *Please. Please stop this.* "Please."

"You know, I really have to thank you. Louis spent years trying to figure out how to discreetly make your other frat brothers disappear. He tried everything. Shell companies, hostile takeovers, relocation efforts. I told him to kill them. But he actually *liked* you people. Then you showed up and well, that all became so much easier."

"Please."

"It's so much better to love what you eat, isn't it? That personal connection makes everything so sweet."

"Please."

"Please? This is what you wanted, wasn't it? If I remember correctly, this is exactly what you asked for. Money, life eternal. Power."

"I don't want to kill the people I care about."

"Well, you don't have to. And I'm not going to judge the fact that you did. There is always collateral damage. Besides, it's not like you killed *all* of your fraternity brothers. Just some of them. The remainder are safe and here with me. Docile, happy as newborn calves."

"Help me." Whatever dignity he might have once claimed ownership over was forfeit now, auctioned away by circumstances, and there was a version of Duke who would have shot himself for what followed: him skidding over the blood-soaked tiling, tripping, then crawling on hands and knees through the gore to the screens. "I don't . . . I was so hungry."

And he still was.

The last tatters of his self-restraint held just enough to keep Duke from laving his tongue over the floor, anything to sponge up one last sip of blood. But he wanted to, nonetheless, craved the idea like an addict.

"I didn't mean any of it." Duke fisted a hand in his hair, face wedged in his elbow. Despite himself, despite the vestiges of his pride, he curled fetally by the electronics, spare arm constricted around his knees. "I didn't want to kill them."

"If only want could be harnessed, we'd have free energy forever," said the old woman, her humor incandescent. "You were so hungry, Marmalade. Of course you meant what you did."

He did not want to look. He did not want to turn. He could smell them, smell the bitter reek of bile, the organ tissue, the piss, the bowels slackening, no longer obligated to withhold their contents. Under all of that, the mentholated, vaguely antiseptic scent of shaving cream. It was the last that broke Duke, the foreign tincturing of normalcy, made him weep in convulsive gasps.

There were his friends. These were people he knew, frat brothers, coworkers, peers, his *network*, sustained over fifteen years of turbulent friendship. Not always the most palatable companions and certainly not always the most sterling of human beings. But they'd always been there for him, nonetheless, a bond better than blood.

Now?

They were meat.

"Please."

"Don't worry, Marmalade. No one in the world will need to know it was your fault. We, as a clan, are very good at dealing with regrettable accidents. After all, life is short and deeply brutal and things sometimes just *happen*, don't they?"

To Duke's shame, it was not horror but relief he felt, a wretched gratitude at the revelation he would not be exposed, incriminated in the slaughter of these men he had called friends. So he bobbed his head and said nothing.

"Thank you. I—"

"Why are you thanking me? I haven't done anything for you yet. I was merely discussing the joys of being what and who we are. Or, rather, of who *I* am. I never said those services would be offered to you."

"The contract—"

"Was in breach practically the moment you signed it. Your little fail-safes . . ." She shook her head. Her voice sweetened then. "But if you say my name, Marmalade, I'll make it all go away for you."

"I don't remember. . . . Please, please help." The begging wore down to a hitching, nerveless whimper, incoherent save for the word *please*.

"Say. My. Name."

Duke could not.

"Please," said Duke, though he knew the word had no weight.

The old woman sighed and her expression, unseen by Duke, his face caged in bloodied hands, gentled, became something almost human. Regret warmed in her eyes, fleeting and astonishingly tender. "That's the thing about power, you know? It's in the little things, the small details, the people you ignore. The clauses you don't read. You should have known better. Look at the world you left behind. Humans sanctify youth and beauty, but who holds the power, Marmalade? It's those behind the curtain, the ones who go unseen. The things you'd like to forget ever mattered."

"Please."

"If only you had been a little less you, this all would have gone so much better."

"Please help me."

"What's my name, Marmalade?"

Duke said nothing, only wept.

"You disgust me, Marmalade. But you still have uses. Clean yourself up and finish the job you were given. In a few months we will have another performance-review meeting." The old woman clucked to herself as she examined her nails, their surface red gold from some angles, rot black from others. "You'll want to do better at that one."

"I'm hungry. . . ."

"Of course you are. But don't expect your Renfields to drop by anytime soon. Mara has taken care of that. You need to focus on what you promised me. You need to focus on remembering who you are to me. On who *I am* and what you are to this clan.

"Because, I hate to say this, but you're definitely living from paycheck to paycheck these days."

The monitors went dead. The silence became as oppressive as his hunger. But he could do nothing about either.

Sobbing, Duke crawled forward to do the only thing left to him.

He began his work.

THE
LAND OF
MILK AND
HONEY

CAITLIN STARLING

NOVEMBER

NIGHT MANAGER

—◆—

It's November in Portland, which means the sun sets around 4:45 p.m. and rises just after 7:00. A lot of people hate this time of year—it's gray and bleak and dark—but it's always been my favorite. It gives me a lot of time to myself before and after my work shifts, with the farm sleepy and silent. I work the seven-hour overnight shift, from 10:00 p.m. to 5:00 a.m., which doesn't sound like much, but this job is seven days a week, fifty-two weeks a year, handling emergencies between the residents, human and animal alike. It's amazing how much happens once the sun's set, and so little of it is happy.

I'll confess to occasionally doing some work in my office before my shift officially starts, when I'm bored enough and the spinning wheel or dye vats aren't calling my name. The quiet stuff only, though, with the door locked and the lights down, so nobody can tell I'm in. I'd honestly rather be out in the fields, gardening, but there's not much to be done at this point in the season. All our raised beds are wrapped up for the winter, there's enough water (and then some) for everybody, and the only things growing are grass, weeds, and garlic. Even the bees are hunkered down, despite the relatively mild weather, and I don't blame them.

But it's a terrible irony that in the summer, when there's the most work to do, I don't have the time to do it.

Tonight, instead of paperwork, I take some time with the sheep, sitting on one of the newly hewn fences, admiring. They're beautiful animals, and I have a knack for reading them, for making them comfortable with me. In Portland, especially these days, you don't need to bring the sheep in for most of the season, though they do stay damp and smell of wet lanolin funk, so you have to keep an eye out for fungal infections. The earth beneath their hooves is mostly mud, but there's still forage for them, so we leave them out, let the lambs get a few extra months on them. It's easier to sell them when people don't think of them as cute babies anymore, but before they get that mutton flavor.

We originally intended to keep goats. Portland *loves* goats, especially after they were evicted so developers could build the nostalgia-themed Goat Block Apartments back in 2015. But while cashmere is lovely to work with, we can't farm it as much as we'd need to turn a profit. Sheep it is, then, a small herd of Merinos, some Bluefaced Leicesters, and mostly Dorsets for the meat market. They'll be lambing in the early spring, and then the commune—the farming side of it, anyway—will be focused on birthing, feeding, weighing.

But before that, the slaughter.

ECOVILLAGE

⬩

We're a small food and arts commune up in North Portland, on just shy of two hundred acres of former industrial land near the airport that nobody else wanted, turning weeds into farmers market gold, wage slaves into artists, and people at the end of their rope into healthier, more "functional" members of society. It's a noble goal, and we do it well. We've been open for just a few years, and already we have over a hundred and fifty members—and a lot more on the waitlist. But we can only get the approval for new houses so quickly, and what we build is *quality*, no double-wides or half-insulated shacks. No, we are going to fit in. We want Craftsman-style looks, and comfortable living. We've even rescued a few from demolition for infill development, picking them off their crumbling foundations and moving them up here to fresh concrete pours, and I've been working on restoring them in my off time. Winter's good for that.

All of this—the commune, the sheep, the houses, my

job—I owe to Lucille. She's an old-timer, one of the rare locals, and she's a great coworker. She understands our mission statement even better than I do. She wrote the thing, after all. It was her idea, to build a collective that's ethical from top to bottom, nose to tail. There are so many people in this city who need help, support, inspiration, structure, and we can give that to them. In return, they work the soil if they want to, create art, and live safer lives. But no matter what, they all contribute to this great moral feast, nourishment without guilt, organized to benefit all.

Around me, the night deepens. My watch buzzes an alarm. It's time to head into the office; there's an applicant due for an intake interview in half an hour, and I don't want to keep her waiting.

THE INTERVIEW

———— ◆ ————

R obin Joy is perfect.
Not her name (the name is unfortunate, but that's the one she prefers, and the one on her birth certificate) but the rest of the package. Her voice is powerful, her words undeniable, her stage presence glorious and addictive. And now she's sitting in the chair across from me, her plump, freckled legs crossed at the ankle, asking to live with me.

"Look," she says, leaning in, "I've never tried anything like this, and I can't say I've always wanted to, either. But it's cool, what you're doing here. It's really good stuff. The outreach, the self-funding, I'm a big fan." Formulaic, perfect interview answers, but coming from her, they feel genuine. They *are* genuine. I can tell these things.

It's early for me, around six in the evening, but I *had* to be the one to interview her. Everything about her, the vibrancy and life she exudes, has been calling to me. I couldn't leave this to Key like I normally would.

She doesn't know that I've watched all five of her most recent performances across town in the last twelve months. That's probably for the best. It means she's open with me, honest, and doesn't expect me to be impressed. Wants me to be, yes, but doesn't expect. Maybe that's real humility, or maybe she's still in that wretched stage every artist goes through, where they're embarrassed people agree that they're good. Or maybe she knows how to work a fresh audience. Live performers are good at that, and even though her work isn't improv (she's done a few podcast interviews on her process, I've listened to them all), I know she's got that special something.

"I want to do the work program," she says, before I can do more than smile and offer her a beer from the minifridge behind my desk. She cracks it open smoothly. That's her blip of bartending experience, nine months backing at a place in Southwest.

"Rewilding or production?" I ask. The collective needs both still, but I can't imagine her working either. No, she's better suited for the farmers market, but we won't be manning a regular booth again until April.

"Where do you need more help?"

I'd planned to give one answer—*focus on your art, we'll find something in the spring, there's no rush*—but my self-control slips. "I could actually use some help around the office," I say.

The one job she is in no way qualified for.

But she smiles, and I'm smitten, and what can I do?

She says yes, she'd love to work in the office. She asks if that means she's been accepted.

"We'd love to have you," I say, and touch her set of

keys, already printed a week ago, that hang beneath my desk.

I knew I was going to say yes when she made the appointment. We almost always do.

We'd—well, I'd—done the homework.

HAWTHORN HOUSE

S he moves in officially four days later. Robin Joy likes privacy, so I put her in Hawthorn House. Right now, she's the only resident. I make it clear it won't be like that forever, and she understands. She's never done this communal living thing, though, and this will be a nice transition.

The house is technically under renovation, but parts of it are finished and livable. There's running water and electricity everywhere except the kitchen, the replastering should all be set, and the laundry facilities are in working order. I've cut corners here and there—the ceiling medallion is Styrofoam from Home Depot—but I doubt anybody but Lucille could tell, and I haven't invited her to be part of the move-in crew.

"There's a mini fridge and hot plate," I say as she drops her bags near the bed. "Yours to keep, even once the kitchen's working."

"Are you sure? Somebody else must need them more. I

can just go out and get my own," she says. "I mean, I know the deal is you provide furnished living, but . . ."

"We're very strict on that," I respond, smiling. I have a hard time not smiling around her. It's a problem. "Everything here, we provide. It helps equalize things. Makes sure we're not appearing to favor anybody, or that we're out to take people's belongings or money. We don't want to look like a cult."

She laughs at that. "You know, if you say you don't want to look like a cult, it makes it sound like you know you're a cult."

"Well, commune, cult . . . it's all in how it's handled, right?" I motion for her to follow me on a brief tour of the house, indicating the work still to be done, and where she can treat the building like it's her own. "We don't have anybody at the top. That helps, I think."

"There's you. You're at the top, aren't you?"

I wave it off. "Just administration. Somebody has to do the accounting and keep everybody from biting each other's heads off."

More laughter. We get along really well. That makes me uncomfortable, when I think about it too long, but why should it? I wouldn't be the first shepherd to have a favorite ewe. And it's not like I feel hungry when I look at her.

Well, that's a lie. Of course I feel hungry.

Her art *suffuses* her, and I can't get enough of it. It's not just a job; it practically drips from her, fills the room on her exhales. And I just want more. Something like this was always going to happen, and really, the guilt I'm feeling should just be pride. Pride that I'm really settling into this job.

How could I run an arts commune if I didn't thrive on art?

"So when's my first shift?" she asks as we run out of rooms to stroll through. We're back at her bedroom door, and she leans on it in that inviting, enticing way that some girls have when they're flirting just a little bit, not quite ready to say goodbye, but not sure yet where they want the night to go.

Well, that makes two of us.

"Tuesday, two in the afternoon," I say. That's when Key is working, and they're solid and reliable.

She gives me a double thumbs-up. "Great, I'll see you then," she says.

"No, I work nights. Key will take care of you."

And that makes her frown. "Oh, I guess I just thought . . ."

That we'd be working together? Yeah, bad idea. Good idea? Fuck. "Maybe once you're more settled, we can revisit it," I say. "But nights are tricky. I wouldn't want to dump you into that first thing. Get to know everybody first, figure out where you fit. Then tell me if you want to spend your nights putting out fires."

"I guess that makes sense," she concedes. But she sounds nervous. Lonely. Everything flirtatious has gone out of her, and I suspect she's realizing that this really is just another place to live, not some exciting adventure.

She'll settle in, though. She'll make friends easily. But this *is* her first night in a new world. "I'll be here most evenings," I say, "before work. Finishing the kitchen and everything. I'll see you tomorrow."

And just like that, Robin Joy's shoulders unwind. "That'll be great," she says.

SOUP

———— ◆ ————

We had our last crop of squash in today. Some of it went into dinner, rice-stuffed roast butternut, and now I'm handling the rest. It's officially shift time, so I left a sign on my office door. I can play loose with the rules every so often, especially when I'm working elsewhere in the building.

This main building is institutional, a little industrial even, but we're working on it. Making it as beautiful as it is functional.

The kitchen and dining room were our first projects, and the large prep counters are glorious to work on. The pressure canner and flats of mason jars are ready, and I have plans for a soup that will cook up easily in a big batch and keep well, shelf-stable. We prefer to have the community members do the food prep—it makes them proud—but we also don't want to overwork them. Some people thrive on overwork, but on the whole, those people aren't here. Or, if they are, they want to use that energy on art.

I'll never stand in the way of art. I am of a line of artists, and I was made for a beautiful world.

It takes the better part of an hour, peeling and splitting and seeding and chopping, but I enjoy the glide of the well-sharpened knife. I love cooking, even when I don't get to eat it. Once all the squash are disassembled, I move on to garlic, bell pepper, and the rest of my mise en place. I measure out a fair amount of nutritional yeast; we have an ongoing problem with pernicious anemia right now with our vegan members, so I'm trying to work the fortified yellow powder in wherever I can.

Finally, I get the cubed, oiled squash roasting in the oven, and sit down at my laptop.

Work can only wait so long, after all.

I pull up our finances. No deposits to record from farmers markets, since they're thin on the ground this time of year (though soon we'll probably make wreathes to sell at the winter craft fairs), but we have plenty of expenses. We're nowhere near self-sufficient, not yet. Give it a few more years. Until then, thank goodness for our patrons.

I hear the footsteps long before their owner arrives in the kitchen, but I'm too focused on reviewing our property tax records to look up. Then I hear, "Leigh?"

Robin. I lift my head. She's been here two weeks already, but seeing her still fills me with pleasure. "Hi there," I say, smiling. And it's a genuine smile, always is for her. "Were you looking for me?"

"No," she says, but comes and sits down across from me anyway. The tables in the kitchen are small, not the long communal deals from the dining room. I can smell her over the roasting squash: already-dry sweat and a hint of perfume, the same she was wearing the first day she met me. "Well, not really. I mean, I didn't go by your office or anything."

"But you want to talk?"

She bites her lip. Nods.

Nervous. Not good. I close my laptop. "Is something wrong?"

"Just . . ." She looks around the room. "I don't know, do you want to go get a drink? I feel weird talking about it here."

Very not good. I stand up and turn off the oven. The squash will keep. I wrap up the bowls of chopped garlic and the rest. "I'm not supposed to go off campus during my shift," I say. She grimaces. "But Lucille's probably up, or Key. Hang on." Lucille isn't my first pick, not normally, but we have a stakeholder coming by tonight around three to pick up an order. He'll appreciate the luxe touch of having the official owner here to greet him.

I grab up my phone and shoot Lucille a text asking if she can come in to work tonight after all. In under a minute she's responded, saying yes. Nothing more than that, no details exchanged, because we're professionals.

I add that I've started some squash soup, if she wants to keep it going.

She won't.

VEGAN

We end up in Southeast, at a bar on Division not far from Ladd's Addition. I drive, because the bus at this time of night only would've made Robin more uneasy. Saturday night TriMet gets weird, and even though Robin has lived in town for a few years, she's relieved to avoid the transfers, the potential incidental nudity, and the bizarre array of substances, teenagers, hipsters, and all the rest.

The bar I pick is entirely vegan, which Robin likes, and loud, which I like. The patio's still open with a haphazard array of radiant heaters, and I tuck us into a corner by an absolutely stunning mural. I haven't been here in a year, and it hasn't changed at all. I can't tell you how much of a relief that is. I love the new bars and shops, all the variety, but sometimes it's just nice for things to stand still for a while.

"So, what's up?" I ask.

She looks down at her spicy paloma. (I just have water. She didn't ask. Either she's used to sober friends, or she remembers I'm technically on the clock.) She fidgets instead of answering. She didn't talk much on the way down to the bar, either. Maybe she's second-guessing herself now that we're off campus?

The important thing, no matter what, is to give her space. To make her comfortable, to make sure she feels she can trust me. Trust papers over a lot of sins.

So I don't fill the silence. I don't fiddle with my phone or look away as if I'm bored, but I don't stare at her, either. I wait. I keep my expression open, easy, a little concerned. When more than a minute goes by, I lean forward and rest a hand on her upper arm. Just as I expect, she finally looks at me, expression all nervous desperation tinged with hope.

(I'm very good at reading people. Community manager, shepherd, and all.)

"Hey," I say, softly. The din of the patio swallows up the sound, but I know she hears it. "It's okay. If it's not working out, it's okay. I'm not going to take it personally."

(A lie. Of course I would. But no need to get ahead of myself, not here, not now, when she needs me. No time to think about the outboarding process, the way we'll have to track her, the paperwork I'll have to fill out.)

"No, it's—that's not it. Not exactly." She ducks her head, takes a swig from her glass. She's going to go through it quickly. "I'm going to sound paranoid," she says.

Shit.

That's all I can think. All my people-reading skills go out the window, all my self-control, and for a moment, I just think *SHIT*. Somebody fucked up. Have I fucked up? What has she seen? What has she heard?

Shit shit shit.

I make myself take her hands. Just for a moment, just a light squeeze, and then I let go. If she's figured it out, if we've fucked up that badly, I don't want her to feel unsafe or trapped. I don't want to cross those boundaries.

But she came to me. To *me*. And she isn't angry. Okay. Maybe this isn't as bad as I thought.

All this takes only a few seconds. She never has a clue.

"Paranoid is okay," I say. "Whatever it is, I want to know."

More of the paloma disappears. She drums her fingers on the table, anxious. "All the blood donations," she says at last.

I stay calm. "What about them?"

"It just seems a little sketchy." She shrugs. "Unethical, I guess. I mean, I can consent or not, sure, but some of the other members . . . they get rewarded for it. And it's weird, seeing it happen at a commune. It's not like we need our own blood bank or something. And it's not like it's open to the public."

Relief floods through me. I can explain this. She's quite close to the truth. That makes the lie easier, that and how practiced my answer is.

"There's some context you're missing," I say. (Understatement.) "You know the medical services we provide free of charge? The needle-exchange program, the low-cost prescriptions—those are a donation as well. The blood doesn't *pay* for that"—it does, although not in a straightforward manner—"but it's part of a reciprocal relationship.

Medical care wouldn't stop if nobody wanted to provide blood, but it's an act of goodwill. We like to provide for the community. Not just *our* community, but the city. Other people who need help."

Snacks arrive: roasted cauliflower with harissa tahini. She picks at the steaming food, turning over my answer. "Sure, okay," she concedes. "But like—you know Ethan?"

Ethan is a fifty-five-year-old man who has been with us since the beginning. Before that, he was sleeping rough for two and a half years. He had a heroin problem when we took him in, but decided to try to kick it last year, and is three months, six days clean right now. Good guy. PTSD, not well treated yet, but we give him the resources he needs to make sure most of his days are okay.

"Yes," I say. "Of course."

"You don't feel like he's being taken advantage of?"

I consider my response carefully.

She doesn't like waiting, I guess. "I mean," she says, waving a cauliflower floret as if it's a wand, "he's not all there. He's erratic. Does he—it just seems like he's being used. Maybe it doesn't do him any harm, but . . . I don't know. Institutional overreach, or something. You shouldn't have to give up parts of your body for a break in rent, you know?"

"Nobody is forced to participate, and we don't reward participants with money, or extra privileges, or rent breaks," I say. "Where did you get that idea?"

"I mean, why else would people donate blood so often? Key had me schedule out the next couple visits, and it just seems excessive."

I make a note to myself to talk to Key later.

"Listen, I get it," I say, "but some of us believe that because blood is a renewable resource, donating when we're able to is a public good."

She stares at me.

"I said something wrong," I venture.

"A *renewable resource?*"

Okay, maybe not the best choice of words. I do make mistakes occasionally. I laugh, rubbing at the back of my neck. "Well, yeah. Like dairy cattle. No, don't—don't look at me that way, I mean it in the most respectful way possible. What if I said, like honey? The product of labor the body does anyway, that can benefit others with careful donations. It's not like a liver. It grows back."

"Livers do grow back," she points out.

"Huh. Well. Taking out a liver would be more invasive." I try to get back on script as quickly as possible. "And at any rate, very few members actually donate each visit," I say. "I can show you the numbers. But I promise you, we do our best to balance encouraging participation against protecting the more vulnerable in our community. It's not like James Marion Sims."

By Robin's shudder, she knows the name. Good. It's nice when people remember history. They know things could always be worse.

"We're not treating people as expendable for the greater good," I continue. "We really do our best to treat every individual community member with dignity, because regardless of what the world thinks, every one of them is human and deserving of the same treatment." I pause, then add, "You know, if you do end up staying in administration, you can help with oversight on that."

She perks up. She eats some of her cauliflower. "I don't think I have the training for that," she says after she swallows. But it's clear she's interested. "I'm not a social worker or anything."

"Right, but," I say, gesturing with my full water glass, "you'll be in a position to know who might be more vulnerable, and to make sure they know they don't need to participate. And you're an incredible writer. I know you don't do marketing-type work—I get that's not where you're comfortable—but maybe you could help our messaging. Make it clear. We can do better together, I'm sure of it."

She leans forward, wholly engaged. Her expression loses its confusion, its concern, replaced with the heady thrill of having a mission. "Do you think so?"

I nod.

"I'd like that," she says. "It'd make me feel a lot better."

Of course it would.

It's called forced teaming, what I did to her, what I do to the whole community. *We're in this together. We all know. We all agree.* I make sure to accept dissenting voices, parrot them back, make people feel *heard*, but in the end, it's all management. And when somebody takes issue, when Robin asks *is this ethical*, I make sure the door is open in case it's best for them to leave, because if they leave easily, they stress the rest of the group less. But it's better still to redirect the dangerous behavior. It's better to fix a problem than to cull it.

Culling is much more noticeable.

We treat every human in the commune with the same amount of dignity, because, in the end, they're all one herd. And it's easier to make decisions when, despite all their individuality, you can treat them as a unit.

Robin finishes her paloma, finishes her cauliflower, and begins talking about other things. Writing, the city, how great a singer Ethan is. I know I have her. She strayed, but now she's a part of the herd again.

And I'm happy.

MESSY

◆

If anybody asks, the bleached, denatured blood residue that will still linger in crevices despite how furiously I'm scrubbing all the tile tonight is poultry blood. In Oregon, if you slaughter less than a thousand birds a year for farmers markets, or any number just for your own consumption, you don't need a license. Which is good, because we don't *have* a license for anything else sold commercially, and we don't have any weanling pigs on private contract with customers this year.

It's true we've had slaughter and processing classes here with some of our residents using last year's lambs. That would more than explain the blood, just not the timeline. But the important thing is that there's been blood in here before. There will be blood in here again. There will be no DNA left to test, and everything here is done up to the FDA standards for a regulated abattoir, even though we don't qualify, even though we'll never have an FSIS inspector here every day. There's nothing here to incriminate us.

But I'm still paranoid.

This is the most dangerous thing we do. Especially on nights like tonight, when things get messy.

This guy . . . this guy was something else. He's always left a mess, but this . . . I'll need to have a talk with him, because he crossed a line. Spread the blood around, made a game of it. It's pathological, and money or no, the commune isn't going to survive if people like him think they can just break the rules because they're donors.

What a mess.

And it doesn't help that I'm on edge, maybe because of going out with Robin earlier.

Robin.

Robin, because she is perfect and incredible and clearly felt alive after our outing, is finishing the soup for me. When we got back to campus, I checked in with Lucille at the office and let her know I'd take care of the rest of the evening. She was gone without a word. That left me to head back to the kitchen until our stakeholder (ugh) arrived. It was only one in the morning, so I had a few hours left to finish cooking before then. I could handle it all, as long as I focused.

And then I found Robin there, waiting for me in the kitchen.

I should have been annoyed. I should have sent her off to bed as kindly as I could. It wouldn't have been hard. She was buzzed and it was late. But instead, we sat up and talked about the city, and about art, while I turned the oven back on. When it was time to load up the color-designated pots half an hour later, she fetched the canned, homemade stock—half vegetable, half chicken, for all our varied nutritional needs—and we were still basking in each other's company by the time my phone buzzed.

The soup wasn't finished. It had another half hour to go, minimum, and then it needed to be pureed and canned after. But it was time. Time for blood and a mess Robin could not be allowed to see. I must have let my consternation show (I must have been too relaxed . . . was *definitely* too relaxed) because she asked if there was a problem.

What I should have done: said no, told her it was almost three in the morning and she should go to sleep, promise her I could finish up alone, then put the soup on the back burner for a few hours.

What I did: hesitated, said I needed to get back to my office (couldn't tell her there'd be a visitor; who visits a commune at three fucking a.m.?) but the soup would keep, and don't worry. And Robin—perfect Robin, drunk Robin—was right there, ready to take over. She didn't even ask if Lucille could step in and finish the soup. (Of course, she wouldn't. She doesn't care for that sort of thing anymore, just old architecture and beautiful books. But that would have given me another opening, if Robin had asked. Another chance to lie and do my job properly.)

So here I am, an hour and a half later, scrubbing blood that isn't poultry blood off the tiles, not knowing if Robin has been reasonable and knocked off to bed, or if she's still waiting, wondering, adding to her list of questions I thought I'd nipped in the bud. What should I tell her when I finish up? Especially since she's already worried about the blood donations, I can't tell her I was cleaning up a late-night mess in the slaughter room.

Something else about the animals, maybe? No, she could figure out that was a lie.

A medical emergency? Even easier to debunk.

Nothing at all, because it isn't her business?

Except she trusts me.

She *likes* me.

When I finally finish bleaching and scrubbing and rinsing and (for good measure) scheduling ten chickens for slaughter the next day under a fake customer number, I go and shower until there's no coppery-sweet scent of blood or tang of bleach left on me. It takes extra time, but not too much, and it's necessary.

My hair is short. It dries quickly. By the time I walk back to the kitchen, there's no trace of damp left, and I'm wearing a T-shirt with the ecovillage logo on it, the exact same logo that was on the shirt I was wearing before.

I find Robin waiting there, asleep at the kitchen table.

I rouse her gently and apologize. I say *I* must have fallen asleep at my desk, and I look embarrassed, and I thank her for finishing the soup. Say it smells delicious (it does, but doesn't quite mask the scent-memory from that damn room). Tell her to get some rest, because the pressure canner will take at least another half hour to come up to temp.

I think for a moment she's going to argue and try to stay, but she's too sleepy and this is all so mundane, the excuse so boring, that it barely registers as anything worth questioning. I simply walk her back to Hawthorn House and bid her good night. I all but tuck her into bed.

And then I go and clean the slaughter room again— and say a silent thanks that there's no body to get rid of.

THE APPLICANT

I have another round of applicants to interview tonight. I'd say it was a mistake coming in early for Robin's, because now Key wants to offload all the after-rush-hour interview blocks to me (I think they're nervous after the talking-to I gave them about what duties it's reasonable to give a new hire), but I can't regret it.

Still, I don't necessarily *enjoy* the majority of these interviews.

We say we accept applicants on a lottery model. That's not true, but we put in the effort to make it *look* that way, and I'm honestly very proud of the system I helped invent. A commune like this needs an exacting balance of personalities, skill sets, skill *levels*. We provide housing and food to those in need, including emerging artists, but we're a humanitarian effort on our tax forms, not an artist retreat.

We don't exclude based on race, sexuality, or health status. Not even addiction issues. We don't *exclude* based on anything, but we do need to keep a balance. Hence the lottery system that isn't a lottery system, and a lot of late nights researching everybody we invite to stay, from the luminary dancer to the active meth addict to the single mother of two (though those specific examples are all based on one person: Julie, over in Columbine House).

I know I do it a lot, and I know it's bad form to compare what I do to managing a flock of sheep, but it's really not so different when you get down to it. A cohesive group makes everybody's lives easier, keeps them healthier, and benefits their shepherd. And I'm their shepherd.

Well, community manager. Same thing.

So I knock out two interviews that are just for show (they're not being accepted), and then settle in at my spinning wheel for some decompression. I've only gotten a few yards spun up when I'm interrupted by a knock at my door.

It's always something.

I look up, expecting Ethan or Julie or half a dozen other members of the community, here to ask for intercession on some interpersonal dispute or for help with a burst pipe, but the face hovering in my open doorway is unfamiliar.

And something about him sets my teeth on edge, just a little.

"Hi there," I say, securing the batt I was working from and getting up off the stool. "Can I help you?" Our community members are, of course, allowed to have visitors on site, but not overnight. The rule gets a little fuzzy in winter, because night falls before dinner's even served. I hope that's what's happening here.

But it's not. He clears his throat, and the motion draws

my eye to a crescent moon tattoo just peeking out of the neck of his sweater.

I straighten to my full height.

"Yeah, uh. I heard about this place, and it seems—seems really cool. I was hoping I could apply for a room here?"

It's so ridiculously implausible of an excuse I want to laugh, but I'm too busy staring, because this is not what my split-second deduction prepared me for. I eye the tattoo once more, then back away from the door, motioning him in without a word.

I'm not sure what I want to say just yet.

"I've lived somewhere like this before," he says, edging inside. "Down in Lents. Nothing formal like this, but a couple of houses on some shared land filled with artists and plumbers and musicians and a couple office workers. Lots of shared labor, productive gardens, and stuff. So I've got skills you could use."

"There's a formal application process," I say.

He colors. Colors, as if this is completely normal. As if *he's* completely normal. "I, yeah, I know, I just—I don't have anywhere else to go right now. Don't have much time to wait. And I thought it was worth a shot."

"I could call around to the shelters in town. You can fill out an application, then wait there for, say, a week"—not enough time, but enough *distance*, it might break his interest, but there's still something *wrong* about this whole scenario—"and then I'll get back to you."

That crescent moon tattoo. It could be a coincidence, feels like it *has* to be a coincidence, but I'm not buying it.

He meets my eyes, finally. He's shy. "They don't want

people like me," he says. And maybe he just means that he's gay, that he's not white, that he's got so many tattoos that the crescent moon barely stands out, gauged ears, "alternative" hair. Portland claims to be progressive, and it is—right up until it isn't.

But I don't think that's all this is.

The longer this conversation goes on without him indicating conclusively one way or another which way his blood leans, the more nervous I get. This could be a distraction. A trap. Anything.

The time has come to end this dance. I bare my teeth.

His eyes widen.

"Oh shit," he whispers. "Oh shit! Fuck, this is your hunting ground, isn't it, shit, I didn't know, I swear I didn't know!" He's terrified. If he were human, he'd be close to pissing himself. He's on the floor now, though I haven't moved an inch, haven't so much as raised a finger.

He didn't know.

He's not here to hunt. He doesn't even want to buy a share. He's applying to *live* here, like a desperate mortal, the kind of desperate mortal he looks just like. It feels wrong, that he stumbled into us. Impossible. But I'm skilled at reading people, and he's well and truly stunned.

"I'll go, I'll get out of your hair, I'm sorry—"

"No," I say, holding up one hand.

He goes preternaturally still.

He's young, looks just like any baby-queer anarchist still idealistic and knocking around Portland. He'd fit right in with our human contingent, and I'd wager, with the way his color doesn't fade now that he knows what I am, he can walk in the sun when it's really overcast out, as long as he bundles up and wears a hat.

He's useful.

Caution says he goes—immediately. But curiosity makes me want to know more. How the hell did he stumble across us? Is he really just looking for someplace to live? So many unanswered questions dance in my head, and one thing is clear:

I'm not ready to make this decision alone.

"What's your name?"

"Kasim."

"Come by next Tuesday, Kasim," I say. "I want you to meet Lucille. Can you bring your papers?"

"Yeah," he says. "Yeah, I've got everything. I'll bring it. Shit, are you sure?"

He's already halfway out the door, too afraid I'll take it back or, worse, snap and tear his throat out.

"It's an audition," I tell him. "Come prepared to show off."

DECEMBER

NEW EMPLOYEE

◆

I half expect Kasim to ghost us, but he's outside my office when I stroll into work on Tuesday, clutching a ragged satchel to his chest. He's dressed up a little for the occasion, and he's nervous. I take my time unlocking the door, checking my messages, straightening some paperwork, before finally addressing him.

"Welcome back," I say. "Follow me."

An interview like this poses a few logistical problems that I'll admit I wasn't entirely prepared for. I don't want to take him to my house or to Lucille's, because I don't need him knowing where we sleep if this doesn't work out, but I can't have him near the humans if we're going to talk shop. I considered the husk of Hawthorn House, but Robin's not allowed to work nights yet, and even if she could, I don't want him knowing where *she* sleeps, either.

That leaves somewhere off campus, the fields, or the barn. I pick the barn, and shoot off two texts: one to Lucille telling her where we'll be, and one to Key telling them

I've stepped out for my appointment, and can they please hold down the fort for the next two hours?

It's still early, so there's a chance some community members will be working in the barn, but it's blessedly empty. Even the sheep are still mostly outside; only a few sick ones are penned in. I check the doors to be sure, then gesture with a lift of my chin to a hay bale. He sits. I extend my hand and he gives me his papers, meaningless to anybody who doesn't know exactly what she's looking for.

I do, though.

He's exactly what his tattoo claims: a duskborn who follows Camarilla law. I didn't know we had any duskborn, but then again, it's not like they're allowed into Elysium meetings, and it's not like I go to Elysium meetings, unless it's specifically demanded of me, so clearly I'm no expert.

I ask him a few questions about his background and his hobbies while we wait for Lucille. After a nervous look around, he starts talking. He was turned only a few months ago and has lived in Portland since he was a young teenager, both on his own and drifting between rough sleeping groups and support homes. For all that, he's still idealistic. Still fundamentally likes people, even if he doesn't trust them. If I had to guess, whoever embraced him was from some of our remaining philosopher-kings, one of the Brujah who stayed in town thinking they could add Portland to the Anarch Free States. But Portland is commercializing its Weird too fast, and we're still Camarilla for the time being.

He's telling me about this old warehouse in industrial southeast where he's been staying since waking up craving blood when Lucille shows up.

Lucille is old, powerful, and profoundly disinterested in everything around her except her art. This is her retirement plan, though she doesn't help me run it at all; hasn't since our first six months. She doesn't dress like a farmer, choosing fine cashmere sweaters and woolen skirts, most of which I made for her. Tonight she has her long blond hair in two French braids and is at least wearing boots.

She takes a seat near us without a word. Kasim cringes away reflexively.

"Well," I say. "Let's get started, then."

Whatever amount of comfort he'd gained from our easy little chat is gone. I told him to come ready to show off, but he doesn't know what that means. And he can tell Lucille is . . . old.

"What exactly am I getting into?" he asks.

I like how direct he is.

"Exactly what it looks like," I say. "Exactly what we say it is. We're an arts commune with a mission to prioritize the forgotten, the disadvantaged, the downtrodden."

"And they're—human."

"Yes."

"Except for you two."

"Except for us two. And you."

He frowns, looks around as if he could see past the painted wooden walls, the pens, the bales of hay, and the farm equipment. "And this is—what, a humanitarian mission?"

Lucille's lips quirk. She's likely thinking of the linguistic relationship between *humanitarian* and *vegetarian*.

"Yes." I watch the confusion, the disbelief, deepen. "And more."

He turns that over in his head. "But not hunting grounds."

"Not exactly."

Another beat.

"Holy fuck," he says, finally, eyes widening. "It's a *farm*."

I grin. He's succeeding at showing off—that he's got some amount of brain between his ears. "It's a farm," I agree. Better than *ecovillage death camp*, which I half expected him to call us. But no, he's not disgusted. He's riveted as I begin outlining the structure of our little enterprise, how the majority of our stock just provides blood donations, the ones Robin was so distressed by. The blood is taken in daytime, by human phlebotomists, the majority of whom are in some way linked to the local Camarilla superstructure of the city. While they do take a portion of the donated blood to its ostensible, official purpose, a certain amount is kept pure. No fractionation, no CPDA-1, so it's a little chunky when it comes out of storage, like unhomogenized, unpasteurized milk, but it's safe.

We keep that blood on-site, far from the human housing, and I make deliveries weekly. We can only support so many customers like that, and even with the general distaste for bagged blood, demand still outstrips supply. Human bone marrow only pumps out new red cells so fast, no matter how much iron-rich food and nutritional yeast I put into the herd.

For live feedings, our supply is even more limited, but we make a good enough product to charge a premium. "We keep records on just about everything regarding our community members," I explain. "Those records are obfuscated by a numbering system that matches our nonhuman livestock; we record share purchases of sheep and deliver human blood along with lamb rib roasts. Physical traits, personality traits, personal histories, current and past medical status including drug habits, religious beliefs, orientation . . . the list goes on. It means we can match buyer with product."

"What do you do with the bodies?"

"We try to minimize loss."

After all, blood is a renewable resource.

"Fuck," he says, leaning back in his seat. "You really have this all figured out."

"Everything except scale," Lucille says.

"We're growing at a sustainable rate," I counter, sweetly.

"So, you do this all yourself." He glances over at Lucille, and he's keeping up well enough that I can guess what he's thinking. He's figuring out she's not hands-on enough to be much help.

But she's not the only set of hands I can trust here.

"The majority of the ecovillage's functioning handles itself," I say, "but for the few tasks that Lucille and I can't manage on our own, we keep retainers."

He doesn't like that. His brow darkens, his shoulders stiffen. I ignore it, continue on. "We pick carefully, people who already trust us, so they're not in too much cognitive dissonance during the day or when we're not around. We currently have five retainers, including Key, who's watching the office as we speak."

The horror on his face, the righteous anger, is growing.

What happened to showing off, sweet boy?

"And you think that's—okay?" he asks, finally.

"I think it's practical," I say. I don't tell him that they're not bound to me, that I rely on Lucille's greater power to keep them held. Again, he doesn't need to know the details, how we sneak our Blood into their food in special one-on-one meals, how we groom them until they're entirely loyal, in love with not just us but the land we're standing on.

I think, briefly, about how wonderful it would be if Robin knew. If Robin were bound to me. But I don't have time for thoughts of Robin now, not with how Kasim's agitation is growing.

"You're drugging them. Forcing them to be—complicit. Compliant."

Actually, he sounds quite a bit like I'd imagine Robin would in this same position.

"They're happy," I say, thinking of Key's undying loyalty, their joy in serving.

"Without the ability to say no, no amount of comfort or happiness is real."

Yes, definitely a philosopher-king. Kasim's lived on the streets for years and still believes in objective good, ideal situations. He has likely killed to survive, if not as a human then certainly as a struggling, desperate lick, but he doesn't yet understand the need to manage, to cull, to craft an environment of success for oneself and those we depend upon.

"And yet the lamb is not allowed to say no, either, nor the herding dog, unless their caretaker allows them to," I say, gently, until I realize gentleness is only angering him more. I change tack. I become cold. "True informed consent is a beautiful dream. And it is a lie. It will always be a lie."

I wait for an argument. It doesn't come.

Ah. I'm influencing him, perhaps unduly. It slips out, sometimes, when I am determined to win; but winning isn't the point here.

This is *his* test.

I back off. Watch him shudder. Watch him glance, desperately, at Lucille, who is looking at one of the sick sheep, at the colors of its shit streaking its rear.

"There is no consent," I say, drawing his attention back to me. "Not for animals, not for humans, not for Kindred. There is only the illusion. There is only our interpretation of what is done to us. If you cannot understand that, you don't belong here."

I expect him to stand, to leave, or to at least shout and argue, but he surprises me. He asks, "And what about me?"

"You don't bind anybody without our permission."

"Not what I meant," he says. "I mean—I mean, are you going to have *me* drinking your Blood? As insurance, or . . . ?"

Not a bad idea, but I dismiss it immediately. "No," I say. "Not unless you think it's necessary. And if it is, I don't want you here."

And really, it's more a matter of resources. I don't want to stretch Lucille's influence too thin.

"Fair," he says. Goes quiet. Thinks. Still doesn't get up to leave, even as I watch him struggle to reconcile his concept of justice and free will with everything we've built. Finally, he rubs at his eyes, laughs weakly. "They don't know, all the rest of them. That you're feeding off them."

"No. But they freely give anyway."

"And they get"—he waves a hand at the whole place—"all this in return. They're not hunted. They're safe."

I nod.

"I guess it makes sense, that some sacrifices have to be made to get something this—this humane."

I smile.

"Glad you agree," I say.

Of course, things are not as idealistic as he seems to think. He is too gentle for us, too hopeful; it will break him soon enough, his love for people, his desire for a better way. But isn't this the better way? More humane, as he said? I think he'll fit in here, better than any other of our kind I could pluck randomly from the streets. It takes a real progressive thinker to switch from what we've been doing to this new system of ours.

"We keep the Masquerade here just like we do everywhere else. Which means you don't tell anybody here, not even the retainers, what you are. You don't tell anyone—period. As far as they're concerned, you're another human working the night shift. And if you break that one rule, you're out. Understood?"

He nods. "Yeah, I understand. But they're not going to notice the whole . . . nocturnal thing?"

"Not unless you make a big deal out of it."

"Right."

"I'm serious. We're an active farm—there's work every day, every season. And you'll be a part of it," I say. He bristles a little. Doesn't like taking orders is my guess, and I can only imagine the intensely shitty ones he must have followed to be approved by the Prince of Portland. "Your choice on what that part is. You can work in the fields like the humans, or take on some light security, surveillance on feedings, running messages, resolving human issues— there are a lot of options."

He subsides. "Got it."

"We'll provide sustenance as payment," Lucille says.

I'm quick to add, "From the bagged product. No live feeding, not on site." That's my own rule, one Lucille isn't bound by, but I'll be damned if I let this unproven child out among my flock. He eats like I do, or he's gone. "And you will stay fed. Drink twice a day, if you have to. I recommend far from the source, because habit is important. I've found it's helpful to abstract feeding from humans as much as possible, in order to take better care of them."

I spend my entire life not just in a world of humans, but intimately involved in them. I resolve their disputes, I clean up their messes, I even handle minor medical issues. A shepherd starving to death would predate upon his own flock out of season.

What a waste of resources.

He nods, quickly. "Yeah, sure. Sure." He's young enough, and likely hates himself enough, that he's not fazed by this, even though bagged blood doesn't taste anywhere near as good as the real thing.

"And you stay away from the sheep," I remind him. "No live feeding."

"Got it."

"Then welcome to the farm," I say as I hold out my hand. "Let's get you settled in."

DOMESTIC DISPUTE

R obin is adapting well. She has made friends easily, and I'm told she is a good listener. She's a quick study, too. Key finished training her in all the basics—who to call for various forms of emergencies, who lives where, how to update our community newsletter—and tonight she's in for her first evening shift. With me.

I start her with the paperwork.

"This is how we track each animal," I say. "Divided into shares." We're looking at a sheet I've pulled up for one of the Dorset lambs. "Contact info for the buyer here, current status of the animal including veterinary history, record of down payment."

She nods, but I can see she's looking at the *shares* column. I imagine what she's going to say, about how unsettling it is to see a life divided up mathematically like that and turned into dollars. But instead she says, "Is it just proportional or is there a specific weight per share? Do we true up later?"

I can't help my smile. Maybe she can't bring herself to

say *slaughter* just yet, but she's being a professional. I appreciate that.

"Proportional. We have a minimum slaughter weight, and we raise more animals than we sell, so if any don't reach the weight contracted for, we keep them. And if they come in more, then that's a bonus." I shrug, leaning back in my chair, drinking in her presence. "We're generous here whenever we can afford to be. And the cost of raising one lamb is more or less the same as another."

She likes that concept. And it's very true, for all the animals. The sheep have rotated pasture and competent veterinary care, our poultry free-range among our gardens, and our humans live a good, enriched life.

Work is optional, and art is encouraged. Medical care is free to our members and we've created a low-judgment environment. Every new member is given their own private room. We have entire apartments available for families, of which we host twelve, and we allow for bunking together in certain circumstances, as long as it's two months from when they join. We want to make sure everybody's more or less settled before such close living occurs. Shared houses can be powder kegs enough. We serve communal breakfasts and dinners, cooked by a rotating list of members. All chores are handled that way, with weekly meetings to discuss adjustments to the roster. We have multiple communal spaces. Two are open use and can be reserved for up to an hour at a time, while the others are themed: painting studios, a ceramics building, a quiet room.

Most of my management is done this way, without any human involvement and barely any conscious notice. Making certain things available with ease, making sure everybody has enough food, making sure they're safe. It's the same tack we take with our sheep: providing solid fences, winter feed, water, all without their notice or care. It increases happiness when intervention seems low.

But there are some limits. We restrict cell phone usage on the grounds. It's optional, which means a surprising number of people participate. We tried banning phones at first (we're careful, but the omnipresence of cameras these days is always a security risk), but that led to people not trusting us and finding ways to keep their phones secretly. By making it just a suggestion and wrapping it up in the rhetoric of reducing distractions and engaging with the land, we have a much higher compliance rate.

Robin still has her phone. She's checking it a few hours later when there's a knock at the office door. I grudgingly get up from where I've been working at the small lap loom I keep for slow nights, but all lethargy disappears when I see Kasim next to a panicked-looking Ethan.

"Oh good, you're in," Kasim says. "I, uh. I found Ethan, wandering. I think he's coming back down."

He's shaking head to toe. I hold out my hands, palm up, not too close to him. He sees them. Fixates on them, ignoring Kasim, ignoring Robin. I have that effect on our members, a combination of comfort, trust, and a habitual use of just a fraction of my less-than-human power of attraction. (I try to keep a hold on it, but at this age, it just slips out. And it has its benefits. Fewer people argue with me when I'm wearing a raiment of calm charm.)

It's enough to bring his desperate guard down a little. He puts his hands in mine. He breathes a little more easily.

"It's okay, Ethan. What happened?"

His pulse flutters. Jumps. I catch his gaze and hold it, and soon his breathing begins to match mine; a measured performance that's enough to keep his panic at bay.

"It's Jason and Bill," he says. "They're at it again. It sounds bad this time." His fists clench and his thumbs scrape at my knuckles, full of tension. Behind me, I hear Robin move; she probably feels she needs to be close enough to intervene. She can't know that Kasim and I have this handled.

"Jason and Bill," I repeat.

He nods. His grip loosens, just a little, because he knows I'll handle it. Jason and Bill don't live in the same building as Ethan because this isn't the first time they've gotten loud and angry, and it sets him off. But I'm glad Kasim found him, glad he's here to tell me, so that I can fix it.

"Right, I'll handle it," I say. I nod at Robin, drawing Ethan's attention to her gently, letting the world back into his attention. "Want to stay here with Robin?"

She's watching the two of us, biting her lip. In hindsight, maybe separating her from the other members wasn't the best idea. She's behind on learning the various dynamics on site.

"No, I just want to go home," he says.

"I can take him," Kasim says. "Unless you think you'll need me . . . ?"

I weigh the options. "Ethan, are you okay walking with Kasim?"

"Yeah," he says. He lets go of my hands and runs one hand through his hair. Kasim's a better fit for him; Robin's clearly a little distrusting still of Ethan's "stability."

"He'll take care of anything you need. Don't worry about asking, okay?"

He nods, and Kasim smiles. It's gentle without being patronizing. I'm glad Kasim found him; he's clearly got experience with things like this.

As they leave the office, Robin asks, "What should I do?"

I glance at her as I put on my coat. "Stay here. Hold down the fort."

"What if there's another . . . issue?"

She's got a point. She's not ready. I survey the room. "Okay. Can you put up a sign with my cell number saying I'll be back as soon as I can, then lock up?"

"I can help," she says.

I can't stop my smile, even though I'm working through a hundred permutations of what I'll find when I get to Bill's. "I know you can," I say. "Meet me at the central housing building when you're done. But if things are at all overwhelming, stay at the edges."

"Do you really think it'll be that bad?"

"No," I say, "but I don't want you to think you have to help me if you feel out of your depth."

And then I make myself leave, because Jason and Bill need me more than Robin does right now.

Central housing is a quick fab apartment building, LEED certified by the barest margin, just across a central plaza from the admin building. I hate it, but we needed a high-density building to start with. I'll replace it down the line. Bill and Jason both live up on the third floor, and there are other community members milling about the halls, looking distressed. Ethan must have been visiting one of them. Better than it spilling outside, I guess.

I can hear raised voices. Jason's apartment door stands open, and I knock only once before stepping inside. Another resident, a woman named Genna, is sitting next to Jason, who's nursing a swelling jaw. Bill is sitting at the kitchen table, head in his hands, the image of contrition.

This is worse than I expected. Bill and Jason both joined the commune about half a year ago, and neither had a history of violence. They lived next door to each other without issue at first. But over the past month or two, they've started clashing. Just verbal fights, and they always sort it out after. But I should have put a stop to it then, not just tried to help. I made resources available, offered to move them to separate buildings, but they didn't want that. Jason is always the target of Bill's aggression, but he said they'd work it out, that it was just an adjustment issue to not needing to work anymore, and I believed him.

See, Bill quit his job, but has never gotten involved in community upkeep, which is objectively fine, but it pisses off Jason. And it isn't good for Bill, either. The removal of responsibility has uncovered something in him, something nasty, and he fixated on Jason. His only saving grace was that it never became physical, which is why I've let it go on for so long.

This? This is Bill's last strike. I have to fight down the urge to rip Bill apart for crossing this last line into violence. It may have been just one punch, but it's proof he is no longer a sheep in the fold; he's become the fox, biting at heels, trying to drag a lamb into the woods.

I could have stopped it. Should have kicked Bill out weeks ago, before it got to this point. It's long past culling time, and if it was just me and Bill in the room, I might have put him down right here, damn the consequences.

But summary justice doesn't work among this many humans.

So instead I sit and talk with them both for half an hour before Robin arrives. She lingers like a ghost by the door, almost a legal observer to the goings-on. Bill's anger surges a few more times, coming out in overblown apologies meant to manipulate, and with Genna and Robin here, I can only use mortal means to corral him. But I do.

In a perfect world (playing by human rules), I would just kick Bill out. But now that he's lashed out physically, I can't be sure he won't return to get back at Jason, or Ethan for reporting the fight, or Genna for intervening. And if he does it during the day, I won't be there to protect them. Which means the best answer is to let Bill stay where he is and give Jason the ultimatum: switch buildings or leave.

That pleases Bill greatly, of course. It'll keep him docile, happy in his freedom from consequences. Once he's had a day to accept it and cool off, I'll tell him he, too, has to move houses. Make it seem like an upgrade. Hopefully it'll take him a while to ramp back up to aggression, the way he did the first time.

Because Bill won't stay long. Bill will disappear into the night sometime in the next week or two. Whatever bullshit he decides to pull to get his way next, it won't matter, because he'll be dead and processed and gone before he can act on it.

Jason decides to leave the commune, sick of dealing with Bill's shit, but I can see it hurts him. When Bill is gone, I'll reach out to Jason and invite him back. After all, it's not his fault I fucked up.

MANAGEMENT

———— ✦ ————

I don't think you fucked up, letting him join the group," Robin says later that night. We're out by the quail enclosure. The long night has left me frustrated, and making sure the run is secure and the shelters are keeping the birds dry helps me focus. Some of the quail rouse and begin cooing their soothing, frog-like songs.

"I try to pick our members to avoid this sort of thing."

"Some people are abusive shitheads. It happens. They're really good at hiding it."

That's not the problem, though. The problem is that our system *encouraged* it somehow. I'll need to take another look at the lack of work requirements. How do I balance that better? Some people need structure and won't create it for themselves. It's like animal enrichment, such as the scratching areas we provide for the quail to encourage natural self-care behavior. They'll never brood their own eggs—humans bred that out of them centuries ago—but at least they'll bathe.

I can't explain it to Robin that way, of course. I set about repairing a section of chicken wire instead.

"I do think you fucked up *tonight*, though," she ventures. "Letting Bill stay here, running Jason off?"

I can't justify that to her, either. Doing that would mean explaining just how I know Bill will be exiting with no chance of return. I want to; I want her approval and her understanding. And I still feel violent. Destructive. I want to go and tear Bill's throat out right this minute, to prove to her I have it under control. (Irony, I know.)

"It's not permanent," I say instead, twisting two sections of wire back together with needle-nose pliers. "I just want to keep everybody safe. Keeping him where I can monitor him is safer."

"Bill assaulted Jason," she says. "Word's going to spread, and now he knows he can get away with that sort of thing. It's going to scare the others. I know you don't want cops here, and I understand that, but . . ."

"But they won't do anything for 'just' a dispute between guys," I remind her. "Not when it's only one punch. Not when he's that good at pretending to be apologetic. He'll normalize it, people will give him a little space, they'll forget."

"Genna and Ethan won't understand, you know."

The others, they'll probably buy Bill's minimizations. Society has them primed to do that, especially since his target was another guy, especially since Jason left. They'll assume *Jason* was in the wrong—or else why would he go, and not Bill? But Robin is right. It will just be for a week at most, this tense cohabitation, but it'll rock the boat, and I won't be there during daylight hours to keep the peace.

"This is going to ask a lot of you, and I apologize for that, but would you be willing to talk to them? I don't think they'll want to hear it from me."

"I don't exactly have any authority beyond my picture on the website. And I can't say *I* understand, either."

"No, and that's why they'll listen. Tell them that I'm handling Bill, and that I hear their concerns. And in the meantime, I'll start making Bill pull his weight. Move him into his own place, so he's farther from the others. I'll drive him off. I'll be the bad guy." Another vicious twist of the wire. "And I'll make sure he forgets all about Jason."

CONTRACT NEGOTIATION

———— ◆ ————

Jolene Ladzka is here for her scheduled feeding. She takes her blood awake and willing, and she has developed a fondness for Ethan. He never remembers her after, but he always sleeps better the night after she's fed on him. Something about her method soothes his inner demons.

After, she tends to linger. Tonight is no different, except that she asks to talk to me privately. And because Robin is on shift, I suggest we go back to my cottage.

She doesn't care a single bit for its ornamentation, the corbels I had made by a local woodworker or the painstakingly restored mullioned windows. Not a moment's attention paid to the entry hall runner, made by an old man in Nepal whose work was coveted by kings, or the perfectly oiled and balanced spinning wheel by the chairs we sit in.

"I want to buy a life," Jolene says after she's made herself comfortable.

"I can put your name in for the lottery the next time a whole stake comes available."

I immediately think about Bill. But though I am primarily an artist and not a businesswoman, I can smell the opportunity on her. The desperation. Money has little meaning to me now; I have most of my needs met, and the ones left to strangle on the vine are there by choice. But the community needs money, and there are other things I could ask of her. Even so, that doesn't mean I need to capitulate eagerly.

She doesn't like my answer, of course. but says nothing, drumming her fingers on the arm of her chair. I try to find a pattern there in reflexive self-protection; she's a thaumaturge, a blood sorceress, and I trust her less than most of our kind, on principle.

"Leigh, please reconsider," is all she says.

I smile my public-facing, fundraising smile. "Jolene, I understand we make a good product, but I can't just give you somebody else's contract." Not only is it unprofessional, it risks severe consequences. Almost everybody on that list is as dangerous—or more so—than she is.

"I'm not asking for somebody else's. I want somebody untapped. This isn't a gourmand asking for her next feast. I need a research subject."

"And I don't provide lab animals."

It used to be that the Pyramid handled this sort of thing internally, never desiring involvement from the outside. Even with how their Blood failed spectacularly last decade, Jolene should still be able to manage her affairs on her own.

"I need a particular profile," she says as if she didn't hear me. "I'm sure you either have it in stock or know where I can get it. I'm willing to pay whatever cost you require."

It doesn't make sense. Why indebt herself for a body she can surely pluck out of an in-patient facility somewhere, or off the streets, or from the Greyhound stop at Union Station? She's fully capable of doing her own research.

So, again I say, "No." I wait for her response. We've entered contested territory now, and I ready myself to feel the push of her will upon mine. She's more formidable than I am, particularly when she's just fed, but this is my home territory, and she knows very well the support *I* have.

Still.

A minute passes, and she doesn't push in the slightest beyond the steel in her gaze. Yet. That I can tell. But she is older than I am and practiced at subtleties I can only dream of (and the horrors to match). She finally leans forward and says, as guilelessly as she can pretend, "Please hear me out?"

I make a production of giving in, because now I'm curious on top of eager for a way to make Bill's culling useful. "And what is the profile?"

If Bill doesn't match, no loss; I can honestly tell her I have nothing available and can simply log her for a future life when one appears that matches her desires—if I'm still interested once she's off my land. But if he *does* match . . .

Two birds, one stone, et cetera.

She grins wolfishly, delighted at successfully piquing my curiosity. "Lurking danger," she says.

Those two words.

Those two words are so precise that I immediately hate her. Those two words suggest she *knows*, and she locks eyes with me, sizing me up. *Then* I feel the push. The swirl and tug upon my mind, so crude that I know she wants me to notice.

And then it's gone. A warning shot. She can take what she wants from me, so it's better if I cooperate.

Maybe I should say *I have no such person*, to prove I am indomitable. Perhaps I should just laugh. But instead, I say, "What will you give me?" Maybe, *maybe*, her influence snuck inside within the Trojan horse of her obvious attack, but I don't think so.

I think it's a longer game than that. A test of some kind. A warning. But this transaction? Simple.

She gives me a figure and the name of a contact of hers who would be more than happy to invest in the ecovillage. And a promise. Her aid in refining the process of preserving blood to give me a few more decades of gentle subsistence. It's likely useless—if a method was possible, some young Duskblood street alchemist would have cracked it—but Jo Ladzka is no mere street alchemist. It's worth taking a shot, especially with the amount of funding she's offering.

And I know my time will run out. I have only to look to Lucille.

We sign the deal for Bill's life, and she even drinks a draught of my Blood. There is no point in drinking hers in exchange to seal the bargain, and she doesn't argue the inequality. She suborns herself to me, just a little, just to prove she's somehow still in charge.

I wonder what she knows.

SYLVIA

Tonight Robin and I check on last year's lambs.

They're almost slaughtering weight now, and I aim to have them dead by January. But until then, we need to keep them fat and healthy. Most of the work is done during the day, but it's always good to have eyes on them at night, too. Robin has never even touched a sheep, so I spend most of the visit orienting her to the barn where I have the nearly yearlings. I've wintered everybody outside until now because barns trap disease, but it's wet, wetter than usual (and Portland is *wet* this time of year), so I need more land per animal as it all gets chewed to mud. The lambs are separated off anyway, since they need fattening, and the ewes are hardy, so into the barn the lambs go.

It's dry and warm in here, a close press of fuzzy bodies. The air is filled with the stink of fresh manure, the aroma of lanolin, the sweetness of hay. The lambs are docile, raised up close to me and the humans, and they mouth gently at Robin's outstretched hands as she reaches into the pen.

"Are all of these sold already?" she asks.

I think back to the spreadsheets and e-mails waiting for me in my office. "About half. I'm hoping for three quarters of them to sell; the rest we'll keep here."

"For breeding?"

"For eating."

Her expression sours and she goes very still, staring at the lamb that lathes her palm with its tongue. "All of them? They're all going to be killed?"

"Not all. There are a couple ewes we're going to keep." I point to a young Bluefaced Leicester, with her tawny curls and silvery head dotted with black splotches. To Robin, she probably looks like all the rest, except for the number on the tag, but I have high hopes for her. Her mother is one of the stronger ewes, in her fourth year of lambing with no troubles yet, and her lambs grow up well for Bluefaces, meaty but still with good fleece. "For the wool herd, or for breeding. That one is both, she's good stock."

"How do you know?"

"Watching them. Careful record keeping."

"Did you grow up doing this? Get an ag degree?"

I shake my head and am about to tell her something about my childhood when I catch myself. It's been just long enough now that my real age and my apparent age are diverging noticeably. "No," I settle on. "Just a hobby."

"*Just* a hobby."

"Well, not anymore." I smile. "A little past that, now. I hope you're still here in spring."

"To see these lambs die?"

"To meet the bees," I say. "But that, too, if you want. Or not, if you don't. That'll happen next month, not in spring, though." Robin eats vegan a lot of the time, though not exclusively. I thought about asking why during her interview, but I've found it's best to be matter-of-fact around the realities of meat eating, of animal raising, of slaughter. Either people have clear opinions on it already and don't need your input, or they're coming to their own decisions actively and it's not my place to sway them by anything other than doing.

"They live good lives, right?" Robin asks after a few minutes of silence, while she wanders over to my special Blueface and gives her a pat on the head. "For as long as they live?"

"That's the idea," I say. "It's a millennia-old arrangement. We keep them safe from predators, from disease, from the weather, and in return, we take sustenance from them."

I swear I'm not trying to smell her while I speak. But I can. I definitely can. Warm blood, right here, and I'm thinking about lambs and humans and this *new* arrangement, this years-old arrangement. Come, live here, live free, and give freely of your blood. A human can consent, as much as anything can, whereas the young ram I'm fussing with can't. I want to tell her, so badly, so suddenly. I want her to share in my pride.

But even though I can see her turning over the concepts in her head, getting comfortable with them, I know it's way too soon. It may always be too soon.

"So," Robin asks finally. "What's her name?"

"She doesn't have one," I say.

"Why not?"

"Farmers don't tend to name their animals."

"Even the ones who will live?"

"Even then. You have to keep a kind of distance. You never know what will happen, and there are a lot of lives depending on you."

"I've lost pets. It's gutting. I don't think I could manage losing—how many lambs are there?"

"Forty-three this year."

"Jesus, I don't think I could take *twenty* deaths a year."

"And that doesn't count illness. Slaughter we plan for, we *hope* for, so it has a sort of dignity. Sickness . . . just feels like failing. As if you failed *them*." Not just sheep and chickens, either; humans, too.

It's nice to talk to somebody about this, to watch them consider, weigh, evaluate. She crouches down, eye level with the sleepy animal. "All the same, I think she should have a name."

"Why?"

She shrugs. "Call me superstitious, but maybe it'll ward off death."

Or paint a target on her. I don't say that. But I think it. Still, the lamb is already my favorite, and I'll mourn her anyway, when the time comes.

"Sure," I say. "Have something in mind?"

"What about Sylvia?"

I consider. The lamb's head *is* mostly silver, with only a few dark spots, and the land she lives on is lightly wooded. It seems appropriate. But I'm curious. "Why Sylvia?"

"After Sylvia Plath."

I stare. "Is this some additional *naming her for the dead will keep death away* type of thing?" I don't understand.

But Robin, perfect Robin, just shrugs and says, "No. Because Plath's words are immortal, aren't they? This girl can't cheat death forever. But we'll remember her when she's gone."

TILLER OF THE GROUND

———— ◆ ————

Caine was a farmer. Did you know that?"

Kasim doesn't answer, just looks down at me. I'm on the ground, ass-deep in mud. I don't remember how I got here, or why Kasim is here, but I'm not bothered. I keep talking.

"A farmer, a 'tiller of the ground,' while his brother was a 'keeper of sheep.' Does that make sense to you?" I ask him. "That Abel was the one who would have known blood and sickness and death, and yet it was Caine who turned to murder?"

He doesn't answer. He does edge closer. I peer up at him, at his crescent moon tattoo and his almost-human pulse. I can't stop talking. "It was Caine who gave humanity its bloodlust, and who ultimately made us into monsters who must be either predator or shepherd to survive. But you know what's funny?" I add, leaning in conspiratorially. "When *they* say vegan, they mean 'doesn't eat animals,' but when *we* say 'vegan' we mean 'feeds off animals, not humans.'" I giggle.

Kasim laughs. He gets it. He *gets me*.

But as quickly as the joke came to me, it's gone. "Why was *Caine* the farmer?" I murmur.

"Can you stand up?"

"Of course I can," I say, and don't. "I have nothing against farming. Obviously. I spent all last night out checking our wintering beds and our cover crops and the garlic shoots. I *like* farming! I enjoy every aspect of food production, of turning life into sustenance."

"Please stand up, Leigh." He sounds—what, scared? A little desperate? I smile broadly, trying to put him at ease. No need to be afraid, Kasim!

"I think it's what makes us human," I continue, sliding my hands into the mud. It feels amazing. Slick and cool and knotted with grass roots. "Farming, I mean. It's hard work, but the benefits far outweigh the struggle. That's pretty obvious. No agriculture means no villages, no towns, no cities, no nations. Abel couldn't have done that. Wandering shepherds can't keep up with demand. So these days, humans grow their meat much like they grow their corn, for better or worse."

He crouches down, finally, leaning in to hear more. I think he's interested, until I see a little furrow in his brow. *Concern.* Still concerned. I think back. Why would he be concerned?

"Makes *us* human?"

"*Us*," I repeat, feeling the shape of the pronoun between my lips. "Makes *us* human. Am I human?" I rub at the soil with my palms, frowning. I sound out my thoughts, slowly, the way they're coming to me. Molasses-thick, not blood-hot. "I was once. I think I still am, but not—not in the same way. Obviously. I drink blood. I don't age. I've got—I've got *powers*."

"Leigh, let's get up," he says, reaching out and gripping my upper arm. "This isn't the right place to—to talk like this. Let me help you to your cottage."

"I know I'm not the same as they are," I say, barely noticing how he pulls at me, except to sit down harder. I'm busy. Can't he see that?

"You're really, really not." What has him so desperate? I look around. We're alone. No humans here to observe us, to mark the difference like I am.

"But I'm not like you, either," I say, finally looking directly at Kasim again. "When I look at other Kindred, like you, like Ladzka, even Lucille, there's a difference there, too. I make the food. I cultivate it. That process, it changes me, makes me . . . better? Stronger?" No, that's not right. "*Human* means the opposite. Doesn't it?"

"*Up*, Leigh. Come on. Don't make me get Lucille." He tugs again. I stand, finally, though the earth does its best to hold me back. It recognizes me. I look at where the mud has sunk into the creases of my hands, plodding along behind Kasim as he leads me toward my cottage.

"Caine was a farmer," I murmur to myself. "I am a farmer of man. But I should be called a shepherd, with my herd, my husbandry, the blood and sickness and death that are all my responsibility. It's all getting jumbled. Caine should have been the shepherd. Or a hunter, a solitary hunter, and yet he worked the soil and found murder *there*. Perhaps it was *because* he didn't know what it was to cull a sick animal. Because he didn't know to respect life in order to gain more from death. Maybe that was why it was murder."

Kasim isn't talking. I look at him; now *I'm* the desperate one.

"Am I upsetting the order of things?" I ask him.

He goes still. "This is the better way," he says, but he doesn't sound like he believes it. Doesn't sound like he's certain.

I'm the certain one. But I don't feel certain, either. I feel dizzy. I waver on my feet. It spurs him to action, and we start walking again, the squelching of my boots drowning out my voice.

"Is this wrong, no longer looking death in the face and naming it murder, and instead calling it farming, ranching, slaughter . . . the abattoir instead of the killing fields?"

We reach the front door. The knob won't turn for Kasim. He lets go of me, glances at the sky. It's getting brighter, bit by bit.

"I need to go," he says. "Can you—can you get yourself inside?"

I fumble with the lock. It turns. The door eases inward. I hear footsteps fading behind me, so I don't think he hears my conclusion.

"There are rumors," I whisper to the empty hallways of my house, "that it was Caine who spread agriculture across the early human world. He planted his crop then, a growing swell of humanity to feed upon, and we have harvested it for millennia since. Perhaps I am only implementing it in a more focused manner."

Yes.

Yes, that seems right.

DEAL-BREAKER

---◆---

I come to the next evening on the floor of my bathroom. I'm lucky; there are no windows in this room, and nobody has found me insensate and put a stake through my heart. Noddist bullshit no longer runs through my head.

All that's left is memories of being foolish, of having a death wish, of lying in the mud in the fields and proclaiming for all the world to hear *what I am*. How did I fuck up this *badly*?

I'm supposed to be in a hidden vault beneath the house. I have only half memories of leaving it maybe an hour before dawn, after I took my morning dose way earlier than normal. I was spun up after spending the evening with the sheep and with Robin, desperate for something to take the edge off. I'd needed it. I'd *needed* it.

So instead of grabbing a bag from my main stock, I'd reached for one of the pouches Jo dropped off early last week. I'd wanted something strong. I'd been hesitant to try it until then (Who wants to try a blood sorcerer's experiment? And besides, it's only been a few weeks since she took Bill, so there's no way it was more than a first draft), but that much intimate time with Robin was—was too much. I wanted something stronger than normal. I figured I *deserved* it, deserved peace.

Except whatever blood that thaumaturge gave me must have been tainted somehow. Because of course it was. That's what I get for trusting another blood-drinker to provide my food for me. She's got no sense of integrity. Fucking stupid, is what I am.

It could have been worse, I tell myself as I down a bag of blood—my *own* product this time, chunks and all—and wash all the caked mud off myself. As far as I can tell, in the disjointed fragments of memory banging around my head, it was only like drinking a batch of blood high in THC, maybe 'shrooms. It could have been far worse.

Once I'm changed, I text an apology to Robin and ask her to handle the office while I deal with an emergency. Kasim's the real person I need to apologize to, but I'm not ready for that. No, first I get in my car and drive to Washington Park.

To Jo Ladzka's house.

It's a gamble; for all I know, she could be out, but I don't want to warn her by calling ahead. I whip around dark, winding roads, up the pitch-black stretches of Cornell, and into the great woods that tower above Portland. Her house perches on one of the steep ridges inside the park, buried in a tangle of unmarked roads, but I know the way.

If she doesn't want to see me, I won't be able to get to her. The house is warded to hell and back. I know about where the first ward will be, and I park my car just outside of it. I test it.

It gives.

She's in, then, and while now she knows I'm here, she's letting me come.

My anger is desperate to have the upper hand, to come roaring in like a vengeful angel, but that is not the tack to take with her. No, better an unannounced visit paired with surprising calm. I master myself as I near the lights of her home, which has none of the old charm of mine nor the modern polish of the other houses in these woods. Instead, it's a haphazard stack of three different building styles, added onto decade after decade. It sprawls. It towers. It makes no sense at all.

I'm met at the front door by two of her Blood-bound servants, older women with fine-boned hands that are decorated with small scars. They don't talk, not out of deference but of smugness; they serve a greater master than I. They beckon for me to follow. I hesitate, but enter, half expecting horrors to line the walls. But it's a very normal house. Boring, even.

Wherever she does her work, it must be tucked away.

I expect I'll have to wait, but Ladzka is waiting for me in her kitchen.

"Leigh," she says, smiling pleasantly. "What a surprise—are you bringing Christmas gifts?"

"Not this time."

"A shame. But I have something for you," she says, and goes to her fridge, kept as polished as any lab equipment. At the thought of her lab, I shudder; I don't want to see what perversions she keeps down there.

For all I know, Bill might still be alive.

I'm caught on that thought—of Bill restrained, hobbled, his veins tapped to deliver the material for blood sorcery on demand—when she holds out another blood bag.

I stare at it.

"Another iteration," she says. "A refinement. I think you'll really like this one."

"No," I say.

She frowns. "No? Are you over bagged blood, then?" She steps closer.

I bare my teeth reflexively.

"You look a little peaked, Leigh," she says. "Sit down. Please, have a drink. It will take the edge off."

"And leave me gibbering out nonsense under the stars again?" I snap.

Fuck. There goes my hand.

Her face takes on an abstracted look of compassion. It's all wrong. In another context, I'd admire it—it's a work of art, that mask—but now I'd rather clutch my head or lunge or leave.

Instead, I take the bag of blood from her, then set it gently back in her fridge. I shut the door.

"The deal is off," I tell her. "No more lives, no more experiments. Find another source."

"Tell me what happened," she says. She watches for my response.

But there's no reason for me to answer her, not even to maintain the relationship. We are transactional. She purchases live feed shares, she gets her blood, we move on. I refuse to be indebted to her, and that's what will happen if I answer her questions, if I keep accepting her gifts, even if they're allegedly as payment for Bill. Bill's only one life. Eventually the value of her experimentation will exceed what I gave to her, and then the scales tilt back in her favor.

And even before that, she will find weaknesses in me. I won't let her do that.

"The deal is off," I repeat. "You can come for your normal feeding on the fourth."

"Leigh—I didn't want to bring this up, but I know you understand that it's hardly good customer service to blame *me* for your own failings." She leans in. "That specimen you gave me, Bill—he's not what I was after. I said *lurking danger*, not childish entitlement. I assume that's why the batch I gave you had such unintended side effects," she says, making this my fault. "I need good material, Leigh, not your castoffs. Not your trash."

I thought I'd hid it better than that. But I refuse to feel ashamed for her.

"Surely you know somebody in your system like that," she says. "Impassioned. Ready to be tipped over the edge. Somebody *glorious*, Leigh. That's all I want."

I think of Robin, and in another instant am relieved that there is no way Jolene would ever think to pay attention to her. What is an artist to a blood sorcerer?

Besides, there is no violence in any bone of Robin's body.

"The deal is *off*, Ladzka."

The corner of her mouth twitches, ripples, but she does not snarl. She only sighs, disappointed, perhaps thinking of severing our relationship entirely. I wouldn't stop her.

But I'm useful enough for her to try to keep. "Are you sure? Just another little donation, and I'll have your problem solved for you."

She might even be telling the truth. But I don't like whatever game she's playing. I don't trust that she didn't know something was wrong with what she gave me until I told her. She was too prepared to ask for more. I consider whatever trust existed between us broken, and I'm already two people down, because Jason has refused to return to the commune.

So I say, "No," and leave.

ANIMAL HUSBANDRY

———— ◆ ————

We need to expand soon.

Bill and Jason's slots need to be filled. We have room for more, too; Robin's the only new member to join in three months (not counting Kasim, for obvious reasons). It's time to grow the herd a little more, if only to absorb the inevitable losses that come every quarter with our existing contracts.

But I'm nervous. I'm worried I'll miss something, like I missed it with Bill. It's winter, too, and the general rule is to never add to your flock in the leanest time of the year. Hell, I preemptively culled the quail population before it started getting dark, since they only lay well for a year or two at most. Fewer mouths to feed. The logic doesn't apply one-to-one for humans (obviously we have enough food and housing), but I'm feeling off-balance. I want to be cautious, and I can't afford to be.

When I'm feeling like this, the only person I can go to is Lucille.

I find her in the community's remote studio, out in the fields, which is empty except for her this time of night. She's working on a painting when I come in: sun-drenched hills, off a batch of photos I assume Key took for her. I've brought wool that needs carding into batts, and we work in silence for a while. I hate the company of most other Kindred—we are always struggling for dominance in some way—but Lucille and I have an equilibrium, a working relationship that is comforting to both of us.

A lot of our kind give up working with their hands. Even those who were sculptors in life slowly turn to patronage and indulgence, leaving behind creation. I'm not sure why it happens; it could be a status thing, left over from centuries when working with one's hands was base labor, or it could be that without the perspective of the sun and looming death, work loses its savor. With an eternity to create, progress becomes meaningless. We are the work that endures, more than any canvas, any sculpture.

But I still enjoy it. On nights when I feel there is nothing human left in me, I still want to create. I want to help bring a lamb into the world, bloody and weak, and I want to spin wool and spread plaster and focus on the magic of the body and mind and soul combining into one singular task.

I've been there for maybe an hour, mind dancing along thoughts of immortality and legacy contrasted with the present, the active, the timeless, when I finally feel like talking.

"Do you think we should expand?"

The soft scrape of her brush against canvas answers me for a long time. My skin grows soft with lanolin and speckled with grass seeds. At last she says, "Of course."

I consider. "I could hold off for a few months."

"New blood is always appreciated," she says. "And we have another mouth to feed with Kasim. It will decrease our stores. If we cannot show growth, you cannot continue the experiment."

She's right, of course. Our operation is not widely accepted or appreciated. Many find it laughable and a recipe for disaster. I've worked to prove them wrong for over five years now, and so far, our luck has held. We haven't had any breaches of the Masquerade, and while we can't disappear members as easily as people off the street, we produce a good product, and that counts for something.

But any faltering, any weakness, and we will be torn apart. The experiment will end. *My* experiment.

I can't allow that. I can't allow any failure. I've been lucky, these last six months or so. Things have been going along smoothly, happily. But that can change so easily. This Bill thing, that was a setback—and a warning. Jolene Ladzka's strange offer likewise.

Lucille doesn't know about the latter, though. I wanted to see how it would pan out first. If it had worked, it would have been an absolute triumph, but Lucille would have told me not to pursue it at all. She would have been right about that, too.

I can't bear to tell her how badly I fucked up.

"And how is our illusion of moral integrity?" she asks, turning to blending colors, summoning sunrise on her palette in a continuous shift of purple to orange. I try not to watch, lest I get entranced by the process.

"Holding," I say.

"Good." Another long stretch of the sound of the brush and the comb on canvas and fleece.

I'm deep in flow when Lucille says:

"It would secure us more if we expanded our portfolio."

At first, I don't understand her meaning. The words sound too new on her lips. *Portfolio*—the language of an investment banker, not a great artist born before the First World War. But then, once I've gathered up the threads of the conversation, I take her meaning.

She's far cleverer than I tend to give her credit for these days.

"We do have room, I think, for more varied types." We have a glut of the frightened and downtrodden, the humans we provide shelter to who had none before, and over time those convert to a peaceful, engaged sort. Some of our clients like that type, while for others it must be getting boring. I go through my mental roster, sorting each community member into categories. The passionate, the depressed, the sedate . . . we lack the angry. Bill *had* fit that profile, thanks to a lapse in my judgment, but I don't want more like him. There are other paths to the same result, though.

"More young idealists," I say. "Like Kasim. Choleric, with a balance of sanguine to keep them from fighting." I don't like those terms—they're too simplistic—but Lucille thinks in them almost exclusively. It's her age showing.

"We are thin there," she agrees.

She doesn't say anything else after that. I stay another half hour, until the batt is organized and ready for the dye vats, then pack up and return to the office.

I cover my desk in pending applications. They've been accumulating for weeks. I want Kasim to do an in-depth pass, looking for kids fresh out of PSU social justice–focused courses. No, better yet—Robin. She'll like that plan. I can spin it as putting into practice what we discussed last month, and it should give me the right blend of passionate idealism with a guard against antisocial behavior. They'll come with risk, a higher propensity to look for injustice, but we can sweep them up in the energy of this place, cloud their better judgment.

Robin's off tonight, though, so I call Kasim instead. There's a good chance he knows somebody.

JANUARY

CULLING

S ickness in the quail. I had to cull four hens today, young ones. I didn't bother bringing them into the slaughtering room, I just cracked their heads on the side of their hutch and snipped their necks with shears right there in the yard. Quail are stupid things, and even if they could smell the blood, I don't think they'd care.

Key is going to be upset in the morning. They're a gentle soul and would have tried to nurse the quail back to health, but we've seen this before and I know how it goes. Slowly the birds will stop walking, then stop eating. Eventually we'd have to force water down their throats with syringes, but even that wouldn't work long term.

Better to have it done with.

It leaves me angry, though. Not that the quail are dead, but that they were diseased, and so I can't work that alchemical magic to turn them into stock, or even food for the barn cats. I thought about draining them myself, but they're small, and I don't know what their illness would do to me.

I bury them deep enough that prowling foxes or enterprising raccoons won't dig them up, far enough from the hutch not to attract more pests. Then I check all the other birds, each one docile in my hands. They're all fine, fat and happy off their feed and kitchen scraps, and they coo their little frog-like songs once I have them back in their run.

They, like the sheep, like the humans, trust me implicitly.

I leave them behind and stalk out into the greater wilds of the commune, past where the dry-built walls end and where our rewilding efforts are underway. Young trees, native species of bracken and vine, careful creation of ponds and widening of creeks—it's enough to take the edge off. This is the way the world goes. Where there is not predator or parasite, there is disease, there is accident, there is loss. Death is constant; even I, in all likelihood, will die one day.

Maybe that thought should upset me again, but instead it brings with it a gentle calm.

And then I see the footprint.

It's human, not animal, and any member of the commune could have left it. Except the footprint is not of a sensible boot, but of a sneaker. Not something any community member would wear this far out, not this time of year. And when I look for others, eyes narrowing in the dark, I find two more, coming from the direction of the closest road.

Somebody was here. Somebody who should not have been.

There are no tracks leading away.

I follow them as far as I can, but catch no scent and hear no movement beyond the usual nocturnal creatures. I am alone, with no clues left to me. I spin half a dozen explanations, two of them particularly unnerving—poachers on my land, or worse, suspicious humans with infrastructure behind them—but I tell myself that, with so few footsteps, it's impossible to reconstruct a path. And it's not far from here to the road; anybody working in this section of the land would have been smart to drive as far as they could and walk in, then back out. There's no reason to enter this far from all the houses, just to hunt my people.

Only a fool, angry over dead quail, would walk across miles of muddy, murky field and wood.

I make myself go back to the office.

THE TOWER

Robin invites me to watch one of her performances, so I rearrange my schedule to get a few hours off. It's tricky, since normally she'd be the one covering for me, but Kasim is happy enough to fill in. We don't have anybody scheduled to visit tonight, and he's not cleared to handle the files yet, so I leave him sitting vigil in case we have another eruption from the human members. (These things come in waves it seems, so since Bill, I've been waiting for another. Not a fight probably, but an overdose, a bad breakup, a suicide attempt—there's a lot that can go wrong.)

I offer to drive her there, but she declines, saying she needs the prep time alone. And that's fair. We're likely closer in my mind than we are in hers, so I give her the space. I drive myself down just before doors open. The performance is part of a larger spectacle that's put up in the theater on Alberta, a variety show featuring dance, lectures, a static gallery in the foyer, a whole arrangement of delights and challenges and beauty. I love it, every bit of it, and it gives me a rush I've been missing lately, being so caught up in the work on the farm.

I love the farm, of course, and it is artwork of a kind, a living piece of craft, but there's something about *spectacle*. I wouldn't be of my own Blood if I didn't crave it.

All of it, though, is pale beside Robin.

She's dressed simply. Loose, baggy sweater that hangs limp around her shoulders, baring her throat, paired with black skinny jeans tight on her wide thighs and delicately patterned Wellingtons still mucked with mud and sheep shit. She sits on the edge of the stage to begin, and even with her mic, she's quiet at first.

Her art is in her speech. In the cadence of her voice, the timbre, the intonation, the emotion and restraint of it. She transports us, the entire room, to a windswept cliffside, to the tower built on top of it. A tower she has guarded, carefully, all her life. She weaves together tarot, astrology, history, architecture, pulling us into the molecular structure of mortar, then back out again to the great expanse of roaring wind, of the storm, of, finally, her body and her tools of iron, helping speed along what nature has already begun.

break down, break down every single brick of it, crush each one beneath my heel, mix every particle of dust with wine and force it through my body, until it is a part of me, force the change and the silence after

I want to own it. To record it, to write it down, to have it forever.

But that would kill its magic. It is her very life that invigorates it so.

I've watched her perform five times already. This is the sixth—the first she knows I'm in the audience—and the selfish, proud part of my soul (or whatever it is I have) thinks that her knowing I'm here is what makes it so much better. Is what *inspires* her. More likely, it's been the time she's had to herself at the ecovillage. No day job, food provided, everything I do intentionally to cultivate art like this. *But normally*, that covetous part of me whispers, *it takes longer to settle in.*

And to that I counter, *She's so polished up there it must have been in the works before she ever came to me.*

However it happened, though, this performance eclipses all her others. I'm entranced. Literally. Can't move, forgetting who I am, what I am. Not even thinking to panic that my guard has dropped so low. I'm silent when everybody else claps, but when she leaves the stage, I scream with joy and the noise is swept up in the continuing applause.

After, we wind up at the same bar on Division where we talked in November. She's high on endorphins and weed, and I'm flattered she suggested we go off alone instead of joining the main after-party that's headed to a service industry–favorite strip club on Morrison. I would go anywhere with her, but tucking ourselves into that walled patio, under the heater, her with another paloma and me with water again, it feels right. Like we're following a narrative.

I'm more than a little in love with her.

I tell her she was amazing, and she laughs and says she knows. We talk for almost an hour about her process, and I watch her glow at having an understanding audience. I think, sometimes, she forgets that I'm an artist, too. That I'm not just a farmer. But I can keep up with her talk of theory and structure and the rush of finding just the right edit to make. And I give her room to lead, to fill the space between us, to keep performing. She loves it.

And then I'm thinking of what it would be like, to drink from her while she's so hyped-up about her own work, full of pride and eagerness and relief. *Incredible* is a bare start, *awe-inspiring* likewise. I jump back from the thought as if it's sunlight, but it won't leave me.

If I let myself drink from her, I would embarrass myself with the high coming off of it. That magic in my gut would transfer her incandescence to me and the whole bar would feel it, would come to worship at my feet the way I want them to worship at hers.

Given all that, what comes next is probably inevitable.

We're back on community land, after a twenty-minute drive where all I can smell is her, all I can hear is her intoxicating, delighted chattering, chattering I respond to, encourage, revel in. I let her out near Hawthorn House, but she wants to walk, and so we go out to the gardens. The paths here are paved with carefully chosen colored cobbles, so even though it's dark and wet, it's safe enough. We can't see the colors of the plants, with all their flowers gone for the winter, so I tell her about each. About the purple-flowering monarda, about the borage that all the bees love with its periwinkle flowers that stay all the way through October, about what thyme and basil look like when they're allowed to bloom. It's her turn to hang on my every word.

She reaches out and takes my hand, and I don't pull away.

I tell her about lemon balm tea and sorrel salads and everything she can look forward to come spring and summer. I show her the garlic beds and explain about the necessity of cold shock to their growth, and the hand-made trellises we'll grow beans on in the spring. I sketch out a whole idyllic life for us. She is entranced, and I am entrancing. She follows me, happily, to the greenhouse where we'll grow our seed starts and where our tenderer plants spend the winter.

And then I push her up against the see-through wall and kiss her.

I don't mean to, but my self-control is frayed, so frayed that I can't even back off far. Just far enough that our lips don't touch anymore, but I make myself breathe, make my heart race, just for her. Her arms go around me reflexively, and she looks into my eyes, searching for—something.

"Keep going," she whispers.

In an instant I'm kissing her again, then nuzzling at her throat. She arches. Every predatory instinct in me screams to life, blood lust and artistic intoxication and some old shreds of human emotion tangling together. It would be so easy to bite her, and I can just make her forget afterward.

But I have rules. I have *standards*. I have just enough presence of mind to know that if I let things go any further, it will put the whole herd in jeopardy.

So, finally, I push her away.

She makes a small noise, confused and hurt, and searches my eyes for some explanation, and I seize the moment. I feel my monstrousness unfurl, like a seraphim's many wings, and she is pinned as surely as she was by my body.

"This never happened," I tell her, and it's as if I can hear the mechanisms of her mind at work, poised to erase. "You took my hand, after I told you about the thyme and basil. We did not talk of lemon balm tea and sorrel salads, we did not go to the garlic beds, we never stepped foot into the greenhouse. I did not kiss you. You did not ask me to continue."

She nods, the tiniest of things, lost in her overwhelmed mind.

I keep her like that, docile and blank, as I walk her back out into the night. Our bodies cool. We go back to the bit of path where she took my hand, and I let go of her physically, though I do not look away. I'm not a natural at memory replacement, not like Ladzka must be, but I am skilled enough from constant practice on the farm. And I know the best way to decrease distress is to make the transition back to wakefulness, back to memory, as seamless as possible.

When I am certain I can control myself, I look away. She blinks. She yawns.

"I'm sorry," she says. "I must have drifted off."

"It's getting late," I confirm. I begin walking in the direction of Hawthorn House, and she follows me, kittenish.

Maybe I shouldn't have made her forget, but I only had the one chance, and it's better if she doesn't know. It would be better still if I sent her away, but I want to give it a little more time. I want to test myself. I thought I wasn't at risk, and I was wrong; so now I need to train up my resistance. Robin Joy is perfect, but she is not unique; there will be another like her one day.

We part at her doorstep, and I fade into the night.

PR

Today, while I was sleeping, we had a visit from the mayor's people.

They want us to take on a much higher number of the houseless population of Portland. The mayor is under pressure to clean up the streets and is refusing to enact any policies that may *actually* help the problem, but he knows we take a large portion of our membership from that group.

But we don't take high numbers, and we certainly don't take whoever gets sent our way. Especially not for human political purposes. Especially not without oversight on who joins; we will be obliterated if I fail to maintain the integrity of the herd, the safety of our stock.

The request came with veiled threats, though, so I have to take it seriously. Worries about "cultlike" appearances. Concerns about how we're using government grants. I can't just say *no*, not when the cleanliness of my operation is at stake.

So I must ask Sebastian Vương for intercession.

Vương is not the Prince of Portland. He's not the seneschal, either. To be honest, I couldn't tell you his exact place in the power structure, which is as much because I stay out of court politics to the best of my ability as it is because he is, undoubtedly, dangerous.

He's not much older than I am, but holds far more sway. He is always calm and focused. I have never seen him flinch or lose his self-control—and I have watched him feed.

He only takes live prey, and Robin matches his profile perfectly. I should have assigned her to him the moment I gave her the key to Hawthorn House, but of course I didn't.

As soon as I've had a moment to think things through, I call ahead to one of his people, who says he's open to seeing me tonight.

I meet him at his house in the Southwest Hills, high on one of the steep cliffsides that wind up and up the great ridge that forms Portland's western boundary, but outside of the arboretum proper. It's a beautiful house, classic modernism, with impeccable landscaping that somehow manages to look beautiful even in the gray Portland winter.

My first hint that he expected me to show up tonight should have been how easy it was to get an audience with him. But it's the second hint that hits home: his guest.

Jolene Ladzka perches on a stool in his spacious kitchen, sipping from a large smoothie that smells of heart's blood.

"Leigh Konopasek," Sebastian Vương greets me, not looking up from the sheaf of papers he's making his way through. "Sit."

He's fed recently, though he isn't bothering with any pretense at a lively blush. It's the power rolling off him that I respond to, that sends my skin crawling. I drop my own charade, the better to be at the ready. This is wrong. This is very wrong.

"I had a visit from the mayor's aide today," I say.

"Yes," he agrees. "You did."

"I was going to ask you to turn his attention from us. Am I correct in assuming that would be pointless?"

"You are."

To the point. He's always to the point. And Jo, she always holds herself so exactly, and I end up feeling like an unwashed hick, even though I'm wearing a perfectly tailored suit with rose-leaf buttons, custom-made for me by an atelier down on Division. My armor.

I try to reassert myself by remaining silent. Waiting.

Eventually, he deigns to set aside his work and look me in the eye. He folds his hands across one knee. "You need to increase production to remain viable. Reducing the vagrant population keeps the rest of the humans happy. Explain to me your disagreement with my solution."

I can't help it. I launch into an impassioned lecture on the safety needs of my flock, the carrying capacity of the land, the available housing, the need to carefully vet each new addition so that the overall quality of the herd will increase. It's carefully rehearsed, at the ready for just such an occasion, honed by bringing in Kasim last month.

But it doesn't sway him at all, and Jo watches with a quirked brow, slurping on her pureed offal.

So I turn to what he *will* care about. "You can't really think this will go unnoticed, can you?" I say. "There's limited demand for bagged blood as it is, so most of them would be marked for active feeding. And that means too many of us on my land, too many opportunities for mistakes and slaughter, and people will notice that. Better to kill them on the streets. One less linking feature between them all. And you're doing it already anyway, aren't you?"

He shrugs and says, "But you make a better product."

"Exactly. And quality requires *care*. We're at capacity. It won't work."

He rises at last, crossing the space between us. The kitchen is beautifully, perfectly white, polished to a mirror finish, and it's like I'm surrounded. My head swims. The bastard brings his whole force to bear on me as he says, casually, "I thought this agricultural initiative of yours was supposed to increase ease of access to sustenance. And yet it seems to decrease the number of available targets. That is the inverse of how this is meant to work."

I want to tear out his throat for threatening what is mine. "Society is the limiter," I make myself say instead, calm and slow. "Society is *always* the limiter. I found a way to fly under the radar and produce good, consistent, dependable product."

"There are other ways, I'm sure. Use your brain," Jo says sweetly. She, no doubt, wants me to cooperate again, to stop being so precious, to hand more bodies to her. More experimental subjects. An active breeding program for certain traits, maybe. Everything I denied her the last time we talked and more besides.

"There *aren't* other ways, not with the sort of facility I run. Not with the outcomes I get."

"Then change the facility. Move to the countryside. Or we will give license for somebody else to."

It would be so sweet, so satisfying, to gut him with my bare hands. But even if I could strike him, it wouldn't do any good. I can't beat him. If I still had need to breathe, I would be panting with the effort of restraining myself. My jaw aches from holding back my snarl.

"There is a reason," I grit out, "that we are historically parasitic instead of predatory. You are being greedy, and you know it. If you want predictable results, if you want this quality you so clearly prize, if you don't want the Second Inquisition coming down on all of our heads, you *respect the method*." I almost mention the footsteps on my land, but stop short, unwilling to add another vulnerability to my apparently long list. "My land, my system, will grow at the speed it will grow. And you will get contracts at the rate you get contracts. Anything else will stress the herd. Will destroy it."

He throws up a hand in disgust. "You are obsessed with your pastoral idyll! Herds of sheep, beehives rented around the city, salvaged architecture—you damned diva, you Toreador aesthete, you have been too long away from real feeding and have lost the plot. *Fix it*. And get out of my house."

CATCH AND RELEASE

◆

I leave the Southwest Hills angry, frightened, and ravenous.

Bagged blood isn't going to cut it tonight.

I have the barest presence of mind left to pick somebody as far from my community members as possible: a high-up tech guy, the kind who wears sweatshirts to the opera because he doesn't give a single shit about tradition or artistry but wants to show off his new money, the kind who drinks Bud Light Lime at an artisanal cocktail bar, the kind who doesn't know how to cook but won't tip the restaurants he patronizes for every meal. But my nature is still my nature: I pick a handsome one, one who works out, probably drinks meal replacements because he doesn't care about the taste of food, but it leaves him nourished, optimized, hideously beautiful.

I find him at this exquisite burlesque place downtown, where Burnside gets close to the river and the street layouts get confusing and half-unreachable. He isn't appreciating any of what's on display: the dancers or their costumes or their music or their choreography. All he's seeing is *tits*. *Queer girl tits*. Straight men always have a hard-on for queer girl tits, can sniff them out even when they don't know what they're doing. I don't know how, but I use it to my advantage. Unbutton my own shirt until only a single one keeps the fabric together before I draw his attention.

I wonder what he thinks of me. Classic dyke haircut, but a fancy suit, not a flannel, and I'm not hiding my simmering rage well. Whatever it is, it's at least a little interesting, and it just takes the promise of some free, good quality weed (because this sort of guy always thinks about going to the dispensaries, never does, doesn't want to admit he has no idea what he's doing because he only ever smoked shit from his college source) to draw him into one of the darker alleyways.

And *fuck*, when I break open his jugular . . .

He isn't what I want. He isn't Robin, isn't full of artistry and fire, isn't soft in my arms, isn't even dotted with freckles. But *fuck*. Fuck. It's been months. I should have done this *before* my meeting, I wouldn't have been so unprepared, and I should not be doing it now, because now all I can think about is how much sweeter blood is when it's straight from the vein, when the heart is pushing it eagerly down my throat. I nearly kill him. Nearly.

I didn't realize I was so hungry. Maybe Vương and Jolene are right about some things. Maybe I'm deluding myself.

I do have an idea, though, driving back over the river via the gorgeous St. Johns Bridge. Maybe it's the engineer blood in my belly, maybe it's the relief, maybe it's just the travel time to let my mind wander.

I'm going to start a catch-and-release program.

IMPLEMENTATION

◆

I tell everybody my plan at the scheduled community meeting two nights later. The rush of the engineer's blood has long faded, but it's left a craving in its wake that makes me feel weak; bagged blood barely takes the edge off. Being in a room with so many living, breathing humans is a struggle. I probably should have waited a few more nights, but Vương doesn't care about my feeding habits. He wants results.

I wait until discussions about chore division and menu requests are over, but before people have begun to drift away. We sit in the communal living room, sprawled on beanbags and couches and cushions on the floor, some snacking on dried eggplant jerky I made last night.

"The city wants us to accept more applicants from the houseless population," I say. Robin is watching me closely. Her brow clouds.

"I like the idea," I continue. There are nods around the room, Ethan chief among them. "But we all know we have limitations. The amount of rooms, the amount of food, and making sure we all like our new community members. And we *also* all know that, for the city, this is a publicity stunt they're hoping will paper over their failings for a little while."

That gets a couple *hear hears!* from the audience.

"We're going to do what we can," I say. "Those of you willing to open your houses, come see me after this. And our farmers' corp, we'll talk about plans for expanding the gardens next year. Sound good?"

Nods all around. I'll admit, I'm adding a bit of extra *oomph* to my words—and it's working. The humans in the room (and Kasim) are just the tiniest bit ensorcelled. They would follow me *toward* a cliff, though not off it.

"But I think what we can do *best*, by our goals and for the city at large, is to provide more services. Food donations. Soup kitchens. Open houses. Providing free enrichment classes to the wider area. Open medical days. It's going to take extra work to make this happen, so I wanted to bring it to a vote. Silent vote, Ethan, no need to raise your hand. There're ballots in the kitchen, with lots of open response space. Take one, think about it, fill it out over the next few days, then drop it at my office. We'll talk about the results next week. Agreed?"

More nods. I smile. I stand up, stretch. "Thanks for coming, everybody."

And then it's time for the management meeting.

That's just myself, Lucille, Kasim, and Key. Robin looks as if she wants to stop me from leaving, but she lets us go without a fuss, without even asking why *she* isn't included if the rest of us are. I'll make it up to her. But she's just not ready to hear what comes next; she still doesn't know about our nature. I've had a hundred chances to slip my Blood into the meals I've cooked her, and I've never taken a single one.

She's just not ready. She's cautious. Passionate, but cautious. Hard to sway, but when I manage it—

I pull my focus back. It's not just her that's not ready; neither am *I*.

We're already halfway to Lucille's place. The pure Queen Anne–style house is barely on communal land, and it is breathtaking. All period. All painstakingly restored. None of the shortcuts and modern approaches I take.

We reach the wrap-around porch and pass through the heavy oak door with its leaded glass transom and side lights. I take precautions, checking windows and doors, though Lucille is careful even in her general disinterest. Once I'm sure the house is secure, we settle in the formal sitting room on vintage furniture.

I tell them about my meeting with Vương (in edited form, without Jo Ladzka, without the insults, without what happened after), and I'm relieved to receive a similar response to my own. Then I outline the plan. "We use these outreach events to develop feeding profiles," I say. "We create a specific method for engaging with our visitors to learn exactly what we need from them to serve our current clientele and allow for expansion. We won't have the authority to sell contracts or shares on such free-range stock, but we can provide a service of information. The best of both worlds. The leadership is happy, bellies are full, and our community members remain safely managed."

Key is nodding.

Kasim is furious.

"Go ahead," I say, and watch some of the fury falter. He still isn't used to being treated with respect by his betters, and it is the easiest tool I have to get his guard down.

"I, uh . . . well, you know I respect you a lot, right? This whole place?" Lucille is impassive, but Key beams, and I feel relief. We haven't talked about what he saw that night he found me in the fields; I haven't come up with a convincing lie, and I don't want him knowing about my short-lived deal with Jo. He could very easily use my weakness that night to undermine my authority now, but he doesn't. "I respect it because you're actually, you know, doing good work. Giving all sorts of people places to live, and jobs if they want them, and safety—I mean, as much as we can, right?—and I don't know how you're pulling it off so well. But, like, you help people."

"We try, yes."

"I mean, we help ourselves first, but then everybody else. And it's not one of those twisted blood doll situations, it's actually symbiotic instead of just claiming to be. I like that."

He doesn't even glance at Key. I can't tell if he's still mad about how we keep retainers, which is good; at least he's keeping his opinions to himself.

"Anyway," he says, hugging his skinny knees to his chest, "this whole thing? It stinks like shit. They want us to disappear homeless people for them."

"They already do it every day."

"I know, and it's fucked up!" He's on his feet, pacing like a mortal, frantic and emotional and desperate. "We're—they're—vulnerable people who don't deserve to be targeted like this. Even if it's 'natural' or whatever. You've *avoided* that here, in a way that makes *sense*, and this doesn't fit. You can see that, right?"

"I can see that," I say. I gentle my voice, but it doesn't pierce his prickling shell. "But we aren't predators, we're parasites. If we kill openly, we are struck down. We have to feed off those who go unmissed, or the system retaliates. I've carved out the space I'm able to, here, because I think it is more humane." A lie, for Kasim's benefit, but not entirely a lie. The real reason is for control over a constant supply of food, well-vetted, tailored to a customer's particular dietary needs. That it's morally better on a human level is a bonus. "But I can't expand it. There will come a day where you and I can't get by on bagged blood anymore and will need to find another solution. This was never going to change the world. Just a corner of it."

"But painting a target on individual backs . . . I don't know, Leigh."

"It does extend them a measure of protection," Lucille points out.

"I don't see how," Kasim says, darting looks at me and Key, hoping for some clue of how to interact with the slumbering beast before him.

We don't offer any help.

"They will be marked as ours, even if they are off our land." Lucille waves a hand lazily. "They are ours, and as long as Leigh keeps us in Sebastian Vương's good graces, that means something. They will not be killed indiscriminately."

She doesn't move to explain further, so I step in. "If they die, there is no easy replacement with a ready-made file. It's a waste to kill them. And I will work with Vương and perhaps a blood sorcerer to find a way to make it clear they're owned to any lick that stumbles across them in the street. Lucille is right. By defining them, we protect them. And," I say, rising from my seat, which has the immediate effect of putting Kasim into a seat of his own, in reflexive fear, "the programs we create will be available to all. Not everybody who comes for an HIV test will be marked for feeding. We'll diffuse the focus. I have thought this through, childe."

He says no more, but I can see he is not convinced. He's angry. He's wrestling with himself, with his own demons, and against logic that will match every predatory instinct he has and hates himself for having.

What matters, though, is that he subsides. He can get right with himself on his own time.

We adjourn for the night.

SLAUGHTER

W e began processing the lambs yesterday.

I was asleep for most of it, of course; there's no way I can insist on slaughtering at night, when the human staff can't see as well and while we have two community members who are more than adept at wielding a bolt gun and a knife. But there are only two, and daylight is scarce right now, so they were only two-thirds through the flock when I rose. I drank quickly, went to them, and helped to separate out each new lamb. We worked with calm efficiency, and as their strength flagged, I stepped in.

By midnight, all thirty-seven lambs slated for death were dispatched. I took over then and let the humans rest. I removed the heads, tied off the esophagi, and hoisted the lifeless carcasses one by one. I skinned them and spilled their guts on the slaughter room floor, erasing any lingering traces of Monsieur Messy Feeder's visit.

That night, I worked until nearly dawn, then left all

the skinless, headless bodies there to cool. It's faster to kill an animal than to piece it out.

All that work kept my mind off the fact that Robin is gone.

She left three days ago, and I have experienced a flood of varied emotions that I haven't felt since when I left Vương's house two weeks ago. No . . . those were far simpler emotions, a narrower band. *This* is old stuff. This is panic and betrayal, anger and shame, desperate curiosity. *Why?* But I know why. Or I suspect. She didn't have the decency to come to me first. She quit during the day. Talked it over with Key, left me a note, and was gone by sundown.

The day she left was the day after the first of our open clinics. She saw the amount of information we were collecting. She must have thought back to our night at the bar, the words *renewable resource*, and put together just enough that she knew something was wrong.

I'm going to have to go after her. I will. I have to figure out what she knows. She's not under the pull of my Blood, and so she's a threat.

But I can't go after her yet. Not until the lambs are processed. Not until I've leashed my vicious heart.

I wish she'd call.

I know that if I go to her, I can convince her that everything is okay. I used logic last time. If it fails now, I have less mundane techniques at my disposal. I can keep her close, find a way to bind her during the day . . . but I don't have the capacity to plan those details right now. So I work.

I spend six hours in the slaughtering room, carefully matching each corpse with its order and specific butchering instructions and transforming life into food with the alchemy of the knife, the bone saw, the vacuum pack. I could leave it to the humans (and do leave over a dozen), but I still need some kind of work, and reviewing records of blood pressure and hobbies and lifestyles would have harmed me more than it helped. So I split the carcasses in two, and break them down into quarters, then to primals. My knife scrapes along bone as I clean up rib roasts and glides smoothly through silverskin seams, unraveling the body into perfect intact stretches of muscle. I bag up cooled and cleaned entrails, kidneys and hearts and tripe and livers, and try not to think about Robin, saying that livers can regrow if a small fragment is left.

She's supposed to be here, and I will admit that last night, in my pettiness, I almost brought Sylvia to the slaughtering room.

But I didn't. She's a good ewe. I have enough self-control to protect my investments. If I ever lose that presence of mind, I will be lost entirely.

NEW LOVE

◆

The next night, I manage to stay away from the processing room, though there's several tasks I could
make for myself. I instead go through applications.
Four new interviews are scheduled for next Tuesday, so I
finish up some light social media stalking for final determination on who will be invited to stay. It only takes a few
hours, though, and then I'm at loose ends again.

The night beckons. Moving will help. I go outside into
the soggy midnight air and start walking. But the greenhouse makes me think of her, and the parking lot, and the
paddock, and—

A figure shifts in the darkness between two residences.

I follow. Whoever it is moves furtively, trying to avoid
being seen, and I think of the footprints out across the
fields. I'd nearly forgotten, with the new initiative, with
Robin, and I can't afford to forget again.

Then I catch a glimpse of tousled hair. I know that
hair.

It's Kasim.

"Fuck," I snarl into the damp night air. Any Kindred sneaking into one of the humans' buildings would be a problem, but this goes past problem into disaster. How did I miss this? I should have enforced feeding *with* me, though fuck if I want him near me while I eat, especially not after my evening under the stars last month. I should have kept a closer eye on him, instead of avoiding him as much as possible out of shame.

I slip into the house by the front door instead of following him in through the kitchen. I sniff the air. He's upstairs. I can't hear his voice or footfalls; he's being stealthy. But I find him.

I find him in Ethan's room.

I find him in Ethan's *arms*. They're both disrobing quickly, quietly, Ethan laughing every so often, Kasim stealing kisses and touching Ethan's scarred, ropey body with clear affection.

I go very still, my silence caught between screaming and laughter.

Of course he isn't here to feed.

I saw this coming. He still craves humanity, craves gentleness and life and soft caresses, and his Blood's thin enough that he can still get it up most nights. Put him near humans, and the urges increase. I thought it would be enough, teaching him to see the community as food stock, but it wasn't.

The worst part is Kasim seems to be as good for Ethan as Jo's visits; he's been doing a lot better in the last month, reporting fewer episodes to his therapist, and I guess now I know why. And I don't want Ethan hurt.

Then again, Kasim is doing enough of that himself.

This is the last thing I need on my plate. The rollout of the catch-and-release program has hit roadblock after roadblock: finding the right people, getting the word out to the right communities, figuring out what information we can ask for without risk of blowback. We need things that are HIPAA-protected, and for people who don't *live* here, the process of getting that information is a little more fraught.

And Robin still isn't back.

And Kasim is about to get Ethan's pants off.

They're too wrapped up in each other to notice when I ease open the door, but they notice when I throw it the rest of the way open. Kasim's off the bed and snarling, ready to lay down his life, but Ethan is just staring, humiliated, unsure of what to do.

"Don't move," I say.

Kasim breaks for the window.

Coward.

I lock eyes with Ethan. "Kasim never came by tonight," I tell him. "You've lost track of the last half hour. You did not see me in your room."

And then I close the door and give Ethan some privacy, descend the stairs as calmly as I can, then take off in search of Kasim.

To his credit, he's not far off. He's waiting for me, and he doesn't look as though he's going to attack. He's just pacing, wildly, tearing at his hair.

I clear my throat.

"No more second story exits," I say, when he looks up.

"Leigh—"

"We're not having this conversation here. Follow me."

I lead him out into the gusty rain, through the mud, past the low fields filled with die-back and cover crop. His Converses suck up the mud as he follows.

He's been here a month and hasn't thought to change his shoes.

At least he has the common sense to take them off on my porch. If he's thinking about the last time we were both here, he has the decency not to mention it. Maybe he understands he's in deep shit.

We go inside, to the parlor. I see him take in the furniture, the rugs, everything Jo ignored. Good for him.

"Sit," I say. He obeys.

"I wasn't feeding," he says quickly.

"I figured that out. What made you pick the Camarilla?"

"Huh?" Any other day, that blurted answer, so human-like, would have charmed me. Here, now, it just makes me angrier.

"You go out past Eighty-Second, that's full Anarch territory. Infiltrates halfway here along Powell and Sandy. You had options, options that would've put a lot fewer restraints on you. So. Why Camarilla?"

He squirms. This clearly isn't what he was anticipating. Good.

"Uh. It made—it made sense."

"Did you know whoever embraced you?" I should've asked this in the intake. I shouldn't have treated him with any respect at all.

"Kind of." He swivels his head, looking for an exit. "She didn't stick around, though. I don't understand what this has to do with anything. What's going on?"

"You *chose* to submit to Camarilla control, but you don't want to leave your human life behind. You tried to apply here as if you were just a normal guy. You still talk to your family." He startles. He didn't know that I've had Key look at his phone, check the numbers he texts against some records I probably shouldn't have access to. He never says anything he shouldn't, but he still talks to his sister nightly. "And now you're fucking a human."

He sits rigid in my chair.

"We don't take well to such close relationships with the meat," I say.

"The meat—what the fuck?"

"It risks the Masquerade. Everything you're doing, it risks exposing us, getting us all killed, and you *choose* to put yourself under Camarilla law while doing it? What's wrong with you?"

"What the *fuck* are you going on about? Who the fuck are you to be angry at me for getting close to a human? Everybody here, you care about them, and don't even get me started on you and Robin—"

I lose my temper then. Just like I lost control in that field, with Robin in the greenhouse, with that tech guy at the burlesque club. This time, I'm full of rage and a perverse glee. I throw him across the room and am on him again before he can stand.

"You're fucking psycho!" he shouts, trying to cover his head. "What is *wrong* with you?"

I don't know what he sees, staring bug-eyed up at me, but I can feel the fury transforming me, combining with the thickness of my Blood to create awe. Horror. Terror. If he'd been human, he would have shit himself.

Let this be a reminder to him that he is far from human.

As it is, he cowers. He blubbers. I fight the urge to crack his ribcage in two, spatchcock him like a roasting chicken, but only because I don't want to clean up the mess. I don't feel a single ounce of shame at the impulse. He needs to get that I'm not playing, that I am not nice, that I am in control.

"Leigh, Leigh, I'm sorry . . . fuck." He wheezes. "I'm sorry . . . shit."

"Give me one good reason not to tear your throat out." I don't know what I sound like, if I'm roaring or hissing or speaking at a calm, even volume. It feels like all three at once to me. It feels *good*. I haven't let out the anger like this since that tech guy, and even then, it wasn't this. That was feeding, not dominance. I *like* that Kasim knows exactly what I am and hates me for it.

His eyes dart around the room, as if looking for relief. There will be none. I bare my fangs, already thinking about how his Blood will taste. Thin, almost powerless, but not entirely. Better than a bag. Better than a human.

"Clots!"

I stop.

"Instead of the catch and release. Or—or in addition, it doesn't really matter, but you know, we have this portfolio, this collection of all this blood, and I'd heard—I'd heard blood can make clots. Powerful things. Right? Can't we refine it? Make it better? Cultivate . . . cultivate it. Into something special and useful and not what you'd find on the streets. That whole bit, that you're a farmer of man— this is like making wagyu beef, yeah? Making a quality—a quality product."

I almost lunge again, but this time the anger is different.

Because why didn't *I* think of that? It's brilliant. Clots. Old name: dyscrasia. Oldest name: animal husbandry. That's what he's suggesting. Not just maintaining the health of the flock and picking good additions, but also nurturing what's already here in specific directions. It isn't entirely dissimilar to what the thaumaturge is after, though it will be a much slower process to do it sustainably.

It runs risks, sure. Such manipulations will be more potentially noticeable, and fostering a choleric or melancholic dyscrasia could put others in danger. But if I'd stopped to think that night at Vương's house, if I'd offered up this?

Robin would still be here.

Robin would still be here, I wouldn't be pursuing goals that run counter to my actual ideals and desires, and we'd all be a hell of a lot safer.

It's worth the risk, now if not before. Things can't get much worse. (A lie, but a powerful one. Things can always get worse.) I let him go and back off, but don't look away. He remains pinned by my gaze as I struggle to darn the thin spots in my self-control.

"All I know," he says, breaking the silence with his nerves, "is based off thin-blood street alchemy but, like, there's got to be something there, right?"

I nod.

He licks his lips, pulls himself shakily to his feet. "Me leaving Ethan, it's going to destroy him. You know that, right?"

I hadn't thought about it. But yes. I do know that, upon reflection.

I can see the next bit of logic hurts him. Good; it ought

to. It might toughen him up. "With his background . . . it could do it. Couldn't it?" he whispers. "Break him hard enough to make a clot."

I'm already mentally going through my contacts list, looking for a customer who will appreciate being offered Ethan on a silver platter. I feel myself smiling.

"Kasim," I purr, "there might be hope for you yet."

CONFESSION

Robin finally calls me.

During the day, of course, so I wake up to a voice mail. It's awkward and uncertain. She doesn't apologize at all, which makes me proud. Instead she says that she's been thinking since she left, and that she wants to see me, talk it over.

I text back while walking to the office, asking if she's free tonight. When she doesn't respond after half an hour, my nerves get the best of me and I go back out. I check on the pregnant ewes, the quail, the chickens, and Ethan, who is, as predicted, devastated. He seethes with pain, and my attempts to help only cause more. It's hard to watch; I never like to see an animal suffer. But the predator instinct in me stirs more and more the higher his agony goes. Tonight it's somewhere between the smell of a barbecue and the lightning strike realization that you've found the weak, abandoned member of the herd, ready to be picked off at your leisure.

Jo Ladzka is going to be pissed that I'm taking away her monthly feed, but what will another drop of bad blood between us hurt? I do the math, calculating when will be a safe harvest window. Jo doesn't drink him to the last safe point, so the three weeks since her visit have probably given him enough time to recover . . . except he hasn't been eating well this week.

I go down to the kitchen to make him a green smoothie and text his new prospective buyer, asking him to follow up with me on the pollination contract he asked about for his fruit trees this spring. I've gotten Ethan to drink half his smoothie of kale, almond butter, banana, and honey when my phone—*finally*—buzzes.

And it's not the buyer.

It's Robin.

I make hurried excuses and run out of the building like a schoolgirl, answering the phone and heading for my car.

"Hi," she says.

"Hi."

"I'm free but I don't want to stay out too late," she says. "I'm over near Peninsula Park. Does that work for you?"

"Of course. I can be there in fifteen minutes. Meet you at the gazebo." She hasn't suggested a bar (*our* bar). No, she's picked someplace quiet. Which means yeah, she wants to talk about things in private. Which means I've been right that she left not because she got bored or because an ex wanted to get back together with her, but because she got scared and bolted.

A park could also mean danger. It could mean a setup. I only realize that once I'm already in the car, but I don't turn back.

Robin's not like that.

The weather is miserable, hovering just above freezing, spitting rain in uncertain gusts. I can't drive all the way to the gazebo and the walk to it through the park takes longer than I expect. I pass tents and huddled figures, worrying that our meeting spot will already be taken, covered as it is. But as I go deeper into the park, there are fewer and fewer tents, until I'm alone.

All alone. I distantly note my relief, that she's exactly like I think she is.

I end up waiting for almost ten minutes for her to show, setting up my phone to give us some light in order to keep my hands busy. I'm just starting to wonder if she's ghosted me when I catch her scent on the wet air. Another minute passes before she emerges out of the shadows, weighed down in a raincoat and heavy boots. As soon as she's under the gazebo roof, she pulls back her hood, revealing dark circles beneath her eyes and chapped lips, as though she's been chewing them. She sits down on the bench without a word and motions for me to join her.

I do. She doesn't say hi, and I don't either. For a long time, we just sit like that. I realize just how much I've gotten used to her physical presence then. Not sure why it surprises me; we've been working together three or four nights a week for over two months. But I can feel myself relaxing just because of the sound of her breathing, when by all rights I should be getting more and more uneasy.

"I should have told you I was leaving," she says at last.

"Not if you didn't feel safe doing so."

She frowns. "Is that what you thought was . . . ?" And then she laughs. "No, I was just . . . I was embarrassed."

I'm stunned. *Embarrassed*—about what? Fear would make more sense than shame.

"I just needed some space," she says. "Needed to figure out how I felt about stuff, and I knew I couldn't be objective near you. You're pretty convincing, you know."

I make myself smile. "I've been told as much. I'm glad you called, though. Do I get a chance to answer your questions?"

"Yeah," she says. "I tried to put it all behind me, move on and stuff, but that whole place is pretty important to me now. It really is amazing, what you do there. You know that, right?"

"Thanks. I try. *We* try."

"That's why I was so embarrassed. How you explained everything should have made sense, but the whole blood drive thing, and the sudden push to do outreach, and the thing with Bill . . . Or I guess it *did* make sense, but not in a way I liked, so I wanted to get some perspective."

"Did you get it?"

"No." She sighs. "No, it's all the exact same as when I left. Except . . . Except I have these memories. Foggy, like a dream, but I remember you, and I remember the greenhouse. I remember . . ." She trails off. I've gone still as death. Literally. I've been thrown enough that I've forgotten to breathe, and my skin has already started to cool when I regain control over myself.

But she sees it.

Or maybe she just feels as desperate as I do. Maybe she's responding to the preternatural charm that rolls off me, whether I want it to or not. How much of those nights on Division were a result of habitual influence on my part? I don't know.

Whatever the reason, she leans in. She reaches out and folds my cold hand in hers. She stares into my eyes.

"Why did I forget, Leigh?"

Because I made her.

"I wasn't drunk," she says. "Not that drunk, anyway. But I barely remember how it felt in the greenhouse, when you—"

"Stop."

If I could've erased it from my own memory, I would have. It doesn't feel so much like a warning anymore, even with Ethan's heartbreak still shuddering through the commune, even after I *just* told Kasim why intoxication with mortals is expressly fucking forbidden. No, it feels like temptation.

And she isn't stopping. She needs to stop.

"I thought it was a dream, at first, but it felt too real. And then I wondered if—if somebody had slipped something into my drink at the event. If *you* had, after. But that didn't make sense, either. You're not like that. You're . . ."

I cling to the shreds of my self-control. I will heat back into my flesh.

She looks down at where our hands are joined. Mine are flushed now. Too hot. I've overshot.

"What *are* you?" she asks, so quietly a human would have missed it.

I force a laugh. "*What* am I? Like some kind of X-Man?"

If she laughs, too, I have an out. I can convince her she's wound up. Overwrought. This is salvageable. This is—

"You're not human, Leigh."

Fuck.

I stare at her. I can't laugh again, can't crack another awkward joke. I can't even say, *Of course I am.*

Maybe she's heard something, from Key or the night of the meeting at my cottage about rolling out the new program, though I swear I would have felt her if she'd been that close to my home. Maybe Kasim had too much conscience, though if he'd told anybody our secrets, it would have been Ethan. Maybe she's just smart.

After all, she just saw my skin lose its pallor. She's heard me talk about blood as a renewable resource. She's seen me with the sheep and with the humans and she must have noticed that there's something similar there, and it doesn't run toward granting that animals have sentience and independence and the ability to consent.

Most humans, when they get close to the truth, run screaming from it. Or simply see *through* it, as if it isn't there at all. The impossibility is so strong that they can't engage with it. That helps us. As long as we're impossible, as long as we're the stuff out of goth kid fantasies and penny-dreadful novels, we can get away with murder.

But she doesn't think this is impossible.

"Leigh, talk to me," she says.

Without knowing it, she's backed me into a corner. I don't know how long she's suspected, and there's a limit to my ability to make her forget—as my imperfect first attempt has now baldly proven. Camarilla law dictates I kill her. We dance on the edge of the Masquerade, and any farther—here or elsewhere, now or later—and she'll step over it.

I didn't want it to happen like this.

I stretch out my awareness as far as it will go across

the darkened park. All I find are deadheaded roses and hunkering squirrels, a few skunks, and the usual scattering of sleeping birds and insects. No humans nearby and no Kindred either.

"What are you trying to say?" I ask, desperate to prolong the inevitable. To prove that I'm wrong, that she's thinking something else entirely.

She lets go of my hands with one of hers, begins ticking things off with her fingers. "I've never seen you during the day. Nobody on campus has."

"I work night shift."

"Not even in summer. They say you don't help with the crops, and that's not like you. You'd be out there in the late afternoon, at least. But you're not."

She's right. She knows me too well. She knows that if I could, I'd be pulling twenty-hour shifts in the busy season.

Another tick. "You live apart from the entire complex."

"I like my privacy."

"You value communal living."

"I wouldn't be the first hypocrite." But my hope is fading. I try to grasp for panicked rage instead, to make this easier. If I can just hate her, fear her, I can kill her. But I don't find anything I can use.

I find only desperation. Desire.

Temptation.

Key knows what I am. Our other retainers know bits and pieces. There are steps I can take here, steps that will let her live. I can mesmerize her, enough to make her docile, enough to send her back to the commune. I can make her drink from my wrist until she has no choice but to love me. I can bind her to me forever.

But it wouldn't be her. Not quite. It would be her plus me. Tainted. Manipulated.

More than I've already manipulated her?

If I were Anarch, I could just *take* her, here, now. Turn her, bind her that way. Consent is an illusion, I told Kasim that myself. So why am I hesitating?

Why am I so soft?

"I've never seen you eat," she says. "Or drink, not even water. You didn't even taste the soup."

The soup. The night she first began to worry something was wrong. The night I made the choice to keep her anyway. I made soup, and I didn't taste it because I didn't want to spare the energy to keep from throwing up. I can cook just fine by sight and smell.

But she noticed. She's attentive. Perceptive.

I thought because she likes me, she would fail to see my faults. Instead, she has collected them all.

"Robin," I warn. "You need to be very careful now."

Her jaw sets. "What did you do to me in the greenhouse?" she asks. "What *are* you?"

Kill her, kill her. The thought pulses through my body, along with pure need, hunger. I can smell her. I could take her. I'd lose her, yes, but it would be sweet—wouldn't it?

I recoil from the impulse, singed, scared. Scared of myself. Scared of what would happen if I give in.

And that's what decides it for me.

I am no monster, and Robin *fits* into the community. She deserves to be there. And if this experiment is going to continue, it's going to take more than dyscrasias and larger ranges of blood types. It's going to take an increase in carrying capacity, a decrease in suspicion.

It's going to take societal change.

It's going to have to go beyond blood inebriation and into real belief. Honest dedication. Key's too addled now to ever be real proof of that, but Robin? Robin is an opportunity. If I am careful, if I cultivate her, I can turn her without spilling a drop of blood. Make her understand, the way I've made her understand how it can be humane to breed animals for slaughter. Nobody can know until I've proven out my theorem, but we're good at lying together, aren't we?

She has a soft heart. That's what I count on, when I say: "You're right. I'm not human."

I let my Blood still again. I let my skin grow dull and pale. She tenses, but she doesn't scream or try to get up from the bench in the gazebo.

I watch the final pieces click into place organically, bit by bit, logical progression after logical progression. The last of her illusions fall away, the last hope she had of ever thinking she lives in a mundane world.

"How many?" she asks. "How many are like you, back home?"

Home. Exultation surges through me, and it must distort my features because she lets go of me and scoots back.

"Not many," I say quickly.

"The blood donations?"

"A renewable resource."

I want her to agree with me without illusions, but I can't stop myself from influencing her. It is impossible to disentangle what I am from what I say; where my vitae stirs in my throat and gentles my words, it is just another form of oratory. Of setting the stage.

And it works, not like the bludgeon of direct control, but like the sweetness of any beguiling speech.

"You need it," she says.

"Yes. Like you need sun and amino acids and sugars and water."

She frowns. "The sheep?"

I shake my head. "I've tried." That's a lie, but a small one. *I* haven't. But I know some who have. It's worse than bagged blood apparently.

"And that's why it exists? The whole community? For . . . you?"

"From one angle, yes. It allows me to take what I need without hurting anybody." No need to tell her that, no matter where she goes, she will never be far from something like me. No need to tell her about the wheels within wheels.

This is her and me.

"Like honey," she says. "Like milk."

"And from another angle, it gives people a home."

"It's a *farm*," she says.

"And you've seen how kindly I treat the sheep."

She looks at me, stricken. "How can you say that's the same?"

I swoop in to soothe her. "Many people would," I say. "From the other direction perhaps, but much of the argument against raising animals for meat or even dairy go back to *inhumane* treatment. Treating animals other than we would treat people. But I don't believe that. I never have. I think you can treat an animal with respect and comfort, and still harvest from them what you need. A bargain. An arrangement."

"But nobody knows what they signed up for," she says. "Nobody agreed to the bargain."

"The sheep never agreed, either."

All or nothing arguments are dangerous. It would be easy for Robin to simply declare both horribly wrong. But she doesn't. She doesn't, because she's worked beside me, and I've already changed her mind about animal husbandry.

She wavers on a knife's edge.

"What happened to Bill?"

"Processed," I say.

"Slaughtered," she counters. She's gone pale. I can smell fear on her, fear and disgust, but not panic. She's still balancing. Still waiting to be swayed. *Wanting* it.

That gives me the confidence to nod. "But he was an outlier. A special case. Normally, it's just like honey. Taken without threat to she who produces it."

She bows her head.

I wait.

"Is it better," she says at last, "than the alternative? Or—or has this always been going on?"

"This is new," I confide. "An experiment. What I hope is a better way."

"And what's the normal way?"

"To hunt. To kill." (I don't want to muddy the water by explaining that many Kindred don't drain until death because society would rebel. Perhaps another night.)

"And if you don't do this, you'll die?"

"I would, yes. There's no textured soy protein or tofu for what I am. Maybe one day," I add, thinking of Jolene, of what could have been, "but not yet."

"Honey or meat," she says. "And you choose honey."

"I choose honey." I smile at her, and she smiles back. Weakly, yes, but honestly. I rise from the bench and don't reach for her, don't crowd her. It's important for her to believe she has a choice in what comes next. "I'm going to head back now," I say. "You can take as much time as you want to think it over."

She takes my hand before I can go. It fits perfectly. It feels right. "That night, the greenhouse—why did you make me forget? Am I missing something?"

I bring back a lifelike flush to my cheeks, enough to mimic a blush in the waxing moonlight. "Embarrassment," I say.

"Not regret?"

I don't answer that, except to say, "Come home soon. Sylvia misses you."

And then I disappear into the night.

FEBRUARY

ROBIN'S RETURN

I hear your songbird has come back," Lucille says by way of greeting. She is at her easel, her current work less purely representational than usual, filled with jarring colors and unsettling, half-shaped forms. It matches how I feel inside.

"Two nights ago," I confirm.

I haven't seen her yet. That makes me a coward of course, but I'm beginning to realize I am not as brave as I once thought, at least when it comes to her. I've gone over our meeting in the park a hundred different ways, and while a part of me—too loud, too childish—is delighted she knows, that she's home, that she trusts me, the rest is certain I've fucked up. My goals are noble, but my methods—

The Masquerade can't be broken. What am I thinking?

So I've come to Lucille, hoping that even in her abstraction, she can be useful. That she will take pity on me the way she used to. All I need to say is *She knows*, and Lucille will take the reins.

And I am a coward.

"Do you know why she left?" Lucille asks. She is making it easy for me by staying engaged. "Was it another altercation among the herd?"

"No," I say. "No, she just—needed some space."

Lucille looks at me, quirks a brow, gestures to the fields outside her window.

"Not space," I correct. "Time. Back with other people. Sometimes it takes a few rounds for new members to really settle in, you know that."

"I had assumed, given the job you gave her, that she was reliable."

"She is," I say, too quick to defend. I rub at my face. I need to just say it. Lucille will understand. She almost certainly won't immediately go to kill her. We can reconsider the issue of enthralling Robin, and I—

She takes my chin in her hand, startling me. "Your eyes," she says.

"My—what?"

"They've changed colors," my sire says, voice blank and cold. She twists my jaw, changes the angle five times, seven, until she's satisfied. "Yes, they've gone from brown to gold."

I pull away and scramble to the nearest mirror, peering in. And yes, she's right. My eyes blaze. They are inhuman. They are beautiful and terrible, and I don't know what this means.

No. No, perhaps—

"Ladzka," I hiss.

"What?"

"Foul-Blooded *thaumaturge*." I storm for the door,

grabbing up my coat, but I'm stopped by Lucille, who slides in front of me easily and grasps my shoulders.

"Explain," she commands.

So I do. I tell her about the blood bag, and about Kasim finding me wandering outside, and about the strange eruptions of anger and hunger I've been experiencing. She listens to it all. She doesn't berate me for making the deal without her, doesn't laugh at my foolishness or worry over me like a mother hen.

But she also doesn't agree with me.

"You're wrong about when this started," she says.

"What?" I'm sure I'm not.

"It started when you hired Robin Joy."

No. No, that doesn't follow, and just like that, the little shreds of courage I'd built up to ask for her advice burn up. She's not going to consider this objectively.

"You don't know what you're talking about," I say, pulling away from her.

"Don't I? You're not the first of us to change, you know. Think back to the last dinner party with the Prince."

The last one I went to was when she'd granted us the privilege to start our experiment. It was a strange thing, both staid and bacchanalian in equal, confusing measures. Half boardroom meeting, half rave.

I remember very few details, despite how important that night was.

"Our bodies change in response to how we use them. Just like humans develop muscle or waste away, our vitae wears channels in us where we habitually direct it."

"And I use mine to look human," I reply, voice strangled to a deadly calm.

"You treat them like cattle, Leigh," Lucille sighs. "Not just like food, but like a commodity. Does it really surprise you that your body would shift in response to that? A human doesn't think of other humans as if they are cattle. It is an unnatural thing. A dangerous thing."

She touches my shoulder as if to soothe, and I tear away from her, snarling. "You're wrong." Not about seeing them as cattle—or sheep—but about what that makes me. Robin understands. Robin's convinced by this logic, and she is a shining beacon of humanity! It's a false comparison, this food versus livestock idea. How can I be worse, more monstrous, than somebody like Vương or Jolene who never even *think* of human needs and desires and comfort beyond their next meal or experiment?

And besides, there was no change when Robin arrived. I've been doing this for five years just the same.

"This *started* when I drank the leavings of blood sorcery," I spit, "and if you cannot see that, then I worry how you will help keep this community safe. Nothing changed when Robin Joy arrived."

"Except for an obsession."

I can't keep from laughing. It's a cruel laugh. It doesn't sound human, and I feel as far from human as I can ever remember. I feel distorted. Monstrous. Animalistic. "Obsession has nothing to do with how I treat the humans under my care."

"Doesn't it?" she asks. Distantly, I'm confused that there's no rancor in her tone. No fury. She has every right to put me in my place, to tear me to pieces.

Instead, she seems only . . . tired.

The fight bleeds out of me.

She goes back to her painting then. That calm, simple rebuke cuts me deep. I watch her paint and feel shame well up in the furrows I have torn in myself, groundwater rising to the surface.

"Whatever the cause," I say after perhaps a quarter hour has passed in her silent work and my fading rage, "I need to fix it."

"I know of no guarantees," she says, "and I suspect you won't listen to me if I offer my advice."

I bow my head. "Please. You have more experience in the world than I do. Tell me what to try, and I will try it."

Anything except handing Robin to her. I'll figure that part out on my own.

She looks back at me and gestures minutely with her brush, slicked with aubergine. "Be kind," she says. "Be human. Be generous."

"They need me to protect them now more than ever," I respond.

"Trust in what you have built."

And she says no more after that.

I stagger home, feeling the prickling pain of the faintest rays of light cresting the horizon, not enough to see but enough to sting. She's wrong about the cause of this being Robin, but I am willing to try her cure. So many things have happened this winter that have left me raw and defensive. And Robin . . . Robin has, it's true, made me more aware of what *I* am, not just what I serve. I've had to make excuses, had to bargain with myself, come face-to-face with rules I've rarely struggled against in the past.

I've broken the Masquerade.

And perhaps that was the right move, even if it arose

for all the wrong reasons. Surely it doesn't actually keep her safer, or me, or the others to struggle on the tightrope when I am far better on the ground. I am at my most bestial when I fight against what I've denied myself. Giving in, at least by small degrees, may help me reconcile what has come loose in me.

AFTERBIRTH

———◆———

One of the ewes goes into labor close to midnight. It is a curious thing, their preference for evening hours. Some of it must come down to their lambing in winter and early spring, when the nights are long, but I've read again and again (and seen myself now) that a preponderance of births seem to happen at night, far more than random chance would allow. I am more involved with lambing and processing than any other phase of meat production, and I appreciate it. It feels right, to be slicked with blood, either from new life or fresh death.

One of the farming crew noticed the ewe's teats swelling six days ago. It's still a few weeks too soon for healthy lambing, so I knew this one was likely to be a problem. She's been in the barn since, under observation, and so I'm in with her when the moment comes. I consider calling the vet, but instead text Robin. She comes to the barn immediately, willing to be another set of hands.

Why Robin and not the vet? It seems as though it will

be an easy birth, no knives needed. The lamb isn't likely to survive, either, so the expense of the vet makes no sense. There are other humans I could have roused, ones who work in the barn during the day. Except even in the drama of the birth, they might notice my eyes.

Still, I could have handled it all on my own.

I could say it just seemed right to bring her in on this process, after she'd missed the slaughter, but that would be only a half-truth. The other half is that I miss her. Lucille wouldn't approve of the way I got here, but it's still worth giving her idea a shot: reengage with a human on a personal level. Remember what it was to be human and try not to think of sheep when I look at them.

So I call her.

She shows up wearing old clothes and Wellingtons, expecting the muck, and I have her wash her hands in hot water and antiseptic. The ewe has already burst her second water, so it won't be long. Together, we help deliver the little creature, slicked in mucous and blood, and watch as it twitches, as its mother tries to lick it clean.

But within minutes of tying off its umbilicus, it's dead.

I deliver the afterbirth, the clotted, bleeding placenta warm in my hands, and take it away so the ewe won't eat it and get sick. When I come back, Robin is stroking the dead lamb's head.

"I missed this," she says.

"The death?"

She laughs, then cringes, pulling away from the body. "No, I mean—being here. Working with you. I guess the death is part of that, though."

The ewe noses at the corpse, and I let her. It will help

her adjust. If the rest of the sheep were lambing, I could give her an orphan to make up for the loss, but she'll have to bear it alone.

"How did slaughter go?"

"Do you want the short version or the long?" I ask, smiling at her. I can't help myself.

She seems to glow in response to my attention. "Whichever you'd like to tell."

So I tell her, leaving out my anger, and it rewrites the whole experience for me. It's like therapy, being able to revisit those long nights and focus on the craft and pride instead of the hurt and betrayal. I tell her about how cleanly the kills went, how none of the meat had any signs of bloodshot, how the lambs hadn't bitten their tongues, how it had been as peaceful as an early death can be. I tell her about how satisfying it is, to take a muscle group apart at the seams, and to deliver sustainably raised rib roasts to our customers. I tell her about the backlog of animals we still have, frozen off-cuts waiting to be processed into sausage, rillettes, charcuterie.

While we talk, we bag up the lamb to go to disposal in the morning. There are rules about what sort of bio-hazardous waste you can have, even—or especially—on a working farm. She handles the corpse with surprising ease.

After, we wash up and go out into the pasture. We find Sylvia, sleeping, and watch her chest rise and fall for a bit. It feels like before, but better, richer.

I don't have to pretend. There's nothing to pretend *about* and knowing that Robin knows what I am takes one last imperceptible weight off my soul. She stays up with me until nearly dawn, and the night is unusually clear and dry. We look at the stars. I tell her a few things about my childhood, no longer needing to hide my age.

She touches my hand, once, and I don't think about the greenhouse. I don't feel afraid.

I just lean into her.

MASQUERADE

⸻ ◆ ⸻

Somebody has gone through the livestock files.
Not the sheep files, the *human* files, which,
though they're kept in code, are sealed in a locked
filing drawer in the office. Somebody opened it, went
through them, and put everything back in order except
they transposed two pages. I don't know how long it's been
that way because I haven't looked with any real attention
since January, and now my Blood is boiling, seething in
my ears.

Because something is officially wrong.

Jolene? This began, as far as I can tell, after I took
that blood bag from her. My strange moods, the footsteps
in the far pastures, everything growing more and more
unstable. But that doesn't seem right; she isn't the type
to skulk. And she hasn't been on site (to my knowledge,
anyway) since December. Getting into the office isn't easy
during the night, not with me here, and Kasim—

Oh.

Fuck.

Our little revolutionary. Our idealist, whom I put in his place *twice* last month, who thinks I've lost my mind—he holds down the fort when I'm otherwise occupied, and I've been *otherwise occupied* for months now, distracted by the ongoing saga of Robin and the drama of the Camarilla's demands. He has the keys. He has the righteous anger.

I found those footprints a few weeks after he moved in— I have to find him.

He's not hard to locate. I almost run straight into him not five feet from the office door. He looks winded. Scared. He knows.

Wait. How could he know? How could he know that I'd find those files *tonight*, and make the connections, and—

"Something's wrong," he gasps. Gasps, as if he's been holding a breath he doesn't need. "Inside, now. Close the door."

I don't move. I'm too angry. I'm too confused.

"Seriously, *right now*," he says, and he pushes me, hands on my shoulders.

I snarl. He jumps back.

"I'm not kidding, Leigh," he manages, and that's at last what makes me move, because he's no great liar, and he must be terrified if he's willing to risk violence.

We go into my office. I close the door, stand with my back to it. I don't let my guard fall even an inch, though, just in case I'm wrong.

He paces. He works his jaw. I search for guilt in the line of his jumping sternocleidomastoid, and think I find it.

Then he says, "It's Robin," wincing, ready for an explosive response.

The anger curdles, overlaid by confusion, worry. "What?"

"Robin has been talking to . . . somebody. She's got a burner phone—Key noticed it a few days ago. It's an old flip thing."

Robin loves her iPhone, hasn't given it up despite the general trend on campus to lock them away. But I've never seen this flip phone. Wouldn't I have noticed?

"Why didn't either of you tell me?" I ask, brain spinning down paths I'd rather it didn't. Robin has been offsite. Robin left, angry and betrayed, but had a change of heart and wanted to come back. Robin has been so kind to me, so gentle, so perfectly everything I want . . .

I feel sick.

"It didn't seem like a big deal, except—except I just heard her talking on it, out in the fields."

It's pouring rain tonight, just above freezing, and the wind is gusty and horrible. If she's out in that, it means she didn't want to be overheard.

But why not go off campus?

And then there's the convenience of it. The sheer, perfect timing of it. Kasim comes running the moment I find evidence that he's betrayed me with the perfect diversion—

But he couldn't have known. And Robin has worked a few shifts alone since coming home, now that she knows what I am. She had access, same as him.

"Who was she talking to?"

"I don't know, I couldn't get close. I only heard her side."

"Which was?"

He relates:

"Yes, I'm settling back in." (Not incriminating yet.)

"No, she doesn't know." (Problem.)

"She's only told me some of what they're doing, but I think I can put the rest together." (Very big problem.)

"No, I don't think I'm in any danger. She's half in love with me." (Fuck.)

"Yes, I can still make that meeting time." (Fucking *shit*.)

Everything slots into place: that night in Peninsula Park and how easily I persuaded her, how when I first *interviewed* her, she was eager to work in the office with me.

What if all her uncertainty, her feints that made me pursue her, was constructed?

She's not Kindred herself, of course. She worked day shifts with Key, and anyway, I would have known the moment she sat down across from me if not long before, those times I watched her shows and studied her character. (Did she know I was there even then? Was that a calculated lure to draw me in? Seed the perfect application, then put on the show?)

(If she is a liar, then she is a perfect one. An actress beyond measure. I want that to be how she got me, and not my own weakness.)

(It's all such a mess.)

But she's not Kindred. And I don't think she's enthralled, either, because even though there are ways to control a human from a distance, I know I'd smell them on her. Some taint that is not mortal, some darkness that would cling to her sinews. As far as I can tell, she's human to the marrow. If I split her open, she would die. If I tied her to a post in the yard, she wouldn't ignite when the sun came up, and she wouldn't lose the pull of her master's voice when there's no master's voice to heed.

She's mortal. She's human. She's exactly what I've always assumed she was. And she's still dangerous.

I want to believe Kasim is making this all up. I want to believe it more than I've believed anything in my long life. But it makes too much sense, and Kasim would have too much to lose to move against me. But *why*? Is she secretly a radical animal rights activist who's here to shut down the *sheep* aspect of the ecovillage? That's so ridiculous in the face of what I told her the other week that I want to laugh. And yet the burner phone suggests she's talking to another human, because very few Kindred would be stupid enough to talk openly even on an unregistered line now that DHS and the NSA are combing every digital footprint and recording for us.

But *were* they talking openly? Without the other side of the conversation, I can't tell. It's just as likely they were talking just around the edge of anything damning, which would point to Anarchs. Or, less likely but still possible, other Camarilla members who want this experiment shut down, perhaps because of the risk to the Masquerade, but there's no way they'd employ a human to that end.

Kasim's the more likely plant in that case. And yet.

And yet.

Is the timing a coincidence? A manufactured crisis to keep me off-balance? Some ploy to separate me from Robin that just so happened to come on the heels of finding that something is very wrong?

"Leigh?" Kasim asks, and I move away from the door, running my hand over my scalp, thinking, thinking. I have to keep us safe. I have to stop the wolves at my door, no matter who they are.

Say it's humans. Why are we still here, then? They don't care about due process when it comes to torching our hideouts, and even with the heavy human population here, they could still take out Lucille and me without raising too much fuss. Not any more than they're used to risking, anyway. It could be that it's humans, but not Second Inquisition gun-toting humans. Investigative reporters? Still a huge, huge risk to the Masquerade. And if it *is* Anarchs, then that might even be worse. They couldn't take this place over and hold it, no, but they could raid it (or have it raided while I sleep) and hurt all my charges in the process.

There's only one answer, and whether Kasim is lying or not doesn't come into it, because the risk is far too great.

Robin Joy has to go.

All my questions, all my theorizing, aren't important enough to delay that in hope of answers. I need to shut this down, and now.

And if Kasim is lying?

Well.

I'll handle him next.

ASSIGNMENT

I oversee the "delivery" of Ethan's fractured heart to a customer the next night.

The timing is horrible for me, but wonderful for the recipient. After, Ethan is taken to an inpatient ward for an apparent suicide attempt that he won't remember, and I have a resounding success to report to Sebastian Vương. Kasim's plan worked. Between that and the roster of free-range humans we've collected useful data on, we have enough to offer the powers that be to win us more funding, less oversight, and, with any luck, a hands-off approach for another two to three years.

But all that success is worthless if Robin Joy lives out another week. It might already be too late; I risk more every minute that passes. I should have killed her before sunup. I didn't. I should have killed her while the betrayal was still hot in my veins. I didn't.

Instead, I have spent nights agonizing.

I want to assign Robin to myself. I really do. I'm nearly

vibrating out of my skin when I sit down in my office, starting the paperwork because I can't wait any longer. I matched her with the tag number for Sylvia just after we named her by the way, because of course I did, because I'm weak and sentimental, and I come so, so close to putting my own customer number down next to her.

More than once.

She even asked me to do it. Two nights ago, before I knew she'd betrayed me, unable to know she was bound for the auction block, she said:

"If I ever say yes, I think it would have to be to you."

"Why?"

"You'd be kind."

"We're all kind. We're not monsters." Not most of us. Not here. But I knew I was lying, because I was thinking about Sebastian Vương, and about Monsieur Messy Feeder back in November. I was thinking about myself. "And you could always choose not to know. Just donate like it's Red Cross day, get a cookie, never find out. And no matter what, like you said, it's up to you. Always."

Lying. When did I get so good at lying?

No, I've always been good at lying. When did I get so good at lying to *her*?

Wouldn't it be the humane thing to do, the moral thing, to take her stated wish and translate that to the reality I'm now faced with? She said she would pick *me*! But the key word there is pick, isn't it? Consent. Choice. It's not ethical, to assume that just because she'd *pick* me means that she'd want me to take her in any other context.

This. This is where humans are different from livestock. They can tell you exactly what they want, and you can extrapolate just how far that goes.

This line of philosophical agonizing should be what stops me, or at least what I pretend stops me, but I'm getting very tired of lying. Honesty means confessing, if only to myself, that I am furious. I am desperate. And that's why I can't assign her to myself.

It all comes down to my rules. I am a selfish, lying monster. I wouldn't be able to feed from her from a plastic bag. I would want, *need*, to hold her in my arms, make her writhe, whisper sweet nothings to her, and remember what it is to feel the struggle of my prey.

I would make it good for her. I could still bind her to me, to prove she was neutralized, truly safe. She would be like Key is to Lucille. She would be my loyal sheepdog, always watching for my command, responsive to my will. And I want that. I want that so, so badly.

Because I am a monster. I am selfish. I am hungry.

But I can't do it. And not because of respecting her free will, but because it would complicate everything. This community only exists because I have ironclad control over myself. I am the shepherd. Sometimes my flock needs to be culled, but I cannot be a wolf hunting among them. She can be enthralled to somebody else, or killed, but she cannot remain here unchecked. She cannot lead the foxes through the gate.

I finalize the paperwork and text Vương at dawn, when I can delay no longer. Spring is coming, and sunrise is drawing back toward my working hours once more. The dream of this long winter is over.

On Thursday, she goes to Vương, doing double service by sating my doubtful patron. I want him here sooner, to end my agony, but it was the first opening he had.

Goodbye, Robin. I would have loved you, if you let me.

ROMANCE

———◆———

The next night, she calls me.

I should let it go to voice mail, but she knows I'm in the office, so if she's calling instead of stopping by, something might be wrong. I answer in one and a half rings. And then I don't know what to say, so I just croak out my name in greeting.

"Leigh here."

"Hey," Robin says, and, yes, there's nervousness in her voice.

"What's up?" I want to ask so many other questions, but not like this. She's got me trapped, calling instead of stopping by.

"Can you come over? When you get a moment? To the house, I mean."

"Is something wrong?"

"It's the plumbing," she says, apologetically. "The water's out. Don't worry, it's not gushing anywhere, but I thought maybe you could fix it real fast?"

My damsel in distress. And I, her tower minder, am supposed to be on call for exactly this sort of problem. I can't say no.

"I'll be there in a few minutes," I say, and hang up.

This is a trap. Even if there aren't Inquisition agents ready to grab me when I come out the door of the office (there aren't, and I don't sense anybody new on the campus beyond), I know that if I go there, my chances at self-control drop. But I'm already weak. I'm always weak when it comes to Robin. I made the right decision, signing her over to Vương, because in another night it will all be out of my hands.

There's only this last night to do more damage in.

I ease open the door without a sound. The kitchen's finally finished, but the living room and dining room have been all but gutted, their flooring pulled up to be refinished. Work that now seems as if it will never be complete, can never be completed, but it will be. Once she's gone.

I climb the stairs. The bathroom door is open at the end of the hall, and I make myself go there first, check the shower. Water flows easily, no knocks in the pipe. My skin prickles all over in warning, shouting at me to run, but I don't. I go to her door. My chest feels tight and painful, feels exactly as it did when Kasim told me what he'd overheard.

Inside, I can hear her typing. Her laptop keys click gently, then pause, then rush forward again. I listen from outside her door, head bowed, muscles taut.

I knock.

For a moment, I hope she doesn't answer, but then I hear her soft footsteps, the gentle creak of the wood. She opens the door and smiles at me, because she doesn't know what's coming for her. She doesn't know we are at war. She doesn't know I've signed the paperwork and sold off her life, and so she is happy to see me.

Despite the danger, I want to pretend, for half an hour, that things are back as they were in December, when I trusted her.

I am a lovesick fool, hurt and longing. I should not have come.

"I checked on the pipes," I say. "The water's working just fine."

I watch her smile falter, just a little. Guilt? Fear that I've discovered her ploy? Then she steps back.

"Yeah, I lied," she admits, sheepishly. "I . . . I just wanted to see you. And you've been so busy that I figured I needed a good reason to get you over here."

If this is a ploy, it is obvious and desperate. I need to leave. But I can't sense anybody else in the house with us, and excitement rolls off her skin like perfume. Anticipation. Desire.

"Come in?" she asks.

Following every Victorian penny dreadful, those words work magic in me, unlock my limbs, and I step into her room.

"I've missed you," she says.

Fuck. I look around for a seat; she points to her bed. It's disheveled, a nest made of pale cream and deep crimson bedding, a riot of patterns and textures, all perfumed with *her.* I hesitate, then sit. "It's a busy time of year," I say, looking not at her but at the rest of the room. At all the art she's hung up along the walls. I look for clues about *her.* Not Robin Joy the performer, not Robin Joy the employee, but Robin Joy the betrayer.

Her walls are decorated with the work of local artists,

artists I recognize, including some who live on campus. Every flat surface is covered, too, in beautiful planters filled with succulents, in found objects, in half-read books. She has a whole shelf of battered romance novels. Half a shelf of queer theory and poetry, spanning decades. A few small books, gently used, likely from Powell's, about sheep husbandry and gardening.

This can't all be a performance. It can't. I begin to second-guess myself. There's no threat here. What if there's no threat at all? What if Kasim misheard, misunderstood? I've already told Vương, he's already penciled the feeding into his schedule, but I could still undo it.

"Hey," Robin says. The bed bows. She's sitting next to me. Her thigh brushing mine brings me back, and I shake my head as if to clear my eyes of tears, tears that refuse to form, to fall.

"Sorry," I say. "Long couple of nights. The rest of the ewes are starting to lamb." I am a good liar, even if I'm sick half to death of it.

I give myself over entirely to my joy in the sheep. That, at least, is simple.

This conversation should be stilted. She certainly knows I'm avoiding something; we've worked together long enough, and she knows my weaknesses well enough. But it isn't. Words flow like milk, like honey. I tell her about a set of twins, delivered earlier that day, healthy and thriving. I tell her about a ewe who, it turns out, has a false pregnancy, no lambs at all. I tell her about everything I've been using to distract myself from her for the last two nights, and she drinks it all in, to all appearances ecstatic to have me back with her.

"And Sylvia?" she asks, though of course Sylvia is not pregnant, will not be for another year. Her eyes sparkle. She is engaged. She's thinking of *our* favorite, our girl.

For a moment, I forget what she has done, really forget. I'm happy, I'm joyous, I'm leaning in toward her. And then I think of writing Sylvia's number on the contract paperwork for Robin's life, and it comes rushing back. The whiplash is agony.

"Leigh?"

It's showing on my face, my desire to drop to my knees and beg her for the truth, to explain. I want to scream. I want to rip her head off.

"I should go," I manage, standing up, running a hand through my shorn hair. She catches hold of the other one. I freeze. I know better. I fight it for half a second, only that, before I give in, docile, letting her tug me back onto the bed. I sit.

She climbs into my lap.

She kisses me.

It is sweet and perfect, because Robin Joy is perfect, and I have been waiting for this moment to come again ever since the night in the greenhouse. My arms wrap around her reflexively, fit her every curve, and if I needed to breathe, I would be lost. I kiss her mouth, her chin, her throat, her collarbone. I feel the pulse of her blood. I feel her hands begin to roam, over my back, along my hips.

"What took you so long?" she murmurs against my hair.

I am weak. Weak like Kasim. I want her, and I want to own her, and I can still hear Lucille's voice in my head. Reconnect with humanity, she told me, and this seems like the solution. *Don't fuck the animals.* I've told that to my-self and others, over and over again, but if seeing humans as livestock is what's stripping away my self-control, if this is all my fault, then this is the perfect balm.

And behind it all, my own animal need.

I can have this, at least, if I can't have her.

It won't undo what's been done. I know that. I don't care.

She wants to be the aggressor, wants to press me back to her bed, but I can't give her that. Even in my wild abandon, I can't trust her, not quite, and so I roll us over, straddle her, let her feel the unnatural strength in my thighs. She gasps. She tugs at my shirt. I let every mask drop as she pulls the shirt from my waistband, as she unbuttons the flannel, as she slides her fingers up beneath my undershirt. My skin is cold, my pulse still, and I don't know if I'm showing her because I've spent too long pre-tending, or because I want her to remember what I am.

And then the world goes red.

TRAGEDY

❖

I taste blood.

A body arches beneath my hands, luscious and familiar.

I know this scent.

I know this voice.

She is screaming, and the sound gives me the sweetest pleasure I have ever known. It smooths out the frantic bursting of fear, of shame, of panic, leaving in its wake only pure need. I forget to struggle. I forget to fight.

She's half in love with me already, I hear her saying, imagine her saying, but the line between reality and fantasy is obliterated. There is only the *now*.

A hand curls around the wooden bedpost. I smell sawdust. I hear a crack of snapping wood. Or is that a footstep on the staircase? I rage. I fear. I react.

And in another moment, the stimulus is obliterated; all that remains is the response. I am a beast, a creature of hunger, something built by nature (or *un*nature) to rend and slaughter and drink deep, and it is the easiest thing in the world to do what I was made to.

The only result is blood.

The Beast is in me, rampant, rearing, and I tear at flesh. I gorge myself on blood. I roll around like a dog in filth, and I am *happy*, happy for the first time in months, in years. I want to howl. I want to laugh. I don't know what sounds I'm making.

I think, *This is how it all ends, this is the end of me, of everything*, but then a part of me, distant, desperate, thinks that if I have the presence of mind to be poetic, I am not all lost. I must get back to the surface. I must regain control.

Because Robin.

Robin.

Sweet Robin, delicious Robin, Robin in my mouth and throat and stomach—Robin—Robin—

No.

I fight. I finally fight, really fight, but the struggle is a serpent, slippery, winding. It is hard to focus, to remember what it is I'm fighting for. Stillness, I tell myself. Stillness, control, quiet. The rustle of the wind in the grass. The beauty of the darkest night, of the bleating of lambs, of the great edifice I have built in service to the beauty of logistics. Slowly, slowly, I come back down, until it is only me, huddled beneath the porch of Hawthorn House.

There is blood in my mouth.

I spit it out. I fight my nature. I shovel dirt between my lips, chew, until I cannot taste anything else. I vomit soil, then claw my way out from beneath the porch, into the moonlight.

The fading moonlight. It is late now. The night is waning.

I stagger to my feet, taking inventory as quickly as I can. My clothes are stiff with clotting, drying blood, and it smells human. I take three lurching steps forward, away from Hawthorn House, toward home, and then I stop.

I look over my shoulder.

A light burns in Robin's window.

I go very still, caught between the need to flee and the need to know. *You know, you know,* the blood on my hands whispers. But I am not ready to accept it, too ready to cling to the impossible. I fall up the porch steps, claw my way inside. The house is still. The house is empty. There is a chance, a small chance, a tiny ember that is struggling against the cold within me, and—

I reach the top of the stairs.

I smell blood, more blood. I smell the shit of the dying. I walk, as if entranced, to the door of Robin's room, hanging open into the hall. I hung that door myself. I painted the walls inside.

I stand in the threshold and see the evidence of slaughter.

There are clumps of curled, tangled red hair, clinging to scraps of scalp. The bed is overturned, the sheets soaked through. The floorboards are fouled. Helpless, I fall to my knees and do the only thing I can; I begin to pry them up, mechanically processing the scene, falling back on a numb need to clean up the mess. To set things right, to set things back to order.

It is the only thing between silent work and useless howling.

I have less than an hour, but I am alive. I am animate

in a way I haven't been in years. I make quick work of the bedroom, bundle up all the evidence of death. I go to my cottage. I bury the evidence, because fire would be too obvious, too suspicious.

I hide myself behind false walls, false floors, a hundred locks between me and the world of humans.

Lucille was right. Vương was right. I am the wolf in the flock. I am a beast, a monster, and every defense I erected between myself and the core of me was a farce. While I played at my pastoral idyll, I was coming ever closer to his moment, this fracture, and now I can taste Robin's blood on my lips and feel her in my veins, and I want to scream.

But there should have been a body.

What the fuck have I done with the body?

PROCESSING

———— ◆ ————

I checked the slaughter room. There's newly made sausage. I don't know who made it.

I hope it's lamb.

FAILURE TO DELIVER

I t's Thursday, and I forgot to cancel the appointment.

I don't know how I forgot. My whole existence has been reduced to *Robin Robin Robin*. I haven't found her body, haven't found any trace of her except the blood that's already boiled from my veins. I haven't found her burner phone, either, and it's left me terrified. Hunted.

I should have remembered to call off Sebastian Vương, but maybe I forgot in order to protect myself. I have no good excuse for him.

But he's here, now, and he will be angry. I race across the fields, sliding in the muck, reduced to something less than human, less than animal. I don't know what I'm going to tell him. I don't know if I can lie, or if I will just throw myself on his mercy. I can't afford either, not really. Maybe I should just hide.

Or leave.

But Kasim took my shift tonight, and that means he'll be the one to greet Vương and have no ready answer for him, and while I still hate him for breaking open this monstrousness inside of me, for proving my foolishness to me, I owe him safety.

I reach the administration building. I pelt down the halls, muddy boots sliding on the linoleum.

I'm too late.

The door to the office is wide open, and I smell blood. My head spins. My stomach aches.

Only Vương would believe so much in his own right to destruction that he'd leave evidence of his rage where humans could see it.

Luckily, the blood is contained to a small pool in the back of the room. And the blood's owner is still alive. Kasim huddles beneath my desk, shivering, glaring up at me with pure, seething hatred. But he's weak and biddable as I get him back to my cottage and break out some of my own blood stores, giving him enough to start his body mending.

"Fuck you," he says when he's drunk his fill, teeth still bloody and eyes still sunken. *"Fuck you."*

I want to apologize, but don't want to acknowledge how badly I've made a mess of things. I avoid eye contact and start cleaning up the mess he made. Always cleaning up messes.

"I'll talk to him," I say. "About appropriate behavior with staff." If nothing else, Kasim is under my protection. The thought makes me stiffen with pain, though, because there it is: more evidence that I can't protect what is mine.

"Doesn't matter, I fucking quit," he says, staggering to his feet. "I should have told Lucille about your *episode* the other month, and I should've packed up and left then, before you lost control over everything. Easy feeding isn't worth all this shit. I'm not covering for you, not when you almost killed me for Ethan and then turned around and—"

He cuts himself off. He eyes me warily.

It's clear from that look that he knows. He *knows*. I told everybody Robin left again, told *him* to step up security in case she brought whatever threat she was spying for to our doorstep, and I thought, of all people, he'd believe me. After all, he was the one to hear the conversation.

But he stopped trusting me the moment I punished him for loving Ethan. He might have pitied me, feared *for* me, after that night in the fields, but instead I mocked him. I let out the beast in me so he could see it, so I could feel strong.

He knows exactly what I'm capable of.

He walks the campus at night for security, just like I hired him to.

"Were you there?" I ask. My voice doesn't break a whisper. "In the house that night?"

"No," he says. "But I saw what you've done to her room. I know how you looked at her. I'm thin-blooded, not stupid."

I should be ashamed, or scared, but all I feel is exhaustion. I'm tired. So tired. I sit down and put my head in my hands. What happened with Robin, it doesn't mean the whole experiment is a failure. But it feels like the end of the world. I can't trust myself, and without me, what's left? Lucille doesn't care enough. Vương would run it into the ground.

It isn't fair, but I ask Kasim, "What do I do now?"

Kasim doesn't answer. When I look up, he's long gone.

I am alone.

MEMORY FOG

———— ◆ ————

I think I see Robin.

  We have been called downtown to kneel at the Prince's feet, and we walk rain-slick streets lit by white string lights on rows of orderly trees. I don't want to go into the building, and I turn away from the doors. Just for a moment, going into the bar across the street, I see a flash of red hair, the curve of a familiar hip as a woman opens the door, shrugs off her coat.

And then the door closes.

It isn't her. Robin is dead.

"Come," Lucille says, touching just one finger to the back of my hand. I master myself and enter the grand lobby.

We have not been called to Elysium; this is not a safe haven or an open call for machinations, but a closed-door meeting in a boardroom downtown in a top-floor law office. The Prince sits at the head of the long, live-edge oak table (beautiful, and laughable because there's no way the

Prince gives a single shit about its beauty or its rarity) with her retainers and advisors. Halfway down, one on each side, sit Sebastian Vương and Jolene Ladzka. Vương radiates anger. It has been two weeks since I shorted his order and I've already given him a replacement, a new transplant from Ohio who nobody will miss for a while. And yet still he seethes.

Jo, by contrast, looks bored.

But she shouldn't be here at all. Her very presence puts me on high alert.

Lucille approaches first, making her obeisance properly, then sits. I stand alone, by the unused Keurig, stage-dressing to maintain an illusion of human business during the day. I've dressed up in my nice suit, my hair freshly washed, my nails cleaned of any dirt or sheep shit. But again, I feel like the provincial idiot.

I bow to the Prince. I move to sit.

"Stop," the Prince says.

I obey without thought. I keep my eyes lowered. They've stayed their strange, glowing gold, proof of my failure.

"We have been kept apprised of your grand experiment, Leigh Konopasek, and while your aims are noble and your results generally worthy, there are many concerns about its longevity." The Prince herself is doing all the talking.

I'm fucked.

"We appreciate the great lengths you go to in order to protect your holdings from outside influences and to avoid breaching the Masquerade, but as Vương has informed you, you do not produce enough of value to balance out the expenses and risks."

"My liege," I say, too quickly, "we are taking steps to correct—"

"Silence. Yes, I have been informed of your efforts at expanding a hunting portfolio. But these efforts will add to disputes about territory and hunting grounds. I have gifted land to those who serve me well, and to now have to restrict their feeding to those not marked by you is laughable. Do you understand me?"

"Yes, my liege. But we—we have added a new initiative, that of fostering specific dyscrasias."

She does not cut me off then, and I can see Jo looking a little less bored. She stops writing on a legal pad and watches me, to all appearances without guile.

"We have already successfully created a strong melancholic dyscrasia," I continue, breathlessly. "His recipient has reported great results, and he is returning to the ecovillage shortly. It will be some time before we can use him again, but—"

The Prince's patience runs out. She lifts a hand. I stop.

"This is promising," she concedes, "but does not address the issue of volume. Bagged blood is useless to me. To everybody in this room except for you, in fact. Your farm produces little of value. It toes the line—and falls short. And everything I have heard you say, and have heard from Vương, says that this will continue to be true. You are soft, Leigh. You blame human society for the constraints upon your enterprise, but we are not human. There are steps that can be taken to increase production, but you will not take them."

"You're stuck in your pastoral fancies," Vương adds, echoing that night in his kitchen. "But you won't bring your herd to slaughter like you do your sheep. It's a farce. We are sick of it. And now we hear that for all your posturing, your conviction that you are somehow better, more humane than the rest of us, you've murdered one of your flock for your own desires? Disgusting. Absolutely disgusting."

The Prince shifts her smooth glare to Vương and he shuts up. I barely notice it, because I'm trying to figure out how he knows about Robin. Kasim—he must have told him. But he didn't tell them about the clots? No, that doesn't make sense. And there's something else, something at the back of my mind, in the motionless marrow of my bones, a laugh, a gap in time—

The Prince interrupts.

"We are hereby relieving you of control over the herd experiment."

If my heart still beat, it would stop. I sink to my knees. "No, please," I whisper. *Show no weakness*; that is the first rule of the Camarilla courts, but here I am, prostrate, near panic. "Please, please, I can do better—"

Ethan. Genna. My cottage and the gardens, everything coming to life in just another month, the lambs being born right this instant—it all flashes before me. And I think of Robin, helping me bag up that stillborn lamb, and the meat in the sausage grinder, and canning soup and sitting in a Southeast bar and the weight, the chaos, of the last four months crashes into me, and I nearly scream.

But I don't.

I simply listen as the Prince rules that Lucille has failed to keep me to heel and has ceded too much of her authority to an untrustworthy brat. A severe offense, but the punishment is, in the grand scheme of things, light; she must be off the property by the end of the week. She is allowed to take her retainers, of course, but is not to use the resources of the commune for anything else. I hear a chair scrape back, feel a soft touch on my shoulder, and then my sire is gone. All is quiet. They are waiting for me to pull myself together. They are laughing, silently, at my misery.

I lift my head. I keep my face impassive. I wait for my own sentencing, sure to be far worse.

"Leigh," the Prince sighs at last, "I was at a loss with what to do with you. You do good work, it is undeniable. But you are not fit to rule. Luckily, Ladzka has proposed a solution. You will remain on your little farm."

I know better than to feel hope, but I feel it anyway. It hurts. It burns. I clamp down on it, force myself to clench my jaw in preparation for the twist, the punishment.

"However," the Prince continues, "you cannot be allowed to remain in charge. Lucille's failure was to allow you to rule instead of serve, and yours was to think yourself capable of ruling; that is a failure easily corrected, and I am willing to give you a chance to prove yourself. You will be kept on as the groundskeeper and general livestock manager, but Ladzka will be responsible for all final decision making."

My gaze slips from a point behind the Prince's head to look at Jo, who looks back at me, pleased and smug. She has her chin pillowed on one curled fist.

"It won't be so bad," Jo says. "I like a lot of what you're doing. But you shouldn't be the one worrying about expansion; you're best at being in the pens, taking temperatures, doing—whatever it is you do. I'll continue the dyscrasia research." She smiles, and it is gleeful. No, she didn't know about that before now. "And the blood bag enrichment program, at least for your benefit."

"What?" I whisper.

"Well, clearly you can't be allowed to feed from your flock," she says, shrugging. "And now we know you can't control yourself when the need gets too great. But here," she adds, and reaches behind her, into her large purse. She pulls out a small bag of blood and comes to my side. "Try this."

I stare up into her eyes but feel no compulsion to drink, only horror. But horror at what? Lucille was right. It was Robin's presence that destroyed me, not tainted blood. Still, anything could be in that blood. It might be fractionated, or poisoned in a hundred different ways. It can leave me writhing, incapacitated.

But at least it cannot bind me.

My servitude will be conscious, whatever good that will do me.

It's shameful, to drink from a bag in front of everybody seated around that table. I am as old as some of the junior attendants to the Prince, but all of them, to a one, drink from live bodies. I'm the only one to debase myself like this. To eat silage instead of fresh grass, by preference instead of need. To drink from this bag is dangerous and will seal my pathetic nature in front of everybody who might one day rule me.

I have come here to be humiliated.

But what choice do I have? What right have I earned to defend myself? I drink. I drink the whole thing down, and it is sweet, and good, and glorious. It is more than bagged blood, so much more, and in it, I catch flashes of Robin, of her curling hair, of her voice soft and then booming, her presence spilling out from a stage and filling a whole theater. I shudder, bent double, draining the plastic to a vacuum, and then I look up at Jolene Ladzka, bloody-mouthed, waiting for the next blow.

The room is silent.

There is no laughter. It's not somber, though; more bored. I stagger to my feet, knowing it's time to go. "I accept," I say, thickly. It is the only answer. It is the best answer for my flock. For my sheep, my humans, my crops. For me. "What sort of housing should I prepare?"

Jo shrugs. "Lucille's house should suit," she says.

One last slap in the face.

I leave.

HARVEST

I have one last week to myself before Jolene lays claim to all that is mine.

I spend it with the animals. Community movie nights, cooking and putting up food, parties under the stars when the clouds clear. I don't leave the grounds. I drink my bags of clotted blood, none of which fulfill me the way Robin did, or the bag Jo gave me, and I try to believe that the meeting downtown was only a nightmare.

But Lucille is gone. I clean the house myself, as dawn draws earlier and sunset later every night. I prepare it for a new host, polishing every element that Lucille wasn't able to take with her when she left. I struggle to choose new retainers to replace the ones Lucille maintained, to fill in for Key and the others. I don't try to replace Robin or Kasim; I'm resigned to working every night, 7:00 to 5:00, for the next year, decade, century if I'm very lucky. I'm angry often, but have nowhere to lose that anger except in the fields. I build half a dozen new stone walls.

Then, finally, I receive a text that the new management will be arriving tonight. Ethan is back from the hospital, but weak, so I can't offer him up on a silver platter to Jolene. I'm stressed and pained enough to qualify, but though I may be too human in some ways, I am still far too monstrous in others. I pick Genna instead, who still hasn't sorted out her feelings about Bill and Jason and worries about Bill's disappearance while she hates herself for caring. I make sure she stays on site.

I wait in my office, wondering if it will still be mine by sunrise.

The hours creep by, uselessly empty. I'm too preoccupied to work and I've already moved my spinning wheel and lap loom back to my house, just in case. So I sit. I stare at the door. I try not to think about any of the last four months, and instead lose myself in memories of the early days.

Just as I'm slipping into the warmth of a late August evening, a breeze coming in off the Columbia as I and three of our earliest members build cold frames for the coming frost, I feel her.

Jolene Ladzka is the approaching storm. The thunderhead. I stand and try not to look angry.

Or afraid.

She strolls into my office dressed like a caricature of a farmer: bespoke overalls and expensive boots, hair in braided pigtails. I want to smear her with pig shit. I want to bury her in the earth.

Instead, I bow. Just a little. Just enough to signal that I'm not going to fight this.

"Welcome to the ecovillage," I say, as if she's a first-time buyer.

She smiles. "And here I thought you'd be off hiding in the barn," she says, no doubt knowing I wanted to.

I smile back. It is tight. It is a threat grin.

"Is my house ready?" she asks.

I want to sneer and ask if she'll really be giving up her house out in the West Hills, with all its hidden secrets—but I am a professional, no matter what they say. "Of course."

"Take me to it."

She knows where it is. She has met with Lucille before, in the early days. She is waiting for me to fight.

I refuse to give us both the satisfaction.

I lead her out through the admin building, adjusting my course when, behind me, she veers toward the parking lot. But she doesn't want to drive, only to retrieve a satchel from the trunk of her shiny SUV. We walk along the paths, me in silence, her chattering about what the fields around her have to recommend themselves. She asks if we have trail cams set up, so that she can see the birds that come when the sun is up. I don't answer. She continues on.

We reach the front door, and I turn to go. If she wants to see the house, let her see it, let her plan whatever changes she wants for it. Without me.

"Give me a tour, Leigh?" Jo asks to my back. She uses her sweetest, gentlest tone of voice, and I have to bite back a snarl. I make myself smile. I nod. I walk her through the halls of Lucille's house.

I think she even halfway listens while I point out all the beautifications and amenities. She admires the murals for thirty seconds, longer than I would have expected of her. But I also keep most of my talk to practicalities. Lucille appreciated craftsmanship, no matter the era, and so the appliances in the house are as functional as they are beautiful. I'm sure Jo will find some horrible use for all of them.

"And there is a vault, I assume?"

"Of course," I say. I show her how to get to it through a sliding bookcase in the study.

"Delightful!" she says. Her eyes unfocus a moment as she no doubt checks for wards and tricks, but the house is empty.

We are alone.

If I lunge, if I move fast enough, maybe I can incapacitate her. But she is older than me, stronger than me, and in a straight fight I have no chance at all. My only hope is that she trusts in my deference. That she doesn't expect me to fight.

And if I lose, what then? Death, or worse. I would never be able to stay. This dream, this nightmare, would be over.

Of course she doesn't expect me to fight. There's nothing left to fight for.

"How long have you wanted this?" I ask.

Her eyes sparkle, but she doesn't answer.

"When you came to ask for a life contract?"

A subtle shake of her head. She wants *me* to do the work. I want to rub my temples, but I can't risk the smallest show of weakness. I think. I try to untangle the hundred threads that led to this moment from the thousand threads of screaming emotion. By the time I saw her at Vương's—yes. Yes, she knew by then. She had planned. Why else be there? I'd assumed it was to complain about my refusal to give her body after body, that her complaints had been what enraged Vương so much, but now, now that

I'm starting to think this wasn't an accident at all, her being gifted the farm . . .

"After I refused to give you somebody else."

"After you refused to give me Robin."

Robin. "How—"

"I have my sources," she says. Key? Kasim? My nails bite into my palms. "I'll admit, it was too much to expect you to translate *lurking danger* to your pet, not when you were so caught up in idolatry, but I really thought you'd understand when I laid it out for you."

"I did." Robin had been the first to come to mind. I'd thought I was crazy. Paranoid.

I wasn't.

"Bill's blood."

"Who?"

"The *entitled child,*" I say, dredging up her own words.

"Oh. What about it?"

"Did you drug it?"

She smiles. Smiles broadly. "What *did* happen when you drank it?"

I jerk half a step forward, fingers clawing toward her, my frustrated anger finally slipping its leash.

She lifts a hand. "Be still, Leigh. Remember who's in charge here. What happened?"

It wasn't so long ago that I nearly broke Kasim's spine. That I ripped Robin apart. I am monstrous. I want to be monstrous. But any further and there will be nothing of me left.

I breathe like a human. It soothes me. Mollifies. I search for an answer for her, because proving my weakness to her is the lesser risk.

"I made a fool of myself."

It's not enough. She leans in. Presses gently on my mind, reminding me that she can take by force what I will not offer. *Consent is an illusion.* I told Kasim that myself. "And?"

"I wandered around the fields yelling about Caine," I say through my gritted teeth. "I nearly broke the Masquerade. Your doing." This time I don't make it a question.

And this time she actually answers me. "My doing," she confirms. "How curious. More dramatic than I would have hoped for, though. I wonder if it's something in your own vitae that responded that way. The performer in your blood." She considers a moment, then points to the nearby chair. "Sit."

I feel no push along with those words, and that absence is worse than any influence could be. She doesn't have to exert herself; I'll do the work for her.

I sit.

Jo doesn't. She walks behind me and I hear her rummage through the satchel she brought. I stare straight ahead, at the delicate crown molding that circles the ceiling of the parlor, using human tricks to contain my inhuman heart.

And then she's at my side. Her hand is on my elbow, light, soothing. The touch of a nurse. "Just a little prick," she purrs.

A needle slides into my arm. She cannot make my heart beat, and so there was no reason for a tourniquet to make my vein stand out; she used her sense of smell instead. I watch as my vitae fills vial after vial. I go numb, watching reality invert itself as *I* become the renewable resource.

"For research," she says, though I haven't asked. "We'll have a session like this once a week, so we'll need to keep you well-fed. We can discuss exact reapportioning of contracts tomorrow night."

I was wrong. I'm no herding dog; I'm just the bellwether, the sheep who leads the flock.

LIVESTOCK MANAGEMENT

—◆—

I leave Lucille's—*Jo's*—with only the most tenuous connection to my body. It feels like dying. It feels like dreaming. She has done nothing to me except take a few vials of Blood, something I have done again and again to all the humans sleeping in the buildings around me. But I feel reduced. Attenuated.

I go to the barn.

It's something between self-loathing and desperation for what I *know* that takes me there. I want to find Sylvia, stroke her head, bury my face in her fleece, but that is not the work that needs doing. The ewes are in the thick of labor, and I find one of them actively birthing in the pen she's been placed in. I get in with her to observe. Things proceed okay. It's a good distraction. Half an hour passes, and I forget, for those few minutes, the reality around me.

Then Robin walks into the barn.

I can smell her over the stench of amniotic fluid and lanolin and shit, but it's off somehow, wrong. She has her hair pulled back and old clothes on, and she climbs into the pen with me. She smiles at me. She helps hold the ewe while I guide out the fluid-slicked lamb, and after, while its mother licks it clean, we watch each other wordlessly.

"You're not real," I say, because I have to. Because I remember her beneath me, dying.

She spreads her arms. "I'm as real as you are."

"I remember . . ." I say, then pause, frown. My head hurts. I remember killing her. I remember my mouth against her throat, her blood on my lips. I remember struggle. Pain. Losing control. I remember—

A narrative.

A narrative with elisions. With gaps. I have been so convinced it's my hunger's doing that I haven't questioned all those lacunae. And I remember other things, incongruous things, flashes of laughter, not mine. Footsteps on the stairs, when I know I was there alone that night.

Think I was there alone that night.

I remember . . . Robin said that night in Peninsula Park.

I remember that night outside the greenhouse, what I told her to substitute for the memory of my lips on hers.

A narrative.

It begins to click. Jolene Ladzka. Sebastian Vương's lingering anger. Performance, all performance, and here I am, on my knees in the muck, no longer in control, and here Robin is, with all the power.

She'd been talking to somebody on a burner cell. She'd "died" as soon as I told Vương she was going to die, though I'd never told him why. Vương didn't kill Kasim, though it was his right to. Jolene was given the ecovillage, though she's not one for leadership. The Camarilla court of Portland has its food source with newer, better management.

Everybody but me got what they wanted that day in my office when Robin sat down across from me, perfectly designed to strike at my weaknesses. Jo might not have set her sights on the farm until that night in her house, but without Robin, I would have been strong enough to resist.

"Shit," I whisper.

Robin winks. She holds out her hand. It is cold when I take it and stagger to my feet.

"You?" I whisper. Robin, Jolene Ladzka's assistant. Robin, embraced, her thirst now slaked with blood instead of palomas.

"Me," she says. "It was always me."

"What happened?" I ask, though I know. I can guess, at least. That night when I was lost in Robin's arms, no longer caring about anything beyond the two of us, she hadn't been alone. It had been planned from the moment I contacted Vương to schedule his feeding, and I was always going to end up with Robin in my arms. Or did that even happen? Because at some point that night, instead of losing control of my will, I lost control of my mind. Jolene Ladzka came and rewrote every memory, and she told me that I'd had Robin in my arms, that I had lost control, because what else would I have done, really? That I'd been a beast. And I had believed it, because it fit everything else, and somewhere in there, Robin had died and been resurrected.

But not by me. There is no bond between us beyond what existed in life, and, now, her dominance over me. Robin ascendant. New to the Blood, but powerful already, set to rule an empire of flesh.

Was it the last of her mortal blood in that bag Jo fed me? Of course it was. I was afraid of sausages when I should have feared medical grade plastic.

"What happened?" I repeat again, numb, incredulous, too stunned and grateful and horrified to be angry.

"Livestock management," she tells me, even as she runs a hand through my hair, ruffles it lovingly. She smiles, and I see a flash of pointed teeth.

"Now back to work. The animals need you."

ACKNOWLEDGMENTS

---◆---

GENEVIEVE

Thanks first and foremost go to my agent, Rhea Lyons, for your confidence in me and your guidance in all things. I don't know what I'd do without you.

To my editor, David Pomerico, for urging me to dig deeper and "lean into the horror" of the World of Darkness, and for challenging me to tackle the larger themes in Clea's tale: Your direction and vision have been invaluable in making this story what it is. Thank you so much for everything, and thank you to the whole team at Harper Voyager for their hard work putting this project together.

A big thank-you to the Paradox team for their insight and feedback as I wrote this tale.

To Erika Ishii, for her incredible audiobook performance of this novella.

To my family and friends for their support during this project, even though they had no idea what I was working on.

And to Cassandra Khaw and Caitlin Starling: I'm honored to have gone on this journey with you two.

CASSANDRA

To Mouse, my most darling of rodents with whom I spent so much time playing in the World of Darkness. To Onyx Path, who were the first to take a chance on me so long ago. To the Paradox team for entrusting me with part of this triptych, and for tolerating every moment I spent squeeing over the project. To David Pomerico, for all his editing help. To Kay, whose faith in me never falters even on days when I can't imagine why anyone would give a damn.

CAITLIN

When I was a teenager reading rule books and clan novels and *The Book of Nod*, I never imagined I would one day be asked to contribute to the World of Darkness. Thank you to Karim Muammar, David Grigorov, and the rest of the Paradox team for the opportunity, and to David Pomerico, the Voyager crew, and my agent, Caitlin McDonald, for bringing it all together.

Thank you, too, to my husband, David Hohl, and to my friends Shy and Kathleen, who put up with my extremely vague brainstorming requests.

And, finally, thank you to the Portland bars I know so well, and TriMet for getting me around town. This story wouldn't feel as real without either of you. I hope we come back stronger than ever from our pandemic shutdown.

ABOUT THE AUTHORS

Genevieve Gornichec may have tried to major in Vikings when she was in college, but she's always had a special place in her heart for vampires. She lives near Cleveland, Ohio, with her partner, several reptiles, and a very grumpy cat. Her full-length debut novel, *The Witch's Heart*, released in early 2021.

Cassandra Khaw is a scriptwriter at Ubisoft Montreal. Her fiction has been nominated for the Locus Award and the British Fantasy Award, and her game writing has won a German Game Award. You can find her short stories in places like *F&SF*, *Lightspeed*, and Tor.com. Her novella *Nothing but Blackened Teeth* is coming out from Nightfire, the new Tor horror imprint, in 2021.

Caitlin Starling is a writer and spreadsheet-wrangler who lives near Portland, Oregon. Equipped with an anthropology degree and an unhealthy interest in the dark and macabre, she writes horror-tinged speculative fiction of all flavors. Her first novel, *The Luminous Dead*, is out now from Harper Voyager. She has written for *Nightmare* magazine and has two new gothic horror projects: a novella, *Yellow Jessamine*, from Neon Hemlock, and *The Death of Jane Lawrence*, a full-length novel with St. Martin's Press, due out in 2021. Caitlin also works in narrative design for interactive theater and games, and has been paid to design body parts. She's always on the lookout for new ways to inflict insomnia. Find more of her work at caitlinstarling .com and follow her at @see_starling on Twitter.